"Who Said Anything About Money?"

"Huh? I mean, I beg your pardon."

He'd managed to fluster Mari entirely. Tony had seldom experienced such a swell of satisfaction. How odd. "You can pay me back by agreeing to take dinner with me this evening."

She stared at him blankly, her eyes going as round as copper pennies. Tony could get lost in those eyes if he didn't watch himself. She narrowed them again immediately, and eyed him in deep suspicion. "Why?"

"Why what?"

"Why do you want me to take dinner with you?"

"It's your punishment for allowing your dog to ruin my jacket."

A gap in the conversation ensued as Mari stared at Tony, and Tony tried to look innocent. At last Mari said, "I don't understand."

With a nonchalant shrug, Tony said, "What's not to understand?" In truth, he didn't understand it either, but he couldn't shake his compulsion to hang out with Mari Pottersby. It made no sense. She was the most aggravating, intolerable, nonsensical female he'd ever met. Yet he wanted to be with her constantly.

When he'd returned to Los Angeles with Martin after they'd negotiated the contract with Mari, Tony had all but pined to get back to Mojave Wells. And, because Mojave Wells was about as hospitable a place as hell itself, he knew it was Mari calling to him. It was all very annoying, actually. Maybe he'd get over it if he spent even more time in her company. He hoped. . . .

D0050309

Dear Romance Reader,

In July last year, we launched the Ballad line with four new series, and each month we'll present both new and continuing stories set everywhere from medieval England to the American West—the kind of passionate, romantic stories you love best, written by the most gifted authors. At the back of each book, we'll tell you when you can find subsequent books in the series that have captured your heart.

Debuting this month with a fabulous new series called *The Rock Creek Six*, Lori Handeland offers **Reese.** The first hero in a series of six written alternatively by Lori and Linda Devlin, Reese is haunted by the war—and more than a bit skeptical that a spirited schoolteacher can heal his wounded heart. If you liked the movie *The Magnificent Seven*, this is the series for you! Next, critical favorite Corinne Everett continues *Daughters of Liberty* series with **Fair Rose,** as a British beauty bent on independence in America discovers that partnership is tempting—especially with the right man.

Alice Duncan whisks us back to turn-of-the-century California, and the early days of silent films, with the next *Dream Maker* title, **The Miner's Daughter.** A stubborn young woman hanging onto her father's copper mine by the skin of her teeth has no place in a movie—or so she believes, until one of the film investor's decides she's the right woman for the role, and for him. Finally, the fourth book in the *Hope Chest* series, Laura Hayden's **Stolen Hearts,** joins a modern-day cat burglar with an innocent nineteenth-century beauty who holds the key to his family's lost legacy—and to his heart.

Kate Duffy
Editorial Director

The Dream Maker

THE MINER'S DAUGHTER

Alice Duncan

ZEBRA BOOKS
Kensington Publishing Corp.
http://www.zebrabooks.com

ZEBRA BOOKS are published by

Kensington Publishing Corp.
850 Third Avenue
New York, NY 10022

Copyright © 2001 by Alice Duncan

All rights reserved. No part of this book may be reproduced
in any form or by any means without the prior written consent
of the Publisher, excepting brief quotes used in reviews.

All Kensington titles, imprints and distributed lines are
available at special quantity discounts for bulk purchases
for sales promotion, premiums, fund-raising, educational or
institutional use.

Special book excerpts or customized printings can also be created to fit specific needs. For details, write or phone the office
of the Kensington Special Sales Manager: Kensington Publishing Corp., 850 Third Avenue, New York, NY 10022. Attn.
Special Sales Department. Phone: 1-800-221-2647.

If you purchased this book without a cover you should be aware
that this book is stolen property. It was reported as "unsold and
destroyed" to the Publisher and neither the Author nor the Publisher has received any payment for this "stripped book."

Zebra and the Z logo Reg. U.S. Pat. & TM Off.
Ballad is a trademark of Kensington Publishing Corp.

First Printing: September 2001
10 9 8 7 6 5 4 3 2 1

Printed in the United States of America

One

With one hand pressing his sore stomach and the other tugging on a lock of hair, Martin Tafft stared at the girl who stood before him. He couldn't believe his ears. "But—but—" He swallowed, a sense of unreality creeping over him. "But I thought it was abandoned."

The girl snorted. An interesting specimen, she. Tall and willowy—sort of rangy, actually—she had her dark brown hair pulled back and stuffed under a disreputable old hat that looked as if it had once—say, twenty or thirty years ago—belonged to a cowboy and then been kicked around for another ten or twelve years before she inherited it. She had fine, regular features and huge brown eyes that might have been lovely had she been in a serene mood. At the moment, her eyes crackled fire.

The most unusual thing about her was that she had chosen to present herself to the world this morning in a pair of men's trousers. The trousers were old, stained, and patched, and they were topped with an oversized khaki shirt that looked as if it, too, had been around the world several times before it had landed on her.

Martin, a natty man who, although not vain, tried to

observe the prevailing fashion, couldn't conceive of a lady wearing such an outrageous costume. From this circumstance, he deduced Miss Marigold Pottersby to be no lady.

"Obviously, you were wrong," she said, contempt dripping from the words.

"My God." Reginald Harrowgate, who had honed his facial expressions to perfection in the few years he'd been acting in the moving pictures, sneered. "I can't believe this is happening, Martin."

"I can't, either."

"You said the matter was concluded and we could begin filming in two weeks." Harrowgate spoke as if he thought Martin had deliberately lied to him for some fell purpose.

"I thought it was."

The pain in his stomach led Martin to fear he was getting an ulcer. He understood people could develop ulcers from having to deal with too much stress. He definitely dealt with too much stress. If Harrowgate would just go away and leave him to deal with this . . . female, the tension might be reduced considerably. But the blasted ham seemed determined to stick, darn it.

Attempting to ignore his audience, Martin tried again. "Listen, Miss Pottersby, can't we at least rent the mine for a few weeks?"

"No."

Martin's stomach gave a hard spasm. This was terrible. Awful. How could he have made such a mistake? He'd gone over this detestable desert with a fine-tooth comb, spending a week and a half in blazing heat, dirt, and overall suffering, and he'd been positive this mine had been abandoned eons earlier. It looked like it. "But—"

"No. You're trespassing. Please go away."

"But—"

The girl turned and whistled through her teeth. The noise shot through the air like an arrow and stabbed Martin's ears.

Great. Now his head could throb along with his stomach. He had no idea why she'd done such a thing, unless it was to make herself even more detestable than she already was. Maybe she was calling on a band of wild Indians to stake him and Harrowgate to the floor of this god-awful desert so the red ants could sting them to death. Maybe she was—

"Good God!" Martin stared wide-eyed at the phenomenon that had popped out of the old mine shaft at her whistle and was now lumbering toward them at an alarming clip.

Reginald wheeled around, shrieked, "Help!" and started running in the opposite direction. He worked up admirable speed, considering the weather.

The girl put one fist on her hip and grinned.

Martin didn't dare move. He'd never seen such a thing in his life. Terror gripped him by the throat and held him tongue-tied for a second. Finally, after swallowing painfully, he asked in a small voice, "Um, is that a dog?"

The creature, black as pitch, gleaming like polished onyx in the vicious sun, and with a head the size of a crate, barreled past him—thank God—and the girl and, with a wagging tail and what looked like a good deal of joy, pursued Harrowgate. The actor peered over his shoulder once, shrieked again, and kept running.

It was no use. The dog, if dog it was, overtook Harrowgate with ease. Martin had to hide his eyes when it leaped at Reginald's back and he went sprawling.

The girl whistled again. With seeming reluctance, the animal ceased washing Harrowgate's face with a tongue the size of Kentucky and trotted back to her. There he turned, sat at her side, panted, and looked up at her as if he expected to be lauded for his performance. Martin would have taken a solemn oath the thing had a grin on its gigantic face.

The girl laid a hand on his neck. "Good boy, Tiny." She grinned at Martin. "To answer your question, yes, this is a dog."

Martin drew in about an acre of scalding desert air. "I've, ah, never seen one quite like it before."

"I'm sure."

They both heard Harrowgate sputtering and cursing a few yards off. Miss Pottersby said, "Better take care of your friend. I don't think he likes the weather here in Mojave Wells."

Martin scarcely heard her. His attention sat squarely on the monster dog sitting beside her. "Um, what kind of dog is it?"

"Great Dane."

"Oh." Great Dane. Like Hamlet. Only bigger. Much, much bigger. Whatever would Shakespeare have done with a dog the size of a brontosaurus?

He shook off the spell of the dog, and made one last stab at convincing this obstinate girl that it would be to her advantage to rent her mine to the Peerless Studio for a few weeks. "Listen, Miss Pottersby, please take some time to reconsider your decision. The motion pictures pay well, and—ah, I understand the mine has been in your family for years now, and nobody's struck anything but dirt so far."

It was the wrong thing to have said. Martin knew it as soon as he saw the expression of fury cross Miss Pottersby's face. He glanced at Tiny with misgiving, hoping she wouldn't set the black beast on him next.

"Get off my land now, Mister, and take that simpering fiddlestick with you."

Martin blinked, confused, until he realized the fiddlestick was Harrowgate. "But—"

"Dagnabbit, go!" She pointed a slender, brown finger in a direction Martin assumed would take him off her property.

He hesitated for one more minute, glanced at the dog, and shrugged. "Very well, but I'll come again. Please take time to think about it, Miss Pottersby. We can offer you a substantial rental for two or three weeks' work. It would be to your—"

"Go away now!"

Her voice seemed to nudge her protector, because the dog stood and frowned at Martin. Hackles bristled along its shiny black back, which came up to Miss Pottersby's waist. Its head almost reached her shoulders. Since Martin had seen it attack Harrowgate with his own eyes, he knew it was taller than a grown man when it stood on its hind legs. Probably weighed more, too. He gave up.

"All right. I'll have to talk to our investors about this, Miss Pottersby." He was also going to look up the records on this stupid mine to see if there wasn't some loophole he could use to his advantage. He didn't understand why the blasted girl was being so obstinate. Heck, if she allowed Peerless to rent the ugly mine, maybe she could buy herself a dress or something.

He could feel the dog eyeing him as he walked away. Its scrutiny made his shoulder blades itch.

Anthony Ewing, son of Maurice Ewing, one of the richest men in New York, sighed. He felt kind of sorry for Martin, whom he knew worked too hard, but he couldn't allow personal feelings to interfere with business. His father had taught him as much in the cradle.

"Listen, Martin," Tony said, "I know she's a tough nut, but you've got to persuade her. Everything's set to start, and you can't change locations now. It would cost another fortune, and my father would be furious."

Poor Martin looked as if he might pull that hank of hair right out of his head if he kept yanking on it. "I'm trying, Tony. Trust me."

"She has a rabid dog that she turns on people when they annoy her," Reginald Harrowgate grumbled. He was at present soaking his scratched right hand in a pot of hot water and Epsom salts. Tony didn't bother to respond to the comment, having learned after five minutes in Harrowgate's company that the man was an effete fusspot.

"Maybe I should talk to her," Tony mused. He didn't want to do it. He neither admired nor approved of moving pictures. Although he believed women had a place in the world, he didn't think it was in running mines. Frankly, he couldn't conceive of such a thing.

Tony's opinion, about motion pictures at least, wasn't shared by his father or by Martin. The elder Ewing had sunk a whole lot of money into this latest Peerless production, and Tony'd been treated to several of Martin's impassioned lectures on the subject of the growing "flicker" business.

Martin considered motion pictures as something akin to the salvation of mankind. If everyone who worked in them was as good hearted, broad minded, scrupulous, and honest as Martin, the pictures might be. But the people weren't, and Tony knew it. Most folks were out for a buck, and they didn't care how they got it. If one needed an example of this, one needed look no farther than Tony's own father.

"Let me check out the records on the mine first, Tony," Martin advised. "If we approach her again, it had better be with more ammunition than we have now."

Tony nodded and mopped his sweaty brow with a once-pristine handkerchief. "Good idea."

Harrowgate muttered, "Why don't you try a loaded gun?"

Although Tony knew the actor was joking, he wasn't amused. "I'm sure that would thrill her."

Harrowgate humphed.

Martin ceased tugging at his hair and commenced fiddling with a pen lying on the table in front of him. "Listen, Tony, I'm really sorry about this. I checked out all the mines in San Bernardino County, and I would have sworn on a stack of Bibles that the Marigold Mine was abandoned. I'm sure it should be. It doesn't look like any profitable silver mine I've ever seen." He lifted his head and grinned. "Not that I've ever seen any."

Tony grinned back. He really liked Martin, whom he'd known since his college days. "It's all right, Martin. Frankly, I'm astonished that you can do half of what you do. It's not surprising that a mistake slips by once in a while."

Martin shook his head and sighed. "It shouldn't have happened. Mistake, heck. I'm the one who's slipping."

"Nonsense. You just have too much to do. My God, you do everything for Peerless. You do all the casting, hiring, firing, write most of the scripts, direct some of the pictures, maintain equipment, keep up with innovations, and deal with the actors." He cast a scornful glance at Harrowgate, who was too busy worrying about his scratched hand to notice. "Add finding suitable locations to shoot the pictures in, and your plate is filled to overflowing. I couldn't do it."

"Well . . ." Martin did look frazzled.

Tony wished he could help, but he didn't know a single thing about the pictures except that he'd been sent out to make sure the money his father had invested in this one came to no harm.

Martin murmured, "Maybe you're right. I love the work, but I've been at it for several years solid now. I'm a little tired." He pressed his lips together. "But that's no excuse for this catastrophe. Where in God's name can we get another mine? And the Marigold is so perfect."

"Give yourself a break," Tony advised. "I'll visit the courthouse with you, and we can look up the records together." He unbuttoned the top few buttons on his shirt. "Damn, it's hot here. Thank God for electric fans."

"You said it."

Although he didn't want to leave the fan-cooled room of the Mojave Inn and walk out into the blistering desert air, Tony knew where his duty lay, and he intended to do it. He was damned well going to do it in shirtsleeves, though. This weather was enough to drive a man out of his mind.

Mari Pottersby sat at the one table in her cabin and idly stroked Tiny's gigantic head as she went through a stack of unpaid bills for the umpteenth time. She couldn't pay them. Her heart felt heavy.

"Shoot, Tiny, it's going to kill me to lose Dad's dream. Maybe I ought to rent the Marigold to those stupid picture people. It would help to pay a few of these." She flipped a couple of the bills. She felt like such a failure.

"Dad was sure there was silver in there, Tiny." A tear crept past the rigid guard she endeavored to keep on her too-emotional nature and slid down her cheek. She wiped it away angrily. She considered her tendency to be softhearted a tremendous handicap to her ambitions. Rich people could afford to be mushy. She couldn't.

Tiny wagged his tail, bumping a chair and sending it toppling over with a crash. He jumped, gave what, for him, was a yip of alarm, but which sounded like thunder, and laid his head in Mari's lap with a whimper.

"Don't be scared, Tiny. It'll all be okay." She sighed heavily and wished she believed it.

A knock came at the door. Mari frowned. Tiny leaped to his feet, almost tipping the table over, bounded to the door, and commenced emitting a series of cavernous barks. Mari heard a man's voice say, "Good God," and would have smiled if she hadn't been so down in the dumps. It was probably those blasted Peerless people again.

She felt a little guilty about having treated that nice Martin Tafft so uncivilly, but his assumption about her mine had offended her. After he'd left, she'd taken a critical look at it, however, and realized he'd had some justification for the conclusion he'd reached. The place was shabby and ugly, and it looked every ounce as unprofitable as it was.

The entrance into the mine itself looked like nothing more than a hole in the side of a smallish hill. It had been built by her father in the late 1880s. The Marigold Mine had been his baby. His dream. His silver-edged hope for wealth and security.

He'd never achieved either. Mari's mother, a long-suffering woman who hadn't lasted long after Mari's birth, had agreed to name their daughter after the mine, but Mari imagined her heart wasn't in it. She'd been worn down by the hardships she'd agreed to endure in this hellhole of a desert for love of Mari's father. Mari guessed she had inherited her father's grit. Or maybe she'd just learned to adapt since she'd never known anything else. Mari didn't mind the desert at all.

She'd sure not benefitted in any other way from her father's obsession with the Marigold Mine. He'd never once struck anything worth mentioning, and he'd refused to sell out to the borax barons when the borax craze hit the Mojave. He was out for silver, and he wasn't flexible enough to alter his dream to suit reality. Mari had found his attitude frustrating, especially when the two of them had been forced to exist on nothing but beans and salt pork for months at a time.

And now she was being as pigheaded as her father. Feeling even more gloomy than usual, she held Tiny's collar and opened the door of the rough-hewn, one-room cabin in which she'd lived for every one of her nineteen years.

Her mouth fell open. Tiny lunged forward, and she managed to keep a grip on his collar, but she did it automatically. Her brain had suffered too great a shock to allow her to think.

She'd expected Mr. Tafft again. Maybe another guy from the pictures.

She hadn't expected Adonis to show up at her door, sweating and looking cross. She jumped when she heard Martin's voice, since she hadn't noticed him standing beside the god.

"Miss Pottersby, please allow me to introduce you to Mr. Anthony Ewing. Mr. Ewing is one of the primary investors in *Lucky Strike.*"

"How do you do," the god said. He sounded as if he didn't really want to know and had only said the words by rote. His brow was furrowed, his tanned face dripped perspiration, and he was obviously uncomfortable. "It's my father who's the investor, Miss Pottersby. I'm only his agent here on the West Coast. He's in New York."

She swallowed and managed to say, "Oh."

Martin smiled kindly. "May we come in, Miss Pottersby? It's blazing hot out here."

She stepped back, suddenly realizing she'd been gaping. "Sure," she said. "It's hot in here, too."

Martin's smile didn't waver. Mr. Ewing looked even grouchier at her words. Both men entered the bantam cabin. Fortunately, Mari had acquired chairs over the years, mostly from kindhearted neighbors who'd felt sorry for her. She didn't like people feeling sorry for her, but she'd accepted the chairs since she needed them. Also, she possessed a sociable nature, and people sometimes dropped by, so the chairs came in handy.

"You can put your hats on the rack over there," she said, regaining some of her composure. It was silly of her to react this strongly to the presence of a handsome man. Shoot, Martin himself was a looker, and he hadn't affected her this way.

"Thanks," Martin said in his friendly tone.

The other man didn't speak, but both hung their hats on the rack. It had been fashioned decades earlier from longhorn cattle horns and was as ugly as the back of a barn, but her father had brought it with him from Texas, and Mari loved it for his sake. He'd once told her that encountering furniture made out of cattle horns was a hazard of the ranching life. He'd been such a jolly man. Mari always felt as if she were dishonoring him when she occasionally entertained the notion that it would have been nice if he'd been practical as well.

"Would you like some water?" she asked the two men. "It's cold."

"Love some," said Martin. "Thank you." He maintained his smile even in the ovenlike heat of the cabin.

"Yes. Thank you." Adonis hadn't smiled yet.

For the first time in a long time, Mari felt puny and embarrassed about her circumstances. She despised herself for it, and felt an overpowering urge to apologize for the way she lived—which was idiotic. Silently commanding herself to cheer up, she said, "I don't have electricity, but there's a real good icebox."

Neither man spoke, and she felt silly. She also felt their eyes on her as she went to the part of her home that passed as the kitchen and got out three old, cracked jelly glasses from the cupboard (the cupboard had come to her from Mr. Francis Marion Smith, when he'd built a huge house after he got rich mining borax). Then she opened the icebox door and retrieved the pitcher of water she always kept in there.

As she poured the water, she ruthlessly banished her feelings of inferiority. Blast it, she wasn't inferior. She was merely poor, and there was nothing wrong in that.

Except that it was mighty uncomfortable sometimes.

Squaring her shoulders, she brought the men their water and went back for her own. Because she felt edgy, she leaned against the icebox and sipped at her water from there. She figured she'd *feel* stronger if she continued to stand while they sat.

"What brings you back here, Mr. Tafft?" She tried not to stare at Mr. Ewing, because she didn't want to give him the satisfaction of knowing his looks intrigued her. He was probably one of those rich, handsome men who were used to women fainting at their feet.

Martin took another gulp of water, cleared his throat, and his smile underwent a subtle change. It now looked apologetic. Mari's heart went cold, in spite of the weather, which was somewhere in the lower hundreds.

"I'm afraid we went through the court records on the Marigold Mine, Miss Pottersby."

Blast. Mari's own smile slipped sideways. "You're afraid of that, are you?" She was the one who ought to be afraid. And she was.

"Yes. Um, I suppose you know what we found." Martin's glance strayed to Tiny, who had flopped down next to Mari and laid his head on her left foot. The dog took up almost a third of the cabin when he sprawled like that.

A stab of guilt struck Mari when she realized Martin was worried that she'd turn Tiny on him. She'd never do such a thing, but he couldn't know it. Even if she did, Tiny wouldn't hurt a fly. He might conceivably knock someone over from an excess of friendliness and then drown him by licking his face, but that was all.

"Suppose you tell me," she said, knowing it was silly to try to evade the inevitable by verbally sparring with the man.

"This is ridiculous." Tony Ewing shoved himself back from Mari's raggedy table and stood.

Worried by the sudden movement and the tone of the man's voice, Tiny lifted his head and uttered a low rumble. Tony eyed the dog suspiciously.

"Is it?" Mari asked, trying to sound cynically amused. There was nothing the least bit amusing about this situation. She supposed she should save her cynicism for something not so perilous, but his nasty tone riled her.

"You know it is," Ewing went on angrily. "You owe back taxes on this place, and obviously you don't have a cent with which to pay them. You're going to lose the mine pretty soon, whether there's silver in it or not. And it's unmistakable to everyone, except possibly you, that you'll never find any silver. There isn't any, or you and your father would have found it thirty years ago. I don't know why you're being so stubborn."

Mari didn't point out that she couldn't have found anything thirty years ago, since she was only nineteen years old. She also didn't know why she was being so intractable. Except that the Marigold Mine had been her father's whole life. He'd lived in it. He'd died in it. He'd bequeathed it to her after exacting a promise that she'd never abandon it. Unfortunately, he hadn't left her the wherewithal to keep it.

"Tony," Martin said in a mollifying undertone. "Why don't you let me handle this."

Tony looked mulish for a second, then chuffed and sat down again. Mari sensed he was sweltering and uncomfortable, wasn't accustomed to feeling like that, and was reacting badly to it. Since he'd clearly been pampered all his life, she imagined this weather must be rough on him. Nevertheless, she didn't approve of his attitude. "Yes," she said. "Why don't you handle it, Mr. Tafft. Your friend's too tactless to handle deal making."

Martin gave a little laugh. "Don't be too hard on him, Miss Pottersby. He's not used to desert life."

"Yeah. I figured that." She tried to sound disdainful.

Tony glared at her. She glared back and wished she were a meaner person; she'd have Tiny go over there and give him a good scare. She'd never do it. Besides, he looked like the type who might carry a revolver, and she'd die if anything happened to Tiny. He was all she had left, except for the mine, and the mine was worthless.

Martin cleared his throat. "So, anyhow, we went to the courthouse today and discovered that you've been experiencing a little financial difficulty."

All of the tact Mr. Ewing didn't have, Martin did, apparently. She was facing ruin, is what she was. She nodded. "Go on."

"Peerless has no interest in disturbing your mining operation, Miss Pottersby. I promise you that we'll leave everything as we found it."

Darn. And here she was hoping they'd improve the place. She nodded again.

"We're willing to pay you five thousand dollars for the rental of the Marigold Mine for five weeks. That's a thousand dollars a week, which is—well, it's a lot of money."

Five thousand dollars? Mari barely stifled a gasp.

It sure was a lot of money. Again, Mari appreciated Martin's tact. He'd been about to say it was more than she could make in that period by working the mine. If he only knew, it was more than she could make in two or three years by working the mine.

On the other hand, he probably did know it. He'd been to the courthouse. She didn't speak, knowing from experience that when a person kept quiet, other people felt compelled to fill the silence.

"I'll tell you exactly how it is, Miss Pottersby. The Peerless Studio, which was established several years ago by Phineas Lovejoy and me, has become a leader in the emerging motion-picture industry.

"Peerless only makes pictures of the highest caliber. While we still produce a lot of one-reel and split-reel shorts, we've most recently been concentrating on what we call featured motion pictures. Featured pictures are longer and have more complex plots than the shorts. They might be likened to stage performances in that whole families can go see such a feature and make a holiday of it, so to speak. *Lucky Strike,* the picture we want to make here in Mojave Wells, will be a featured motion picture."

He paused. Mari wondered if he expected her to say something. At this point, she had nothing to say. If she kept quiet for long enough, maybe he'd increase his offer, and she'd be able to pay all of her creditors and keep the mine going for another little while.

Until the money ran out again. She sighed, knowing that she was always going to need money. And she wouldn't always be able to depend on Martin Tafft to require a mine for a motion picture, thereby pulling her out of the soup.

Martin took another drink of his water, emptying the glass. "I came out here a few weeks ago, searching for a suitable location to make the picture. Your mine is perfect. I had thought it was abandoned, but I know better now." He gave her another apologetic smile.

It was difficult, but she managed not to smile back. She sympathized with him, but this was too important for her to give in to her indulgent nature. She attempted a basiliscan stare. She didn't know if she achieved it or not, but Mr. Tafft's buddy's frown deepened, so she imagined she'd come close. She remained silent.

"Anyhow, this place is perfect." Martin eyed her steadily for another moment. Mari got the uncomfortable feeling that he was sizing her up for something other than a financial deal. "Say, Miss Pottersby, you've never considered acting in the pictures, have you?"

Two

Mari jumped a foot, startling Tiny, who leaped to his feet and growled at her visitors. She laid a soothing hand on his back, and his hackles gradually smoothed out. He flopped back down, creating a smallish earthquake in the tiny cabin.

After clearing her throat, she said, "No, Mr. Tafft. I have never entertained the slightest wish to act anywhere, including the motion pictures." The notion had never entered her head, for that matter. The pictures? Her? Marigold Pottersby, a miner's impoverished daughter? What a laugh!

He continued squinting at her, and Mari became edgy. "Why?" she snapped. "Do you think offering me a part in your picture instead of paying me for using the mine will work? It won't. Trust me."

"No, no," Martin said quickly. "It's not that."

Mari let her gaze drift to Adonis and realized he had begun looking at her speculatively, too. She felt heat creep up her neck. Mari's exposure to people outside the extremely small community of Mojave Wells was limited to a couple of trips to San Bernardino each year. Since San Bernardino was about as far from being a thriving metropolis as it was from Cincinnati, she had met very few people as sophisticated as Martin Tafft and Anthony Ewing. They made her feel inconsequential and even more like a poverty-stricken hick than usual.

"Of course not," Tony said. Mari heard the scoffing note to his voice. "We're not chiselers, Miss Pottersby. We're trying to make a motion picture."

"Yes, yes," Martin said. He sounded distracted. Turning to his companion, he said, "Say, Tony, do you remember the description of the heroine in *Lucky Strike?*"

Tony frowned at Martin. "Vaguely."

Martin's scrutiny returned to Mari, who felt like squirming but didn't. "The description fits Miss Pottersby perfectly. Absolutely. I don't think we could find a more perfect match."

"Hmmm," Tony mused.

"What?" Mari asked, drowning out Tony's murmur. The word came out as sort of a screech and embarrassed her. She swallowed and tried again. "I beg your pardon, Mr. Tafft. I don't believe I understand what you were trying to say."

For a tense second, Martin continued to eye her without speaking. Mari's nerves almost crawled out of her skin. Then he cleared his throat and spoke, and Mari decided she hadn't gone daft. He had.

"Would you consider acting in this picture, Miss Pottersby? We'll still pay rent for the use of your mine, but you'd be perfect for the part of the leading lady."

"Provided she can act and looks all right on film," Tony growled.

Mari's glance careered wildly between the two men for a moment before she convinced her innards to settle down. Tiny was apt to become disturbed if he sensed uneasiness in her, and she didn't want to frighten these fellows, no matter how much they scared her.

"Oh, yes," agreed Martin, not waiting for Mari to respond. "Of course, we'll have to do a test first."

She swallowed again. "Oh." For the life of her, she couldn't think of anything intelligent to say.

"Would you consider acting in the picture, Miss Pottersby? For the leading part, we could pay you another five thousand."

That would make a grand total of ten thousand dollars. She was standing here listening to a man offer her ten thousand dollars for five weeks' work. Unless this was a dream. Ten thousand dollars could keep Mari and the mine operating for at least three years. Four or five if she was careful, and Mari was accustomed to being careful. Her largest daily expense was for Tiny's upkeep. She grew her own food, and shot whatever didn't grow in her garden.

There had to be a catch in here somewhere. "What would I have to do? You said something about a test?" What kind of test would an actress have to take?" Mari had been under the impression that actresses were all fluffy headed nitwits who couldn't pass a test if given the answers along with the questions.

"It's not a written test," Martin assured her, as if he were used to answering this question. "It's a test to see how you look on film." He smiled at her kindly. "Sometimes, a person will look perfect in person, but comes across as wooden on film."

"I see." That made a certain kind of sense, she guessed.

"Well?" Tony asked gruffly, as if he were restless and wanted to get this over with.

Mari frowned at him. "Don't rush me. I'm thinking." She didn't appreciate it when he rolled his eyes. He was as handsome as the very devil, but she liked Martin better. Martin at least was nice.

"I don't think you could lose if you take Peerless up on its offer, Miss Pottersby," Martin assured her. "Peerless has a spotless reputation in the industry."

"I see." Mari thought hard for a moment, wishing the two men would go away so she could mull stuff over in peace. Something very important occurred to her. "If I agree to this and somebody strikes ore by accident while you're making your picture, the ore's mine."

Tony said, "Good God," as if he couldn't have imagined anything more illogical or improbable if he'd tried for the rest of his life.

Again Mari frowned at him. He was getting to be a royal pain in the neck, and Mari contemplated asking him to leave.

Before she could, Martin again came to the rescue. "It's a good point, Tony. I applaud Miss Pottersby for thinking to secure her interests."

Tony said, "Right," and shut his mouth. Mari wanted to stamp on one of his highly polished, though dusty, shoes.

Martin rose. "Why don't we leave you to think about it, then? Please take your time. We're staying at the Mojave Inn. Perhaps you'd like to join us for dinner this evening, and we can further discuss the matter in a relaxed atmosphere."

Relaxed? Was he kidding? Any time Mari had to dress up and dine in a restaurant—something she'd done only thrice in her life to date—she was as nervous as a frog in a skillet. Grand manners weren't something she'd had a lot of practice with. On the other hand, he'd probably not have asked her if he hadn't intended to pay, and it might be nice to eat something she hadn't had to grow or kill.

She decided to make sure. "Your treat?" The heat crept from her neck to her cheeks, but she couldn't afford to take chances with the few dollars she had left.

Tony snorted. No big surprise there. He might be as rich as one of those Greek gods, and as handsome, but he was as rude as anything.

"Of course," Martin said.

He, Mari noted with gratitude, didn't seem to despise her just because she hadn't grown up in a big city with money and fine clothes and society manners. She wished Tony's attitude didn't make her want to sock him. Or sic Tiny on him. Not that she could, since Tiny could never be persuaded to sic anything except as a gesture of friendship and welcome, which wasn't what she had in mind.

"Fine," she said with a nod. "I'll think over your offer, maybe think of more questions I'd like you to answer, and we can talk about it tonight. There may be other things I'll need written into any contract."

"Of course," said Martin. His smile was warm and comforting. Mari wished Martin's smile could visit Adonis's face, just once. "Peerless is only interested in making the picture. We have no interest in the mine itself, and naturally will turn over any findings to you."

Martin, Mari noticed, unlike Tony Ewing, didn't smirk as he said it. She liked Martin Tafft a lot. Again unlike Tony Ewing. "What time?"

"Eight?" Martin said.

"Eight?" Shoot, Mari was usually in bed by eight. Mining was hard work and didn't allow for late nights. She remembered reading somewhere that city folks had dinner at eight, but she'd probably starve to death before then.

Martin, who apparently had detected a note of dismay in her voice, amended his offer. "How about seven? Would that be better for you?"

She saw Tony give Martin a sour look, and she felt more like a bumpkin than ever. Nevertheless, she lifted her chin—it wasn't her fault Tony Ewing was a darned snob—and said, "Seven would be fine. Thank you. I'll meet you at the hotel."

She'd probably starve to death by seven, too, but she

wasn't going to give that blasted Tony Ewing any more ammunition to shoot her with. Blast him.

"The girl's impossible," Tony grumbled as he and Martin made their way back to the Mojave Inn. "She's rude and crude and hasn't a single thing to recommend her except her looks, and they need all the help they can get. I'm afraid it would be a mistake to hire her to act in the picture, Martin."

Not only that, but she'd been completely unimpressed by Tony and his money. It galled him that her attitude mattered to him. He'd believed himself to be above such things. He knew that, while money made the man—in his father's cynical words—money didn't matter a hill of beans when it came to character, ethics, or moral worth.

Yet Mari Pottersby's attitude of indifference toward him had peeved him. A lot. She'd stood there, squinting at them in that condescending way she had, with that monster dog lying next to her waiting to pounce. Arms folded over her breasts, she'd eyed Martin and Tony as if they were a couple of scummy worms. Tony had never been treated thus. He wondered if his father's money had protected him from the real world a trifle too much.

He imagined he'd find out. He'd been on his own for years now, but not in such rough company in such a rugged place. He unbuttoned another button on his shirt—he'd shed his celluloid collar hours earlier—and scowled as he scuffed up dust. His shoes were probably ruined by this time.

"I think she's got a lot of guts," Martin said. "I hate to contradict you, Tony, but look what she's had to face in her life."

"I've already looked," Tony growled as he did so

again, scanning the scenery, or lack thereof, with loathing. "And I agree that this is a hell of a place. That doesn't excuse her . . . her . . . her arrogance." A prince of arrogance himself, Tony didn't know why hers had irked him, but it had.

Martin chuckled. "Give the girl a chance. She's fighting mighty big odds."

"She's a fool to fight, if you ask me, and an even bigger fool to hesitate about taking your offer." Tony detested pigheaded people. "Obviously, she's never seen ten thousand dollars in her life, she'll never be offered ten thousand again, and I can't understand why she doesn't just snap it up."

"Well," Martin equivocated, "it's only ten thousand if she agrees to play the lead."

Tony stopped in his tracks, turned, and threw his arms out. "Why wouldn't she?" he demanded. "Why, in the name of all that's holy, would a young woman on her last legs—she's about to lose that precious mine of hers, as you well know—make a fuss about such a splendid offer as the one we just made to her?"

With a shrug, Martin said, "Don't know, although I have a hunch."

Tony pulled in a lungful of incinerated air and dust. "Please enlighten me. Her attitude is completely beyond my understanding."

Martin grinned at him. Tony liked Martin. He also respected him a good deal. Martin wasn't hot tempered like him, and he seemed to understand his fellow man a good deal better than Tony did. The latter quality was often a blessing and sometimes a pain in the ass. Like now, for instance.

"I think it has to do with her father. She considers the Marigold Mine his legacy to her."

"Some legacy." Tony wheeled around and recommenced the trudge toward the hotel. This place was hell, and there were no two ways about it.

"I know. It's not your kind of legacy."

In spite of the heat, Martin looked kind of perky. Evidently, Tony thought sourly, their recent encounter with the Pottersby witch had invigorated him. It had infuriated Tony. Made him want to punch things, in fact.

Martin went on, "Your kind of legacy is millions in stock shares and bonds, and a life of blissful prosperity."

"What's wrong with that?" Tony jammed his hands into his trouser pockets. Why would a young woman who looked like Mari Pottersby want to run around in men's britches? They made her seem common and crude and unfeminine. Why, the girl looked like Calamity Jane or another of those hellcats out of the Old West.

A gray and toothless prospector leading a tired, elderly mule was coming down the road toward them. Tony shook his head. Until recently, he'd believed scenes like this were the product of a dime novelist's imagination. He wondered if the old coot was going to pay a visit to Miss Pottersby. Probably. He looked like the type she'd fall for.

By God, he was really in a bad mood. Martin deserved better from him. So did his father, although the truth of it made him queasy. Tony made an effort to cheer up, but it didn't help much. He was too hot, too sweaty, too mad at Mari, and too uncomfortable to be cheerful.

"Nothing's wrong with your kind of legacy," Martin assured him. "I'd be willing to bet that Miss Pottersby would kill for one. But that wasn't the hand life dealt her. She was born to a father with a dream, and he passed it on to her."

"He ought to be shot," Tony said bitterly.

Martin grinned. "Too late. He's already dead."

"I still think she's insane not to jump at the chance we're giving her."

"She'll probably come around," Martin said with a shrug. "I suppose she won't be able to help herself. Money's like that."

Tony eyed Martin briefly. "You sound as if you disapprove."

"Oh, no. It's just that—well, I feel sorry for the girl. She's young and pretty and bright. Most girls her age are going to school or getting married or working at jobs designed for women. She's trying to keep a dying mine alive for the sake of a man who was probably nuts, but who was obviously a good enough father to have inspired devotion in his daughter. The guy couldn't have been all bad."

Dammit, Martin was making him feel like a bully and an old meanie. Simon Legree Ewing. That was him. Tony sighed. "All right, I'll grant the girl has a few good qualities. I only hope this dinner idea will work."

"I hope she photographs well and can act. Not only does she look perfect for our heroine, but she needs the extra five grand."

"You're entirely too nice, Martin."

"Nuts. She'll be perfect."

"I hope so."

Tony, who'd never thought much about his own blond good looks, had to admit that if anyone took the effort to scrub Marigold Pottersby clean, slather some cream on her to get those rough hands soft, give her a manicure, send her to a hair salon, and clothe her in something besides dirty dungarees, she'd be a looker. She'd never be one of those petite things who simpered and fainted every other minute, but at least she wouldn't look like a scarecrow.

Actually, she could be damned near striking if she ever tried. "I wonder how she'll dress for dinner," he mused aloud.

"Me, too. I expect she'll try to look nice."

"Do you?" Tony wasn't so sure.

He and Martin spent the remainder of their day in the fan-cooled parlor of the Mojave Inn, discussing how *Lucky Strike* was to progress. Martin seemed sure that they'd secure Miss Pottersby's permission to rent her mine. He sent a cable to the Peerless Studio, requesting a cameraman be sent out as soon as possible so that a screen test could be made for Marigold Pottersby.

Tony still had his doubts.

If she had any money, Mari thought glumly as she hiked up her skirt in an effort to keep it out of the dust, she'd be able to buy a car. Even an old, beat-up rattle-trap held together with baling wire, like the heap driven by her buddy Gordon Shay, would help in times like this.

Not that she expected there would be any more times like this. Her heart rattled against her breastbone like dice in a cup, her nerves hopped and skipped like Mexican jumping beans, her mouth was as dry as the surrounding countryside, and she wanted to turn tail, run back home, hug Tiny, crawl into her narrow cot, and pull the covers over her head. She'd stay there until Martin Tafft, Anthony Ewing, and the entire Peerless Studio either left Mojave Wells or finished their project without her, whichever came first.

There wasn't a chance in heck of that, though. No matter how scared and nervous she was, Mari wasn't going to turn her back on the prospect of ten thousand dollars. She wondered if they'd meant it.

The whole thing sounded highly unlikely to her. On the other hand, she'd read something somewhere about Peerless; she'd even seen a couple of their pictures when Mr. Purdy at the grocery store had invited people over and projected some moving pictures against his back wall. Mari'd especially enjoyed an opus called *One and Only.*

Every time she considered watching herself in one of those pictures, however, she felt a mad compulsion to turn around and run, screaming, into the night.

She hoped she looked passable. It was too much to ask of the Fates that she look good. Her face was brown from years of working outdoors, her hands weren't soft and lovely like the hands of beautiful women were supposed to be, she was too tall, too thin, and too—not perfect.

She'd washed her hair, however, and pinned it up. When she wasn't holding her dress up out of the dust, she was disconcerted by the way its long skirt buffeted against her heels as if it were chasing her. Obviously, she'd spent too much time in trousers and not enough time in dresses. Not that dresses were appropriate to her way of life, but Mari acknowledged sourly that her way of life wasn't appropriate to a lady.

When she'd surveyed the result of her efforts in her mother's old hand mirror by the light of the kerosene lantern, she'd decided she hadn't turned out too bad. At least her face was clean and her hair was shiny. A couple of people had told her she had pretty hair. One of them had been Gordon Shay. Big deal. On the other hand, it had been a compliment delivered by a man.

The dress she wore was one of the two she owned;

both had belonged to her mother. That made them at least twenty years old, but Mari had tried to update them, using pictures from ladies' magazines she'd borrowed from the librarian, Miss Winters. She had a sneaking hunch that Miss Winters felt sorry for her, Mari didn't really blame her for it. Lots of people did.

Anyhow, the dress was old. Fortunately, the fabric was a good, sturdy calico. Unfortunately, fashions had changed a good deal in twenty years, and the calico had faded in spots.

Mari told herself to stop finding fault with herself. She'd done the best she could, and that was all that could be expected.

Oh, but she was so nervous!

Fortunately, she still possessed a pair of her mother's evening slippers. Unfortunately they, too, were at least twenty years old. And too small for her. She'd have blisters before the evening was over, or she'd be much surprised.

Fortunately, the Mojave Inn was only a mile from her cabin. Unfortunately, that mile was dry and dusty and Mari had to pass by the homes of several of her friends along the way.

Fortunately, they'd be through working in their mines and gardens for the day. Unfortunately, they'd also be finished with their dinners and probably, given the heat, sitting outside to enjoy the relative coolness of the evening.

"Stop it!" Mari commanded herself. If any of her neighbors saw her and asked what she was doing, all duded up and headed for town, she'd simply explain it to them.

They wouldn't believe her. They might believe the part about Peerless wanting to rent the mine, but they'd never believe anybody wanted her to play a part in the picture, much less the leading lady's role.

But that couldn't be helped. It was the truth, and Mari had often found it necessary to stand on the truth even when explanations sounded skimpy. It occurred to her that existing on the truth was a perilous and generally unprofitable business.

And that's exactly where the promised Peerless money would come in handy. She tried to encourage herself with the prospect of ten thousand dollars. Or five thousand, when that nice Mr. Tafft realized she wasn't cut out to be an actress.

Unless he'd been spoofing her about that part of his deal. The more she thought about it, the more it seemed likely that he had been. Who'd want her, of all people, to act in a motion picture?

Such a trick, if trick it was, was really unkind of him, though. Mari hadn't believed him to be unkind; he acted so nice. She pressed her lips together and reminded herself that the only reason confidence artists succeeded was that they'd mastered an air of sincerity.

Oh, but it would be a bitter pill to swallow. What a disappointment! She'd thought so highly of Martin Tafft.

That Anthony Ewing fellow was another kettle of fish. Mari figured this sort of thing was exactly what she should have expected from a man who looked like him. He was too handsome. All that thick, dark blond hair and those blasted classical features. Why, that nose of his made him look like he was sneering even when he wasn't.

What a rotten trick to play on her! It wasn't enough that she had to endure poverty and the prospect of never being able to run the mine properly, but now she had to put up with men trying to exploit her. Imagine, offering her money when they only meant to divert her from their true motives. The two of them were so slick, they slid. Drat them.

What a fool she was to have rigged herself out as if she believed their sweet talk. And making her walk a mile to their supposed dinner conference was a pretty dirty prank, too.

Mari was hopping mad by the time she reached the Mojave Inn.

The dining room at the Mojave Inn wasn't like any decent restaurant Tony'd ever been in. Which made sense, since it wasn't one. It was more like a hole in the wall, and the menu carried two choices for the main course. Steak and pot roast. Tony watched the waitress, a buxom lass named Judy, as she carried food to the tables, in an effort to determine which entree looked tastier. He finally decided it wouldn't make any difference. They both looked awful.

Tony didn't recognize Miss Marigold Pottersby when she first appeared at the door to the Mojave Inn's dining room. He noticed a tall, lovely, dark-haired, dark-eyed woman standing in the doorway, fingering a small beaded bag, and his interest perked right up. He hadn't expected to encounter such a fine specimen of womanhood in this hellhole.

When Martin rose and started for the door, Tony frowned and opened his mouth to ask him what he was doing. Only then did he understand.

Good God. Could that attractive female possibly be Miss Pottersby, the grubby miner's daughter? He narrowed his eyes and peered closely at her.

By God, it was. Tony slowly rose from his chair and started to follow Martin.

But this was uncanny. Impossible. A miracle, even. That the untidy, trouser-clad ragamuffin he'd met this morning could have been transformed into this stunningly shy violet was incredible. Inconceivable.

It must be some kind of trick.

At once he realized he was being foolish. It couldn't be a trick. There was no way on Earth Mari Pottersby could have known Martin wanted to use her mine before the Peerless folks spoke to her about it. And she certainly never expected Martin to want to use her in the picture. Therefore, she couldn't possibly have made herself look good in order to deceive Tony into wanting her.

No. This astonishing transformation must, therefore, be the result of one of those freaks of nature that kept mankind constantly confused.

But, good God.

Martin got to Mari before he did. Tony saw Mari and Martin smile at each other. It wasn't until Mari held out her hand in the same slightly self-conscious manner Tony had noted earlier in the day that his insides fully reconciled themselves to the fact that this comely female was really, honestly, and truly Marigold Pottersby.

The fact that she was clearly as nervous as a cat also clued him in to her true identity. He couldn't recall another such interesting instance of feminine metamorphosis. When he got to where she and Martin stood, her glance for him was as apprehensive as hers for Martin had been friendly. Tony begrudged her that look.

"How do you do?" she asked him politely.

"I'm well, Miss Pottersby. And you?" His voice, he noticed, had chilled considerably in his walk from the table to the door. Interesting. Why should she make him want to be impolite? Was it merely because she so plainly liked Martin better than him?

She stiffened visibly. "I'm fine, thanks." Her words, too, sounded clipped and frosty.

Snippy little thing, wasn't she? Tony jogged Martin

out of the way and held his arm for Mari. He was a trifle embarrassed when Martin looked at him strangely, but he hid his discomposure. "Here, Miss Pottersby, let me show you to our table."

Now that he was standing right next to her, Tony saw that she wore no paint or powder. Probably didn't own any. If she did, she wouldn't know how to use it. She was a nobody from nowhere, in fact, and didn't have a sophisticated bone in her body.

It seemed a lovely body, though. His senses recognized its slender beauty even as his conscious mind attempted to find fault with it.

Her gown looked as if it were a million years old.

Tony's finer nature told his critical one not to be so damned snooty. Not everyone could be born with a silver spoon in his or her mouth, as he had been. Poor Mari Pottersby had been reared by a lunatic in dire circumstances. Tony should be treating her courteously, not seeking ways to find fault with her.

Mari murmured, "Thank you."

As she walked, she lifted her skirt, and Tony saw dust coating its hem. And those shoes. They were antiques if he'd ever seen any and they, too, were so dusty, he couldn't make out what color they'd been to start with. He frowned. "Did you walk all the way over here, Miss Pottersby?"

Her color, which was deep to begin with, deepened still until a rosy flush crept into her cheeks. Tony watched, fascinated. He'd never, ever have dreamed that she could be so attractive.

"Yes, I did," she said, her tight tone implying she considered him a fool for asking. "How else was I supposed to get here?"

Martin, hurrying behind them, said, "I'm so sorry, Miss Pottersby. I should have thought to send a car for you."

Dammit, Tony wanted to be the one to have said that. Too late now. He said, "You ought to have told us this morning that you had no transportation, Miss Pottersby. We didn't expect you to walk here."

She looked him straight in the eye. Her eyes, Tony noticed with a sudden clenching in his chest region, were huge and dark and sparkled like jewels. "I have transportation. It's only that I didn't think the donkey would have been appropriate to the occasion. I don't generally expect folks to provide transportation for me, you know. Besides," she added with something like a smirk, "one ass at a time is my limit."

Dammit, she was too fresh for this world. "Meaning me, I suppose."

"You know yourself better than I."

Tony heard Martin snort as if he were smothering a laugh, blast him. He decided to quit firing her wit with fuel, dropped the ass question, and went back to the original point, which she was either too stupid or too stubborn to perceive. "Don't be ridiculous, Miss Pottersby. We're hoping to conduct business with you. We'd have been happy to send a car."

Martin held a chair for her. At the same time, he grimaced at Tony, signaling him to stop quarreling with the mine owner. Tony knew he should. They needed her, and they'd succeed more easily if she liked them. But something foreign seemed to have taken possession of his common sense this evening, and he couldn't have stopped tiffing with Mari if he'd wanted to.

As Mari sat in a huff and a fluff, she barked, "Then you should have told me you could send a car sooner, shouldn't you? How am I supposed to know what you big-money, picture-backing people do and don't do? I've had to *work* for my keep all my life. And I can't read minds."

Tony heard Martin's stifled moan of despair even as he growled, "Most people who work for a living generally have some common sense." He managed a fairly decent sneer. "At least that's what I've always been told. I wouldn't know from experience, would I?"

She was glaring in earnest now. "It doesn't look like it to me."

By the time Martin sat and began trying to soothe ruffled feathers, Tony was so mad, he could have punched something. Preferably Miss Marigold Pottersby, who was protected by an act of nature, being female and therefore unpunchable.

Tony felt cheated. And very, very annoyed.

Three

If Mari ever got the opportunity, she was going to give Tony Ewing a great, big, fat piece of her mind, the intolerable snob. What she'd like to do is knock him flat with the big cast-iron skillet she used to cook dinner every night. Except this one.

The only other times Mari had eaten in a restaurant, someone else had done the ordering. She'd been very little at the time, maybe five or six, and no one had expected her to be anything but shy, naive, and reserved.

It was her misfortune to be a grown-up woman now and unable to retire into the security of childhood. People naturally expected a child to be inexperienced. She still knew nothing about dining out, but she no longer had any good excuses for her ignorance. Except poverty and unsophistication, and they didn't count, being more apt to be ridiculed than understood.

Thank God she and the waitress who was serving their table this evening were friends. Judy Nelson, whose parents operated the Mojave Inn, and Mari had gone to school together. Mari smiled up at her. "Hi, Judy. How's Pete doing?" Pete, Judy's brother and twelve years old, had recently broken an arm when he'd fallen out of Mr. Nelson's wagon as they were driving to San Bernardino.

Judy eyed Mari in obvious amazement, a fact that

went unappreciated by Mari herself. She did, however, vow to attempt to make herself look more like a lady from now on. If seeing her in a dress had this effect on her fellow Mojave-ites, it was past time she did something to boost her image.

"Pete's doing pretty well, Mari. He's tired of being laid up and is being a perfect pig, though." Judy grimaced, thus demonstrating her filial devotion. She went on, "My goodness, but aren't you all dolled up tonight? You look swell." Judy sounded as if she'd never encountered a more flabbergasting sight in her life than Mari looking swell.

Mari felt her lips pinch together and made an effort to relax them. No sense advertising her discomposure. "I'm here tonight on business." She tried to make it sound casual, as if such things happened to her all the time. Judy, of course, knew better and let all three of them at the table know it with the dubious lift of her eyebrows.

"Oh. How nice." Judy gave up on Mari and turned to the men. Mari blessed her silently. The waitress's gaze seemed to get stuck on Tony. She simpered and tugged her apron straight, and Mari retracted her silent blessing. "You want the steak or the pot roast?"

With a roll of her eyes, Mari decided it would be a good thing if Judy got out more, saw more of the world. A body would think this was the first time she'd ever seen an attractive man, the way she gawked at Tony Ewing. She was so obvious, Mari wanted to hit her. She also wanted to hit Tony, who gave Judy one of his winning smiles. He had never smiled at Mari like that. The only smiles Mari ever got from the big snooty moneybags were nasty ones.

"Do you have a preference, Miss Pottersby?"

Mari jerked her head in Martin's direction. She'd forgotten all about him, which had been a big mistake since he was the nice one of these two men. She undertook to deliver a gracious smile. "I don't think it makes much difference. I hear they're both pretty bad."

Judy muttered something that Mari didn't catch. Served her right, though. Judy had no business flirting with the customers. Mari sniffed and tried to look superior. Since she'd never done such a thing before, she wasn't confident about the outcome.

Tony sent her a scowl. Mari scowled back. It would serve *him* right if the food here made him sick.

Martin cleared his throat. Mari got the feeling he wished he could clear the air so easily. She felt guilty for a second, before she remembered that these men were here to try to cheat her. She sat up straighter in her chair and said, "I believe I'll have the pot roast, thank you."

"One pot roast." Martin smiled with relief and turned to Tony, who was still frowning at Mari. He said, "Tony?"

His dining companion started in his chair. "Oh. Oh, yes. Well now, let me see." He glanced up and gave Judy another gorgeous smile.

Mari wished she could kick him under the table, but he'd probably misunderstand and think she was jealous. As if she'd ever be jealous of so odious a specimen of mankind as he. His smile, the one he reserved for people he liked, transformed his face and made him look charming and approachable and almost deliciously masculine. It wasn't fair.

After a moment of his stupidly smiling at Judy, Tony said, "I believe I'll try the steak." He shot a mean glance at Mari. "I'm sure both main courses are delicious."

Mari said, "We'll see," under her breath.

Judy cast her a triumphant glance.

Martin hurried to say, "I guess I'll take the pot

roast." It sounded to Mari as if he were trying to counter everyone else's bad mood and worse manners by being especially festive. Another tiny stab of guilt smote her.

But that was neither here nor there. She had to keep her wits about her because this evening might make or break the Marigold Mine. At least temporarily. The depressing truth was that no matter how much money Mari poured down the ravening maw of her father's mine, it was played out. In her heart of hearts, Mari knew it, although she'd never admit it aloud, even to herself.

It was too depressing to dwell on right now. She smiled sweetly at Martin. "I'm sure you'll enjoy the pot roast." Transferring her attention, but not her smile, to Tony, she said, "I hear the steaks are always as tough as an old boot."

"So," said Judy, interrupting mercilessly and looking as if she could cheerfully kill Mari, "that's two pot roasts and one steak. Thank you." She marched off, and Mari knew she needed to do some fence-mending in that quarter. She hadn't meant to be rude to Judy, darn it. It was all Tony Ewing's fault.

Before Tony could use the breath he took to shower her with intemperate words—not that she didn't deserve them, she supposed—Martin rushed into the breach. What a brave man he was.

"So, please tell us, Miss Pottersby, have you lived at the Marigold Mine all your life?"

Mari gave him points for attempting to salvage the evening. "Yes. All my life."

Tony said, "Hmph."

Martin said, "You'll have to tell us about how mining operations go forward. We'll need to study up on the subject for the picture."

"I'm sure that's so." Mari made sure she pitched her

voice to sound honey-sweet for Martin, whom she liked even if he was probably going to try to gyp her.

"I've cabled to the studio in Los Angeles to send a cameraman out here, Miss Pottersby," Martin went on. "As soon as he arrives, we'll have him take some moving pictures of you. I'm hoping you'll look as good on film as you do in person."

Mari told herself not to get swell-headed; he probably only said such things to gull his audience. Once he got them feeling good, he'd strike like a rattler. Since she hated to think such things about Martin Tafft, she shifted the blame for such sleazy business tactics onto Tony Ewing's broad shoulders, where it fitted more naturally.

"I'm sure I'll be very nervous," she told Martin. Shoot, she was already very nervous. To counteract her jitters, she sat taller and lifted her chin. Out of the corner of her eye, she caught Tony observing her. She wished he'd take himself off somewhere so she could calm down.

"You needn't be," Martin assured her. "People don't generally realize it, but a person either looks good on screen or he doesn't. It's the camera that decides. That's not universally true, of course, but it's the case more often than not. If your loveliness doesn't come through on film, it's the industry's loss."

And hers, Mari thought glumly. Five thousand dollars would be a gigantic loss to her.

To keep from being disappointed, she reminded herself that the offer was probably a lot of hooey to begin with. She wasn't altogether successful. Even the thought of so much money thrilled her.

"Would you like a glass of wine, Miss Pottersby?"

Tony had asked the question, breaking into the conversation abruptly. Mari thinned her eyes and peered at him narrowly. Wine? Good grief, was she going to have to drink wine? Were they going to ply her with liquor to get her to sign some contract detrimental to her financial situation? Not that there could be any situation much worse than the one she already occupied.

Then again, wine drinking was probably expected at these business dinners. All sophisticated people drank wine. Since she was about as unsophisticated as a human female could get and had never even thought about wine, much less tasted it, she wasn't sure about that, but she read widely and recalled a lot of wine being drunk by rich people in books and magazines.

She swallowed uncertainly, hoping this wasn't an evil plot on the part of her dining companions to weaken her resolve. "Thank you. That would be nice." She hated being even this courteous to Tony Ewing, but knew it would be worse to show her dislike openly. Except when he was being mean to her. Then she could be mean back. That was only getting even, and that was allowed.

Or was it?

Lord God Almighty, Mari was so jumpy, she wouldn't have been able to recite the Twenty-Third Psalm at the moment, even though she'd recited it every day of her life until her father died. He'd liked her to say it as an evening prayer.

Thinking about her father and his favorite psalm made her sad, so she ceased.

"When did your father die, Miss Pottersby?" Tony asked as if he'd tiptoed into her brain and known she'd been thinking about her father. As he spoke, he poured from a bottle of red liquid into a glass the likes of which Mari had never seen in person. It had a stem and was a glass especially designed to hold wine. Mari recognized it from pictures she'd seen.

Trust this rat to bring up her innermost thoughts and

spill them all over the dinner table. She frowned and said, "He's been gone for six months now."

"I'm sorry." This gentlemanly comment came, naturally, from Martin, who had a shred or two of human compassion in his soul. "His passing must have been very difficult for you."

"It was. Thank you." Mari lifted her glass, took a largish drink of wine because she felt insecure, and nearly choked to death. She set down her glass too hard, and some of the liquid spilled onto the white tablecloth, thus adding humiliation to her already skittish state. Blast it all.

As she wiped her teary eyes with her dinner napkin, she noticed Tony eyeing her from over his own wineglass. She sensed him smirking at her, although he was too suave to do so openly. She hated him then.

Once her nerves settled somewhat, she admitted that this latest gaffe on her part eliminated any necessity to pretend a sophistication she didn't possess. Nobody'd believe her at this point, whatever she did.

In order to show Tony Ewing that she had a sense of humor as well as the mine he wanted so darned badly, she grinned at Martin. "Can you tell I've never drunk wine before?"

Martin grinned back and lifted his glass in a salute. "It takes some getting used to."

It sure did. Although she didn't want to, she shot a peek at Tony. If he'd been smirking before, the expression had tipped upside-down, and now he frowned. Fortunately, his frown wasn't aimed at her. In fact, he didn't even mention her abysmal table manners when he next spoke. "Maybe we should get down to brass tacks."

Mari blinked at him. What brass tacks? The mine? Are those the brass tacks he meant? She was willing, although she'd sort of expected the Peerless people to try to curry her favor awhile longer before they talked business.

"Tony . . ." Martin appeared displeased.

"I don't think a dinner in this place is going to soften Miss Pottersby's heart," Tony said in a tone that told Mari exactly what he thought of her: Nothing. He did do her the honor of looking at her when he next spoke. "If she has a heart."

Mari almost wished he hadn't looked, his face was so hard and unyielding. She experienced a humiliating urge to cry. It wasn't fair that he should be so heartless to her. What had she ever done to him? Well, except refuse to rent him her mine, but that didn't sound like any sort of crime to Mari. She gazed back at him with as much serenity as she could muster. "You're so right, Mr. Ewing."

Martin heaved a gusty sigh. "Listen, Miss Pottersby, I'm sure Tony didn't mean to be rude—"

"Oh, I'm sure he did," Mari broke in. "He's been rude to me since the moment we met." There. She felt better now. She added, "Quite frankly, his conduct seems to me unlikely to help you in your business endeavors, Mr. Tafft. You ought to leave him at home next time." If she'd been six years old, Mari might have appended a "Nyah, nyah, nyah," to her assessment. It was implied, though, and she suspected Tony Ewing knew it. She had the satisfaction of seeing him look first startled, then embarrassed, and then furious. Unless that was her imagination.

"Yes." Martin gave Tony a thin smile. "I'm afraid he's not used to the weather out here, and the heat's made him somewhat short tempered."

Mari said, "Oh?" and eyed Tony glacially.

"You have to admit the heat's not awfully hospitable," Tony said, pushing the words out through clenched teeth.

With a witheringly condescending smile, Mari said,

"I believe it's universally acknowledged that deserts are hot and dry, Mr. Ewing. Or did your teachers in New York fail to teach anything about geography and weather patterns?"

Martin uttered a pathetic little whimper and reached for the lock of hair he liked to tug when under stress.

Tony snarled, "No, my teachers did not fail to teach geography, Miss Pottersby. And whether deserts are hot and dry or not isn't the point. The point is the weather here stinks."

Mari nodded grandly. "Indeed? I see the condition is contagious. It's apparently made a stinker out of you."

She and Tony were squaring off to fight some more when their meals arrived. Mari wouldn't have known it until Judy plunked her plate in front of her if Martin hadn't sighed and whispered, "Thank God."

When she glanced around to see why he was thanking his Maker, she beheld Judy, who was again staring at Tony Ewing. The fool. Mari had never suspected that Judy could be so silly as to fall for a pretty face. She peered at Tony and amended her assessment slightly. Okay, so the guy was more than a pretty face. Actually, if one judged by appearances alone, he'd be a grand and glorious sight. Kind of like seeing the flag waving on the Fourth of July.

Elegantly clad in a lightweight, light-colored summer suit, he seemed the very essence of masculine elegance. Mari knew that he wore a sporty straw hat, because she'd seen it on the hat rack and known it belonged to him because it looked cosmopolitan and out of place here in Mojave Wells.

His face had the lightly tanned effect that went beautifully with hair like his. His hair was thick and wavy, dark blond with lighter streaks that spoke of days spent out-of-doors. Probably on his yacht, damn him. His eyes were hazel, leaning toward green, and were large and luminous and exactly what Mari's second cousin Joan, who lived in San Bernardino and was much more worldly than Mari, called "bedroom eyes."

It seemed a dirty shame to Mari that his good looks and fine clothes hid the soul of an ogre. As Judy absentmindedly laid her plate before her, Mari said pointedly, "Thank you, Judy."

Judy, who had been lost in a contemplative fog as she gazed wistfully at Tony, jerked, and her attention shifted to Mari. "Oh, sure, Mari. Hope you like your food."

She seemed to have forgotten Mari's earlier sniping about the fare at the Mojave Inn. Mari considered this a piece of good luck, although she didn't expect it to last. The next time she came to town, Judy would assuredly complain to her about her bad manners. And she'd be right about them, too.

Mari told herself she could feel contrite and apologize to Judy later. Right now she had to keep her wits about her. It was a darned good thing the wine tasted like vinegar, or she might be tempted to gulp it down to steady her nerves.

Because she felt kind of blue for saying sassy things about the food, Mari said, "I'm sure we will, Judy." She was sure of no such thing, having heard from others about the fare served at the Mojave Inn.

"Ah," said Martin, gazing at his plate and obviously trying to maintain a calm demeanor in the face of trying odds, "food."

Mari considered it an optimistic statement under the circumstances.

Tony Ewing lifted about a pound of fried onions with his fork, peered beneath to discern what they'd hidden, and said, "Um . . ."

If Mari hadn't been so angry with him, she might

have laughed. Nobody'd warned him about the onions. Judy's mother claimed that any kind of meat tasted better when smothered in fried onions. Since hers was the only restaurant in town, nobody dared contradict her for fear of being barred for life from her dining room.

After making sure Judy was beyond hearing range, she hissed to Tony, "I told you so."

He glanced up from the pile of onions, and Mari wasn't sure if he was mad at her or not. She thought she detected a twinkle in those magnificent eyes, but didn't dare stare into them for long enough to be sure. Lordy, the man's eyes ought to be outlawed.

"You didn't, either. I distinctly recall you telling me the steaks were as tough as an old boot. You didn't mention word one about the cook's penchant for onions."

In spite of herself, Mari smiled. "I guess I forgot."

"Um, I kind of like fried onions." Martin slipped his comment into the fairly tense atmosphere, using a chipper voice in which Mari perceived an undertone of apprehension.

"Want some of mine?" Tony obligingly lifted his fork, from which dangled a tangle of limp onion rings.

"Ah, no thanks, Tony. I appreciate the offer."

Poor Martin. Of course, he might be a legitimate good guy, but Mari didn't feel it would be wise of her to let down her guard yet. He still might be out to trick her into some deal she'd regret.

Tony shoved most of the onions into a pile beside his steak. "I like onions, too, but not quite that many." He tried to saw off a bite of his steak and found it rough going. Lifting his knife, he glanced first at its edge and then at his plate. Gingerly, he stabbed at his steak with his fork. The tines didn't even make a dent in the meat. He glanced up at Mari, looking rueful. "I'm afraid you were right about the relative tenderness of this steak, Miss Pottersby."

Mari refrained from another "I told you so." Rather, she said, making an attempt to be agreeable, "Maybe you can get one of those steel carving knives from the kitchen. It'll probably taste all right if you can ever cut it up."

Tony shook his head and resumed gazing at his steak. He looked both sad and hungry, and Mari took pity on him. She told herself she was being a jackass to give in to her tender heart. After all, Tony Ewing had enough money to buy the whole town of Mojave Wells if he took it into his head to do so.

Nevertheless, she said, "Please excuse me for a moment," rose from her place, and walked to the swing door separating the dining room from the kitchen.

Even though she'd never bought a meal in their restaurant, she'd been to the Nelsons' kitchen often enough to know the way. She returned a few moments later, bearing a sharp knife in her fist. Because she was feeling kind of jocular, she repositioned the knife as if she aimed to stab Tony in the heart with it. The blasted man didn't even have the decency to pretend fright.

With a sigh, Mari decided she should have expected nothing better from him. He was too darned contrary to play along with her joke. "Here, Mr. Ewing. See if you can kill the cow with this."

"Thank you, Miss Pottersby."

"No problem." She sat, smiled at Martin, and began on her pot roast.

Mari was no kind of cook, but she decided after the first couple of bites that the meat she cooked up in her one cast-iron skillet along with potatoes, carrots, and onions grown in her garden, tasted a heck of a lot better than this piece of dried-out shoe leather. She chewed, swallowed, took a sip of water to chase the roast down, and sighed. "I'm sorry we don't have better accommodations for you movie folks here in Mojave Wells. We don't get a lot of tourists or people who want to shoot pictures here."

"Think nothing of it, Miss Pottersby. This is great fare compared to some of the places I've been."

Mari gazed at Martin for a moment, trying to catch him in the lie. At the moment, however, he was diving with evident relish into his pot roast. As his portion of beef undoubtedly came from the same cow and had been cooked in the same pot as had Mari's, she acquitted him of subterfuge. "You must have been in some mighty rough places, Mr. Tafft."

Martin laughed, took a sip of his wine, and said, "I have. The picture business isn't all glamour."

Tony snorted. Before Mari could say something nasty about his behavior, deportment, and general moral laxity, he said, "So far, I haven't seen any glamour at all, and this is only my first time around a motion picture."

In spite of herself, Mari was interested. "Is that so? I'd believed you to have been connected with the picture business for quite a while." Her ignorance of motion-picture making was so acute, she didn't even know enough to ask questions about it. Fortunately, Tony relieved her of that burden.

"Nope. I'd never even been to California before. Poor Martin bears the brunt of the work. He has to do everything that needs to be done for the studio, from hiring actors to finding locations. And wherever he goes, he has to eat the local chow. He's been everywhere and done everything." Giving up on his steak for the moment, he asked Martin, "Didn't you have to travel rough in Mexico once? I remember hearing something about fried ants and a donkey."

"Fried ants?" Mari, who loathed, detested, and despised ants, stared at Martin, horrified. "How awful!"

Martin chuckled. "They weren't ants, Tony. They were grasshoppers. They weren't half bad, either."

Yuck. Although Mari didn't hate grasshoppers with the same vehemence she reserved for ants, she didn't think she'd want to eat one. "Did you really have to eat them?" Her nose wrinkled before she could stop it. She hadn't had much of an appetite when she arrived at the Mojave Inn because of her general state of anxiety. She was rapidly losing the little appetite she'd had to begin with.

"I don't suppose I *had* to, but I had no objection, and I always try to blend in. Besides, it made them happy, so I did it. Honestly, they weren't bad. Very crunchy. If they'd had a little salt on them, they might have tasted something like French-fried potatoes. The folks in this particular village didn't use salt. Don't know if that's because there wasn't any, or what."

"Oh." Mari's tummy gave a little leap that didn't do anything for her peace of mind.

"Sounds abominable to me," Tony said flatly. "I don't know how you can keep it up, Martin."

Martin heaved another sigh. It sounded heartfelt to Mari. "I don't mind the food part, but I do have to admit I'm getting a little tired."

"A *little* tired?" Tony guffawed and drank more wine. "I'd be dead if I'd had the job you've done for the past eight or nine years." As if he expected Mari to say something wicked, he turned and gave her a straight look. "Don't say it, Miss Pottersby."

For some reason, Mari suddenly felt like laughing. So she did. "I wouldn't dream of it, Mr. Ewing."

He grinned back, and Mari almost fainted on the spot. A girl could get used to being grinned at by Tony Ewing. Which was a very bad thing. Mari immediately went back to her pot roast, even though she didn't think she could fit one more bite into her already over-wrought stomach.

After they'd finished as much of their dinner at the Mojave Inn as seemed appropriate for good health, Martin suggested they retire to the hotel's small parlor to discuss business. Mari had almost begun to relax with the two men by that time, but her nerves sprang to attention as soon as Martin mentioned business.

For some reason, her gaze flew to Tony Ewing. His face told her nothing. It looked to Mari as if he was bracing himself for an unpleasant encounter. She resented that. She wasn't unreasonable. She was merely trying to protect her interests.

Who was she trying to kid? She'd probably be better off if she sold these men the Marigold Mine outright, moved to San Bernardino or some other decent-size city, and got a regular job for regular wages.

Tony's spirits were in an uproar as he walked Mari Pottersby home after their wrangle in the parlor of the Mojave Inn. He still resented her a good deal, both for being pretty and not taking care of herself, and also for being too damned smart for a woman. Women were supposed to be meek and yielding. This hard-hearted, hardheaded female was about as far from being meek and yielding as they both were from the Rock of Gibraltar.

Yet he couldn't hate her. In fact, although it gave him no pleasure to admit it to himself, he found her fascinating.

His company made her nervous, though. He could tell. Her voice was brittle and breathy, and it seemed to him as if she were attempting to run some kind of race. She'd tried to get him to stay at the inn and let her walk home alone, but he'd refused. She might not like him, but he knew his duty as a gentleman. He held a kerosene lantern, the light guiding their way in fits and starts. He was unused to carrying such a primitive lighting tool, and it took him a while to learn to control it so that the light didn't bounce all over the place.

"Are you worried about your dog?" he asked curiously, speeding to keep up with her.

She slowed slightly and turned to gape at him. "My dog? Why should I be worried about Tiny?"

He shrugged. "I have no idea. I only wondered why you were hurrying so much."

"Hurrying? Am I?"

There wasn't light enough for him to tell, but he thought she might be blushing. "You needn't be afraid of me, Miss Pottersby. I don't bite." Although a discreet nibble here and there on the comely Mari's bare flesh held some appeal.

"Don't be ridiculous," she advised sharply. "It's late, and I have to get up early to work in the mine."

He considered asking her why she bothered, but he didn't want to rile her unnecessarily. "I see." He was glad when she slowed down, though.

She turned her head and gazed at him, a hint of rebellion in her expression. "I suppose you think I'm a fool to keep working the mine, don't you?"

"Um, well, that's not my call."

"Right. I can tell you do."

Tony decided silence would be prudent.

"Well, it's not," Mari declared hotly. "You're out here working for *your* father, aren't you?"

"Yes, I am." Prudence also dictated that he not remind her of the differences between their respective sires. Maurice Ewing was a multimillionaire. Mari's father had been a lunatic.

"There. You see? We're both carrying on for our fathers."

"Right."

They walked along without speaking for a few minutes until Mari let out a huge breath and said, "Oh, very well. You're right. The mine's probably played out, and I'm an idiot for trying to keep it going."

"I didn't say a word."

"You didn't need to." She sounded bitter. "And I suppose I am stupid. But I can't bear to quit. It was Dad's dream."

"I understand." He didn't understand for a second, although he pitched his voice to what he hoped sounded like a soothing tone.

"I'll just bet you do."

They had come to within dog-sniffing distance of her cabin, and Tiny set up an ear-splitting racket, so Tony couldn't try to redeem himself in Mari's eyes. It was probably just as well, since he couldn't figure out why he even wanted to.

Four

Mari was so concerned about her appearance, it took her five minutes to work up the nerve to open the door and step outside. The camera awaited her there.

"Am I really supposed to look like this?" She heard the despair in her voice and hated it. But, honestly! She looked like a ghost. A ghoul. She looked really, really bad.

The makeup artist who had accompanied the cameraman to Mojave Wells laughed. "Trust me, Miss Pottersby, this is exactly the way you're supposed to look. Because of the nature of the celluloid film, white makeup is the only type that looks natural."

She didn't believe him, although she couldn't think of any reason he'd lie to her. Unless this was all part of an elaborate plot to deprive her of her mine.

Don't be any more of a fool than you can help being, Mari Pottersby, she commanded herself. Why would Peerless want the Marigold Mine? The place was a worthless piece of dirt in the middle of an even more worthless desert.

"It'll be all right," the makeup man assured her. "I think you'll look wonderful on film."

That made one of them. Mari took a deep breath, stiffened her backbone, and turned the doorknob. Staring straight ahead, she flung the door wide and marched out into the heat of the day. That had been a mistake she discovered immediately when she stubbed her toe on a huge trunk in her path.

"Ow!" She grabbed her foot and hopped up and down. "Who put that thing there?"

"Oh, golly, I'm sorry, Miss Pottersby." Another man—what his job might be, Mari couldn't even guess—rushed up and shoved the trunk aside. "I meant to move that before."

Feeling extremely gloomy, Mari said, "That's all right. I don't suppose it matters." It wouldn't matter if she broke her neck, if it came to that, and it might spare her a whole lot of future misery.

Which was no way to think. She scolded herself some more as she tried to iron out her rumpled composure. Thank God Martin Tafft possessed a compassionate soul. He hurried over.

"Gee, I'm sorry about the trunk, Miss Pottersby."

"That's all right," Mari repeated dully. This was stupid, and she knew she'd be humiliated when Martin discovered it too. She was no more an actress than she was a princess.

Martin stepped back from her and gazed at her face. Mari hoped the thick makeup hid her blush. "Boy, you look swell!"

Disappointment smote her. She hadn't truly believed Martin Tafft was a liar until this minute. She said, "Right."

Martin laughed. "Oh, I know. You don't believe me. But you'll see. I have a feeling a new career awaits you in the pictures, Miss Pottersby. Motion-picture actors make a lot of money, so don't sneer until you see the results of this test."

"Okay." Mari figured she might as well comply meekly, rather than make a fuss. Her failure would be less mortifying if she didn't stir up a lot of bother as she achieved it. The sooner this was over, the better.

Great. Perfect. There was Tony Ewing. Why did he have to be here?

Stupid question. It was his father's money at work on every aspect of this idiotic venture. Mari was surprised when he rose from the camp stool he'd been occupying and came up to her, holding out his hand and smiling. This was a change, indeed. Glancing up at the sky, she had to acknowledge that the weather seemed cooler today. Maybe his bad moods really *were* a result of the sweltering heat.

"Good morning, Miss Pottersby. You look swell."

Hmmm. That made two swells and one abysmal—her personal assessment. Mari decided to withhold her final judgment until she saw what Martin called the test.

"Thank you." The two words were mechanical. It was a darned good thing these silly pictures were silent, because Mari knew from bitter experience that she couldn't emote worth a darn. Her teacher had told her that more than once, during the catastrophes that passed for class plays.

"Ready, Ben?" Martin called to a man who stood behind the motion-picture camera, an intricate contraption the likes of which Mari had never seen before. It was big and boxlike, had a crank on its side, and stood on a tripod. Martin had explained during their meal at the Mojave Inn that great advances were being made almost daily in the motion-picture industry. Folks were developing fancier cameras and better lighting. They were even building huge motion-picture palaces in cities large and small across the nation.

Mari wondered what would happen to the world if all those geniuses spending their brain power on the pictures were to turn it to something useful. Like medicine. Eliminating poverty and famine. Mining engineering.

She was nervous. That was the only reason she was finding fault here; she was sure of it.

The man named Ben stepped out from behind his camera, signaled to Martin that he was ready with a wave and a grin, and Martin took Mari's arm. "Now, try not to be nervous, Mari. We're all on your side."

He'd called her Mari. She blinked at him, so surprised he'd used her given name that she forgot to be scared of the camera. She wondered if that had been his intention. After the cameraman started turning the crank, a huge grinding noise erupted, and Mari whirled around to see what was going on.

"Good!" Martin cried. "Now walk up to Ben. He's the guy behind the camera."

Well, heck, this wasn't so hard. Mari even smiled a little as she did as Martin had instructed her. A big pop startled her, she saw a sprocket fly out of the camera, and she worried for a second that something terrible had happened. Martin's voice at her back reassured her.

"That's natural, Mari. Those sprockets chunk out every few seconds. It's the nature of the filming process."

"Oh. Okay." She wondered what she was supposed to do now. Fortunately, Martin also directed motion pictures from time to time, and he told her.

"Can you walk over to the fence now? Pretend you're picking flowers or something."

Picking flowers? In Mojave Wells? Mari shrugged and did as directed. She felt silly bending over to pluck imaginary flowers out of the air, but she'd built a fairly sizable bouquet before Martin gave her another direction.

"Wonderful. You're doing swell! Now, can you turn quickly and look frightened, as if someone you fear is creeping up on you?"

"Sure. I guess so."

"I'll help," came a voice she recognized from behind her.

She stood abruptly and turned to see Tony Ewing stalking toward her like the villain out of a nightmare. She backed up, honestly frightened for a moment as she took in the grim expression on his face and heard him snarl wickedly.

"You don't have to pretend so hard," she muttered, and put up a hand as if to ward him off.

"Who's pretending?" he growled.

He sounded as if he meant it, and Mari experienced a moment of real panic. She felt her eyes open wide, and she backed up until she bumped flat against the fence. Still, he came at her. She cried, "No! Stop it!"

"Never!" His voice had taken on a timbre Mari had never heard in a human being. He sounded like a human version of Tiny when he was seriously irked.

This wasn't funny anymore. It got less funny when Tony reached out, grabbed her shoulders, and wrenched her away from the fence and into his arms. She reacted automatically and violently.

"Ow!"

"Stop being such a baby."

"Dammit, that hurts." Tony swatted Mari's hand away from his forehead.

"Serves you right," Mari grumbled as she plopped the wet rag she'd removed into a bowl of water and handed him a wetter one to press against the lump on his skull.

"For the love of God, I was only trying to help you do well in the test."

She lifted her chin. "You didn't have to try so darned hard. You might have warned me first, anyhow."

"You're a frightening woman, Miss Pottersby, did you know that?"

"Fiddlesticks." Disgruntled, Mari took the bottle of iodine from Ben, uncorked it, and poured some of its contents onto a wad of cotton wool. "Here, move that cloth and let me put some of this on the cut."

"What did you hit me with, anyway?"

"A rock. And it was your own fault. You shouldn't have grabbed me like that."

"We were doing a test!" Tony sounded furious.

In a way, Mari didn't blame him. In another way, she did. "How was I supposed to know what to do? I've never done anything like this before!"

"God."

"Mr. Tafft didn't warn me you were going to butt in and scare me to death."

"For the love of . . . I can't believe you really thought I meant to do you harm. The whole thing was being captured on celluloid!"

"Hunh." He was being such a pill, Mari almost wished she could hit him again. She felt kind of silly, though, since she ought to have known he was pretending. But she was right, too. This was all brand-new to her, and she wasn't accustomed to strange men creeping up on her, looking as if they wanted to strangle her and then do horrid things to her. Or vice versa.

He jerked away from her extended hand, giving her an excuse to snap, "Stop being a baby and let me dab this iodine on that bump."

"A baby! I bet I'll have a black eye tomorrow, blast you."

"Fiddlesticks. It's only a little bump."

"A little bump? You might have knocked me out!"

Mari smirked. "It would have served you right."

Fortunately, Martin rushed up to them, sparing them both increased hostilities. "Mari! Come on inside. I've seen the test, and I think you're wonderful." He slowed down and grinned at Tony. "You were pretty splendid, too, Tony. You really did look like you were bent on murder. Want a part in our next movie?"

Tony muttered, "God."

Mari smirked again. "See? I told you so. You ought to have said something. Then I wouldn't have been frightened."

Martin laughed, which went some way toward dispelling the bad feelings swirling in the air. "Cut it out, you two. You look great together on film. I'm almost sorry we've already signed Harrowgate to the leading male role."

Tony took the hand Martin held out to him. Although she felt more like giving Tony a big shove from behind than assisting him, Mari took his other arm and helped him to his feet. She really had given him a pretty good wallop. She was darned proud of herself, in fact.

"When we get inside the inn, maybe I can rustle up some sticking plaster and gauze," she offered. "He probably ought to keep that cut covered, at least until it stops oozing."

"Oozing?" Tony grabbed his arm away from her as if he suspected her of membership in some demonic cult. "Oozing? Good God, that sounds as if my brains are leaking out!"

Mari batted her eyelashes and shrugged, as if she were silently asking him what he expected.

"I can walk by myself." He then let out an inarticulate growl, yanked his other arm away from Martin, and stormed off ahead of them to the inn. They watched him in silence for a moment, then Mari spoke.

"I didn't mean to hurt him. I don't know why I got so scared."

Martin chuckled softly. "I do. You were already

frightened about the test, didn't know what to expect, and then Tony tried to help you along."

"Humph. Well, if the test was to see if I could act scared, I expect it worked out all right. He scared the heck out of me."

Fudge. She shouldn't have said heck out loud. With a sigh, Mari guessed she had a lot of practice to do in order to fit in with the motion-picture community. The rough-and-ready mining environment in which she'd been reared hadn't prepared her for polite society.

But Martin only chuckled some more. "Whatever happened, the screen test looks very good. If you always come across that way on film, it looks as if you were born for this."

She turned and gawped at him for a moment before she realized he was kidding her. Trying to make her feel good about making such an idiot of herself. It was nice of him, but unnecessary. Mari had no illusions about herself—or about life, if it came to that.

Gazing at her in turn, Martin said, "You don't believe me, do you?"

Now she was embarrassed. But she told the truth anyway. "Actually, no. I don't."

"Why do you think I'd fib to you?"

Good question. Mari thought about it. "To get my mine?"

"You've already agreed to rent me your mine, Miss Pottersby. I told you the truth when I said you look exactly the way the heroine in *Lucky Strike* is supposed to look."

She thought some more. "In that case, I don't know why you're fibbing to me."

Martin shook his head. "I wish you weren't so suspicious of our motives, Miss Pottersby. All we want to do is make the best motion picture we can. If you're right for the part, it will help us along."

That made sense, even to Mari. Still, she couldn't feature a man-about-town like Martin Tafft or a stuck-up rich boy like Tony Ewing actually needing *her,* Mari Pottersby, to act in a picture. It didn't make any sense. Such a scenario was too far out of Mari's experience to be believable.

She decided to shut up about it. It was going to be hard enough watching herself on film without making herself miserable ahead of time.

They found Tony slumping in an uncomfortable folding chair in a darkened back parlor of the Mojave Inn, looking grumpy with his arms crossed over his chest. The pose of granitelike grievance didn't last long since the rag kept slipping off his head and he had to keep uncrossing his arms to slap a hand to it. When she saw him trying to keep up appearances thus, Mari's heart did a teensy jump, and a twinge of compunction attacked her.

"Oh, dear," she murmured. "I'd really better fetch some gauze and sticking plaster before we watch this test thing."

"I'll help you." Martin was laughing as he said it.

Tony didn't think there was one single little thing funny about this latest outrageous behavior on Miss Marigold Pottersby's part. The woman was a walking disaster. He'd only been trying to help her, dammit.

She had looked so small and alone and scared when the camera started grinding that Tony had felt an overwhelming compulsion to help her make good. And then the fiend had seized a rock and tried to kill him with it. Damn her and all uncivilized females to perdition.

He glared at her and Martin when they entered the room where they were going to screen her test. He wished the damned washrag would stop slipping. He rose abruptly when they turned around and walked out again.

"Damnation, where are they going now?"

But they were already gone. They'd left him. They'd taken one look at him, turned around, and left him all by himself.

Fine. This was just fine. First she tried to kill him, then she opted to leave him alone to die by himself with no one nearby to give a damn. All right for her. See if he cared.

He'd sat back down and resumed stewing in an even more powerful grump when the door opened again. His heart did a crazy hitching leap when he beheld Mari, armed with scissors, tape, and gauze, heading his way, although he wouldn't show his pleasure to her for all the world.

"Here, Mr. Ewing. I've brought a bandage for you."

Her voice was soft and musical; it didn't fit her. She was anything but soft and musical. She was a stringy harridan, and she was crazy, obtuse, and dangerous. "Thank you. You needn't bother." He made sure his voice was as hard as rocks.

The insane woman didn't seem to care. "Don't be a baby," she commanded, as if his voice hadn't put her off at all. "You can't keep slapping that rag on your head for the rest of your life. I'll just bandage it with gauze and tape and you can forget about it."

And exactly what did she mean by that? Tony would never forget that she'd beaned him with a rock. Why, he might well have a permanent scar from this. Not that he cared about scars. Still, she seemed mighty nonchalant for a woman who'd recently attempted murder. Not to mention the fact that it was terribly humiliating to have allowed himself to be conked by a female.

"I doubt that I'll be able to forget about it entirely, Miss Pottersby, since I have no doubt the wound will take some time to heal." Lord, he *did* sound rather like a small child, didn't he? Trying to cover up, he said with an assumption of graciousness, "You needn't bother. I can bandage my own head."

"You'll need a mirror to see yourself," she pointed out.

Nettled, Tony snapped, "I'm sure I can manage."

"Oh, stop being such a darned snot!" Mari had the grace to blush and press her lips together.

Tony merely glared at her, so indignant his head began to pound, which he was pretty sure wasn't doing his wound any good.

"I'm sorry," she said almost immediately. "I didn't mean that. And I'm sorry I hurt you. Even if you did deserve it."

It's as if she couldn't bear to make a sincere apology. Livid, Tony said in measured tones, "I was trying to help you."

She sighed. "Yes, yes, I know. Now shut up and let me cover that knot."

He gave up. "Very well."

"You might want to try to relax. You're sure to get a headache if you stay all mad and tense like that, Mr. Ewing."

"And exactly how much medical training have you had, Miss Pottersby?"

She sighed again. "Go ahead, belittle me. But I've learned how to doctor most injuries and illnesses in my life."

"I'm sure." He hoped he sounded disparaging, because that's how he felt.

She didn't argue. Her fingers handled the gauze and scissors deftly, and she created a perfect pad for his poor head. The wound throbbed, and Tony wondered if she was right about him getting a headache if he didn't calm down. Dammit, he didn't want her to be right. About anything.

"After I get the pad taped in place, I'm going to massage your neck," she told him.

He jerked away from her, spoiling Mari's aim and getting a piece of plaster stuck to his nose. He yanked it away furiously. "You're going to *what?*"

"Will you stop that?" She ripped another length of tape from the roll and snipped it off. She was sticking the strips to one of the arms of his chair.

He wasn't sure he trusted her. "Why are you doing that?" he asked suspiciously.

"So they'll be ready when I need them."

That made sense. "Oh." He still didn't like it.

"Stay still, or we'll never get this done."

But Tony wasn't so easily mollified. "You said something about massaging my neck. What was that about?" It was outrageous. It was scandalous. No proper female put her bare hands on a gentleman's flesh, massage or no massage, wound or no wound.

"For pity's sake, calm down and stop being such a sissy," Mari commanded.

"Sissy? *Sissy!*"

"Yes. Sissy. You're thinking it's improper for me to massage your neck, aren't you?"

Tony clamped his mouth shut and didn't answer her sarcastic question, mainly because he'd have had to say yes.

"Well, for your information, Mister, massage helps relax a body. When you have to live rough, you learn not to be fussy about maintaining all of the silly airs and graces people who live in towns think they need to survive. They're wrong, you know. All of those things are unnecessary luxuries."

Airs and graces? Was the woman mad?

Stupid question. Of course, she was. Although he hated it, the notion of Mari's fingers massaging his neck appealed to him. Tony sat back in his chair and glowered at her. "Very well. If you must."

"I swear, men are such babies," Mari muttered as she dabbed more iodine onto his cut head.

He winced inside, because it hurt. But he'd be boiled in oil before he'd let her know it.

"There. Now don't move again, or we'll never get this done." She gently placed the pad over his wound and held it there while she plucked one of the pieces of tape from the arm of his chair.

In order to bandage him properly, she had to lift her arms, thus giving Tony an up-close and perfect view of her bodice. She had a nice shape. And she obviously didn't go in for corsets and a lot of boning. Although she was slender, the curves he could see were all hers. He could tell, because her nipples pressed against the calico. Tony swallowed and couldn't decide if he was more happy to have found that out, or just the opposite.

She worked fast. Too fast, in Tony's opinion. He wanted to investigate her attributes for a while longer.

No such luck. He had just about decided that the size of her breasts was probably perfect—not mere fried eggs and not balloons, but a delicious handful—when she sat back, lowered her arms, and said, "There. All done." She sounded intolerably self-satisfied.

"If I get an infection . . ." his voice trailed off, because he didn't want her to accuse him of being a baby again.

"You won't get an infection," she said with conviction.

He wanted to argue, but held back because he didn't want her to think he was sniveling. In truth, he was only furious and wanted to lash out at her for catching him unaware and beaning him. He was a man, blast it, and she was a skinny little snippet of a female.

Perhaps not skinny . . .

At all odds, she was female, and females were supposed to be weaker and less capable than men. They weren't supposed to bash men over the head with rocks.

Miss Marigold Pottersby was about as weak and incapable as a grizzly bear. With elaborate courtesy, he bowed to her from his chair. "I'm sure you're right."

Her head tipped slightly to one side, she gazed at him through slitted eyes. "And if you do get an infection, I'll be more than happy to lance it for you."

Her smile was as evil a one as Tony had ever seen. For some reason, it made him want to laugh out loud and hug her hard. Good God, insanity must be contagious. "Thanks a lot."

"Think nothing of it." She gathered her medical accoutrements together, rose from her chair in a more stately manner than Tony would have guessed her capable of, and trounced off to Martin's side.

Martin, Tony noticed with interest, was grinning at the two of them, as if he thought they were as cunning a pair as he'd ever seen. Tony's urge to laugh vanished. Miss Marigold Pottersby was a very dangerous female.

"Ready to watch this thing now?" Martin queried in a friendly, let's-all-be-pals voice.

Mari set her tape, scissors, and gauze on a table. "I guess so." If she was enthusiastic, she hid it admirably.

"Let's get it over with," Tony growled.

Mari frowned at him. He frowned back. So they were back to square one.

Martin had already arranged chairs for them. While she was doctoring Tony's wound, Mari had moved a couple of them out of line. She pushed them back, then sat in the one on the end, leaving a chair between herself and Tony. Although this didn't surprise Tony, it did disappoint him. He couldn't have said why, since he really wasn't keen on being close to a woman who was evidently out to kill him if she got the chance.

"I thought you were going to massage my neck," he said stiffly.

"I'll do it after this is over." She sounded grim.

He had to be satisfied with that.

The screening was to be done against a wall of the parlor. Ben and Martin had removed two paintings—very bad ones—from the wall and propped them up next to the sofa. The wall was more or less white, and would make a passable viewing screen. The accommodations around this place were pretty pathetic, Tony thought with an internal sneer.

Then he told himself not to be a snob. Then he told himself he wasn't a snob, and that Mari Pottersby was dead wrong about him. Nevertheless, he felt slightly ignoble about having had disparaging thoughts about the Mojave Inn. After all, nobody came here. Why would they? Unless a person had business with the miners hereabouts, why visit Mojave Wells? It was a terrible place. A ghastly one. One that no right-thinking individual would ever visit on purpose, unless he were forced to. As Martin and Tony had been.

Sighing happily, Martin sat in the middle chair. Eyeing him, Tony decided Martin, at least, was glad Mari had chosen to sit apart from Tony. The poor man probably feared a fight would break out if they sat next to each other.

That was silly. Tony would never strike a woman, not even one as irritating and hazardous as Mari Pottersby.

"Can you get the lights, Ben?"

"Sure thing, Martin."

Tony watched as the cameraman went to the light switch, pressed the off button, and returned to his camera. The room wasn't awfully dark, but it was dark enough that Tony wished Mari were sitting next to him. He still didn't know why. But he'd have liked to watch her face as she saw herself on film. He was curious to see her reaction.

"Okay," said Ben from behind the projector. "Here goes. It's rough and unedited."

"That's fine," Martin told him. "All we need to see is how Miss Pottersby projects herself on film."

Tony thought he heard a noise from Mari, sort of a cross between a moan and a sigh. He looked her way, but only saw Martin. Damn it.

A mechanical sound started, a tunnel of light flickered from the projector, and images began appearing on the wall. There were several frames of test patterns, and then nothing. Into the nothing, a woman walked.

Mari gasped. "Mercy sakes, is that me?" The question had been asked in a whisper, and held a world of wonder.

"That's you." Martin, on the other hand, sounded about as happy as a man could sound.

Watching the wall, Tony guessed he understood why Martin sounded so damned happy. Mari Pottersby looked good on film. Very good. Appealing. Delicious. Almost ethereal—which was a laugh, since she was about as ethereal as a dynamite blast.

Unable to stand not knowing how she was taking this, Tony leaned over and peeked at Mari. She was sitting as straight as an iron rod in her chair. It looked as if her hands were strangling each other in a tight knot in her lap. She stared at the Mari projected on the wall as if in horror. Her mouth opened slightly, and it looked as if she wanted to say something, but she didn't. She licked her lips.

He couldn't wait any longer. "What do you think, Miss Pottersby? How do you like yourself on celluloid?"

She didn't turn to look at him, being too occupied in staring at the wall. "I—I don't know. It doesn't look like me. I mean, it doesn't look like what I think I look like. I mean—oh, bother."

Tony understood.

So, apparently, did Martin. He chuckled easily. Everything about Martin was easy. Tony usually enjoyed Martin's company, but sometimes he acknowledged a faint twinge of envy. Tony wished he could be as personable as Martin. Martin got along with everybody. Tony struggled with people who weren't as quick as he, or as knowledgeable. It wasn't a pleasant personality characteristic, and he tried to hide it. He figured he'd inherited it from his father, who was as impatient as a man could be.

"It's probably going to take you some time to get used to it," Martin went on to say. "Lots of people have a hard time when they first see themselves on film."

Mari wouldn't turn and face Tony, but she had no trouble facing Martin. Tony frowned as he saw her face, chalk white from makeup and the darkness, stare with those huge, beautiful eyes at his companion.

"Really? You mean, everyone looks strange on film?"

Another chuckle. Then Martin said, "You only think you look strange. The truth is, you look great. You're absolutely a perfect fit for the heroine of *Lucky Strike,* and I wouldn't be at all surprised if there were many more opportunities for you, should you want them, after this picture comes out. You're a natural."

She was a natural, all right. As Tony watched himself appear on the wall, creeping toward Mari, Mari backing up in terror, and then picking up a rock and walloping him over the head with it, he decided she was a natural disaster.

Five

Two weeks later, the town of Mojave Wells was under siege. At least that's how it looked to Mari, who watched with trepidation as trucks and wagons loaded to the rails with picture props, cast, crew, scenery, cameras, and trunks and boxes filled with mysterious stuff, rolled into the small town.

The Peerless Studio had taken the place over. Mojave Wells had grown to twice its normal size in a single day. The Mojave Inn was full to overflowing. Judy had even been forced to give up her own room to accommodate Peerless crew members. Citizens had been recruited to rent rooms to some of the actors.

Nobody minded. This was the most exciting thing that had ever happened in the small desert community. It beat the tar out of borax mining.

Everyone who had lived in the town for more than a year or so marveled at the prospect of one of their own actually getting to play a part in a moving picture. Mari had never entertained so many visitors in her short life.

Tiny, who loved company, was thrilled.

Mari, who enjoyed the camaraderie, was as nervous as a rabbit facing a stew pot.

She held onto Tiny's collar as carpenters moved in on her mine. Her heart thumped like a bass drum. "Oh, boy, Tiny, I hope I'm doing the right thing."

How could ten thousand dollars possibly be the wrong thing?

Mari didn't know, but she'd struggled to survive for long enough to doubt the existence of good luck. Luck was what a person worked like the devil to achieve and then generally didn't. It wasn't something granted by a passing good fairy from Peerless who decided to whack an individual on the head with her—or, in this case, his—magic wand.

Oh, sure, Mari had read about the chance soul who happened to find a vein of rich ore in his backyard. She understood some guy in Australia had found a rock that had turned out to be a gigantic diamond while out walking in a field.

That kind of luck had never visited Mari, and she didn't expect it to show up at her door. She'd had to work like heck all of her life and didn't anticipate that aspect of existence changing anytime soon. As a matter of fact, she couldn't rid herself of a taint of mistrust about this whole motion-picture venture with which she'd gotten herself entangled.

"Oh, good. There's Mr. Tafft."

Walking toward her waving and smiling, and dressed to the nines as usual, Martin was the first real bright spot Mari had encountered today. She smiled back tentatively, wondering if he was going to bring her bad news. She couldn't imagine what it might be. That he'd found another girl who looked better than she did on film? That he'd decided not to use her mine after all?

But no. Those guys with the picks, hammers, saws, and shovels were now clustered around the Marigold, talking to each other. They must be going to do something. Mari hoped they'd shore up the rickety structure of the mine shaft, which had been in place for far too long without repairs. She wasn't holding her breath, however.

"Good morning, Miss Pottersby!" Martin called when he was still several yards away. He looked peachy in a tan sack coat and sporty knickerbocker pants. He was quite the dresser, although he always managed somehow to appear tasteful and not at all gaudy. Mari feared if she tried to be fashionable, she'd stick out of the crowd like a bandaged thumb. You couldn't turn a sow's ear into a silk purse, as she'd been told all her life. Which was sort of depressing.

She forced herself to smile at Martin. "Hi, there, Mr. Tafft. I see you're ready to begin working on the picture." She tried to sound confident. She swore to herself that she wouldn't cry when he told her they were pulling out and that she'd never see a dime of Peerless money, much less the ten grand she'd been promised.

Martin strode up, grinning. Before he responded to Mari's comment, he held out a hand for Tiny, who demonstrated his obliging nature by washing it for him.

Mari said, "Tiny!"

The dog merely wagged his tail, thus stirring up a cloud of dust, assuming Mari had spoken his name as a sign of approval. Tiny never anticipated unpleasantness in people. She wished she could be more like her dog.

Martin laughed. "He's a friendly cuss, for so enormous a dog, isn't he?"

"Yes." Mari sighed. Heck, even her dog, who looked like he might eat a person as soon as look at him, was a teddy bear in disguise. Maybe she should have got herself one of those ratty little Chihuahuas. They were mean as the dickens. But she loved Tiny, good nature and all, and couldn't bear even to think about giving him up. That was another reason she was going to be miserable when Martin told her she wasn't going to get that pile of money.

Martin straightened, still smiling. Tiny's eyes took on the mournful cast Mari could never resist, so she took over petting him after Martin gave it up.

"The first thing we're going to do is test the strength of your mine's main tunnel, if that's all right with you." Martin gazed happily at the crew clumped around the mine's entrance.

Maybe they *were* going to use her mine, and maybe they'd even shore up the shaft. Mari licked her lips and mentally crossed her fingers.

"Sure. I mean, you explained that to me before." She'd even had him spell it out in the contract. Unfortunately, she'd managed to develop grave doubts in the ensuing weeks. Mari had gotten the feeling, while they'd been negotiating, that Anthony Ewing had been impatient with her. But she'd never done anything like this before, and aimed to make darned sure she didn't encounter any unpleasant surprises. Anything might happen, however, and she swore she'd keep a stiff upper lip when it did.

"Right." Martin nodded. "But I want to make sure you always know what's going on, because I know how much this mine means to you."

He didn't even sound sarcastic, and Mari appreciated him for it. "Thank you."

"Thank *you.*"

So much for that. Although she hated herself for it, Mari asked, "Um, is Mr. Ewing going to be here during the filming?"

"Tony?" Martin seemed surprised. "Oh, sure. He's going to be here the whole time. This is his father's first picture investment, and Tony's going to be an integral part of the entire process."

"Oh."

"In fact," Martin went on eagerly, "I think I see him coming right now." He walked a few paces away from

Mari, lifted his cupped hands to his mouth, and called out, "Tony! Over here!" He raised his arm and made sweeping gestures of welcome.

Great. Now she could have Tony Ewing sneering at her.

Mari told herself to stop it. She'd been mooning about the man for two solid weeks now. Why was she pretending not to want him here now?

Simple, she answered herself. She was afraid of him. Oh, she wasn't afraid of *him* exactly. She was terrified of what he represented, which was everything she'd ever dreamed about for her life. Mari had adored her father, who'd been a decent, hardworking, lovable, witty, and lighthearted fellow. She wished more people in the world were like him, in fact.

But, oh, sometimes she really, really longed for stability and security. Even a luxury or two might be nice every once in a while.

Tony Ewing, the son of a man as wealthy as Mari's father had been poor, epitomized every good thing in the world to her. He had money, looks, breeding, intelligence, business sense, and an effortless ability to fit into society. Any society. Even her fellow natives of Mojave Wells claimed to like him. Mari had asked, since she'd found him so alarming. Not to mention annoying.

She'd discovered herself to be the only one who had this reaction to him. All the rest of her friends thought he was a pip.

Yes, indeedy. Tony Ewing had everything. Mari had nothing. They were poles apart in every particular, and he made her so skittish, she could hardly stand it.

As he got closer, she tried not to stare at him in awe. He looked good enough to eat today, in his seersucker summer suit and jaunty straw hat, with his easy stride eating up the distance between them. She couldn't figure out why his appearance today should move her so much. She'd certainly not forgotten how good looking he was; yet seeing him in person rattled her.

She braced herself for the encounter, unwilling to let him know how much his presence affected her. He was conceited enough already. He didn't need to add her to his trophy list. She imagined her head, stuffed and mounted, in the reading room of some elegant Ewing-owned castle somewhere, her name engraved on a small brass plaque underneath. She'd not be given a place of honor. That, she was sure, he'd reserve for someone of greater social standing, poise, beauty, and wealth than she.

In fact, he might not even bother to mount her head. Shoot, he must have millions of women under his belt by this time. Therefore, she didn't greet him with a smile as he approached her and Martin. She watched his pleasant expression harden as he joined them.

Unfortunately, her concentration on ignoring Tony Ewing caused her attention to slip from Tiny. The dog stood up, wagging up a hurricane with his tale, and she jerked sideways, not having anticipated the sudden movement. When Tiny let out an ecstatic bark and lurched away from her, her hand slipped from his collar, and Tiny bounded off to greet Tony.

"Tony! I mean *Tiny!*" Mari shrieked, as she watched her dog barrel straight at the approaching millionaire.

"Oh, Lord," murmured Martin.

"Damn it!" bellowed Tony as Tiny, in a display of rapture so great it surprised even Mari, leaped upon Tony, putting his giant black paws on his white-clad shoulders. Formerly white-clad shoulders.

Mari whispered, "Oh, dear," and pressed her flaming cheeks with her hands.

Martin chuckled.

"Damnation, Miss Pottersby, call off this beast!"

At least Tony didn't fall over backward under the dog's exuberant greeting.

"I've already said I'm sorry," Mari snapped. *"I* can't help it if my dog has no discrimination."

Tony glowered at her, so furious, he could scarcely get his brain to form words and his lips to speak them. "You might train the damned thing not to maul visitors."

"He didn't maul you. He greeted you with affection. Here. Try this."

Tony eyed the dripping rag in Mari's hand with distaste. He'd never had to live so rough in his life, and he didn't like it. Why people actually ventured into the wild, where there were no accommodations, and even worse beasts than this woman's dog, baffled him. "What did you put in the water?" he asked suspiciously.

"Only washing soda. It'll probably get the dirt out. It's *only* dirt."

Only dirt. "Right." He snatched the rag from her hand and scrubbed a dirty shoulder. He ought to have known better than to wear a new suit in this disgusting wilderness. It only made him more furious to know he'd done so to impress Mari Pottersby.

Where had his brain gone begging? Why, *why* did he care what the ridiculous chit thought of him? Why did it gall him so to know that she despised him. *She* despised *him,* for the love of God! She didn't have two cents to rub together. Why, Tony Ewing could buy her precious mine right out from under her, and she wouldn't be able to do a damned thing to stop him.

Except bash him with a rock.

Which made *him* want to laugh out loud. And then turn her over his knee and spank her the way her father should have done.

And that was another thing. Her loyalty to a man who'd obviously been deranged irked Tony. It wasn't a quality with which Tony was familiar, loyalty. He could recall his father, many times, cutting men off at the knees who'd been his staunchest supporters only a short time earlier.

That's the way Tony had been taught to believe the world worked.

Until he'd met Mari Pottersby, who seemed willing to undergo the torments of hell out of loyalty to a dead father who didn't deserve such reverence. Hell, if it had been *his* father—but Tony, shocked by the turn his thoughts had taken, desisted. His father might be a bastard, but he was a shrewd businessman, and Tony honored him for it.

Not for Maurice Ewing the mawkish sentiment displayed by Mari for her dead parent. If old Maurice had met Mari's father, he'd have set him straight with one or two painful home truths. Then he'd have taken the Marigold Mine and done something with it, sending Mari to the poorhouse along with her old man.

"Do you need another rag?"

Tony's troubled thoughts had led him away from the damage Tiny had done to his formerly immaculate summer suit. Mari's snappish question dragged him back again. "What? Oh." He glanced down to see that he'd been rubbing one dirty patch of his left shoulder for several seconds without paying attention to his job. "Yes, I guess so." Because she irked him so damned much, he frowned at her.

She frowned back. "Here." She thrust a rag at him.

"Watch out!" He jumped back too late to avoid soapy water dripping onto the knee of his trousers. "Damn it, are you determined to drown me today, or what?"

"Oh, stop whining. Anybody with an ounce of sense

knows better than to wear light colors out here in the desert."

Tony practically threw his old rag at her as he grabbed the wet one out of her outstretched hand. "That's nonsense. Light colors reflect the sun. You're wearing white." So there.

She lifted that stubborn chin of hers and glared into his eyes. Her own eyes looked large and luminous in the blazing sunlight. How did she always manage to look so clean and cool in this ghastly climate? She was probably used to it. Tony started in on his other shoulder. When he squinted down at the one he'd just scrubbed, his temper spurted up again. These rags of hers were doing no good.

"I may wear white, but I'm not silly enough to wear a fancy city suit out here," she retorted.

"Of course not," Tony growled through his teeth. "You don't have one." He added furiously, "Dammit, this will never come clean."

"Fiddlesticks."

Nevertheless, she appeared doubtful as she viewed his jacket. She even tutted softly. "Take it off, will you? Let me look at it. Maybe I can soak it clean or something."

"I don't trust you," he said nastily.

"Oh, for Pete's sake!"

"Listen, Miss Pottersby, it isn't *my* dog that attacks visitors and mauls them—and don't tell me he doesn't maul people, either. Your dog's a menace. It ought to be destroyed." Tony would never, ever destroy a dog for being friendly, even if it was too large and too exuberant. His annoyance with Mari, however, was so great that his tongue ran away with his better sense. He'd seldom spoken rashly to anyone either, because he'd always been a prudent man. Until now.

Mari drew away from him as if his very presence

offended her; as if he were a monster out of her worst nightmare. Her lower lip trembled. Tony watched, fascinated.

"You—you wouldn't." The words were only a hoarse scrape against the blistering air.

Good God, she was going to cry. Tony couldn't believe his eyes.

"You beast." She swiped a hand across her cheek as if she were mad at herself for succumbing to tears. "You can't hurt Tiny."

Probably true. Hell, he didn't even want to. He was only peeved with himself for allowing the dog to get the better of him. He actually kind of liked Tiny. He was a good dog. And friendly. A little too friendly, given his size.

Tony didn't want to admit it. Let the insufferable woman worry for a while. He said coldly, "The animal is a menace. If you can't control it, it ought to be put away."

"No."

If her eyes got any bigger, Tony might just fall into them and drown. She was going to be spectacular on film. Magnificent. The public was going to fall in love with her. She'd have all the men in the United States wanting to marry her.

For some reason, Tony's temper erupted again. "If you want to keep that monster dog, Miss Pottersby, I suggest you figure out how to control it."

"If you so much as lay a finger on my dog, I swear, I'll—I'll—" Her voice started shaking as if it were being disturbed by a strong wind, and she had to stop and clear her throat. "I'll shoot you."

Tony scoffed. "Don't be ridiculous. It's only a dog." He'd never been allowed to own a dog. His father didn't like them.

For some time now, Tony had wondered if his father's

distaste stemmed from the possibility that a dog in the house might garner attention, thus deflecting it from Maurice. Tony prided himself on being a realist. He knew his father's ego needed constant pampering.

"Tiny is all I have, you *horrid* man."

Good Lord, her voice had gone positively lethal. Miss Marigold Pottersby could be a volatile female without half trying, couldn't she? "I thought your precious mine is all you had," he said, feeling spiteful as he did so.

"It is. The mine and Tiny. If you do anything to either one of them, I'll—" She stopped speaking abruptly.

Tony thought he knew why. He sneered down at her. "You'll what? Kill me? Don't be silly. You signed a contract."

"There's nothing in the contract that says you get to do anything bad to my dog," she hissed. "And you'd better not."

This conversation was becoming more preposterous by the second. Tony would never hurt an animal for no better reason than that it got his clothes dirty. He couldn't understand why he'd threatened Mari with the destruction of Tiny. Such tactics were underhanded and mean; they made him sick.

He wouldn't admit as much to Mari in a million years. He yanked his jacket off. "Here. You said you might be able to clean this." He shoved it at her.

"Not until you promise me you won't hurt Tiny." She hugged his jacket to her bosom, and her face held a combination of terror and defiance that made Tony feel unpleasantly guilty.

"Oh, for God's sake, I'm not in the habit of hurting dogs."

"That's not what you said. You said—"

"Damnation, I know what I said!" He hated getting

trapped in situations of his own making. His father never got tangled up like this.

Of course, his father was the meanest son of a bitch on the eastern seaboard. "I promise I won't hurt your damned dog. Are you happy now?"

She sniffed. "No." Her eyes went slitty. "And I'm not sure I trust you. I'll talk to Mr. Tafft about it. Maybe he can write an amendment to our contract or something."

"For the love of—" Tony sucked in a couple of bushels of air. He leaned over and thrust his face close to Mari's. He awarded her a mental gold star for not flinching away from him. Rather, she stood her ground and glared back at him, although she still held his jacket the way she might hold a shield. "I will not hurt your dog. I promise. Cross my heart and hope to die. There. Are you satisfied now? You don't need to talk to Martin."

"Well . . ."

"I swear it."

Mari held her rebellious pose for another second or two, then gave it up. Tony felt an irrational surge of triumph. It really wasn't much of a victory to manage to intimidate an impoverished girl. He was ashamed of himself.

With a toss of her head, Mari turned. "I'll see what I can do for this jacket."

"Fine." Tony propped his fists on his hips and glowered after her. "You do that."

Damn, she had pretty hair. It shone like the richest mahogany in the fierce sunlight. Today she'd brushed it back from her face and knotted it at the nape of her neck, a practical style for the place she lived in and the kind of work she usually did. She wore no hat, which didn't amaze him. She was absolutely devoid of any sense of propriety. Any proper female wore a hat outdoors. It was de rigueur. Expected. Polite. Not to mention necessary in this hellish desert.

Not Mari Pottersby. Defiant as ever, she. Tony wished like thunder that he didn't feel like throwing his head back and laughing—and then thanking God he'd met her.

The darned jacket would never be clean again. Mari had soaked it in water and washing soda, then scrubbed it on the washboard on which she did her own laundry. "Blast it, Tony—I mean Tiny—why did you have to take a shine to *him?* I can't afford to replace his expensive clothes when you ruin them."

Hearing his name, Tiny lifted his hamlike head, grinned, and wagged his tail. Mari sighed. "Oh, I know. You were just being friendly. But I wish you wouldn't jump on people."

If she were worth a grain of sand, she'd have trained him not to leap on people before this. But had she? Heavens, no. Mari had thought it was fun to have a dog that scared the bejesus out of people, but was as gentle as a dandelion puff.

"I can really be stupid sometimes, Tiny," she mumbled, scrubbing hard.

When she lifted the jacket out of the soapy water and inspected it, Mari sighed heavily. "It's better." She hoped it wouldn't shrink. Then again, if it did shrink, she guessed it wouldn't matter much. It was probably ruined already.

On that happy note, she lugged the tub over to her sparse kitchen garden and dumped it out to irrigate her food supply. The carrots, cabbages, tomatoes, and onions growing there were used to being watered with leftover wash water. Everyone's garden around Mojave Wells was used to it. People joked about not having to wash their vegetables because they were already clean from all the soapy water dumped on them during the growing season. Soap was supposed to be bad for plants, but Mari guessed it was diluted enough not to affect these hardy specimens.

She was ashamed of herself for thinking how nice it would be to have running water and indoor plumbing. That sort of idle dreaming resulted in nothing but discontent, and Mari didn't need it. She had her father's mine to run. And if some of that money Peerless seemed to heave about by the truckload landed on her, that's what she'd do with it.

It was stupid to think about installing hot and cold running water. Nonsensical. Folks didn't need such luxuries, especially around here, where there was hard work to do and no slacking allowed.

With a sigh, she lugged the heavy tub back inside the dingy cabin and hung it on its peg above the sink. As she wiped a hand across her sweaty forehead and scanned her earthly possessions, she told herself not to waste time in idle daydreams.

Unfortunately, she spelled the word wrong in her head, and it came out *idyll*.

"Blast! Stop it this minute, Mari Pottersby!"

Tiny lifted his huge head and peered sleepily at her. Mari said, "It's all right, boy. Only a momentary aberration. I ought to take lessons from you on how to live. You don't crave what you can't have. All you do is enjoy each day as it comes."

And eat. Tiny ate tons, sometimes more than Mari could easily provide. The Peerless money would come in handy for feeding Tiny, too.

In order to keep her mind from dwelling on useless fancies, Mari started singing. She couldn't carry a tune in a bucket, but she loved music anyway. The only time she ever heard music was when she went to church, so most of her repertoire consisted of hymns.

She sang them loudly until, when she took Tony's jacket outside to hang on the line, she noticed the Peerless crew who were pounding the mine shaft into shape had all stopped pounding in favor of looking at her. They were probably all pausing to be thankful motion pictures were silent, given her voice. Like a dog with its tail between its legs, she scurried back into her home, embarrassed and put out.

"Oh, Tiny, I'm not used to people being around all the time. I'm used to my privacy." In fact, she felt invaded and violated. The sensation was most uncomfortable.

Mari also wasn't used to making painful confessions and asking for forgiveness. Two hours later, as she neatly folded Tony's once-fashionable jacket and braced herself to take it back to him, she rehearsed the confession she'd have to make to him. She continued all the way to the Mojave Inn.

That was the easy part. The hard part came next, when she was supposed to ask him to forgive her for allowing her dog to ruin his clothes.

"Forgive, heck," she muttered, building up quite a head of steam as she walked. "What do *I* have to be forgiven for? *I* wasn't the one who wore a fancy suit to Mojave Wells. It isn't *my* fault my dog likes him."

This was the first instance since Tiny had come into her life that she'd looked on him as a traitor. Still, she'd known for a long time that although Tiny might be very big, his brain wasn't. Anyhow, it still wasn't her fault the silly dog had taken a liking to the blasted millionaire.

It was her fault she hadn't trained Tiny not to jump on people. Mari knew it. And she hated knowing it.

By the time she spotted Tony Ewing—clad in an-

other fancy suit—seated on the porch of the Mojave
Inn and sipping an iced drink, Mari was mad enough
to chew nails. He and Martin Tafft were talking, probably about the darned picture they were going to make
here.

Six

Tony didn't say anything to Martin when he spotted Mari Pottersby tramping up to the hotel, carrying a bundle. He presumed the bundle was his jacket, and he wondered if she'd managed to fix it. He doubted it.

Not that he gave a rap on a personal level. What did he care about one measly jacket? Hell, he had enough money to buy Bloomingdales.

Since her dog had attacked him, Tony's grudge against Mari had been growing by the hour, however. He wanted her to suffer for the animal's unseemly behavior. He couldn't have said why, although he thought it might have something to do with her illogical loyalty, her damnable lack of respect for him and his money, and her smart mouth.

It was a pretty mouth.

Damn, he hadn't meant to admit that.

"Say, Tony, isn't that Miss Pottersby?"

Tony squinted at Martin and acquitted him of subtlety. Martin's open, honest face didn't betray a hint of sarcasm.

Well, and why should he be sarcastic? It was Tony who had the problem with the Pottersby wench, not Martin. Martin didn't ever have problems with anybody.

"Yeah. I think it is." He spoke casually, as if the two men were chatting about espying a lone eagle in the sky. In Mari Pottersby's case, it was more like a lone buzzard. Which might be why Tony often felt like carrion in her presence.

She was a graceful buzzard, though. Even though the weather stank—the rusty thermometer hanging outside the Mojave Inn's back door registered 105 degrees—her back remained straight, and she seemed to glide across the dusty ground. Tony wished she were ugly. It would be so much easier to hate her if she weren't so darned pretty.

At least she wore a hat this afternoon. Evidently, not even she could tackle the midafternoon desert heat without headgear. She might even turn out to be human. Maybe. Unlikelier things had transpired. Or so he'd been told.

While Tony was still sneering, Martin rose from his chair and called out a cheery greeting. "Good afternoon, Miss Pottersby! Good to see you. Let me get some iced lemonade for you. You must be dying of heat prostration if you've walked all the way here from your home."

Her home. Tony very nearly snorted. If that painfully rustic cabin was a home, Tony'd eat his hat.

Mari trod lightly up the steps of the porch and gave Martin a friendly smile. "Thanks. I'm dry as a bone and awfully hot." She ignored Tony.

"You really ought to allow us to drive you around, Miss Pottersby," Martin said. "We've got cars and drivers, and it would save you a good deal of walking in the heat."

"That's okay, thanks. I can't afford to get soft."

"Suit yourself. I'll be right back." Martin took off, gracious man that he was, to fetch Mari some lemonade.

She hadn't said boo to Tony. Tony noted this lapse in particular and resented it. It occurred to him that he hadn't spoken to her, either, but he quickly thrust the thought aside. He wasn't the one at fault here, after all.

He observed with interest as Mari watched Martin until he was out of sight, then took a deep breath, as if she were preparing herself for an unpleasant task. She turned and looked down at him, since he hadn't bothered to rise politely, as a gentleman ought to do when a lady approached. He justified his bad manners by telling himself Mari wasn't a lady.

Thrusting the folded lump of fabric at him, Mari said abruptly, "Here. I'm afraid I ruined it."

Tony finally pried himself out of his chair. Only when he was standing did he take the jacket from Mari's hands. He didn't speak until he'd flapped the folds out and held the jacket at arm's length for inspection. "It shrank," he noted in a neutral tone.

She clasped her hands behind her back. If she'd been wearing trousers, Tony had no doubt she'd have stuffed them into her pockets. "Um, I noticed that."

He glanced from the jacket to her. "What am I supposed to do with this? I can't wear it."

"Um, I don't know. Donate it to charity?"

"The stain didn't come out of the right shoulder, either," he pointed out.

"I know. But a poor person probably wouldn't care."

"I'm not a poor person."

It was very interesting to Tony to watch the way Mari operated. Now, for instance, she was barely containing hot retorts to his innocent comments. She looked rather like a pot about to boil over. Her face, a beautiful golden-tan color from the sun, had taken on a deeper reddish cast, and her gorgeous eyes had thinned ominously.

"I know you're not poor." Her tone of voice had become harder, too, and she was clipping her words.

"Most poor people can't afford to care about a tiny stain or two."

"Tiny?" Tony lifted the jacket and held out the right shoulder so it was a mere inch away from Mari's pretty eyes. "That doesn't look tiny to me. Although," he added smugly, "Tiny did it."

She expelled a huff that made the jacket's arm flutter. "Darn it, I know Tiny did it. I'll pay you back."

"Oh?" Tony flipped the jacket away from him. It landed half on and half off the chair he'd vacated. He watched Mari watch the jacket's flight, her expression a priceless combination of incredulity and rage. "And will you pay only for the jacket, or does your offer extend to the suit, which is no longer whole and, therefore, unfit to wear?"

"Darn it! I'll pay for the whole suit!" She sniffed and lowered her voice. "You'll have to wait until I get paid."

"Will I? And what if I don't want to wait that long?"

Ah. Tony grinned inside. He'd finally made her lose her temper entirely. He couldn't account for the feeling of joy that invaded him when she stamped her foot and hollered, "Dagnabbit, I'm sorry my dog got your blasted suit dirty. I'll pay you back when I can. There's nothing I can do in the meantime but say I'm sorry. What do you care, anyway? You've got more money than God!"

"True," Tony agreed calmly. "But I think you ought to pay for the damage your dog does when asked to do so. Do other people have to wait for months—"

"Months?" Mari shrieked. *"Months!* What do you mean, *months?* Dang it, Mr. Tafft said this would only take a few weeks!"

"Calm yourself, Miss Pottersby. You probably won't have to wait months for your money."

She expelled another gust of air and whispered, "Thank God."

"But I think you should pay me for the damage to my jacket sooner than that."

Her shoulders went back, her spine stiffened, she lifted her chin and glared at him. "Well, that's just too bad, because I don't have any money."

He cocked his head slightly. "Who said anything about money?"

"Huh? I mean, I beg your pardon."

He'd managed to fluster her entirely. Tony had seldom experienced such a swell of satisfaction. How odd. "You can pay me back by agreeing to take dinner with me this evening."

She stared at him blankly, her eyes going as round as copper pennies. Tony could get lost in those eyes if he didn't watch himself. She narrowed them again immediately, and eyed him in deep suspicion. "Why?"

"Why what?"

"Why do you want me to take dinner with you?"

"It's your punishment for allowing your dog to ruin my jacket."

A gap in the conversation ensued as Mari stared at Tony, and Tony tried to look innocent. At last she said, "I don't understand."

With a nonchalant shrug, Tony said, "What's not to understand?" In truth, he didn't understand it either, but he couldn't shake his compulsion to spend time with Mari Pottersby. It made no sense. She was the most aggravating, intolerable, nonsensical female he'd ever met. Yet he wanted to be with her constantly.

When he'd returned to Los Angeles with Martin after they'd negotiated the contract shoals with Mari, Tony had all but pined to get back to Mojave Wells. And, since Mojave Wells was about as hospitable a place as Hell itself, he knew it was Mari calling to him. It was all very annoying, actually, and he trusted he'd get over it if he spent even more time in her company.

In the meantime, he could tell she believed him to have an ulterior and portentous motive. He could almost hear the little gears in her brain turning. Pasting on a bland smile, he pretended to reassure her. "My intentions are pure. I promise I won't try to compromise you, Miss Pottersby. You needn't be afraid."

From a dull brick red, her cheeks bloomed fire. The process was fascinating to behold, and Tony watched it with pleasure.

"I'm not afraid! Not of *you.*"

He lifted an eyebrow. He didn't like the way she'd said *you,* as if she couldn't imagine anything less plausible than an attractive woman being subverted by him. Hell, women were always plying their wares on him, trying to get him into compromising situations so he'd be forced to marry them. This female didn't know with whom she dealt, if she believed women to be immune to him, Tony Ewing. Damn her anyhow.

"No? Then why hesitate?" He forced himself not to grind his teeth, but to smile in a winning way.

"Here's the lemonade. Nice and cold."

Both Tony and Mari jerked at the sound of Martin's voice, cheerful and obliging. Tony turned and found Martin at his elbow, holding out a frosty glass full of lemonade to Mari. He saw Mari blink several times, as if she'd been as startled as Tony by Martin's arrival.

Which was stupid. They'd both known Martin would be returning with lemonade for Mari.

"Um, thank you very much, Mr. Tafft," Mari said after a quick overhaul of her emotions. She even managed a gracious smile as she accepted the glass and sipped. "Mmm, this is good. It really hits the spot."

Martin beamed at her for a second, then swept a hand out. "Sit down. Sit down! Tony and I were just going over the shooting schedule."

"The shooting schedule?" Mari sat, looking puzzled.

From which, Tony deduced she was unfamiliar with the language of picture making. He tried to clarify. "That's the order in which the scenes will be filmed."

"Oh." She frowned at him, as if to tell him she didn't care to have him explaining things to her. Too bad for her.

Mari didn't know about any of this. She watched a bunch of actors walk over and clump around the mine's entrance. They all carried picks on their shoulders and had their white makeup smudged to make them look like people who actually worked for a living, instead of actors. Mari, who'd been a miner all her life, had never seen a miner look like that, but she held her tongue. It was apparent that motion-picture folks didn't go in much for reality.

At the moment, she sat on a folding camp chair under one of the umbrellas that had been set up to protect the cast and crew from the blistering sun. She'd been impressed by how early these people got up to work. She'd assumed they'd all sleep in and let the better part of the morning pass before they did anything. But they'd all started gathering at least an hour and a half earlier. Mari had joined them about twenty minutes ago. She'd left Tiny in the cabin to prevent any misunderstandings.

Nothing happened.

The actors shuffled around. A couple of them lowered their heavy picks to the dirt. Some of them peered into the distance, toward the town of Mojave Wells, as if they were anticipating someone's arrival. Mari wondered who they were waiting for. She craned her neck and looked, too, seeing nothing but the barren desert stretching for a mile or so in all directions. So she sat back again, ready to wait some more.

For several minutes a whole lot of nothing ensued. Grumbles swelled from the cluster of actors/miners. Mari crossed her arms over her chest and sweated along with them, although she at least was protected by the umbrella's shade.

If whoever it was the actors were waiting for was late, she didn't blame them for getting huffy. It was too darned hot to stand around doing nothing.

After talking amongst themselves for some minutes and probably melting all that ugly makeup off their sweaty faces, the actors finally decided they needn't suffer heatstroke while waiting for whoever wasn't here. They began straggling over to the line of chairs and umbrellas. Several of them saluted Mari politely. She smiled back.

A young man, breathing heavily, flung his pick to the ground, collapsed into a chair, and said, "I hate this heat."

"It's mighty hard to take, all right," Mari agreed. To make him feel better, she added, "It's cooler inside the mine."

"Hunh! I wouldn't know. And I may never find out if the director doesn't show up pretty soon." He sounded crabby and irritable.

For that matter, Mari herself was feeling a trifle antsy. She wasn't accustomed to hanging around twiddling her thumbs, waiting for people to show up. She'd worked independently all her life, and she'd worked like the devil—for all the good it did her. She didn't like having to wait for idlers to make an appearance in order to begin her workday.

Shoot, if she hadn't rented the Marigold to Peerless, she'd have had half a day's work done by this time. She squinted up at the sun and estimated the time to be somewhere around nine o'clock. Way past time for any respectable person to get to work.

Which, for some incomprehensible reason, spun her mind around to Tony Ewing. She heaved a sigh and wished it hadn't.

After the jacket debacle, she'd had dinner with him at the Mojave Inn. Fortunately, Mrs. Nelson had offered chicken and dumplings on the menu last night, so at least they could cut the meat. It actually hadn't tasted half bad. The Nelsons bought their chickens from Mari, which supplemented her meager income, and she'd had an illogical sense of satisfaction to know that Tony Ewing was helping to support her, even in this little way and without knowing it.

More surprising, she'd enjoyed herself. Every time she remembered the evening, a shock of amazement smote her. Imagine, enjoying herself in Tony Ewing's company. It didn't make any sense. Especially since they'd spent most of the evening taking verbal swipes at each other. She grinned now, recalling the various strikes and parries each had executed. She'd had a hard time getting to sleep afterward, because her senses had been zinging from the stimulation of the evening's conversations.

The throb of a motorcar in the distance jogged her thoughts and propelled her to turn and look again. Finally. A car was coming, all right. Mari wondered if it contained Tony Ewing.

Exasperated, she told herself to get her fancies under control. She hated when she entertained useless daydreams, because they only led her to be dissatisfied with her life. And, since there wasn't much she could do about it, she'd decided long since that she didn't need the aggravation of unfulfilled daydreams plaguing her.

Most of the actors playing miners rose from their camp chairs and squinted into the distance. Mari asked the young man who'd spoken to her, "Is it the director?"

He shaded his eyes and peered off into the distance, reminding Mari of a big-game hunter on the African veld, surveying the bush for lions.

Ack. There went her imagination again. She gave herself a mental smack on the back of the head to capture her attention.

"I can't tell," her companion said after a moment or two of observation. "Probably."

"Too bad he's late," she offered, hoping it would make him feel better to know someone else disapproved of the director's rudeness.

"I'll say. It's too hot to play these games."

These games? Whatever did the young fellow mean? Mari didn't ask, supposing the reference to "games" pertained to the pictures. Although she really didn't care a whole lot, she'd as soon not broadcast her ignorance to the world. She offered a neutral grunt, and hoped the young man would consider her to be on his side.

"By Jupiter, it's not the director. It's Martin!" the young man cried.

Mari got up and peered at the motorcar, too. "Weren't you expecting him?"

"Oh, sure, but not today. I thought he was going to drive to L.A. and get some costumes for the leading lady."

L.A.? The leading lady? That was her! Oh, my. Mari's heart sped up. "Um, what's L.A.?" she asked, because she was curious.

"L.A.?" The young man turned and looked at her as if he believed her to be joshing him.

She wasn't. Rather stiffly, she said, "I've never heard of it."

He laughed. Mari didn't find anything amusing

about not knowing something, and she deplored people who ridiculed other people's ignorance. Before she could say so, the young man said, "It's short for Los Angeles. That's what all the picture folks call it."

"Oh." L.A. Los Angeles. That made sense.

The car rumbled onto the plot of land that had been marked off as the Peerless set, and the actors began ambling over to talk to Martin. Mari discounted the stab of disappointment that struck her when she saw Tony wasn't with him as a touch of indigestion.

She'd never been troubled by indigestion in her life.

Something was wrong with the picture, though. She heard a couple of "Sorry's" and one or two "That's too bad's" as she approached Martin. He saw her, and she thought she saw relief enter his eyes. "Oh, good. I'm so glad you're here, Miss Pottersby."

He was? How nice of him to say so. "What's the matter, Mr. Tafft?"

This time she heard several people exclaim, "Mr. Tafft?" as if they'd never heard his name before. She glanced around, frowning.

Martin gently took her arm. "Don't pay any attention, Miss Pottersby. Everyone calls me Martin. Picture making is pretty casual. In fact, I'd be pleased if you'd call me Martin."

"Oh. Sure. Everybody calls me Mari." In fact, except for the Peerless people, nobody ever called her Miss Pottersby.

He gifted her with a broad smile. He had a really nice smile. He was a mighty good-looking man, actually. Mari couldn't figure out why he, who was nice and polite and exuded gentlemanliness, should leave her unmoved, while Tony Ewing, who was rude and impolite and exuded sarcasm, made her want to leap on him and kiss him to within an inch of his life.

Oh, dear.

"Thanks, Mari," Martin said. "Say, we've had a disaster this morning."

"I'm sorry to hear it." Her heart plummeted. Could something have happened to Tony? Food poisoning, maybe? Terror gripped her momentarily.

"Yes, it's a pain in the neck."

Hmmm. That didn't sound too bad. If Tony had died, surely Martin would have been more upset than this. "Oh?"

"Our director, John Gilman, has taken sick. I don't know what's the matter. He was fine yesterday. Today he's sick as a dog."

"I'm sorry to hear it. Do you need the name of a doctor?"

"Mrs. Nelson got the doctor for us, thanks. But now it looks as though I'm going to have to take over the direction of this picture."

"Oh." Mari had no idea on Earth what a director did or didn't do in connection with a motion picture. "Um, is that a problem for you?"

Martin heaved a big sigh. "I guess I can handle it. But it means I'll have to spend all my time here, and won't be able to do other things I'm supposed to do. Which brings me to you." He smiled again, winningly.

Mari felt her heart, which had calmed down considerably since she and Martin had begun talking, speed up again. "Me?" She pointed to her chest.

"I'm afraid so. Say, Mari, would you be able to go to Los Angeles with Tony today? I was going to go myself and bring the costumes back to the set, but now I'm going to be stuck here. Since Tony's never dealt with costuming before, I think it would be easier on everyone if you were to go with him."

"Go with him? To Los Angeles? Me?" Mari decided she was babbling and shut her mouth. After swallowing, licking her lips, and taking a deep breath, she tried again. "I'm sorry, Martin. But—you want me to go to Los Angeles with Mr. Ewing? For costumes?"

"I'm really sorry about this, Mari." He looked as though he meant his apology sincerely. "It's only that Tony's so new at this."

"And I'm not?" She tried not to sound as bewildered as she felt.

His quick grin reassured her. "Sure, I know you're new to the pictures, too, but you'd be doing me a big favor if you'd go with him. That way, you can try on anything that needs to be tried on. If alterations have to be made, we'll know right away. I spoke to the costumer on the telephone a couple of weeks ago—as soon as we knew you'd be playing the part, in fact—and I'm sure she's got everything under control, but . . ." He gazed at her pleadingly.

"And you think if I go with him, there won't need to be alterations?" Mari wasn't sure about this, since most of her clothes came to her secondhand, but there seemed to be something slightly askew with Martin's reasoning here.

"What I meant was that, since Tony doesn't have my experience, he won't know, without you there, if things need to be altered. I've done this so many times, I'm pretty good at judging fits without the actors there."

"Oh. Yes, I see."

His eyes took on a pleading cast, not unlike Tiny's eyes when he was longing for something he couldn't reach. Which didn't happen often. "So, can you do it?"

Mari swallowed again. "Um, sure. I guess I can go." Whatever would she do with Tiny? "How will we get there?"

"Tony's machine."

Mari didn't know much about the sophisticated life,

but she knew that a "machine" was a motorcar. "He has one?"

"Sure. It's big and comfortable, too, so at least you won't be bumping around in a horse-drawn cart or anything." He laughed his friendly laugh.

Los Angeles. Mari had never even dreamed about traveling all the way to Los Angeles. Why, it was miles and miles away. It was, by her standards, a big city. A metropolis, even. Mari felt like a yokel when she ventured as far as San Bernardino. She couldn't imagine how she'd feel in Los Angeles—and with Tony Ewing. It sounded scary.

"Um, well . . ."

"Please? You'd be doing me a tremendous favor." Martin seemed to think of something and added brightly, "Say, I know you weren't expecting to have to travel in connection with your employment for Peerless. How about I tack on another hundred dollars if you make the trip?"

Another hundred dollars? Mari couldn't conceive of a person's having the financial wherewithal to fling a hundred dollars around for no better reason than because another person had to take a trip to Los Angeles.

She flapped her hand in the air, feeling stupid and greedy. "There's no need for that. You're paying me plenty already."

"Nonsense. I know you can use the money, and I'm asking a big favor. Please accept the money."

Bother. She sure could use the money. For a moment or two her pride fought with her needs. Eventually pride lost. "Well—okay, I guess. But you really don't need to do that. I don't mind going to Los Angeles." Or, if she were to speak the language of the movies, L.A. A tiny bubble of excitement caught up with the ache of fear in her chest.

A motor trip to a fairly big city. With Tony Ewing, the most handsome, albeit the most aggravating, man she'd ever met. Scary, indeed. And very, very intriguing.

"That's swell." Martin's smile seemed less forced, and Mari could tell he was relieved that she'd capitulated. She felt kind of guilty about worrying him. "Tony will be here as soon as the doctor sees John. Can you be ready to leave today?"

"Today?" Good heavens. "Um, sure. I don't know why not." Except for Tiny. She gasped when she remembered her dog. "Oh!"

"What's the matter?" Martin started looking worried again.

She felt silly. How could she forget Tiny? "Um, I forgot about my dog. I don't suppose I can take him with me?"

From the look on Martin's face, she knew she couldn't. She hoped this wasn't going to prevent the trip to L.A. All of a sudden she really wanted to go.

"I'll be glad to feed him for you."

He wouldn't be glad, and Mari knew it from the tone of his voice. He was such a nice man. To make him less sorry he'd offered, she said, "You can keep the hundred bucks if you take care of him." What the heck. A hundred here, a hundred there. What was it to Mari?

She couldn't believe she'd actually thought that. A hundred dollars to Mari Pottersby was akin to a million to Tony Ewing. But, since she'd yet to see a single penny of Peerless money, it felt sort of like throwing confetti around or making deals with play money.

"Don't be silly, Mari. I'll be happy to feed Tiny for you. I'll even take him for a walk, if he needs it. And you deserve the money. You're being asked to do way more than the contract calls for."

She eyed Martin for a long moment. "Um, you don't need to walk him. He can walk himself if you open the door."

"Do you think he'd run away if I didn't go with him?" Martin looked worried.

Mari sighed. Where would he run to? There was nothing around here. "Oh, no. He always comes back." Often with a jackrabbit carcass carried proudly in his huge jaws. Mari decided Martin didn't need to know that much. City folks made a big to-do over the jack-rabbits, but they were really only pests. Mari approved of her dog's willingness to eliminate vermin.

"Good. I'd never forgive myself if I lost your dog."

How sweet. Mari smiled at him. "Well, then . . ." She knew she was going to accept. She didn't know why she was even pretending to hesitate.

Martin said, as if trying to persuade her, "It will only take a day. It takes several hours to get there, and you'll be an hour or so at the costumer's place, and then you can turn around and come right back."

She nodded. That's what she'd feared. She'd be going to a real city for the first time in her life, and she wouldn't even get to see it. She sighed. "Sure, I'll do it."

"Great. That's great. Thanks, Mari."

"Sure, Martin. No problem."

The rumble of a distant motor propelled them both to turn around and investigate. Another motorcar, followed by a gigantic plume of dust, headed toward the Marigold Mine.

Martin shaded his eyes. "That must be Tony."

And there, in a nutshell, was Mari's problem. Darn it.

Seven

Tony waited impatiently for Mari Pottersby to hug her outrageous dog and join him in the motorcar. He frowned at the pair, which he could scarcely discern in the gloom of the cabin, unable to understand the bond between them. It seemed silly for a young woman as pretty and sprightly as Mari to bestow all of her affection on a dumb animal.

He could not, therefore, account for the yearning that attacked him at odd moments to rush out and buy himself a dog. A big dog. A friendly dog. A dog to walk with and talk to. A companion. A loyal friend. Perhaps a Great Dane.

Damn it, this was stupid. He called out, "Are you ready yet?" The internal disruption he was feeling crept into his voice as a nasty note.

Mari heard it, too. She turned and gave him a vicious scowl. "Wait just a minute, can't you? I have to make sure everything's ready for Martin to come and feed poor Tony—I mean, Tiny."

If she confused his name with that of her dog one more time, Tony didn't know what he'd do, but it would be drastic. "Poor Tiny," he mimicked. "We're only going to be gone for a day."

She'd called Martin Martin. When had that happened? Why was Martin on a first-name basis with her, when Tony wasn't? Were those two closer than he had suspected? Had some surreptitious courtship been going on under his very nose, and he'd missed it? Was Martin wooing her? Was she wooing him?

Good God, were they lovers? Jealousy, green and as monstrous as Tiny, swelled in Tony's bosom. He told himself not to be an ass, which didn't help much.

"I know that, and Martin knows that, and you know that, but Tiny's never been left alone before, all by himself."

Tony rolled his eyes. He'd be safer if he didn't contemplate any possible relationship between Mari and Martin, but concentrated instead on how ridiculous the girl was.

So, back to dogs.

At once he decided there were to be no Great Danes mucking up his life. His own dog wouldn't be as big as Tiny. Tony'd get himself a nice, largish—but not too large—friendly dog that wouldn't knock folks over when they came to call. He didn't know much about dogs. Maybe he could pick up a book in L.A. Something that described the various breeds and things like that.

He caught himself up short. What in the name of holy hell was he thinking about buying dog books for? For the love of God, he lived in New York City. If he ever decided to get a dog, he'd do it there.

It was all because of Mari. She'd rattled his senses so hard, he could scarcely keep his wits together. If she and Martin *were* a courting couple, Tony considered it mighty sneaky of them not to mention it to him. Were they trying to keep it a secret because they feared his reaction?

That was arrant nonsense. What did he care if Mari loved Martin and vice versa? It was nothing to him. *She* was nothing to him.

His entire insides clenched as if he had a cramp, and

it was all he could do not to double up with pain. He fought off the spasm, gritted his teeth, and remained upright.

Damn it, would the girl never be through in there? He contemplated squeezing his horn, but feared the noise would frighten Tiny so much, she'd refuse to leave him. Then he considered stomping to the cabin and hauling her out of it, but again, he didn't quite trust her dog. She claimed Tiny was as gentle as a lamb, but he was a hell of a lot bigger than any lamb Tony'd ever seen. And he had sharp, pointy teeth, too. Tony decided not to chance it.

At last! Mari came out of the cabin, carrying a carpetbag that looked as if it were at least a thousand years old. She wore a dress about that old, too, and Tony recognized it as one she'd worn before. Didn't the girl have any decent clothes at all? She looked like a damned ragamuffin.

He was ashamed of himself when the reality of Mari's poverty crawled through the resentment clouding his senses and tapped on his brain to get his attention. She probably didn't have any decent clothes because she couldn't afford them. Anyhow, she wouldn't need them out here, would she?

Not only that, if she decided to get some new clothes, she'd indubitably have to make them herself. Tony's heart squinched when he considered Mari's blistered fingers as she wearily sewed into the night by the light of a single sputtering candle.

Damn. He hated when sentiment got in the way of rational thought. He had no business feeling sentimental about Mari. She wouldn't thank him for it. She'd be more apt to slap his face for insulting her.

The notion made him grin.

Mari appeared troubled as she lugged her carpetbag to the machine. When she saw him grinning, she stopped walking and frowned. "What are you laughing at?"

He threw out his hands. "I'm not laughing at anything."

"You're smiling." She said it as if it were an accusation.

"Is that a crime?" Her interrogation had squelched any inclination to smile. He walked up to her and started to take the carpetbag. She didn't release her hold on it. "Give me the bag, for heaven's sake."

"I don't need your help."

"For crying out loud, you may not need it, but I'm giving it to you. Let go of the stupid thing."

"No."

"Damn it, I've got to put it in the tonneau."

Reluctantly, she released her hold on the bag. "I don't like to be laughed at."

"For God's— I'm not laughing at you!" He jerked the bag up roughly and flung it into the big car's backseat. "You get the strangest ideas in that head of yours."

"You were smiling."

He turned and glared down at her. Since she was a tall girl, it wasn't that far down. "What's wrong with smiling? If you're going to tell me I can't smile when I feel like it, we're never going to get along."

She sniffed. "I don't suppose we ever will, no matter what I tell you." She flounced to the passenger's door and reached out to open it.

Tony beat her to it. "Here, damn it. You may not be a lady, but I was raised to be a gentleman, and gentlemen open doors for females." He yanked the door open and stood, fuming, as Mari settled herself on the luxurious leather seat.

As ever when they fought, she lifted her chin. Tony had begun to recognize this gesture as an act of defiance from a woman who had nothing but her basic character with which to tackle the world and everything in it. She didn't have money to talk for her, or a male relative, or anything else. She had her wits and her honor, and she possessed an intolerable amount of pride.

She was cute as a bug.

As Tony cranked his motorcar and then jumped into the driver's seat, he couldn't believe he'd actually thought that.

It was ridiculous for her to be this nervous. No matter how many times she told herself, Mari couldn't halt the anxiety eating away at her self-possession. Blast it, what was it about Tony Ewing that bothered her so darned much? Just because he was handsome? Just because he was as rich as Midas? Just because she wanted to leap into his arms and kiss him?

Probably. Darn.

"I don't know why you brought that big bag with you, anyhow. We're not going to be there overnight."

If her chin rose any higher, she'd be staring into the backseat. Mari lowered it reluctantly and gave an imperious sniff. "It's best to be prepared. I might not have been reared to be a lady, but at least I know that much."

"I didn't mean that," Tony growled.

"You didn't mean what?" She didn't think it was her place to give this awful man an inch. He already had all the money in the world. The only thing she had was her dignity, and she wasn't going to let him take that away from her—or not more often than she could help.

"What I said about being a lady. I didn't mean that."

"Oh." She turned her head away from him and stared out the window.

If she were to admit the truth, she'd have had to tell him she'd seldom been this excited. Imagine her, Mari

Pottersby, driving to the metropolis of Los Angeles in a big, fancy car with him, Tony Ewing, the richest, most handsome man she had ever set eyes on.

"And you still won't need that bag."

"It's always wise to be prepared for the unexpected." She'd heard tales about these fancy motorcars breaking down. Or sometimes they drove over tacks and blew out their tires. Their engines overheated, too, especially in the desert. And what if they ran out of fuel? Unless he kept a supply with him, Mari didn't know where he'd get any more.

He grunted. She could tell he was exasperated. Too darned bad. She squinted through the window, spotted something unusual, and cried out, "Oh, look over there!"

"What? Where?"

The machine swerved wildly, and Mari, grabbing the seat to keep from slithering to the floor, shrieked, "Oh! What's the matter?"

"What's the matter? What are you screaming for?" The automobile screeched to a stop by the side of the road.

She stared at him, wide-eyed, and demanded, "Why did you do that?" Was he trying to kill her? Maim her? Punish her for being nasty? Good Lord, she'd never have guessed him capable of these sorts of tactics.

He stared back at her for a moment, then turned toward the front and bowed his head. His hands gripped the steering wheel so tightly that his knuckles shone like polished marble. "You screamed. I thought something had happened to you."

"I didn't scream."

"Yes, you did."

"No, I didn't."

He drew in a huge breath and held it.

Mari bit her lower lip. "Um, I guess I did speak sort

of loudly. A little bit. It's only that I wanted you to see the two roadrunners."

He slanted a glance at her without lifting his head. "Roadrunners?" The word came out hard, reminding Mari of sharp knife blades and hatchets and things like that.

"Um, yes. I didn't mean to frighten you." That was polite of her, wasn't it? To acknowledge a slight lapse—although she hadn't known it to be a lapse—and apologize for it?

"I thought you'd suffered some kind of attack or seizure."

"I beg your pardon."

"Please don't screech like that while I'm driving."

"Very well." She was beginning to feel put-upon. She hadn't meant to scare him, after all. It wasn't her fault he couldn't drive and look at things at the same time. It wasn't her fault his nerves were bad. She decided to say so. "You might want to consider drinking a glass of warm milk at night before you go to bed. I understand it does wonders for the nerves."

This time he lifted his head when he stared at her. "My nerves?"

She tilted her head, again lifting her chin. "Yes. You seem a trifle jumpy."

"Jumpy? I'm not jumpy, Miss Pottersby. You shrieked like a banshee."

"I did not!"

He sucked in another breath and let it out slowly. "I suggest we begin again. Perhaps we should go over a few rules—rather, suggested modes of behavior—before we do so."

She'd seldom felt this stupid, and it was an intensely uncomfortable experience. Nevertheless, she knew she'd been at fault. Sort of. In a way. It still wasn't her fault that his nerves were bad. Because she didn't want to fight all the way to Los Angeles, she decided not to press the issue of his fretful disposition. "Very well."

"If you wish to point out some entity in the countryside that you believe will be of interest to me, please don't . . . speak loudly."

He'd been going to say, *Please, don't screech at me.* Mari could tell. She also resented it, though she deemed it prudent not to say so. "Very well."

After another moment's pause, during which Mari could almost hear him battling with his urge to holler at her, he said, "I appreciate your willingness to show me flora and fauna native to this area. I've never been to California before, and I've never seen a roadrunner."

"Well," she said, feeling crabby, "they're gone now, so you won't see those two."

"I'm sorry about that."

He didn't sound like it.

Mari held her tongue as he restarted the motor and the machine lurched once more onto the rough road. None of the roads in Mari's life were paved, although she'd read about paved roads. She expected she'd see some in Los Angeles.

They hadn't been traveling for very long before another pair of roadrunners began racing beside the car down the road. Very quietly, Mari pointed them out to Tony.

He grinned. "I've never seen any birds like that before."

She couldn't help grinning, too, because the birds were so silly looking as to be adorable. "No. They're unique, all right."

"There seems to be a lot of uniqueness in this neck of the woods," he murmured.

Mari squinted at him, but could perceive no ulterior meaning to the words. A desert tortoise captured their joint attention then, and she elected to stop worrying about surreptitious meanings to Tony Ewing's pronouncements.

The scenery was pretty dull, at least to Mari, who was accustomed to it. She was surprised to discover how many items of interest actually dwelt in the desert. She pointed out jackrabbits, more tortoises, vultures, cottontails, ground squirrels, tarantulas, tumbleweeds, more roadrunners, a small herd of wild donkeys, several prairie quails, an old bummy looking prospector, who waved his tattered hat and grinned toothlessly at them, two red-tailed hawks, and an eagle.

Tony leaned forward and squinted through the windshield. "That's an eagle?"

"Yes. You don't see too many of them anymore."

"I'll be damned. I've never seen an eagle before."

"Not many city folk have, I expect."

He glanced at her. Mari pretended not to notice, but continued staring through the car's window.

"Thanks for showing me all this stuff, Miss Pottersby. I drove out here with Martin and didn't see half so much."

"That's only because you didn't know what you were looking at, and he didn't either, I imagine."

"I'm sure you're right."

Silence fell between them, although "silence," under the prevailing conditions, with the machine's motor roaring fit to kill, didn't really describe it. Muteness was more like it, Mari supposed. She didn't know what to say, that was for sure. They were driving through a stretch of absolutely bleak desert, so there weren't even any points of interest to mention. A couple of sagebrush. Some creosote bushes. A mangy old Joshua tree. A tumbleweed or two.

She told herself there was no reason to be nervous. Just because she was alone in the middle of nothing with the most attractive man she'd ever met was no reason to fall into a dither.

Tony cleared his throat, and Mari jumped a foot. "So, Miss Pottersby, I don't suppose you'd consider calling me Tony. I think we've known each other for long enough that it wouldn't be considered improper."

She stared at him, then swallowed. "Oh. Sure, I guess that's okay." Darn it, she could feel heat creeping up the back of her neck, and she knew she was going to be blushing in a second. Hoping he wouldn't notice, she turned her head and looked out the window. "Call me Mari."

"Thank you. Mari."

She liked the way her name came out of his mouth. Probably because he had such a nice mouth. He also had a great voice. Deep, smooth, kind of velvety. He had a caressing sort of voice.

Good Lord, wherever had that thought sprung from? She prayed hard for something interesting to tiptoe onto the scene. Something that would distract them both. Something—

"My God!"

Mari jerked around, and found Tony staring out his own window and jamming his foot on the brake. She looked, too, and gasped.

"Merciful saints in heaven! What in the name of glory is happening?"

A swarm of mounted Indians, bedecked with war paint and feathers, had just galloped over a rise in the near distance on Tony's side. Mari gaped at the scene, her brain trying to assimilate this odd intrusion of somebody else's history into her own personal world.

Tony, staring hard, didn't answer immediately. After a moment, he seemed to relax. "I think I know what it is."

"You do?" Darn it, he wasn't supposed to know anything about her native California. He was a blasted easterner. "Then please, let me in on it." Her voice was as dry as the desert outside the car.

"I think it's another motion-picture operation."

Mari blinked, thought for several tumultuous seconds, and said, "Oh."

"I heard Biograph was sending a company out here to do a picture. There's a fellow named DeMille who's been horning into the scene, too."

"Oh. My goodness. I, ah, hadn't realized that people were doing so many pictures in the area."

He turned and gave her a rather sardonic smile. "Peerless was the first to recognize Southern California as ideal for the picture-making process, but I don't suppose the others will be left behind for very long." He gestured at the whooping band of Indians. "As you can see."

"Yes. I see."

Sure enough, as they watched, a motorized truck, with a cameraman cranking energetically at his machine in the back, rolled over the rise, following the Indians. Tony shook his head. "It'll never work."

She gazed curiously at the scene, then again at Tony. "Why not?"

He shook his head. "Landscape's too bumpy. The image will be all over the place. There's no way you can shoot a moving target from a moving vehicle and get a clear picture."

"That makes sense. Why do you suppose they're doing it?"

"If it's Edison and his gang, they're probably experimenting with a newfangled spring-mounted camera or something. They're willing to try anything."

"I guess that's a good thing," she said doubtfully.

"Oh, yeah, it's a good thing. For Edison. The bastard's—sorry, Mari—the buzzard's such a tyrant and so single-minded and exclusive, that nobody else will ever profit from his inventions, though."

"I didn't know that."

"Oh, yeah. He won't let anybody or anything leak out of his studios back east. Anything he discovers will remain his exclusive property. He keeps the patents on anything his employees invent, too. If anyone leaves his company, he has to sign a pledge in blood not to use any of the products of his imagination that Edison's patented. I don't know what the penalty is. Death, I suppose."

"That's pretty drastic."

"I'm joking about the death part, but not about anything else. Edison's a real pip."

Mari thought about it as she watched the Indians. They'd stopped whooping and racing, had pulled up their ponies, and milled about in the dust, waiting for the truck to reach them. Now that they were closer, Mari perceived that they didn't look much like any Indians she'd seen pictured in books. They looked more like white folks painted up to look like Indians.

"Well," she mused, "I guess if I were Edison, I'd want to keep close tabs on my inventions, too. And if he's paying those guys to invent for him, I suppose he has a right to their inventions. At least—well, I don't know." The notion of inventions and rights to creative ideas was a new one to her, and she had no clear opinion on the issue.

"I'm sure I would, too," Tony agreed. "But his protectionism is going to turn around and bite him on the butt one of these days."

She glanced at him, sure she shouldn't want to giggle at his choice of words but finding them funny anyway. "What do you mean?"

He shrugged. "He's got everybody annoyed with him. I mean, he's not just protecting himself. He goes after everyone else's ideas like some kind of octopus. He snatches anything he can get, patents it, and calls it his own. One of these days, he'll get his." He grinned at her. "At least, I hope to blazes he will."

She considered for a moment, then grinned back. "Can't say as I blame you."

They started up again. Mari watched through the back window until the Indians and the truck and the camera were out of sight, wondering about the intricacies of making a motion picture. It hadn't occurred to her that filming from a moving vehicle might not work, although it made sense now that she thought about it. There was a whole lot to this picture-making stuff that she didn't know beans about. She wondered if Tony knew any more than she did.

"Um, so, did you study the industry before you came out here to help Martin with this picture?" she asked after the Indians faded into the desert behind her.

"Oh, yes. I studied a lot about it." He frowned. "Can't say that I had much interest initially, but when my father decided to invest in this picture and asked me to travel out here to watch over his investment, I learned as much as I could."

"It's all so new. It must be sort of fun to be in at the beginning of a new industry." Was that a dumb thing to have said? Too late not to say it now.

Tony's eyes thinned, and he looked sort of like he was frowning. It wasn't one of the kinds of frowns he directed at her when she irked him, so Mari didn't get nervous. Yet.

After a moment or two, he said slowly, "I guess it's all right."

"All right?" Shoot, that was tepid praise. "I thought everybody nowadays was in love with the pictures."

"Most people are." He still frowned.

Watching him curiously, Mari said, "But you're not?"

He shrugged. "Oh, the pictures are all right, I suppose. I'm not really interested in getting involved in them, though. I prefer other business pursuits."

"Oh? Like what?"

"I don't know. Things I understand." He glanced at her and grinned again. His grins were enough to send a girl into a swoon. "I'm interested in mining, actually. Studied mining engineering in college."

Mari stopped wanting to swoon. "Mining?" Her voice had gone sharp. "What do you mean?"

If he'd come out here to get her mine away from her, Mari'd have something to say about it. Damn him, anyway! How dare he lull her into talking civilly to him and then as much as tell her he aimed to deprive her of her father's dream?

She told herself to calm down. She told herself he hadn't said that. She told herself he probably didn't even *want* to own the Marigold Mine. Why should he? It was an unproductive hole in the ground.

As if he'd read her mind, he said wryly, "Don't worry, Mari, I'm not aiming to snatch your mine away from you. I'm only interested in profitable ventures."

She jerked as if he'd slapped her. "That was a mean thing to say." True, probably, but mean.

He had the grace to look apologetic. "You're right. I beg your pardon."

She sniffed. Restraint blossomed between them once more. Disheartened, Mari wondered if it would always be thus, or if, before the end of this stupid picture, they'd be able to talk to each other as friends. Or at least as acquaintances with no particular grudge between them.

Probably not.

"I'm sorry, Mari."

She was so startled by the words, which Tony had spoken very softly into the lull, that she whipped her head around to stare at him. She couldn't believe her ears. After considering asking him to repeat himself, however, she decided against it. He was so darned touchy. Those nerves of his.

"Um, that's all right," she said, although she might have been lying. She wasn't sure.

"No, it's not."

Oh. Well, that settled that, she guessed. She didn't know what to say now.

He solved that problem. "I didn't mean to say anything unkind about your mine. It wasn't polite, and I apologize. I know how much it means to you."

That was nice of him. "Thank you." For some reason she couldn't fathom, her throat tightened. She'd have said more, but was afraid she'd blubber and embarrass herself.

The motorcar purred along for another few minutes. Neither Mari nor Tony spoke. Finally, Tony heaved a big sigh and said, "Listen, Mari, I think we got off on the wrong foot. I don't want to fight anymore. Do you suppose we can try to get along?"

Well, now, she wasn't sure about that. She'd sure like to get along with him. She could imagine all sorts of uses for a rich friend like Tony Ewing. Unfortunately, she couldn't quite picture herself fitting in with his city pals.

That was stupid. He wasn't asking her to join his crowd. She eyed him thoughtfully, and said, "Sure. I suppose so. I guess we have been kind of snapping at each other since we met, haven't we?"

"You could call it that."

She had a feeling he was remembering the rock incident, and her lips tightened. That hadn't been her fault, darn it.

"Anyhow, I'd like to bury the hatchet, if that's all right with you. Maybe we could just start over."

Maybe they could. Then again . . . Mari said, "Sure. All right." It was worth a try, she supposed.

He turned the full glory of one of his beautiful smiles on her, and Mari had to swallow hard. "Good. I hope you'll allow me to take you out to dinner in Los Angeles. I've spent a good deal of time there these past several months, and I've found where all the important picture people hang out. It might be fun for you to see where the stars do their glittering at night."

She blinked at him. "But—but, I thought we weren't staying there overnight."

He turned to face the road ahead of them again, still smiling. "Changed my mind."

As he began whistling a merry tune, Mari's mind started churning out all sorts of scenarios. None of them were very flattering to Tony's character, but they all sounded like a good deal of fun to her.

Which went to show that she was only inches away from being a fallen woman.

It was a lowering reflection, and Mari hoped neither her father nor her mother was watching her from above.

Eight

Mari's first impression of Los Angeles wasn't one of awe. Far from it. From her perspective, it was a dull brown city much like San Bernardino, only bigger and full of orange groves. Just a little bit bigger, though. It was mostly crops and cows and cactus, like everything else in the vicinity.

"Doesn't look like much so far, does it?"

She turned to see if Tony was laughing at her, or if he'd been making an honest statement of fact. She gave him the benefit of the doubt. "No, it sure doesn't."

After thinking for another few seconds, she decided to say something else. Maybe he'd laugh at her. Maybe he wouldn't. Ever since he'd made an overture of détente back there on the desert, they hadn't been sniping at each other nearly as much as before. Mari decided an experiment was worth the effort. "Um, I'd sort of been hoping for something more grand."

He smiled, but he didn't laugh. "If you want grand, you're going to have to head east. L.A.'s pretty much a desert town now. If it's ever going to grow up to be a big city, it'll have to find a good source of water somewhere."

She surveyed the dusty town and nodded in agreement. "You're probably right. I guess water's the most important thing, if a city expects to prosper."

Still, Mari could see a glimmer of prosperity here and there. One or two big houses with elegant grounds hove into view and impressed the heck out of her. She wouldn't mind living in a house like one of those. They were castles compared to her tiny shack.

As they drove deeper into the city itself, she noticed a good deal of what she recognized as Spanish influence prevailing. Many of the buildings were low white structures and had tile roofs. Soon they were driving alongside a sprawling plaza with a huge church at one end.

"Want to stop and look around? This is a good place to get something to eat, too, if you like Mexican food."

"I'd like to look around, but I don't know if I like Mexican food or not. I'm used to my own cooking."

She glanced at him sharply when he chuckled, but he didn't look disparaging, so she decided not to get indignant. He turned the automobile down a brick-paved road lined with stalls where everything from hats and belts to turkeys and chickens to apples and oranges was being sold. Mari asked curiously, "Is this market day?" Thursday was market day in Mojave Wells, but it wasn't nearly as elaborate as this. On Thursdays a few outlying farmers brought their vegetables and chickens to town. This looked sort of permanent.

"I think every day's market day here. This will give you a chance to see if you like the cooking in these parts. They use a lot of beans and rice and chilies. I find it tasty. Not at all like what we're used to on the East Coast."

The only thing Mari could think of that she knew for certain came from back east was a kind of shellfish called a lobster. She'd heard folks rave about lobsters, but she didn't imagine she'd ever get a bite of one. "I expect that's so. I suppose different parts of the country use whatever grows there."

"Right."

"And what's easy to cook." She cleared her throat and wished she'd stop feeling like such a hick. "We use lots of beans in Mojave, too. It's because they keep when they're dried, and it's hard to keep stuff cold there. Dried beans don't spoil."

He parked the automobile under a shady pepper-tree—Mari knew it was a peppertree, because she'd seen them in San Bernardino—and its engine rattled to a stop. "That makes sense. It must be hard to keep things like milk and eggs fresh in that insufferable heat."

"It is for me," she admitted. Of course, if she had a few extra dollars, she might be able to afford a better place to live, with electricity and fans and electrical iceboxes and things like that.

There she went again. She hated when she started wishful thinking, because it led to nothing but unhappiness, and she couldn't afford that any more than she could afford electricity. To distract herself, she surveyed the busy street and noticed large flowered pots with huge bouquets of bright flowers. The flowers didn't look real to her, but they were lovely. "Gee, it's pretty here."

"I like it, too."

There were lots of people in Los Angeles, at least in this part of it. Most of them were strolling or lounging, a sensible concession to the heat, which, while nowhere near as extreme as in Mojave Wells, was still intense. Women in white cotton dresses and men in white cotton shirts and pants spoke Spanish to each other. Many of them eyed Tony's motorcar with interest. A few children, barefoot and also clad in white cotton, walked over and stood several yards away, peering at the newfangled contraption as if they'd like to come closer but didn't dare. Mari smiled at them.

Tony noticed her smiling, opened his mouth to ask her what was funny, understood the small gesture she made with her hand, and turned to behold the children. He smiled, too, and Mari's heart flipped over.

He gestured for the children to come closer. After exchanging looks of trepidation, they did so, grinning shyly. Mari clasped her hands and watched, intrigued to see Tony interact with children with whom he had nothing whatever in common.

"Want to see the car?" he asked softly.

The children conversed in Spanish for a moment, then one little boy, bolder than his mates, stepped forward, removing a huge straw hat and bowing. *"Sí, señor.* The car." His accent was thick as molasses. Mari was charmed.

Her state of charm transformed into one of astonishment when Tony opened the front door of the motorcar and said, *"Es un Pierce Arrow Grande. Quieren,* um, *ver a dentro?"*

The little boy nodded. He, too, appeared surprised that Tony could speak his language, if only a little bit, and he smiled in appreciation. With a gesture, he called his friends over.

Mari moved closer to Tony. "I didn't know you could speak Spanish."

Smiling and watching the children peer with fascination inside his amazing machine, Tony shrugged. "I don't know it very well, but I'm good with languages. I never took Spanish in school, but it's hard to avoid it here in California." He squinted down at her. "At least, I haven't been able to avoid it."

She flushed. "We don't have so many Spanish folks in Mojave, I guess."

"Probably not. Los Angeles was originally settled by the Spanish. I reckon that's why so many still live here."

"Probably."

The small flock of children investigated Tony's car with care and respect. It didn't look to Mari as if any of them dared do more than touch the plush leather of the seats, and none of them tried to climb inside or sit on a fender. They were awfully cute.

After a few minutes, Tony said something to the boy who'd assumed the position of leader of the group, and the boy nodded eagerly. Reaching into his pocket, Tony pulled out some coins and handed them over to the boy, who accepted them with thanks.

Taking Mari's arm, Tony said, "There. I asked them to watch the machine while we stroll around for a little while and get some lunch. I'm hungry."

How enterprising of him to enlist the natives in his cause. Although she wasn't sure it was a good thing, Mari's respect for Tony's ability to deal with people outside his rich eastern set rose a few points. She also wondered why he hadn't been so tactful with her when they'd first met.

Then again, she'd been in a relatively sour mood that day herself. Maybe he'd taken his cue from her. It wasn't a possibility that sat well with her, and she shelved it for the nonce. Much better to enjoy the day, his company, and these fascinating new surroundings than dwell on her possible shortcomings.

"This is Olvera Street," Tony said. "I understand it's the oldest street in Los Angeles. That church is pretty old, too, I hear. All the Spanish settlements were built around churches, or so I've been told. When I took the train out here, it stopped in Santa Fe, in the New Mex-

ico Territory, and it's the same there. All activities centered around the church and the plaza."

"My goodness." A few of the women she spotted
wore gaily colored skirts. Pretty painted pottery stood
beside doors, and Mari saw that her impression of the
flowers had been correct. They seemed to be made out
of crepe paper. They were sure pretty, and she considered making some to enliven her own dismal corner of
the world. Crepe paper was cheap, and she could find
sticks to tack the flowers onto, probably. Her mood
edged up.

They walked past a stall where a woman sold striped
capes and cunningly painted statues of saints. Mari
wished that her father was alive, and that she had some
money. He'd have loved to have one of those cape
things.

The thought both saddened and gladdened her. She
liked thinking of her father as a dear man who
adored bright colors and funny jokes. It was much
preferable to thinking of him as a lousy businessman
with a single-minded mania for the Marigold Mine.
She paused and fingered a striped cape. "It feels
like heavy cotton," she murmured.

"Probably is." Tony, smiling at the woman behind
the stall's counter, lifted one of them down for Mari
to inspect more closely. "See? I imagine they use
wool and cotton both. Wool for the winter, and cotton for summertime. I think they're called serapes."
He glanced an inquiry at the stall's proprietress, who
nodded and smiled, showing a glimmer of gold-filled
teeth.

"Serapes? I've heard that word."

"That old miner we saw by the side of the road was
wearing one."

"Oh, yes, I remember now." She was surprised Tony
did, though. She guessed she hadn't given him enough

credit. He really did pay attention to the rest of the world. She'd assumed, from their first few encounters, that he sat on his throne in his ivory tower and scorned those of his fellows who weren't as lucky as he was. Maybe she'd been a little hard on him.

"You ought to get one of these blouses, Mari."

His words captured her attention with a jolt, and she turned to gape at him. He held out a pretty white cotton blouse with a white ruffle around the neck, and decorated with colorful embroidered flowers. She looked from the blouse to him, and knew she was blushing. Blast it.

She'd love to have that blouse. Mari, who'd never had any clothes to speak of except hand-me-down trousers and shirts from the church basement sale and the two dresses she'd inherited from her mother, had always tried not to want things. Wanting things only led to wishful thinking, which led to dissatisfaction, and she didn't need it. She also didn't need a pretty white blouse.

"I can't use it," she said, wishing she sounded more like she meant it. "I mean, what would I do with a white blouse in a mine?" She managed a laugh.

He shrugged. "I don't suppose you'd wear it in the mine. Here. Let's see if it fits."

Mari jumped several inches when he held the blouse up to her shoulders. She was mortally embarrassed but didn't want to show it. The vendor was beaming at her, and Tony was smiling, and she couldn't figure out what she was supposed to do.

Not that it mattered. She didn't have money to spend on a blouse she didn't need. Anyhow, what would she wear it with? She didn't have a skirt that would go with it, and it would look silly with the battered old britches she wore.

"Then," Tony said, as if he'd been reading her thoughts, "we'd have to get you one of those skirts."

Oh, Lord, Mari hadn't noticed the skirts. They were so pretty, all bright stripes and patterns. Greens and reds and yellows and blues. They no sooner met the eye than they cheered up the spirit.

With a sigh, she supposed she might as well not fight the wish to own such charming clothes. She couldn't afford the blouse or the skirt, so she might just as well want both.

Which was pretty discouraging, actually.

"And you'd need a sash to tie everything together," Tony went on, as if he didn't know how much Mari yearned to possess the finery he was dangling so casually in front of her.

She wished he'd stop it. She felt like a bull being baited by somebody flashing a red bandanna in front of its eyes. She *wanted* nice things. She *wanted* to be attractive, to wear pretty clothes, not to have to work so hard for so pitifully little recompense.

But that wasn't in the cards God had dealt her. Sometimes she wanted to have a sit-down, heart-to-heart chat with God and ask him why, but she knew that was sacrilegious thinking. God's will was God's will, and people had nothing to say about it.

Still didn't seem fair.

Her mind was in such a fluster that she didn't realize what Tony planned until he turned to the stall keeper and said, "We'll take these."

She returned to reality with a painful thump. *"What?"* Blast, she hadn't meant to screech. She could tell neither Tony nor the woman had expected it of her when they both turned and stared at her, the woman with surprise, Tony with thinned lips that denoted to Mari, who'd come to know that expression, burgeoning anger.

"No need to holler, Mari. I'm paying."

"That's scandalous!" she hissed, becoming angry in her own right. What did this man think he was doing? She'd thought his intentions were honorable, even if he didn't like her very much. "I'm not going to let you buy me clothes. Why, it's unheard of!"

"Nonsense." His voice was as crisp as burned toast. "If we're going to be seeing the nightlife in Los Angeles, you're not going dressed like that." He cast a scornful glance at her mother's ancient dress, and Mari's embarrassment grew to monumental proportions.

"If," she said in a voice of stone, "I have to sink to the level of allowing you to buy my clothes, I prefer to skip Los Angeles's nightlife, thank you very much." She turned and stalked off several yards, primarily because she couldn't bear to be so close to those pretty things and to know that in order to possess them she'd have to be at a man's mercy. She could recall very few times in her life she'd been this humiliated. Damn Tony Ewing!

Tony watched her march away from him with narrowed eyes and a narrower mind. What was the matter with the chit? Did she think he was going to squire a woman who looked like a tramp around town?

The stall vendor murmured something to him in Spanish. He whipped his head around and stared at her. "I beg your pardon? Er, *cómo?*"

"Se dijó, usted le a sentimientos lástimas, es un bruto, y no merete una mujer con tanto espirito."

He'd hurt her feelings? He'd acted like a *brute?* And he didn't deserve a woman with Mari's spirit? Tony's gaze traveled from the shopkeeper, whose chin was tilted up in much the manner as Mari's, to Mari, who had commenced fingering some crepe-paper flowers. She seemed to like those flowers. Tony experienced a mad impulse to buy out the flower supply on Olvera Street and lay them all at her feet.

Shoot, he hadn't meant to hurt her feelings. He guessed he should have phrased his reasoning more persuasively. He guessed he had been a little rough around the edges. And maybe in the middle as well.

It was only because he wasn't accustomed to having to use subtlety when dealing with women. And he'd never had to deal with a woman of Mari's stamp. Most of the females he'd known thus far had been grasping creatures who believed men owed them everything they wanted.

Of course, that meant they weren't anything at all like Marigold Pottersby, whose pride was monumental, especially if one considered her circumstances. Or perhaps she was so damned proud because of her circumstances.

"Dammit," he grumbled. "Here. Wrap 'em up." He tossed the woman behind the counter several dollars without counting them and hurried off to unruffle Mari's feathers. She heard him coming, turned, armed herself with a bunch of flowers, and glared daggers at him.

"Listen, Mari," he blurted out before he'd reached her. "I didn't mean what I said back there."

She said, "Ha," and hugged the flowers closer to her bosom.

It occurred to Tony that if he played his cards right, she might eventually hold him close to her bosom. He told himself not to be stupid. Theirs was a business relationship and nothing more.

If he felt a tiny stirring of lust in his loins for the girl, it was only because he was a man and she was a goddess. That is to say—good God, Mari was about as far from being a goddess as she was from being a plutocrat. What he'd meant was that he was a man and she was an attractive woman. That's it. That's all. End of story.

"Honest," he went on. "I mean it. It was a lousy thing to say, and I'm sorry. But I really think you ought to allow Peerless to buy you something to wear besides—" Dammit, he'd gone and done it again: talked himself into a hole. He heaved a gusty sigh. "I mean, look at it this way," he continued, fumbling helplessly. "Don't you think you owe it to Peerless to look your best?"

"No."

No? *No?* Well, hell, now what? He recalled Martin telling him about several new magazine ventures featuring stories and photographs of motion-picture actors. He decided to use them to forward his cause.

"Listen, Mari, there's going to be a lot of publicity about this picture. It's the most ambitious project Peerless has yet tackled. *Motion Picture Story Magazine* is going to do a big spread about *Lucky Strike*. Martin told me they're sending a photographer and a staff writer to Mojave Wells to take shots of the cast and the location and to write a story about the whole thing. They're making a big deal out of it."

"So what?"

In spite of her tone, which was ice cold, and the words, which were clipped, Tony began to take heart. Her eyes no longer exuded loathing; they actually seemed to contain a modicum of interest. He decided to fan the flame, if it was there. "So what? So they're going to make a big deal out of you, too."

"What?"

Now she sounded horrified, and Tony wished he had an extra set of legs, so he could kick himself for being a clumsy ass. He drew in another breath and expelled it harshly. "You're the female star of the picture, Mari, and a brand-new one. It's part of the excitement to have you playing opposite Reginald Harrowgate, who's already famous. They're going to want to write a whole lot about you and take lots of pictures."

The flowers hit a counter with a smack, and her fists went to her hips. "Nobody told me anything about all of that!"

Tony eyed her. "Oh, come on, Mari. You don't expect me to believe you've never seen a movie magazine, do you?" He didn't buy it.

"I don't give a hang what you believe!" Her voice had risen. "When you and Martin came to my door and asked to rent my mine, you never said anything about sticking my face up all over town."

"The nation," Tony muttered, peeved. "Peerless's influence extends to the entire nation by this time."

She gasped, irritating Tony's already rattled senses. "Don't tell me you didn't anticipate public interest," he demanded, "because I *really* won't believe that one!"

"But—but—" She seemed to run out of steam. Lifting her arms and letting them drop in a gesture of futility, she murmured, "But, honest, Tiny—I mean, Tony—"

Tony gritted his teeth.

"I never even thought about—about—publicity. Photographs. Stuff like that."

Her eyes started glittering. Tony watched them with dawning horror. Good God, she wasn't going to *cry*, was she? Tony hated when women cried at him. He never knew what to do. What's more, he'd assumed the only females who used tactics like tears were conniving bitches. No matter how much she aggravated him, he couldn't convict Mari of being one of those.

He made sure his voice sounded sympathetic when he spoke again. "I'm sorry about that, Mari, but it's a fact of this business."

"Oh, God." She sounded as if despair had completely overwhelmed her. Turning around, she covered her face with her hands and bowed her head. He wasn't sure, but he feared she might have succumbed to her urge to bawl.

Tony didn't know whether to trust her or not. On the one hand, he couldn't conceive of Mari Pottersby being untruthful, especially about something like this. On the other hand, what had she expected?

She was a smart cookie. Surely she knew moving pictures were the latest, greatest fad, and not merely in the United States. The whole world was falling under the influence of the pictures and picture actors. Why, Tony wouldn't be at all surprised if public adulation lifted Mari out of her blasted mine and into some upper stratosphere of fame and glamour.

The notion didn't sit particularly well with him, since he liked her the way she was.

That is to say—dammit, he wished he'd stop getting his thoughts all kinked up like this—he admired her fighting spirit. That's what he liked about her. Even though that same spirit had gotten in his way more than once. He feared if she ever became rich and famous, she'd change, and that would be too bad. At least, he thought it might be. It could be.

"Listen, Mari . . ." He didn't know what to say. He didn't know what to do. He felt very awkward. "Um, are you crying?"

"No!"

Now he really didn't believe her. The one word had been so thick, he'd barely understood it. Some unfamiliar compulsion overtook his good sense, and he reached out to place his hands gently on her shoulders. For a second, she stiffened up like cement setting, then let her shoulders sag.

"Say, Mari, I'm sorry. I didn't mean to upset you like this. I figured you already knew that you'd be in for a bunch of publicity hounds coming after you."

He heard her suck in a ragged breath. "I probably should have realized it," she whispered. "But I didn't. I'm really stupid, aren't I?"

Stupid? Well . . . "No. Heck, no. You're not stupid. Just—" Great, now what? "Just innocent." Yeah, that was good. And truly, Tony supposed it wasn't stupid of her not to have anticipated publicity. She'd had her mind wrapped around money, not fame. She'd been so desperate to keep that blasted mine working.

He gently tugged her around and into his arms. She felt very good there. Swell, even. "Please don't cry, Mari."

"I'm not crying!"

Yeah. Right. He patted her on the back, attempting to be brotherly about it, but hampered by the fact that he didn't feel at all like a brother. He felt like drawing her away to some flowered bower and making delicious love to her.

She'd scratch his eyes out if he even tried such a maneuver. "I didn't mean to upset you."

He kept patting and murmuring into her glorious hair. She kept not speaking. At last she heaved a fierce sigh, which lifted her bosom and pressed it into his chest, much to his delight, and tried to pull away from him. He held on for as long as he dared, but eventually had to release her. She didn't lift her head to look at him, and he reached out to tilt her chin up. That uplifted chin of hers had irked him so often, he later marveled that he'd made the gesture.

"Better?" he asked softly.

"I think so." She yanked a handkerchief out of her pocket and tackled her eyes with vigor.

"Will you let Peerless buy you a nice outfit to wear to dinner in Los Angeles?"

Another sigh, deeper and more soulful than the prior

one, escaped her. "I suppose so." Her tone let him know what she thought about letting other people buy her things.

A tiny tug—virtually a mere pinch—of irritation swept through Tony. It was ludicrous for this impoverished chit to balk at receiving gifts from a company with as much money as Peerless. What did she think Peerless wanted from her in return? They only wanted her to act in a movie. The studio wasn't going to compromise her, blast it.

Now, if it had been Tony who was offering to clothe her, it might have been different. He'd probably really enjoy compromising her, as a matter of fact.

But, he told himself, he was only doing this for Peerless. For the sake of the studio's newest acquisition. If one could call human beings acquisitions. One of the amendments to the Constitution had put a halt to that sort of thing fifty years and more ago, hadn't it?

He hollered at himself to stop quibbling. Mari Pottersby had become a valuable commodity to the Peerless Studio. It was worth it, both to Peerless and to Tony Ewing, whose father's money he was supposed to be watching, to clothe her appropriately. So she wouldn't disgrace the studio. Or his father's money. Or something like that.

More heartily than he felt inside, he said, "Great. Let me just go pick up those things."

Racing back to the stall—he didn't trust Mari not to change her mind due to an excess of pride—he shook his head when the stall keeper tried to give him change back, grabbed the package she'd wrapped up for him, and rushed back to Mari. She was fingering the crepe-paper flowers she'd slammed down on the counter and looking gloomy.

Feeling inspired and not caring if Mari appreciated the gesture or not, Tony grabbed the big bouquet, threw some more money at that stall's vendor, and shoved the bouquet into Mari's arms. "Here. Take these. If you say one word about not wanting me to buy them for you, I swear I'll turn you over my knee and paddle your behind."

Which didn't sound like a half-bad idea.

Fortunately for him, Mari didn't know his mind had wandered onto a sordid path. She even gave him a weak smile and said, "Thank you, Tony."

He grinned at her gratefully, and not merely because she hadn't called him Tiny. "You're more than welcome. Now, let's get some lunch. I'm famished."

"Okay. Thanks."

He led her to a restaurant with an outdoor patio that he'd discovered on one of his earlier jaunts onto Olvera Street. They decided to take their noon meal inside, since the air was cooler in there and stirred by electrical fans. He noticed how much more fun it was to explore new scenes with a companion. Even a companion like Mari, who was apt to argue with him every time he opened his mouth, beat the tar out of venturing into new territory solo.

Actually—he wasn't sure it was a good idea to admit it—he'd rather be in Mari's company than anyone else's.

Damn. That was silly. He didn't mean it.

His confused thoughts scattered upon the arrival of a waiter. With a smile for Mari, he said, "I can recommend the tacos and the chiles rellenos. Haven't had anything else."

"My goodness, I've never even heard of most of this stuff. I know what an enchilada is, I think."

"Oh, yeah, I had one of those, too. They're good."

"I think I'll have the— Oh."

Bother, now what? Tony sighed and peered at Mari, who looked stricken, with her menu clutched to her chest. Her eyes were huge and beautiful in the dim indoor light. He tried not to allow his vexation to seep into his voice. "What is it, Mari?" Tact. He had to remember he needed to use tact with this prickly female.

She lowered the menu and swallowed. From the expression on her face, she'd just received a message filled with tragedy and doom—it must have been delivered telepathically, since Tony knew damned well nothing physical had happened.

"I don't have any money."

He stared at her for at least thirty seconds before a "Good God" leaked out of his mouth.

That made her chin tilt up, her eyes thin, and her mouth pinch into a straight line. At once, Tony scrambled to recover lost ground. "I mean, that's not a problem. I have plenty of money."

"I don't expect you to pay for my lunch."

He couldn't help it; he rolled his eyes in exasperation. It was the wrong thing to have done. Naturally. What was the right thing to do with this cantankerous female? "Listen, Mari, I don't care what you expect. My expectations for myself are every bit as great as yours are for you. Whether you want to admit it or not, I am a gentleman. I asked you to dine with me. The gentleman *always* pays."

"But—"

To stop her, he pointed a finger right at her nose. Her eyes crossed, and she blinked. "And don't you even think about arguing with me. You've come to Los Angeles on business. It's *my* business to see that you're fed, clothed, and housed appropriately for as long as you're working for Peerless. And don't forget it again."

There. He felt better now. Although he withdrew his hand and stopped pointing at her, he didn't drop his tough-guy attitude. He saw her swallow again, prayed briefly that she wouldn't fight him on this, and breathed an internal sigh of relief when she said only, "Oh. All right. I guess I understand."

Thank God. He wondered how long her new understanding would last. He wasn't optimistic.

Nine

Mari changed into her new duds at the costumer's studio. Madame Dunbar's place wasn't actually in the city of Los Angeles. Rather, it was located in a foothill community called Altadena, which was north of Pasadena, which Mari'd never heard of, either, so it didn't make any difference.

Altadena and Pasadena were both gorgeous places, full of grand homes and magnificent vistas. Orange groves and poppy fields abounded, and the San Gabriel Mountains loomed over them all as if keeping a kindly watch on things.

Madame Dunbar's studio consisted of a suite of rooms in the upstairs of her magnificent home on the corner of Foothill Boulevard and Maiden Lane. The house was a palace to Mari's eyes. She suspected it would seem so to anyone who'd lived her life in a one-room cabin. It took all her strength of will not to tiptoe around the edges of the carpeting for fear of doing something hicklike. She was very ill at ease.

Also, it was embarrassing to have Tony staring critically at her every time she walked out of the dressing room into the fitting parlor, clad in another costume she was supposed to wear in *Lucky Strike*. One of the ensembles consisted of trousers and an old plaid shirt, not unlike the clothes Mari wore on a daily basis. For some reason, while she'd never been embarrassed to be seen clad thus in Mojave Wells, today she felt like a flaming idiot when she had to parade in front of Tony and Madame Dunbar.

The fact that Madame D stood against a wall, tapping her foot impatiently, arms crossed over her chest, and scowling up a storm didn't soothe Mari's nerves. It didn't help, either, when the seamstress would huff something in French that sounded vaguely blasphemous, storm over to Mari, and tug at a pleat here or a seam there.

Mari felt like a child's toy, being yanked this way and that. Independent her whole life, feeling like somebody else's property was a new and unpleasant experience for her. She got through it, but not without her mood sinking until it wallowed in a swamp of dismal thoughts. She'd seldom been so glad as she was when the fitting session ended, and Tony and the artiste left her alone in the fitting salon. She felt like a soggy mop as she put on the clothes Tony had bought for her on Olvera Street.

However, as she gazed at the transformed Mari in the mirror of Madame Dunbar's elaborate dressing suite, she decided she'd been too hard on Tony Ewing.

Maybe.

She guessed she could buy the part about Peerless wanting its newest actress to dress like a success, both on and off the set. But it still didn't feel right to be having a man buy clothes for her. She had a feeling her mother would have been shocked. Mari sure as heck knew *she* was shocked.

It was difficult, though, when she saw the image of herself reflected in the polished glass, to care much. She'd never looked this good before. And the ensemble was really plain, too. Heck, she could do this, and it wouldn't even cost much. The smashing effect had been created by a simple peasant blouse, a brightly colored skirt, and that red sash, which, as Tony had predicted, brought the ensemble together as a whole. All she needed now was one of those crepe-paper flowers behind one of her ears, and she'd look so exotic, she wouldn't even recognize herself.

She produced a mental image of herself waltzing into the Mojave Inn one evening—make it a Friday or Saturday night, when more of her neighbors were apt to be dining out—and knocking everyone dead with her new and stunning self.

"I wish Pa was here to see me," she murmured at her reflection.

But he wasn't. And her mother wasn't here. And none of her friends or other relatives were here. The only person she'd be able to impress here in Altadena was Tony Ewing. Didn't sound likely to her.

Nevertheless, with that thought in mind, Mari sucked in a deep breath, made sure everything that was supposed to be tucked in had been, patted her hair, which was knotted at the back of her neck as usual, lifted her skirt, noticed her scruffy shoes, lowered the skirt again, and sighed.

"Fiddlesticks." She wished, as long as Tony was flinging money around, he'd thought to fling some at a shoe salesman.

But there was nothing to be done about her footwear at this point, so she squared her shoulders and headed for the door. She knew that Tony and Madame Dunbar awaited her in the huge parlor. To get there, she had to descend a flight of stairs leading to an enormous front reception hall. So be it. At the head of the staircase, she gripped the banister and, after thinking about it for a second or two and deciding it would be worse to tumble down the staircase than reveal her shabby shoes, she lifted her skirt and started down the stairs.

Tony stood at the foot of the staircase. Mari frowned

when she saw him gazing up at her. "I thought you were going to wait for me in the parlor."

"I heard the door open upstairs and decided to anticipate your arrival. Madame Dunbar has tea for us in the parlor."

Mari'd been kind of hoping she'd walk into the parlor and Tony would be struck speechless by her amazing transformation. She was disappointed to discover that life hadn't taken a magical turn for her. Tony looked the same as ever. Handsome as sin and impervious to any charms Mari might possess. It was quite discouraging, actually.

The staircase flattened out into a small polished platform—Tony had told her the staircase had been designed specifically for the display of Madame Dunbar's creations during her semiannual fashion shows—and three more stairs set to the left of the platform led into the hall. As Mari reached the platform, Tony held out his arm for her. She laid her hand on his arm in a way she'd seen illustrated in pictures, and walked in as stately a manner as she could summon.

On the inside, she felt crummy. She'd so hoped to make some kind of impression on this wealthy man of the world. Only went to show—one more time—how stupid she was.

"You look gorgeous, Mari," Tony said conversationally. "I knew you would."

His words stopped her in her tracks, although they didn't stop him, and he kept walking. Their elbows locked and jerked, and he glanced back at her with his eyebrows raised. Mari scurried to catch up with him, embarrassed. "Thank you."

He'd *known* she would? Look gorgeous? Was he kidding her? She wanted to ask, but knew she'd only appear foolish if she did. It was hard keeping her mouth shut, though. She'd not had much practice in keeping her thoughts to herself. Of course, it didn't generally matter, since the only one around to hear her unless she had visitors was Tiny. Tiny didn't care what anybody said, as long as they said it around him.

Even Madame Dunbar, who sat ramrod straight in a fancy medallion-backed armchair, lifted one of her aristocratic eyebrows and nodded her approval at Mari's altered state. Was this a triumph? Mari was so darned nervous, she couldn't tell, although she was glad she looked okay.

"Thanks for seeing us today, Madame Dunbar," Tony said, oozing politeness.

Mari squinted at him and wondered why he never sounded that nice when he was talking to her.

"Bah! Is nothing." The woman waved Tony's apology away as if she were shooing off a pesky fly. "Peerless has been good to me."

For some reason, the dressmaker's artless comment made a bunch of things come together in Mari's head. It was the first time she'd fully recognized the impact the motion-picture industry was beginning to have on the overall economy in those places where pictures were made.

It only made sense. Picture people needed sets, costumers, makeup artists, camera people, cameras, automobiles, hair stylists, set designers, set builders, story writers, artists to paint the subtitles, and God alone knew how many other folks besides actors to create their product.

Not to mention the businesses cropping up on the sidelines, trying to profit from the public's fascination with the pictures and the people in them. Why, there were magazines, theaters and people to operate them, writers, and who knew what else besides. Goodness gracious, the enormity of it boggled Mari's mind.

"Don't you think so, Mari?"

Mari, who'd been occupied with her own thoughts and not paying attention to the conversation between Tony and Madame Dunbar, jumped in her seat and spilled some tea into her saucer. Doggone it! She cleared her throat, tried to pretend she wasn't blushing, and said, "Um, I beg your pardon? My mind was, um, wandering a little." She gave Madame Dunbar a smile she hoped was sweet. The woman didn't acknowledge it by so much as a twitch of her nose, the witch.

"I said," Tony said, sounding exasperated—nothing new there—"that it would be a good thing for Madame Dunbar to create a couple of dresses for you to wear in public. Like the one you're wearing now, only for different occasions."

Mari stared at him, holding her cup and saucer very still in her hands. What did this mean? Was this a legitimate business suggestion, or was he trying to batter away at her integrity by bribing her.

She scoffed even as she thought it. Why in the name of glory would he do that? He'd thus far demonstrated no interest whatever in her, except as a commodity.

"Um . . ."

Tony turned to Madame Dunbar. "She's too damned independent, you see, Madame. She thinks we're trying to corrupt her or something."

"Now, wait a minute, Tiny—I mean Tony. I . . ."

Madame Dunbar laughed. Her laugh came out a silvery tinkle, which didn't go with her stern demeanor, and Mari's confusion mounted. "Silly little thing."

"But—"

"Precious, though." The dressmaker gave Mari the approving look she might bestow on a cunningly crafted ensemble.

Mari gulped audibly.

"She doesn't yet understand that the public's eye has become focused on the pictures and on the people who play in them. A studio, in order to protect and promote its product, has to have attractive stars."

"But . . ." Good God, did that mean he considered her unattractive in her native state? Mari's heart pinged painfully. But she couldn't be too hideous, or Martin would never have asked her to act in his silly picture. Would he?

"Ah, the child is young," Madame Dunbar said to Tony, ignoring Mari. Which was all right, since Mari couldn't produce a coherent thought to save herself. "She'll learn. And I shall be happy"—she pronounced it *'appy*—"to create two gowns for her. I'll 'ave them ready in a week."

"That's great. Thanks a lot." Tony grinned at the dressmaker, jerked his head in Mari's direction, stood up, and said, "We've got to be going now. Thanks for all your help, Madame."

"Certainly." Madame Dunbar rose, too.

Mari wondered if they'd even notice if she remained where she was, fading into the upholstery along with her teacup and her red sash.

But, no. At last, after blathering for another few minutes about costumes and pictures and other things Mari didn't understand, Tony turned to her. "Ready, Mari? We've got to get back to L.A. I telephoned the Melrose Hotel from Madame's telephone room and reserved a couple of rooms. We can stop there to wash up, and then I'll take you out to eat. There are some pretty good restaurants in L.A. They're nowhere near as good as those you can find in New York or San Francisco, but you probably won't care about that."

The smile he gave her took some of the sting out of his words. As Mari arose from her chair—quite gracefully, if she did say so herself—she thought morosely that he was right, no matter how much his words hurt. She wouldn't know a first-class restaurant from a hole in the ground except that she'd not yet been intimidated by a hole in the ground. The mere thought of dining in a fancy restaurant sent shivers up her spine.

Tony held her arm as he led her through Madame Dunbar's sun porch, out onto the flagged patio, and onward to his great big Pierce Grand Arrow parked on the circular driveway. She was thinking hard the whole way and didn't utter a peep. Neither of the others seemed to notice. They were too busy blabbing.

After Tony had started the engine, the motorcar had roared to life, and he took a sweeping turn around the drive, past a lovely rose garden lined with some kind of plant with small white flowers that smelled heavenly, Mari decided to say what she'd been thinking. She didn't want to, mainly because she didn't trust her present companion not to make her feel ridiculous for speaking of such things.

"Um, Tony?"

He peered at her. He looked happy and relaxed. Mari wished she were. "Yes, Mari? Did you like Madame Dunbar?"

Glad for a brief reprieve, she shrugged. "What's not to like? I guess she does a good job."

"She does a great job." He glanced at her again, and his smile vanished. "You sound glum. What's wrong?"

Another shrug. "Nothing's wrong. I—well, I just wanted to ask you something."

He appeared taken aback for a couple of seconds, then said, "Sure. Ask away. Is something bothering you?" He sounded honestly concerned, and Mari appreciated it. She felt stupid and awkward.

"Well, I—" Darn it, she was going to cry! She hated her emotional makeup. It was so demeaning to cry in front of people like Tony Ewing; people who already thought she was a dumb bumpkin. She swallowed hard and forced herself to hold back her tears. This was so embarrassing. After taking a deep breath and holding it until she was pretty sure her voice wouldn't break, she blurted out, "Would you teach me how to act?"

He stared at her. "Teach you how to act?"

Not trusting her voice, she nodded, trying all the while to appear casual.

He frowned and turned back to survey the paved road in front of him. Most of the streets in Pasadena and Altadena over which they'd driven were paved. "I'm no acting coach, Mari. That's Martin's department. I'm only here to watch my father's money."

Bother. She hadn't expressed herself correctly, and he'd misunderstood. "That's not what I meant."

"No?" Again, he turned and looked at her. She wished he wasn't so darned good looking. It would be ever so much easier to ask this of a plain man.

"No."

Squinting at her once more before returning his attention to the road, Tony said, "I don't think I understand."

"I know you don't." She heaved a dispirited sigh.

"Want to explain? Act what? Act how? I don't know what you mean."

Mari's frustrations finally bubbled over. "Darn it! I'm asking you to teach me how to behave!" Now she felt beleaguered, put-upon, and angry, and the focus of all of her feelings sat behind the wheel of his expensive car, pretending not to understand what she was telling him. Mari turned on him. "Darn it, Tony Ewing, you're the one who keeps calling me a rude country bumpkin."

His eyes popped wide open. "I don't, either!"

"You do, too! You criticize me constantly. Everything I do is wrong to you! You even think you have to buy clothes for me to wear, because I'm not good enough to be seen in public with you otherwise."

"Well . . ."

"And it's not fair! I can't help it if I grew up poor. It's not *my* fault my father wasn't a rich millionaire!"

"What other kind is there?" Tony muttered under his breath.

"Don't you dare make fun of me!"

Even though she was looking at his profile, she saw him roll his eyes.

"And don't do that, either! I'm asking you to do me a favor, blast you! And it isn't an easy thing for me to do, either, since I know very well what you think of me."

"I doubt that."

"Oh, yes I do." She lowered her voice to a menacing pitch. "You hate me. You hate the very *thought* of me. You think I'm beneath you."

"Oh, for God's—"

"Don't interrupt me!" She'd gone shrill again. "Well, instead of picking on me all the time, why don't you teach me what to do? Huh? Why don't you try *that* for once?"

Mari threw herself back against the seat cushion, huffed furiously, crossed her arms over her breasts, sucked in a gallon of air flavored with the sweet smell of orange blossoms, clamped her teeth together, commanded herself not to cry, and fumed. She felt so god-awful stupid about her tantrum she couldn't bear to think about it, so she dwelt instead on the injustice Tony Ewing had done her ever since their first meeting.

The conceited so-and-so. Who did he think he was, anyway? God Almighty? Well, he wasn't. He was just the stuck-up son of a city snob who had more money than brains, and Mari wasn't going to take it anymore.

"Okay."

Mari's whole body jerked as if her bones had been replaced by clock springs. She jumped about a foot and swiveled on the plush seat so fast, she nearly gave herself whiplash. *"What?"*

Tony turned his head slightly and frowned at her. "You needn't screech anymore, Mari. I said okay. I think that's a good idea."

What? What did he think was a good idea? Mari's brain was so scrambled, she couldn't even remember what she'd hollered at him.

"I reject absolutely that nonsense about me hating you, but I do think you have a sound idea there. If you're taught what's expected of you in public, you'll be less apt to feel uncomfortable when the picture opens and you have to attend premieres and parties and so forth."

"What—" She had to stop and clear her throat. "What's a premiere?" For that matter, what was a party? The town of Mojave Wells, whose inhabitants were sociable and liked each other, didn't go in much for formal parties and so forth. Somebody'd host a picnic or a barbecue from time to time, but a party? Mari couldn't recall ever attending one.

Tony honored her with a brief smile. Mari recognized the smile as the type a teacher might bestow on a slow student who was performing slightly better than usual. Her heart, which had been racing and hammering and behaving in a manner not generally accepted of hearts, slowed and started to sink.

Good God in heaven, what had she done now? Why had she opened her darned mouth? And, if she had to open her mouth, why had she yelled at Tony? No matter how foolish and inadequate she felt in his company, it wasn't his fault. If there was any fault at all in the circumstances separating them, it was accidental. He couldn't help it if she'd been born poor any more than she could help it that he'd been born rich.

It was for darned sure that neither of them could go

back before their births and make their backgrounds more equitable. Mari had a wretched feeling that's what she was really mad about.

She wanted to be Tony Ewing's equal, socially, intellectually, and financially. She wanted to know if he could care for her if their backgrounds weren't so blasted different. She wanted to stand a fighting chance to win his affection.

What a miserable truth to discover at this point. And there wasn't a single, solitary thing she could do about it, because she'd already opened her foolish mouth and asked her stupid question. And he'd accepted.

Darn it, sometimes life just stank.

In spite of Mari's most recent attack on his character, honor, and moral fiber, Tony felt pretty good about life. And about her.

So, she was beginning to understand the necessity of appropriate dress and behavior, was she? And she'd actually, honestly and truly, asked for *his* help. What a change. What a coup. What an astonishing about-face. Watching her out of the corner of his eye, Tony knew he was going to enjoy this process. He'd been longing to get his hands—so to speak—on Mari Pottersby ever since they first met. Now he had her approval to do it.

He couldn't wait to begin shaping her into a proper lady. It would be his great pleasure to beget—so to speak—a new Mari. Working closely together, they could fashion her into something special. Why, once they got entangled—so to speak—with each other, who knew what might happen?

Hell, as Tony squinted at her slantways so as not to upset her any more than she was already upset, he thought that one of these days, if she was willing to follow his advice and guidance, she could be a truly remarkable lady. She was already a remarkable female. It was the *lady* part that needed work.

"We'll begin tonight," he told her with glee.

She jumped and clamped her hands together in her lap. "What? I mean, I beg your pardon?"

He frowned. There was no need for her to be nervous about this. He didn't intend to be an unkind tutor. "I said, we can begin tonight."

"Begin what?"

Her huge brown eyes, opened wide and staring at him, were one of her best assets, and Tony intended to see that she used them well. The passenger-side tire rattled over something, and he swung his attention back to his driving. Shoot, he'd better watch out, or he'd crash the car, kill them both, and all of his hard work on Mari's behalf would go for naught. Not that he'd done any yet, but he intended to.

"I said we can start your education tonight. After we wash up at the Melrose, I'll take you out to dinner and maybe a club."

"A club?" A fearful note had crept into her voice.

"You know," Tony said, grinning at the notion, "a nightclub. A nightspot. Where there's dancing and music."

"Um, I can't dance. Very well, I mean."

"No problem. I'll teach you. There's nothing to it."

"Oh." He could tell she didn't believe it. She would. He'd see to it.

He heard her swallow and turned to peek at her. He didn't let his gaze linger, no matter how much he wanted to, because he didn't want to cause an accident. "It'll be fun."

"Will it?"

"Sure, it will. And, don't forget," he added, in case she thought to ask if her Peerless duties included nightclub patrol, "this is all for your education and for your future. If you do a really good job in *Lucky Strike,* and the public comes to love you, you could make lots more money in the pictures."

"Oh."

Most of the women he'd met would kill to get into the pictures, except those excruciatingly proper ones from back East who believed everything and everyone in the world who didn't belong to their set were beneath them. He couldn't conceive of why Mari seemed indifferent.

Oh, yeah, now he remembered. That damned mine of hers. Tony wished she could get her mind away from that useless pit.

"Um, I don't think I really want to do any more pictures after this one," she said in a soft voice. "I don't think it's—um, up my alley or something."

Damn. Tony commenced scowling, wondering how he'd overcome this one. Then he brightened. It didn't matter. She still wanted to learn how to behave in public; that part hadn't changed. If she didn't have the added motivation of the moving pictures to spur her education, it didn't matter. He could still have a lot of fun with her. So to speak.

"That's okay," he said. "We'll still start your education tonight. If you don't like the nightclub, we don't have to stay long."

"Thank you."

"You don't have to sound so darned miserable, Mari. I'm not going to beat you or anything. I thought you wanted to do this."

She heaved another sigh. "I do, I guess."

"Well, then. Just trust me. I'm a good teacher for this sort of thing."

"Are you?"

He shot her a grin. "Sure."

She didn't appear reassured, but Tony's mood had

been rising ever since they'd left Madame Dunbar's place, and he wasn't worried. He'd treat her kindly, she'd learn, and who knew what might happen? Several interesting thoughts flitted through his mind, but he decided he'd best not dwell on any of them. For one thing, they might lead to disappointment for him. Worse, they might lead Mari to consider him a cad, and he'd lose her forever.

He didn't mean *lose* her, as when a man loves and loses a woman, of course. He only meant . . .

Well, he knew what he meant.

Motoring south on Fair Oaks Avenue, they'd left Pasadena and civilization behind and were now driving past an extensive sycamore grove. Tony breathed deeply, enjoying the fresh air of the country.

After several miles of quiet, Tony said, "So, do you like it here, Mari? I've thought about maybe moving to Southern California. It's—oh, I don't know. It's nicer than back East. At least the weather is."

It would also remove him from the octopuslike influence of his father. Tony'd been writhing under his father's thumb for much too long. Not that he worked for his father. He'd long ago made sure that he had his own business interests. What's more, they'd prospered and he was now a rich man in his own right. But his father was always after him to go into the family business.

Tony would rather kill himself. Not that he didn't respect his old man, but he knew him too well to want to work with or for him. Maurice Ewing was a master manipulator, a conscienceless bastard, and an almost unstoppable money-making machine.

The reason Tony had agreed to this plan, to come out here to watch over Maurice's investment, was mainly that it would give him a chance to investigate a part of the country that intrigued him. Tony even had investments of his own out here. Several orange processing plants, oil refineries, health spas and resorts, borax mines, and fish-canning factories owed a good deal of their founding monies to Tony Ewing.

Now that he was here and was seeing Southern California for himself, he liked it even better. There seemed to be something invigorating in the very air.

"You didn't like the weather in Mojave Wells."

He turned, distracted from his happy daydreams, to see Mari eyeing him resentfully. With a sigh, he turned again to the road. "I know. I don't like the weather in Mojave Wells. Too hot. But look around here. Isn't this nice? Sure, it's warm, but look at all the shady trees and all the green stuff growing. It's very pleasant. Don't you think so?"

She sighed, too, and admitted, "Yes. It's very pleasant."

It sounded to Tony as if she wished it weren't, and he wondered why. Then, again, he remembered that damned mine of hers.

That must be it. She didn't want to like it here, because that would make going back home and tackling that hole in the ground even more of a wretched business than it already was. His heart twanged painfully, before he made it stop. She'd made her bed. If she didn't have sense enough to climb out of it when it became obviously worthless, that was her fault.

Hers and her father's. Damn. Tony wished he hadn't thought about her lunatic father.

In an effort to keep himself out of the rut Mari seemed determined to occupy, he said cheerfully, "I'll bet there are all sorts of opportunities for a bright young lady in these parts. I understand there are lung hospitals all over the place. I'll bet you could nurse in one if you wanted to."

He could feel her staring at him. Darn it, it wasn't

his fault she was stupidly single-minded. He said somewhat tartly, "Yeah, I know you're not a trained nurse. You're a miner. But the mine isn't paying, and never will, and you might as well face it and decide to do something else."

She sniffed. He couldn't tell if it was a disdainful sniff, but he had his suspicions.

"Okay, okay. I know you promised your old man you'd work his mine, but honest to God, Mari, you can't keep on sacrificing yourself for him forever."

"It's not a sacrifice."

He gaped at her, incredulous. "What do you mean, it's not a sacrifice! Look at you! You're a beautiful young woman, and you're killing yourself in that damned mine! That's not only a sacrifice, it's a pointless one." He took in her hard expression, set lips, and indignant eyes, and slammed his hands on the steering wheel. "Oh, hell, it's useless to talk to you about anything."

After a few moments, Mari said quietly, "It's not useless to talk to me about how ladies behave."

He squinted at her again before turning back to the road. "Yeah. Okay. I'll talk to you about how ladies behave."

Big deal.

Ten

Mari awoke the morning after her very first night on the town—any town—feeling like a princess in a fairy tale. Last night had been a dream come true.

First, Tony had brought her to this incredible hotel. She blinked into the pale dawning light in the luxurious room and, if she hadn't felt the sheets around her, would have believed herself to be dreaming yet. He'd been utterly casual about it, as if he stayed in places like the Melrose Hotel all the time and it was nothing special.

That was probably true of Tony, but it was special to Mari. She tried to imprint every detail of its elaborate architecture, fine furnishings, lavish carpets, hoity-toity bellboys, and everything else in between on her brain so she'd never forget it, even if she lived to be a hundred and ten.

Then he'd escorted her to dinner at a restaurant so fancy, Mari's heart had quailed even as they'd walked up to the door, arm in arm. Tony had been sweet to her, too, anticipating her anxiety and trying to put her at ease. He did a fair job, handling the snooty maitre d' with his own, superior brand of snootiness, and securing them a table in a tucked-away corner. The table sat next to a gorgeous palm tree, and from their vantage point, they could see everyone entering and leaving the restaurant.

Tony had pointed out several local, even national,

celebrities. She'd seen Mr. Huntington, the railroad magnate, and a newspaper man whom she'd never heard of, but who Tony said had all but started the Spanish-American War a few years back. He'd indicated a burly fellow he called Lucky Baldwin and told her a number of stories about him, too, until she began to wonder if all rich men were unscrupulous vultures.

Vultures or not, Mari had been pop-eyed with fascination. Until Tony's civics lesson, imparted at that classy little tucked-away table, she hadn't understood how great an influence other people's money, and other people's newspapers, could have on politics. Tony reinforced Martin's lectures on the potential power of the motion-picture industry. And she was part of it. In a way.

Dinner had been superb. Mari had never before tasted half the stuff she'd eaten last night. Heck, she'd never even heard of scallops or endive or of the process Tony called sautéing. She'd always called it frying, but he'd explained the subtle differences between the processes to her. She wasn't altogether sure she understood them yet, but she was willing to take what he said on faith.

And that was a revelation, too. She trusted him. Tony Ewing, who had grated against her pride from the moment she'd first seen him, she saw now as a friend and adviser. Perhaps not a friend. In truth, Mari feared her feelings for Tony Ewing went far deeper than friendship.

But that was nonsense. Nothing in the world was greater than friendship. She'd be greatly honored if Tony were to consider her his friend.

Opting to forget about her feelings in favor of savoring her memories, Mari ran over her own personal menu in her mind so she wouldn't forget anything she'd eaten. She aimed to impress the tar out of Judy Nelson the next time she saw her. Judy'd probably never heard of a scallop either, and Mari would bet her boots she'd never heard the word *sauté*.

The dinner and the fancy surroundings were only a lead-in to the main event, however. When they'd entered the restaurant, Mari had observed an area devoid of tables in the center of the room. The dark crimson carpeting ended at the edges of the round, polished-wood flooring. Tony told her that was the dance floor, and that they were going to dance after they ate. He pointed out the band to her then, its members sitting on a platform at one end of the room and looking every bit as dressed up as the diners.

The very idea of dancing in those cosmopolitan surroundings alarmed Mari. And that was putting it mildly. Heck, she'd only danced once or twice in her whole life, and that had been at square dances at outdoor picnics with other yokels like herself.

She'd told Tony so and begged to be excused. "Can't I just watch this time?" she asked, trying to keep the quake out of her voice.

He'd laughed at her. For the first time, his laugh didn't make her want to slap his face, probably because he'd reached for her hand, held it gently in his own, and patted it tenderly. "Don't worry, Mari. By the time we're ready to dance, you'll be fine. You'll see."

She hadn't believed him, but he'd been right. This morning, the fact astounded her.

"Must have been the wine," she muttered at her empty room.

But it hadn't been only the wine. It had had more to do with Tony's kindness and gentle instructions. The delicious food had helped, of course, as had the hour or so they'd sat at the table dining, talking, and watching others dance.

By the time Tony held out his hand for her to take,

and led her to the dance floor, Mari's heart had hardly hammered at all. And even that small remaining trepidation had faded quickly, because he'd started out with a simple two-step. By the time Mari'd graduated to the turkey trot, she was completely relaxed and having more fun than she could ever remember having.

It didn't hurt that she looked better than she ever had, up to and including her footwear. A pair of evening slippers had mysteriously appeared at her hotel doorway earlier in the afternoon, wrapped in a beribboned box and held out to her by one of the upper-crust uniformed bellboys. Apparently Tony had decided she needed a flower in her hair, too, because he'd arrived at her room with a real one, a red rose. Mari felt very stylish as they swept into the restaurant, and, wonder of wonders, the feeling stayed with her all evening.

When she swung her legs over the side of the bed and stood up, her feet ached. She smiled what she imagined was a silly smile as she limped over to the dressing table. Her feet were sore from dancing the night away, and she'd never felt so good. Ever.

When she took a hot bubble bath in the Melrose Hotel's magnificent bathroom, using toiletry products she had a sneaking suspicion Tony had purchased and made available for her, she felt even better. There was a lot to be said for luxurious living, even she had to admit it.

Her ecstatic mood began its slide back to normal when she donned her mother's old dress, preparatory for the trip back to Mojave Wells. And the heat. And the shabbiness of her cabin. And that empty mine.

And Tiny. She shouldn't forget Tiny, the thought of whom made her happy again. She loved her dog very much.

Still, she knew she looked less than glamorous when she answered Tony's knock at her door, clad in her hand-me-down dress and clunky shoes. She'd polished the shoes, but it hadn't altered their disreputable condition noticeably. She'd tried to improve herself by tucking one of her crepe-paper flowers behind her ear—and it did help a little bit. It made her feel slightly perkier, even if it didn't show.

Tony didn't glower, though, which she took as a good sign. In truth, he didn't seem to notice her much at all, except as a being he had to transport from one location to another. He said, "All ready?" in a businesslike voice as soon as she opened the door.

It took her only a second to regain her balance, which teetered precariously at being so abruptly confronted with reality. But she'd lived nineteen years as an impoverished nobody. One evening of grandeur couldn't wipe out a lifetime's worth of nobodyhood. She swallowed hard and said, "Sure am. Let me get my bag."

"I'll get it."

She wasn't surprised when Tony barged past her, grabbed her shabby carpetbag, and hefted it up. Rather weakly she said, "Thanks."

"No problem."

At least he honored her with a sort of cocky grin. Evidently, he hadn't retreated altogether into his former aloof pose as king-of-the-world.

But that wasn't fair. He hadn't assumed the position on his own. Mari'd put him there because she'd felt so inferior to him. Bother. Sometimes she absolutely detested her penchant for recognizing her own shortcomings. She'd established him on the blasted pedestal, and it wasn't his fault, but hers.

She followed him out of her room, still starry eyed, but trying to hide her condition. She did venture to say, "Um, I had a real good time last night, Tiny. You were right. It wasn't so scary after I got used to it."

He cast a brilliant smile at her from over his shoulder. "See? I told you I was a good teacher."

She silently thanked her Maker that Tony had opted to ignore her slip of the tongue. She really wouldn't have blamed him for not wanting to be called by her dog's name. "Right. You sure are." And she was an idiot for wishing he could see himself as something more than her teacher.

"And you're a terrific student, too."

It was nice of him to say so. Mari didn't respond.

"Say, are you hungry, Mari? If you can wait for an hour or so to eat breakfast, we can stop at a little place I know on the way to Mojave Wells. It's in the community that calls itself Arcadia. Lucky Baldwin has a big ranch there, and there's a place called Baldwin's that serves great food."

She hadn't yet taken the time even to think about food because she'd been so busy reliving the night before. Now, she realized she was a little hungry. But she could wait. Heck, she'd been waiting all her life, hadn't she? What was one more hour?

Telling herself to cease being irrational and dismal this instant, she brought herself up short and said, "Sure. That sounds nice."

"It's a great little village, Arcadia. I wish we had more time. I'd take you to Lucky's place. He throws some pretty good parties."

Must be nice. Mari wasn't sure what to say to an unproffered invitation, so she remained silent. Tony didn't seem to notice, which was par for the course.

Tony told himself he felt particularly well today because he'd come to an understanding with Mari. She'd finally recognized his superior knowledge of the world, and he'd agreed to be gracious and introduce her to it. He wasn't floating on air for any other reason.

The fact that last night had been almost perfect, and that he'd never had a better time with a woman, out of bed, didn't have anything to do with his mood of good cheer. Not a bit of it. He was only pleased that Mari was proving herself to be an apt student of the finer things. Why, she'd become a gracious lady in no time at all at this rate.

She could dance, too, which had surprised him. It's true he'd had to demonstrate the steps to her, but she'd learned quickly. And no amount of instruction could impart the natural grace she'd then demonstrated.

Now wasn't that a funny quirk of nature? Imagine, a girl like Mari Pottersby, who'd been wearing britches and grubbing in a filthy mine all her life, having all that natural grace and talent. He breathed deeply of the fresh morning air and started whistling. The tune that came to his tongue was one they'd waltzed to last night: "Beautiful Dreamer."

The appropriateness of the selection made him interrupt his merry whistle with a chuckle.

"What?"

Mari's one-word question prompted him to turn and gaze at her. Her gorgeous brown eyes were wide upon him, and the blue flower she'd selected to stick behind her ear set off the ivory of her skin to admiration. She was quite a looker, Mari Pottersby. Tony couldn't understand why he hadn't noticed her intrinsic beauty in the beginning of their relationship. No, not relationship, business partnership. Yeah, that was better. Business partnership. It didn't feel like quite the right phrase, but Tony felt sure it was.

"What what?"

She smiled slightly at his silly question. "What's funny?" she elaborated. "Why are you laughing?"

"Ah. I see. I was only thinking about the tune I was whistling. It seemed appropriate, somehow, what with us being associated with the pictures and all. If ever there was a dream-making business, the pictures are it."

"I see. Yes, I guess you're right."

Tony's gaze kept sliding over to Mari. He could hardly feature this lovely young lady—shabbily clad this morning, to be sure, but she was still lovely—digging in the dirt in search of nonexistent silver. It wasn't right. It wasn't proper. She belonged in much more refined circumstances. He frowned. Life played some mighty unpleasant tricks sometimes. Tony didn't approve.

Mari deserved better than that played-out mine. She deserved—well, hell, she deserved money. A nice home. Pretty clothes. A good man to take care of her.

The notion of a good man taking care of Mari didn't sit well, and Tony discarded it roughly.

All right, so she got along quite well independently. She didn't need a man. But she sure deserved an easier life than the one she had now.

He wondered if she'd let him help her out. Just a little bit. He could show her around, introduce her to people, get her settled into a job where she didn't have to work so hard.

The notion of Mari working at some plodding job didn't sit well with him, either. Dammit, there must be something she could do that he'd approve of.

She could go to bed with him. He'd approve of that.

The truth hit him so hard, he nearly drove off the road.

"Oh, what is it?" Mari cried, clinging to the hand grip of the Pierce Arrow. "Did you hit something?"

Tony cleared his throat. "Ah, no. I, ah, had to swerve to avoid hitting a rabbit."

"Oh." Mari let go of the hand grip and relaxed in the seat. "I guess I didn't see it. I was looking out at the orange grove. Don't the blossoms smell heavenly?"

Sweet-smelling orange trees grew on both sides of the road, and Tony blessed them for it. "Yeah," he said, his mouth gone dry. "Those little critters are quick."

Good God, was he really in lust with Mari Pottersby? He sneaked a peek at her from out of the corner of his eye. She sat erect on the motorcar's buttery leather bench, her head turned so that she could watch the scenery as they sped past it. She had an elegant carriage, vivid features, splendid hair, and a shape any man would lust for. She was smart and quick and funny, when she wasn't being defensive. She could dance. She was ambitious, foolishly so, since her ambitions centered around an unproductive hole in the ground. She had honor and integrity by the ton.

And he really, really wanted to make love with her. He wanted to carry her off to somewhere private— maybe an island in the South Pacific replete with palm trees and coconuts and dusky natives serving them iced drinks—and teach her more than how to behave in society. He wanted to teach her the pleasures of the flesh. He already knew she had a passionate heart. He'd like to redirect her passion toward him.

Impossible. The only way Tony could even imagine Mari capitulating to an affair of the flesh would be if marriage were attached, and that was impossible. Ludicrous. Laughable. They were so far apart socially, it wasn't even funny. Tony had known men who'd fallen for actresses, but he'd never known a fellow to marry one.

Of course, technically, Mari wasn't an actress, but a mine owner.

He gulped, that notion having put a liaison with her in a totally different light.

But, marriage? To Mari Pottersby? Tony Ewing? He'd never even thought about marrying anyone. He had a couple of friends who'd gotten married, but they'd done so more for financial reasons than anything else. Oh, he guessed Harvey Morgan had liked Alicia Britton all right, but Tony hadn't detected anything so exalted as deathless love between them. He shook his head and told himself not to be foolish.

There was no need to think about marriage merely because he found Mari Pottersby attractive. Lots of women were attractive. A man didn't have to marry all of them in order to appreciate them.

The Marigold Mine elbowed its way into his mind, and Tony frowned when he thought about what would happen a month or so from now, when the Peerless crew deserted Mojave Wells, and the little community went back to its old ways. And Mari went back to working in that black pit. His heart lurched sickeningly, and the notion made him shudder.

"What's the matter, Tony?"

He glanced over to find Mari peering at him with concern. He said, "Nothing. Just thinking about the picture."

She nodded. "I'm a little nervous about acting in it."

"No need to be. You'll do fine."

"Do you really think so?"

"Sure." Because a curious sensation of loss had started crawling through him, and all because he'd thought about Mari slaving away in that dratted mine, he added, "If you want any coaching or anything, I'll be happy to help."

"Thank you. I thought you said Martin was the one to help with the acting stuff."

Dammit, he hated having his own words used against him. "He is, but I'll be happy to help, too."

"I see. Thank you."

They breakfasted in Arcadia, which was a pretty little community. Mari was impressed by all the greenery surrounding her. Tony could understand that, since she probably didn't see any green growing stuff for months at a time on that ugly desert where she lived. After breakfast, the drive back to Mojave Wells went smoothly. No tires blew out, the engine didn't overheat, and nothing rattled off the chassis when they left the paved civilization of the Los Angeles area for the dirt roads of the desert.

The nicest part for Tony, though, was when Mari nodded off to sleep in the car and slid sideways in the seat. He drove for miles and miles with Mari's head on his shoulder and a smile on his lips.

Martin knew to the second when Tony and Mari returned to town, even though he'd been inside the Mojave Inn for hours, trying to figure out how best to solve the latest hitch in the progress of *Lucky Strike*. There were so few automobiles in Mojave Wells that as soon as he heard the throb of the Pierce Arrow's engine, he dashed outside to greet the returnees.

He ran down the hotel's porch steps in spite of the blistering heat and hurried to open the driver's door. "Tony! I'm so glad you're back. There's— Oh."

Rubbing her eyes and looking as if she'd just awakened from a deep sleep, Mari, holding onto Tony's arm, blinked at Martin. Then she glanced down, saw how close she was sitting to Tony, and scooted backward across the seat, blushing up a storm. Tony frowned at Martin, and Martin could tell he'd interrupted something, although he didn't know what.

Before responding to Martin's worried speech, Tony

turned to Mari and said gruffly, "It's all right, Mari. You only went to sleep."

"I'm sorry," she stammered. "I didn't mean to . . . to . . ."

Martin got the feeling she wanted to apologize for sleeping against Tony. He also got the feeling Tony wasn't at all sorry that she'd done so.

"Don't be silly," Tony snapped. "I didn't mind at all. You were tired and needed a rest."

Martin saw her swallow, open her mouth, shut it again, and decided he might as well speak. "I say, Tony. I'm sorry to barge in on you like this, but we need to talk about some queer things that have happened since you left."

"Let me get Mari settled first, will you?" Tony said peevishly.

Martin wished he'd been less precipitate about approaching the returning travelers. But, honestly, he hadn't meant to interrupt anything. Besides, the last he'd seen of these two, they'd been at each other's throat.

That should have been a clue, now that he came to think about it. When people honestly disliked each other, they avoided conversation. These two seemed to go out of their way to get together and squabble. With a sigh, he said, "After you're settled and everything, come into the parlor. We've got to talk about this."

"All right." Tony had gone to Mari's side of the car and opened the door for her.

Martin was both amused and interested to note that Tony took Mari's arm to help her from the motorcar. If there was any woman on God's Earth who didn't need help entering or leaving an automobile, it was Mari Pottersby. She was probably the most independent female Martin had ever known, which, of course, meant she'd be perfect for Tony, who was likewise independent.

In fact, Martin had been surprised when Tony'd agreed to Maurice Ewing's request that he go to California and monitor his father's investment. Martin and Tony had been friends ever since their college days, and offhand Martin couldn't think of another time when Tony'd done his father's bidding.

Tony'd explained it to him, though, and it made sense. Desiring to remove himself as far as possible from his father's sphere of influence, Tony had decided to use this opportunity to become acquainted with the West Coast. Ever since Martin had met Tony's train at the Los Angeles Depot, he'd been encouraging Tony to move to California. L.A. was a great place. Martin was only sorry Tony didn't have more interest in the pictures.

Still, a fellow couldn't have everything. Martin would be happy to have his old friend nearer than New York even if they would never be business partners. It would be lovely if, along with discovering a practically perfect place to live, Tony were also to find his life's partner here.

But that was jumping the gun. As Martin went back to the Mojave Inn's parlor, he told himself to tackle one problem at a time. Anyhow, Tony and Mari's relationship was none of his business. Martin didn't have time for romance, so he certainly wasn't the appropriate person to advise Tony about its pursuit. Besides, Martin had a feeling Tony could take care of himself with the ladies.

About ten minutes after Tony and Mari's arrival in Mojave Wells, the door to the hotel's parlor opened, Martin glanced up from the catalog he'd been poring over, and Tony Ewing stalked in, looking like a thundercloud about to burst. "What's the matter, Tony?"

"Nothing," Tony snarled.

Martin lifted an eyebrow. Tony noticed, dropped into

an overstuffed chair near the one Martin occupied, and sighed heavily. "All right, it's Mari. *She's* the matter."

"How's that?" Martin forced himself not to grin. He recognized the same symptoms in his friend that he'd seen in others. If Martin were of a diagnostic turn of mind, he'd have said Tony was coming down with a case of lovesickness, but he'd never say so. He appreciated both Tony's temper and his musculature too much to rile him.

"Dammit, the woman's impossible."

"That's not awfully informative, Tony. What makes her impossible?"

"Oh, I don't know." Tony slapped his driving gloves on the table beside his chair. "She's just so damned . . . proud."

Nodding judiciously, Martin murmured, "Too much pride can be a bad thing." He was neither surprised nor annoyed when Tony swiveled his head and glared at him. If Martin remembered correctly, it was better to say nothing when a man was in a state like that which Tony appeared to be in.

"It's better to have pride than to have no self-respect at all," Tony retorted, as if Martin had accused Mari of being a coward or a sniveling weakling.

"Absolutely," Martin said in an effort to redeem himself.

"But not like hers."

Deciding he'd be better off not speaking at all in response to this comment, Martin only nodded.

"Dammit, she won't let a person do anything for her."

Interesting. Martin cocked his other eyebrow. "Did you try to do something for her?"

Tony threw his arms out, almost knocking over the lamp sitting on the table. Martin caught it before it crashed to the floor. "Dammit, I only told her I was going to drive her home, and she wouldn't let me!"

"Oh. That does seem a little, um, excessive. And you chalk that up to pride, do you?"

"What the hell else could it be?"

Since he didn't have any idea, Martin said so. "I don't know."

"It's because she was embarrassed about going to sleep on my shoulder." Tony slouched in the chair, sticking his long legs out in front of him. "Silly girl."

"Well, I guess I can understand her point."

It was the wrong thing to have said. Martin knew it at once, and sighed inside. He'd forgotten that when a man was in Tony's condition, nothing was the right thing to say.

"Dammit, I don't!" Tony bellowed. "I don't understand it at all. What's wrong with going to sleep if you're tired?"

"Um, nothing?"

"You're damned right. Stupid chit. What was I supposed to do? Shove her away?"

"Um, no."

"That's right. Dammit, if the woman needed sleep, why shouldn't she sleep? And it was only an accident that she sort of leaned up against me."

Studying Tony's disgruntled features, Martin decided that had been a bald-faced lie, but he wouldn't mention it. He did, however, feel compelled to say something, if only to ease his own conscience. "Well, now, Tony—and don't take this wrong, because I know you'd never do anything untoward—but I'm sure a pretty girl like Mari Pottersby, especially one who, like her, has few resources and no parents, might feel especially vulnerable when alone with a man."

Tony vaulted out of his chair, fists bunched, and glowered down on Martin as if he were some sort of repellent monster. "What the hell do you mean by that, Martin Tafft? Do you think I'm the kind of bastard who'd take advantage of a helpless female? Dammit, Martin, you're my friend, but I swear to God I'll belt you a good one if you don't take that back."

Interesting. In the space of seconds, Mari Pottersby had gone from being too proud and independent to being helpless. The phenomenon of love puzzled Martin mightily. He held up a placating hand. "I didn't mean it that way, and you know it, Tony. I know you're not the kind of man who'd do anything unsavory to a girl, and especially not one like Mari. I'm only trying to point out how it's possible that *she* might feel . . . vulnerable."

Tony towered there for another few seconds, looking as though he really wanted to punch something. Martin hoped he'd choose another target than his own cherished body if he succumbed to the urge. Then Tony's shoulders slumped, his hands unclenched, and he sat again, drooping like a wilted flower. "Yeah. I know. You're right. I'm sorry. Didn't mean to be so touchy. Don't know what's wrong with me."

Martin suspected he knew, but he didn't say so in order to avoid another outburst on his friend's part. Instead, he said, "Say, Tony, I need to talk to you. We've got some problems."

Eleven

An hour later, Tony looked at the remains of Peerless Studio's camera equipment in befuddlement. They sure did have some problems.

"How in hell did it get both cameras?" Tony scratched his head as he examined the wreckage of the expensive machinery. The cameras had been stored in a locked shed behind the hotel.

Martin shook his head. "I don't know. We locked 'em in here yesterday, after you and Mari left for Los Angeles, and they were found like this at eight o'clock this morning. We were going to do some site testing today to get the lighting and filters ready for shooting in the mine."

Tony squinted around the shed. It wasn't a handsome place or a new one, but it appeared about as secure as anything else in Mojave Wells. Yet there were the crushed cameras, and there was the beam from the ceiling still lying on top of them. "How in heck did the beam fall? Do roof beams just fall down by themselves? Was there an earthquake or something?" Tony'd heard about earthquakes, but he hadn't yet experienced one.

"I don't know, and no, there wasn't an earthquake. I called Phin." Phineas Lovejoy was president of Peerless Studio. "He's got an insurance fellow coming out early tomorrow to look at the mess."

"Shoot. How much will it cost to replace them?"

"Almost a thousand dollars. I'm hoping insurance will cover most, if not all, of the cost."

"My old man's not going to be happy about this." Tony wasn't eager to tell him the news either. Maurice wasn't known for his easy-going disposition. He'd be more likely to throw something. Like, say, a tantrum. Or his butler out the window. Tony experienced a moment of gratitude that he'd be out of ashtray-hurling distance when he made the call.

"Nobody's happy about it."

Walking farther into the shed and maneuvering around the wreckage—it was difficult to avoid stepping on the accident site because the shed space was small—Tony glanced around some more. "Has anyone gone over this with a good light yet?"

"We're waiting for the insurance man to show up. We didn't want to move anything, in case it turns out to be vandalism or something."

Tony snorted. "Even if it is, what's anyone going to do about it? Do they use that newfangled fingerprinting method out here in California?"

"I have no idea. Probably not."

"Yeah. California's kind of behind the times, isn't it?"

"Indeed. That's one of its many charms." Martin chuckled dryly.

"Right." So far, California's primary charm for Tony was a pigheaded mine owner. He was almost glad for this latest catastrophe, because it at least took his mind off Mari for a few minutes. Probably no more than that, but at least a few.

He turned around to see a huge furry black head heave into view. His heart did a double back flip and a forward somersault, and he tried to keep from shouting out with joy. Tiny! If Tiny had come to town, Mari couldn't be far behind.

"Good God," he said, trying not to let his elation leak into his voice. He'd thought he wouldn't see her again today, and here she was! Almost. "There's that blasted dog."

Martin turned to see what was what, but he was too late to prevent Tiny leaping on him and kissing him, doggie-fashion. "Blech!" He grabbed the dog's feet and lowered him to the ground. "Tiny, you're a menace."

"Good grief! Tony! I mean, Tiny! Come here this minute!" Mari rushed up and captured her dog by its collar. "I'm so sorry, Martin. I only came here to thank you for taking such good care of Tiny while I was away."

Laughing and wiping his face with his handkerchief, Martin said, "You were only gone for a couple of days, Mari. It was no trouble. As you can see, Tiny and I have become fast friends."

"I wish he wouldn't jump on people, though. He's—" Mari peered into the shed, where Tony still stood behind the pile of expensive rubbish, enjoying the view of her, although he wished like thunder she'd stop calling her dog by his name, and vice versa. "Good heavens, what's that? What happened?"

Tony let Martin answer her. He was too busy feasting his eyes. He didn't understand his reaction to her. Sure, she was pretty, but there were lots of pretty women in the world. His heart and soul didn't light up when he saw *them;* only Mari gave him this feeling of pleasure.

When he tried to be objective, which he couldn't be, he guessed his reaction might have something to do with the mere fact of her existing here at all. Mojave Wells was the very devil of a place. Yet this bright light of womanhood had been born and reared here. Watching her now, slender and fine boned with her classic features and dark, shiny hair, it was difficult to imagine her handling that dog. And mining for nonexistent silver. And being all alone in the world.

Tony's heart pinched painfully. Fortunately, Martin began explaining the camera disaster to Mari, and Tony was able to pay attention to him for a second or two.

"I'm so sorry, Martin." Mari squinted at the ceiling of the shed. "I've never heard of ceiling beams just up and falling down like this. I'm sure it hasn't happened to anyone else in town. It's generally too dry for termites to flourish."

Martin's smile vanished as he, too, peered up at the ceiling. Tony decided to make it unanimous and he looked, as well. "You don't think it has anything to do with the dry weather out here, do you?" he asked without much enthusiasm for the idea.

"Well," said Mari. "Like I said, I've never heard of it happening before. Do you mind if I take a closer look?"

"Not at all. Come on in," Tony offered, delighted at the notion of her getting close to him.

"Why not?" said Martin. "Just don't step on anything. I want the insurance man to see it as it is."

"Sure." Mari turned to her dog and said in a stern voice, "Tiny, sit!"

The dog wagged its tail harder, slapping Martin on the leg so hard, Tony was surprised Martin didn't object.

Mari sighed. "Come on, boy," she pleaded. "Please do what I tell you to do. Just this one time? It's embarrassing, the way you constantly defy me."

Tiny let go of an excited yip, which on him sounded like the boom of a cannon. Tony put his fists on his hips and grinned. He didn't know why, but he'd come to like that dog.

"Tiny!" Mari said sharply. "Stop playing and sit!"

Tony would have sworn on a stack of Bibles that the dog grinned at his mistress. "Why don't you try to hold him back, Martin," he suggested. "We don't want him running in here and trouncing on the evidence."

Another sigh leaked out of Mari. "Would you mind, Martin?"

"Not at all. Come on, Tiny. Sit beside me."

Instantly, Tiny trotted to Martin's side, turned so that he could observe the action inside the shed, and sat. Just as if he were a good dog. Mari scowled at him.

Tony laughed. "You've got a sure touch with the dogs, Martin."

"Right." Martin grimaced, then laughed out loud. He patted Tiny's head. "Good boy, Tiny."

The dog glanced up, grinned again, and proceeded to create a dust storm with his tail.

Mari shook her head and went inside the shed. "It's awfully dark in here. Do you think we should get a lantern?"

"Martin doesn't want to muck around with the mess until the insurance people have come and gone." Tony held out a hand to help her maneuver around the wreckage. Not that she needed his help, but at least she didn't argue with him before accepting his hand this time.

"Here. Let me open a window, at least. Might give us a little more light on the matter." She followed her words with the action, and a stream of sunshine flooded the scene of the catastrophe. As she batted dust out of her eyes, Mari squinted at the floor.

Tony squinted at her. Lord, she was an appealing creature. She still wore that thousand-year-old dress

SPECIAL
INTRODUCTORY
OFFER!
4 FREE
Ballad
Historical
Romance
Novels!
A $22.00 value
absolutely
FREE!
Passion...Adventure...Excitement...Romance...
Ballad Historical Romances

Introducing Ballad,
A New Line of Historical Romances

As a lover of historical romance, you'll adore Ballad Romances. Written by today's most popular romance authors, every book in the Ballad line is not only an individual story, but part of a two to six book series as well. You can look forward to 4 new titles each month – each taking place at a different time and place in history.

But don't take our word for how wonderful these stories are! Accept our introductory shipment of 4 Ballad Romance novels – a $22.00 value – ABSOLUTELY FREE – and see for yourself!

Once you've experienced your first 4 Ballad Romances, we're sure you'll want to continue receiving these wonderful historical romance novels each month – without ever having to leave your home – using our convenient and inexpensive home subscription service. Here's what you get for joining:

- *4 BRAND NEW Ballad Romances delivered to your door each month*
- *25% off the cover price of $5.50 with your home subscription.*
- *A FREE monthly newsletter filled with author interviews, book previews, special offers, and more!*
- *No risk or obligation...you're free to cancel whenever you wish... no questions asked.*

assion-
dventure-
xcitement-
omance-
allad!

To start your membership, simply complete and return the card provided. You'll receive your Introductory Shipment of 4 FREE Ballad Romances. Then, each month, as long as your account is in good standing, you will receive the 4 newest Ballad Romances. Each shipment will be yours to examine for 10 days. If you decide to keep the books, you'll pay the preferred home subscriber's price of $16.50 – a savings of 25% off the cover price! (plus $1.50 shipping & handling) If you want us to stop sending books, just say the word...it's that simple.

A $22 value – **FREE** No obligation to buy anything – ever.
4 FREE BOOKS are waiting for you! Just mail in the certificate below!

BOOK CERTIFICATE

Get 4 Ballad Historical Romance Novels FREE! ❖

Yes! Please send me 4 Ballad Romances ABSOLUTELY FREE! After my introductory shipment, I will receive 4 new Ballad Romances each month to preview FREE for 10 days (as long as my account is in good standing). If I decide to keep the books, I will pay the money-saving preferred publisher's price of $16.50 plus $1.50 shipping and handling. That's 25% off the cover price. I may return the shipment within 10 days and owe nothing, and I may cancel my subscription at any time. The 4 FREE books will be mine to keep in any case.

Name _____

Address _____ Apt. _____

City _____ State _____ Zip _____

Telephone (____) _____

Signature _____
(If under 18, parent or guardian must sign)

All orders subject to approval by Zebra Home Subscription Service.
Terms and prices subject to change. Offer valid only in the U.S.

DN051A

If the certificate is missing below, write to:

Ballad Romances,
c/o Zebra Home
Subscription Service Inc.

P.O. Box 5214,
Clifton, New Jersey
07015-5214

OR call TOLL FREE
1-888-345-BOOK (2665)

Passion...
Adventure...
Excitement...
Romance...

Get 4
Ballad
Historical
Romance
Novels
FREE!

PLACE
STAMP
HERE

ll..l..ll....lll...llll.l...lll.l...l.l..l.l.l.l.l.l.l..l.ll.ll..l

BALLAD ROMANCES
Zebra Home Subscription Service, Inc.
P.O. Box 5214
Clifton NJ 07015-5214

that looked as if somebody'd swum the English Channel in it, but she also still had the blue crepe-paper flower behind her ear. And the sunlight, which made dust motes shimmer like precious metal chips as they wafted in the calm, hot air, cast its golden aura upon her, too. Her skin glowed like deep ivory, her hair shone with copper and mahogany highlights, and her eyes were as deep and dark as rich chocolate. Unless that was his heart making him think so.

Good God, he hoped not. Tony'd never had trouble controlling his heart before. This might get out of hand if he didn't do something.

What he did was hold out his hand to her again. "Come over here. You can see where the roof beam came from. It almost looks as if somebody took a saw to it, but you might be able to tell better than I."

Mari didn't bother to fault him for his logic, probably because she was curious and felt more like investigating than arguing. She merely took his hand and stepped gracefully around the mess in the middle of the floor. Shading her eyes so the encroaching sunlight wouldn't interfere with her view, she craned her neck and stared at the ceiling. "I really can't see much from here."

"I can lift you up, if you want to see more closely." It was pure inspiration that made him say that. He hoped she'd fall for it.

She didn't immediately. Instead, she frowned, glanced around the shed, and muttered, "It would be easier if there was something for me to stand on."

Tony shook his head. "Nope. The only stand-onable thing in here is the camera, and Martin would have a fit if you climbed on top of the remains before the insurance people show up."

"Hmmm. I guess you're right. But—"

"Come on, Mari. You sure as the devil can't lift me, and somebody ought to check out the ceiling." He forced himself to sound austere, in an effort to make her think she was being unnecessarily balky.

She fell for it that time. Tony's heart gave a happy hop when she said, "I guess so. Okay. Lift me up."

"Turn around." He held his smile in until she'd done so. He didn't want her to think he had any ulterior motives, like putting his hands around her waist or holding her close to his chest or anything. As soon as he was sure she was secure in his grasp, he hefted her up.

"Say, you don't weigh much, do you?"

A muffled snort from outside the shed prompted him to turn his head. Shoot, he'd forgotten all about Martin standing out there and watching them both. Oh, well. He frowned at Martin's impish grin, then gave it up and grinned back.

"I don't have any idea how much I weigh, but I don't suppose it's much. I work too hard to get fat."

Mari's artless comment brought Tony's attention swerving back to her. "Can you see anything?"

"Not very well. The light doesn't get this far. Can you lift me any higher?"

"How about you sit on my shoulder? I can balance you there."

"Well . . ."

"Oh, come on, Mari. We're trying to solve a mystery here. Hold on tight." He heaved, and by God, she sat on his shoulder. Tony was pleased with himself for his cunning and foresight under the circumstances, when Mari's nearness and the feel of her lithe body under his hands was stirring him to things other than investigating camera crashes.

"Can you see anything?" Martin asked from outside.

Tony felt Mari shake her head. She said, "Not yet. But I don't think it's been sawn."

"No?" Damn. Tony had been hoping she'd stay up there for long enough that he'd be able to catch a peek of her ankles and calves.

"No, but there's something . . ." She reached up and teetered on Tony's shoulder. "Oh!"

"I've got you. Don't worry. I won't let you fall." He expected he had a relatively stupid smile on his face, because her attempt to balance herself had prompted her to throw her arms around him. At the moment, his face was pressed smack into her bosom. And a delicious bosom it was. He praised his Maker that Mari was too poor or too independent for whalebone.

"I'm so sorry," she said. Tony suspected she was blushing.

"Don't even mention it." Tony hoped she wouldn't guess at how titillating he found this experience. He was disappointed when she pulled away from him, and sighed when he lost his soft pillow.

"I didn't mean to . . ."

He suspected she was too flustered to mention the unseemliness of having shoved her bosom at his face and, because he didn't want her to spoil the moment by bringing it up and promoting constraint between them, he said, "Did you say you saw something amiss?" He tried to sound merely practical.

She cleared her throat and got back to business. "Um, I think so. Let me look again. I'll try not to move so quickly."

Darn. But Tony knew he couldn't expect his luck to last very much longer. For one thing, even though Mari wasn't fat, she was a full-grown woman, and his shoulder and arms were beginning to tire.

Mari called out, "Martin, I think you'd better tell the insurance guy to take a look at this. I'd swear somebody went at it with an ax."

"An ax? Good God, who'd do that?"

"I don't know." Mari tapped Tony on the head. "Thank you, Tony. You can put me down now."

He'd been afraid of that. But it was probably a good idea, given the state of his muscles, which had started quivering. "Okay. Let's take it easy now. I'll get you around the waist and let you down slowly." As slowly as possible.

He did so, making sure he held her as close to himself as he could without giving her an excuse to get mad at him. He felt every inch of her body as it slid against him. His blood raced, his sex thickened and grew hard, and he wanted to slam the door of the blasted shed, rip that old dress off her, and make love to her here and now.

"Thanks, Tony."

"Sure." He marveled at how nonchalant and unruffled she seemed as she stood in the beam of light, patting her hair and straightening her skirt. Was she honestly as impervious to him as all that?

"I'll be sure to tell the insurance people about the possible axing of the beam," Martin said.

His troubled tone made Tony wrench his thoughts from Mari, albeit painfully. Since he was supposed to be accomplishing something other than a seduction here, he bent over and inspected the floor. "I don't see any wood chips or sawdust."

"How can you tell? There's so much rubble in the way." Mari, too, bent over and stared at the ground.

Because she was so close to him, and since his blood was high, Tony turned his head slightly. At the same instant, Mari did likewise, and he found himself staring her straight in the eyes. He felt more than heard her tiny exhalation of breath. They were so close, he could have kissed her if he'd only moved a little bit. He saw her eyelids flutter and her mouth open slightly, and the temptation was so great, he very nearly succumbed to it.

Martin brought him back to harsh reality with a jolt. "See anything?"

Tony heard the worried note to Martin's voice, and suddenly realized that Martin was trying to protect Mari. Dammit, Tony resented that. He was no despoiler of virgins. He stood up abruptly. "No. Can't see anything for the mess of metal and dirt that was brought down when the beam fell. At least, I guess that's where it came from."

Mari, who'd also risen quickly and who now appeared chagrined and nervous, said, "Right. I think so, too."

She bent at the waist again and stared hard at the floor of the shed. Tony figured she'd done so as a bluff to take her mind away from other, more earthy matters.

"But wait a minute. This might be—" She reached down and delicately fished in the rubble.

"What might be what?" Martin asked anxiously.

Tiny, who was attuned to variations in the human voice, stood and stared into the shed, for all the world like a sentient being, curious about their investigations. *Good pose, Tiny,* Tony thought, caught somewhere between frustration and amusement.

Nevertheless, he was glad for the presence of Martin and Tiny, because his senses were so on edge around Mari, he wasn't sure what he might do if left to his own devices. Deciding if that idiotic dog could act smart, he could put on an act, too, he joined in Martin's query. "What is it, Mari?"

She held out her hand and showed him a wood chip. It appeared to be freshly hewn. Frowning, Tony took it from her. "By God, it does look like there might be more to this affair than dry rot."

"What is it?" Now Martin sounded impatient. Tiny

let out a lusty whine, as if to spur Mari and Tony into some kind of action, preferably involving him.

"I wonder if there are more of these under the rubble," Tony mused.

"I don't know. Look at that."

Tony followed the point of Mari's finger and got another jolt. "I'll be darned. It looks as if someone tried to sweep stuff up."

"What? Somebody swept something up? What's going on in there?" Exasperated, Martin came to the door of the shed, blocking out a good deal of the light. "Will one of you please tell me what's going on in there?"

"Here, let me show him. I don't think we'd better muck around anymore in here." Mari took her wood chip back.

Tony figured that was fair, since she'd found it. He grasped her arm, though, and helped her sidestep around the wreckage. He figured this would be the last time he'd get to put his hands on her unless he figured out something of a clever nature to do soon.

Handing Martin the wood chip, Mari said, "Here, Martin. It looks like the kinds of chips I get when I chop wood for the stove."

She chopped wood for her stove? As he carefully skirted the remains of the two expensive cameras, Tony's mind boggled momentarily until he mentally smacked himself and asked who the hell else would be chopping wood for her.

"By gum, I think you're right." Staring hard at the wood chip now residing in his own palm, Martin looked worried.

Tony figured he'd start pulling at that lock of hair next. He'd begun thinking of that particular tress as Martin's worry totem, sort of like the worry beads some Indian tribes were said to use. He said, "I think we'd better lock this place up again."

"Right," muttered Martin, clearly distracted. "Right." He glanced up and frowned at the shed. "I wish we had someone to post as a guard. Now I'm worried about the rest of our equipment."

"Oh?" Mari lifted her eyebrows as she attempted to subdue her ecstatic dog, who'd begun gamboling around her as soon as she emerged from the shed. "What other kinds of stuff do you have that might be vandalized?"

Tony felt a pang as he wondered how it would feel to have another being be so happy to see him. He'd prefer a being like, say, Mari, to a dog like Tiny, but even a dog might be nice.

"Oh, gosh," Martin said. "There's tons of stuff. We've got all the backdrops and the set frames and— good God."

"What is it?" Mari gripped Martin's arm.

Tony, too, was alarmed when Martin's face drained of color and he appeared stricken. "What's wrong, Martin?" He grabbed Martin's other arm.

Martin shook them both off. "I'm okay. I just happened to think of the cans of film. Good God, we already have a whole reel made of the set shots."

"Set shots?" Mari glanced up at Tony, who shook his head. He knew more about the pictures than he had when he came out to California, but he still knew very little.

"We always do at least a part-reel of scenery shots before we begin shooting the feature. That's why we shot footage of the miners working yesterday. It's good to have them in case we need them when we begin putting the picture together."

"I don't think I understand, but it's all right. I don't guess I need to," Mari assured him.

"We'd better check it out," Tony said. He didn't know set shots from a hole in the head, but he knew good and well his father would be unhappy if anything else happened to interfere with the picture before it was finished. With a sigh, he decided he'd really rather not work in the pictures, if this sort of thing happened very often.

"Right," said Martin, who instantly took off for the inn. He stopped walking, wheeled around, tossed the key to Tony, and hurried off again.

"I'll just lock up," Tony muttered. "Wait for me."

Although he didn't anticipate obedience from Mari, he was gratified when she didn't immediately hare off after Martin. Tiny might have had something to do with her remaining in Tony's company, because he didn't budge when Mari tugged at his collar. Grinning at the dog, Tony wondered if he'd got himself an ally. He hoped so.

A few minutes later, Martin stood in the small parlor, hugging a can full of film to his chest, and said, "God, I hope it's still all right."

"Don't we all." Tony's mind, which he'd reluctantly dragged from concentrating solely on Mari Pottersby's trim form and elegant features, was troubled. "Say, Martin, if someone *is* trying to undermine the picture, do you have any idea who it is?"

Martin, who didn't need help with very many things pertaining to his life and his profession, had opened the can and was now threading the celluloid film onto a projector. He and Tony had set up the projector in the small parlor, as they'd done when they'd viewed Mari's screen test. He shook his head. "Haven't the foggiest."

"Does anybody have it in for you or Mr. Lovejoy?" Mari asked. She'd taken the chance of letting Tiny enter the hotel with her. To everyone's surprise, the dog was being obedient. At the moment, Tiny looked rather like a lumpy floor rug; he'd sprawled himself out in front of an electrical fan that was buzzing away and stirring the hot air.

Martin looked up from feeding film through the projector to gaze at her in astonishment. "Have it in for us? Do you mean does somebody hold a grudge or something?"

She shrugged. "I guess so."

Pausing for a moment with film dripping through his fingers, Martin let his gaze drift into a middle, ambiguous distance as he thought about her question. After a couple of seconds, he shook his head. "Can't think of a single person who'd want to interfere with a Peerless production."

Tony added his two cents. "When I started studying the pictures prior to coming out to this coast, I found Peerless to have an almost spotless reputation among the various production companies."

"Almost?" Martin peered at him sharply. "What do you mean, almost? As far as I know, Phin and I have never done a single unscrupulous thing. Where does that 'almost' come in?"

Tony grinned. "Cancel the almost. Peerless's reputation is spotless. Absolutely." He liked it that Martin took so much pride in the honorable reputation of his company. So few men did. Take his father, for example.

But Tony didn't want to think about his old man now. "So, if it's not a disgruntled competitor, who might it be?"

"Oh, well . . ." Martin finished his task and stepped back from the projector. "As to disgruntlement, I don't suppose Peerless has any control over what anybody else thinks of us. We're doing very well, and without resorting to the underhanded tactics practiced by some of the other companies."

Tony was pretty sure Martin's comment was an unvoiced dig at Edison's operation. Made sense to him.

Edison was a tough customer. Still, Tony had never heard of him sinking to these types of tactics.

Martin went on, "I suppose it's possible that some lunatic might try to subvert one of our productions."

"You don't look as though you believe it," Mari observed.

She was right. Tony, too, detected a note of disbelief in Martin's speech and attitude. He heaved a sigh. "Let's look at the film and see if it's been tampered with. We can go into a huddle later and talk about everything."

"Right." Martin walked to the wall switch, pressed the button, and the room went dark.

Deciding to take advantage of the low light, Tony sought a chair next to Mari. In doing so, he barely missed stepping on Tiny, who let him know it with a deep, rumbling growl. "Say, Tiny, I didn't mean it." He turned to Mari. "He wouldn't bite a guy just for stepping on his paw, would he?"

Mari laughed softly. The sound curled through Tony like fine brandy fumes. "I don't think so, but you can't blame a dog for asking people not to step on him."

"I suppose not." He wanted to take her hand in his. To kiss it. To caress it.

He didn't, of course. Mari knew how to do lots of things with those hands of hers, and he wouldn't be at all surprised to find out she could slap a fellow's face with them.

Back at the projector, Martin turned on the switch and began cranking. Tony could feel Mari stiffen at his side, as he did the same. He hoped the film was all right, for his father's money's sake, but mainly for Martin's. Tony didn't want Martin to suffer. He was too fine a person. An attack on Peerless would be an attack on Martin Tafft, and that would be wrong. If it was an attack and not an accident.

The director's mysterious illness occurred to him, and he frowned into the darkness. Had that been an accident, too, or had it been caused by something sinister? Or had it perhaps been staged?

Good God, he was turning into one of those fellows who saw conspiracies around every corner. Pretty soon he'd be blaming all these happenings on the Communists or Anarchists. He told himself to get a handle on his imagination, sat back, tried to ignore Mari, which was impossible, and stared at the wall.

After a moment or two of grinding noises, a spray of light shot out of the projector and hit the wall. Several frames of test patterns flickered, and then the town of Mojave Wells hove into view. Tony, Mari, and Martin all sighed with relief.

"Thank God," Martin whispered.

"Amen," said Mari.

Tony's thanks were as heartfelt as those of the others. "Better keep that can in your room from now on," he suggested.

"You bet I will," Martin agreed.

"Is there anything else that's vulnerable? Any other equipment?" If, of course, this wasn't all coincidental. Tony, who had no problem with coincidences in, say, Dickens's novels, wasn't much of a believer in them on an everyday basis.

"I can keep the projector in my room, too."

"What about the sets and so forth?"

Martin flicked off the projector. "I don't know. That's something we'll have to talk about."

"Right." Tony turned to Mari. "Say, why don't you stay for dinner, Mari, and we can go over all of this stuff right now?"

She hesitated. "Well, I've got Tiny with me."

"Pshaw." Tony had never said *pshaw* in his life. "Tiny won't mind. He can—" He could what? Again inspiration sprang to his assistance. "He can stay in my room!" Brilliant. He was proud of himself.

"Well . . . All right."

So they hauled Tiny upstairs and stuck him in Tony's room. Tony guessed he wouldn't mind a few black dog hairs on his bedspread, should Tiny decide to take a nap. He'd rather have Mari there, but at least he'd be able to enjoy her company for a few more hours today.

Twelve

Halfway through dinner, Mari realized she'd come to feel absolutely comfortable in the company of these two men. What a change this was. At first, she'd not only mistrusted them, she'd felt like an unwelcome, interfering insect in their presence, kind of like an ant at a picnic. She'd felt as though they were merely tolerating her for the sake of her mine.

Not any longer. Now both Tony and Martin talked to her as if she mattered, and they included her in their discussions as if they cared about her opinion. The sensation of belonging was a new one to Mari, and she cherished it.

She feared she was also coming to cherish Tony, and it worried her. She didn't need another complication in her life, and falling in love with a millionaire from New York would be a definite complication. For her. She was pretty sure she wasn't important enough to Tony to count as a complication, even if they were getting along together much better since their trip to Los Angeles. He was being very nice about imparting social lessons to her, which she appreciated.

Maybe they could at least be friends. The notion gave her a chilly sensation around her heart that she chose not to think about.

Martin drew Ben, the cameraman, and George, the set designer, into their security discussions after dinner.

They met at a table Mr. Nelson had set up in the parlor. Mari felt like an interloper in a political meeting, only they weren't in a smoke-filled room because none of the men smoked. That was something of a miracle, and one for which she was glad.

She was terribly impressed when Martin divulged that George was Brenda Fitzpatrick's brother-in-law. Brenda Fitzpatrick was one of the most famous actresses in the whole world. Mari had never stood close to royalty until the Peerless folks came to town. Now she knew both a millionaire and the relative-by-marriage of one of the nation's most beloved actresses. Brenda had retired from stage and celluloid a year or so ago, but Mari still had trouble containing her awe. She wanted to press George for details about her. She didn't, though, because even though she didn't know squat about society manners, she knew better than to pry into another person's business.

George said, "You don't know for certain that anything's amiss, Martin."

"You don't consider the destruction of two state-of-the-art cameras as something amiss?" Ben glared at George as if he'd just denied the existence of God.

George, an amiable lad of twenty or so, grinned. "I didn't mean that, Ben. Of course, it's something. It's a disaster. What I meant was that we don't know if a person's behind it. Maybe it was an accident."

"We found fresh wood chips in the shed," Martin said darkly. "It looked a lot like someone went to the trouble of hacking that roof beam away from its moorings."

"Also," Mari said, having just remembered something else, "for the beam to crush the cameras, the cameras had to be moved, didn't they?"

All four men gawked at her for several seconds. She felt heat creep into her cheeks and blurted out, "Didn't they? I mean, they weren't just sitting there in the middle of the shed to begin with, were they?"

"By God, you're right." That was Tony, who smiled at her so warmly, her blush deepened.

"You *are* right," murmured Martin. "Why didn't I think of that?"

"That's right," confirmed Ben. "We even discussed it ahead of time, trying to decide the best place to put them." He turned to Martin. "Say, was the canvas still on top of them?"

Martin's eyebrows shot up. "No! It wasn't, by God. Somebody took it off. I didn't see it anywhere."

"I did."

Again, they all turned to look at Mari, who'd spoken.

She continued, "I remember now that when I picked up that chip, it seemed to me that the rubble was sitting on some kind of canvas flooring. I didn't think anything of it. Until now, when you mentioned a canvas cover. There sure was no canvas on top of the mess."

"Good heavens." Martin's lips flattened out into a straight, white line. "Good heavens."

"I think we ought to go out there and take one last look." This, from Tony. "We won't disturb anything, but I know I'll rest better for knowing one way or the other whether this was an act of malicious vandalism or an accident."

Without another word, they shoved their chairs back from the table and arose. Mari, who knew her way around the Mojave Inn better than the others, muttered, "I'll get a lantern." She did so, and they trooped outside together.

Tony had retained the key Martin had tossed to him earlier in the day, so he unlocked the door. "I'll go in. You can stay outside. There isn't room enough for all of us."

The weather, hot as blazes during the day, always

cooled down at night. Mari shivered and wrapped her arms across her chest, although she believed at least some of her chilly feeling came from trepidation. She really didn't want to know that some evil person was out to get Martin Tafft or the Peerless Studio.

"Mari's right," came Tony's voice from inside the shed. He sounded exceptionally gloomy. "The stuff's lying on the canvas that used to cover it, and she's also right that the cameras were moved to this position."

Martin uttered a soft curse and stuck his head inside the doorway in order to see better. George's curse was more audible. Ben only sputtered and fumed. Mari's heart sank into her mother's old shoes and sat there, lifeless and cold.

All at once, the still night air was ripped to shreds by the thunderous roar of Tiny's barking. All five people at the shed jumped several inches off the ground.

Tony said, "For the love of Pete, what's that?"

"It's Tiny." Mari, who knew her dog too well to believe he was carrying on like that for fun, took off at a dash for the hotel. She presumed the others followed her, but didn't turn to see.

"Hold on!"

She was surprised to find Tony Ewing beside her. He must run fast. "It's Tiny," she gasped, fright plain in her voice. "Something's wrong."

"Dammit, I know there's something wrong, but you're not going up there to check on it all by yourself."

They'd reached the back door of the hotel and she yanked it open before Tony could stop her. This was no darned time for him to play the gentleman. Something was wrong with her dog. Mari thought she'd die if anything happened to Tiny.

"It's *Tiny*," she cried, as if that explained everything. And it did, to her. She was too frightened to think about anyone else at the moment.

"I know it's Tiny, dammit."

To Mari's dismay, Tony raced past her and took the stairs three at a time. Mari's legs were kind of long, but they weren't as long as that. It took her more time to get up the stairs. When she reached the top and saw the door of a room halfway down the corridor gaping open and Tiny standing sentry, barking his head off and holding down something with his huge paws, her heart careened crazily.

Tony got to the dog before she did. As she ran, she was vaguely aware of doors opening on both sides of the corridor and people peeking out to see what all the commotion was.

She heard someone mutter something about hotels allowing pets indoors to interfere with other people's sleep, but she paid no attention. From talking with Judy Nelson, she knew all of the guests presently occupying rooms at the Mojave Inn were employees of Peerless.

And they'd better not complain about Tiny, or they'd have to deal with her. Since she owned the precious mine they were all so eager to use, they'd just better watch their step.

By the time she reached Tony and Tiny, Tiny was in the middle of one of his ecstatic greetings, and Tony was trying to fend him off. Mari said, "Tony! I mean, Tiny! Here, boy. Stop that." To Tony, she said, "Can you tell what happened?"

Of the two male creatures cluttering up the doorway, Tony paid attention to her. He'd managed to pry whatever it was that Tiny had been guarding out from under the dog's heavy feet and held it out for Mari's inspection. "It looks like a coat or jacket of some type. Get away from me, dog!"

Ignoring Tony's rudeness to her precious pet, she took the cloth from his fingers and inspected it. "Is it yours?" It sure didn't look like anything Tony would wear unless he was playing the role of pauper for a Peerless production. Of course, that might have something to do with the fact that Tiny had evidently tugged the garment from the body of whoever had been wearing it. There were clearly discernible doggie teethmarks on and around its hem.

"God, no. I've never seen it before." He finally managed to persuade Tiny to sit still and merely wag his tail.

"I wonder—" Mari broke off abruptly as something awful occurred to her. "Good Lord, you don't think Tiny hurt the person who'd been wearing it, do you?"

Tony glanced from her to Tiny, and turned to look into his room. "You know him better than I do."

"Do—do you see a body on the floor?"

"No."

That was a relief. Mari asked, "Is anything missing?"

"I don't know. The window's open. I know I left it shut to keep the bugs out."

Mari opened her windows at night in spite of the bugs to get a cross draft and drive out the heat of the day. She noticed the electrical fan in the room and guessed some people didn't have to do things like open windows in spite of bugs. It was amazing what money could buy. Comfort, for example. She told herself to snap out of it; there were more important things to think about right now.

"Do you think someone might have climbed in through the window?" she asked, moving farther into the room. She left the door open, because it was shocking for a single female to enter the room of a single male.

"I'm not sure." Tony strode to the window and was inspecting the sill and the wooden siding of the hotel outside his window. The room was on the second floor.

If a person had ventured to climb through the window, he'd have had to climb the wall first, unless he'd brought a ladder with him.

"Is there a ladder or anything out there?"

"Don't see one."

Mari frowned and, tossing propriety aside in favor of satisfying her curiosity, joined Tony at the window. "Oh, but look." She pointed at the earth beneath them. "Doesn't it look as if the ground's been disturbed?"

Tony squinted for a moment and said, "How can you tell?"

Mari leaned farther out of the window. Actually, it was pretty difficult to tell if the dirt below was disturbed or not. "Um, I'm not sure. It looks a little lumpy."

"It always looks like that," Tony grumbled sourly. "This is the god-awfullest place I've ever been in. Don't know how you stand it."

Mari tried not to take offense, remembering for the umpteenth time that a gentleman accustomed to luxurious surroundings, including green growing vegetable matter and mowed lawns, might find Mojave Wells a little hard to take. "You get used to it," she replied calmly. She craned her neck to look up at the roof, balancing herself halfway out the window.

Tony huffed. Tiny had joined them. Sensing a game in which he desired to take part, he jumped on Mari. She lost her grip on the windowsill, felt her balance teetering, and cried out.

"Damn!"

That was Tony, and as he said it, Mari felt his big, strong hands go around her waist. He pulled her back inside the room, and she was safe. From falling. She discovered she wasn't safe from Tony when, as soon as her feet were on his bedroom floor, he tugged her around to face her and wrapped her in his arms.

"Damn that dog of yours," he said savagely. "He's going to kill somebody someday from sheer exuberance."

Although she enjoyed the sensation of being in Tony's embrace, Mari knew it wasn't proper and pulled back. He didn't release her, which gave her a good excuse not to do that anymore. "I'm okay," she said in a voice that shook only a little.

"The hell you are. You're all alone in the world except for that damned dog, and he seems determined to injure you."

"That's not fair." She had an almost ungovernable impulse to wrap her arms around him and snuggle closer. The sensation of being protected was as new to her as it was exquisite.

"The hell it's not." Tony's voice had gone softer and less ferocious.

Mari felt his hands, which had been clutching her tightly, loosen and start to caress her back, and she was almost positive his lips were kissing her hair. She was as close to swooning as she'd ever been. She felt wonderful. Superb. Magnificent. She wished he'd keep on stroking and kissing her in just that way until sometime next week. Maybe next year.

It was Tiny who came between them, nudging them both with his cold, wet nose and whining piteously. Mari gave a start. So did Tony, who released her so suddenly she nearly fell backward out of the window. Sticking her arm out and grabbing the window frame just in time to prevent disaster, she stood upright, licked her lips, and straightened her skirt.

Tony cleared his throat and glared down at Tiny. Mari was sorry the infinitesimal idyll had been so abruptly terminated, but she knew it was for the best. She patted Tiny's head and muttered, "Good dog."

She didn't mean it. If it weren't for propriety's

sake—and for the sake of her heart, which had never been tested and was, therefore, most likely vulnerable to breakage—she'd as soon stay here with Tony in his bedroom, come what may. Which probably meant she was a hussy underneath. She sighed.

"Well, I can't really tell if a ladder was propped against the wall or not, but if somebody *did* come through the window, it would explain the ruckus Tiny caused." Because she meant it this time, she added another pat on Tiny's head and a more hearty, "Good dog."

"I suppose so." Tony ran his fingers through his hair a couple of times, as if he were trying to reestablish some sort of inner composure.

It was a gesture Mari found interesting, since she couldn't imagine why he should have been discomposed by her, of all people. Why, he must have women by the score. By the hundreds. Thousands, even. She tried to work up some indignation that he had taken a liberty with her, but couldn't. Being in his arms had felt too darned good for indignation to get a toehold.

That made her think of something else. "Say, let me look outside again."

"Be careful this time," Tony growled, and took Tiny's collar in a hard fist.

That wasn't fair. She'd been careful. It had been Tiny who'd almost caused a calamity. She opted not to point out the obvious to Tony, sensing he'd pick a quarrel if she did. Instead, she leaned out the window again, making sure Tony had a tight grip on Tiny's collar, and inspected the clapboard siding. "There are marks out here. Look, Tony."

She indicated some scratches and dirty scuff marks on the wall directly beneath the window. Tony said, "Hmmm."

"Does it look like maybe a ladder had been placed there?"

"Maybe." He drew back and frowned into his room. "But if some thief climbed a ladder and got in here, wouldn't the ladder still be there?"

"Not if he climbed back down again when Tiny scared him."

He shook his head. "Then how do you account for the open door. I know the door was locked when I left."

"Oh." Mari felt foolish. Naturally, Tiny couldn't have opened the door. "I see what you mean." She thought for a second and posed a tentative question. "Maybe there were two of them?"

"How do you figure that?"

"One to hold the ladder and one to do the dirty work?" She shrugged. "It's only a suggestion."

Silence settled over the trio as they pondered Mari's suggestion. Martin showed up at the door, along with George and Ben, and Mari smiled and gestured at them to enter the room. She was glad as all get-out that they hadn't arrived a couple of minutes earlier, when she and Tony had been wrapped up in each other.

"What's going on in here?" Martin asked, panting. "Why was Tiny carrying on?"

Observing his newest friend, Tiny bounded over to greet Martin. Martin handled it well, Mari thought, petting and talking softly to the huge beast, while easing his paws from his shoulders and setting them on the floor. She approved of people who weren't intimidated by Tiny's size but knew him to be a pussy cat underneath.

Really, Tiny was much more amiable than, say, Mrs. Glenfelder's dachshund, who tried to murder Tiny every time they met. Mari had thought for a long time now that it was a very good thing Tiny had a sense of humor, or Mrs. Glenfelder's dog would have been lunch by this time.

"We're not sure," Tony said, still frowning in

thought. "Somebody might have climbed through my window. He left a jacket behind." He lifted the jacket up and showed it to the new arrivals.

Martin looked grave. "I don't recognize it. Do you know who it belongs to?"

"No."

"Did he take anything?"

"Haven't looked yet. I'll do that now." As Tony started with bureau drawers, he said, "I think Tiny scared him off before he could do anything."

"Oh!" said Mari, having had another thought. "What about footprints in the hall?"

"I don't know. Why don't you go look?"

So, as Tony opened the door to the room's small closet, she excused herself to the men and went out into the hall again. She didn't notice any footprints on the carpeting and was disappointed until she spotted something a couple of yards down the hall in the direction opposite that of the stairway. When she went to investigate, she saw a small shiny object lying against the wall. She picked it up and carried it back to Tony's room.

When she reentered the room, she guessed Tony hadn't found anything missing, because he was standing there shaking his head. He looked up when she entered. "What did you find?"

"I don't know. It looks like a token or a coin or something." She held it out for general inspection.

The four men gazed down at the gold-colored object in her palm, then Tony picked it up, narrowed his eyes, and peered at it closely. "It's Canadian," he announced after a moment. "It's old and worn, but it's definitely Canadian. We see a lot of these in New York and up north, closer to the border."

"Canadian? Honest?" Mari reached for the coin

again. "May I look at it? I've never seen a Canadian coin before."

"No, I don't suppose you have. You're more likely to get Mexican coins in this part of the country."

She shrugged. "Haven't seen any of those, either. I expect Canadians are richer than Mexicans." It was supposed to have been a joke, but nobody laughed. She didn't care, but squinted hard at the coin. "Oh, yes, I see it now. Oh, my! Is that Queen Victoria?"

"I expect it is."

She looked up sharply because she'd detected amusement in Tony's voice, and she'd be darned if she'd let him laugh at her. *He* might not find anything interesting in a coin with a queen on it, but *she* did. Heck, she'd dreamed for years about visiting England and seeing how royalty ran things. "Do you mind if I keep it?"

"Not at all." He stopped grinning and frowned again. "I don't suppose we can be sure if our intruder dropped it."

"I suppose not." Mari wished she'd unearthed some more telling clue than this. Still, at least she now possessed a Canadian coin, which was something of an oddity. She dropped it into her pocket. "You didn't discover anything, I suppose."

"No. Thank God nothing's missing, but whoever it was also didn't leave anything behind by which to identify him."

"Too bad," Mari muttered.

"Do you think this has anything to do with the cameras?" Martin asked in a voice tight with worry.

Tony shook his head. "Who can tell? This whole thing is getting very mysterious."

"It sure is."

"How can you secure things?" Mari asked. The men all turned to stare at her, and she got embarrassed. She persisted, though, because it was important. "I mean, you can't always have Tiny in your room in case somebody's out to steal stuff or interfere with the making of the picture. For one thing, there's not enough of him to go around."

"I'm not so sure about that," Tony muttered, eyeing Tiny without favor.

"Don't you dare say anything bad about my dog," Mari told him, lavishing pats upon Tiny. "He saved the day, don't forget."

"Yeah, yeah. You're right. Good boy." Tony gave Tiny's head a perfunctory pat. Tiny, who had no discretion whatever, wagged his tail as if Tony had fed him a steak bone.

"Stupid dog," Mari whispered, hugging Tiny hard. She loved her dog, even if he wasn't the brightest candle in the box.

"You know, Mari has a good point," Martin murmured. "We're going to have to do something about securing our rooms if there's a thief around, even if he isn't out to undermine the picture. I'm sure no one wants to return to his room after a hard day's filming and discover he's been robbed."

"I'll be happy to talk to Mr. and Mrs. Nelson," Mari offered. "They're good friends of mine."

"Thanks, Mari." Martin beamed at her. "That would be very good of you. Please let them know that I'll pay for any added security measures they take. Like, locks on the window and so forth."

She grinned at him. "That'll make them happy."

"Are you going to do that now?" Tony asked her. "I'll go with you. That'll make it look more official."

Mari looked up at him, wondering what his game was. "Why does it need to look official? Or is it that you don't trust me to carry out my mission?"

"For goodness' sake! Of course, I trust you. So does

Martin. I just thought you might like someone to tackle the Nelsons with you. You know, to give you some support."

He scowled at her, but the expression looked to Mari as if it were meant to cover something else, something he didn't want to acknowledge openly. She didn't understand what it could be, unless he really *didn't* trust her and that possibility rankled. And it hurt.

As if something had suddenly inspired him, Tony added, "Besides, I'm the one who suggested you leave that dog in my room. I don't want you to catch any blame for that."

"The Nelsons know me, Tony. They won't blame me for anything. They'll probably be grateful to Tiny for preventing a burglary." She frowned. "Or whatever that intrusion was meant to be."

"I'm going with you." His voice had gone louder and harder. "And I don't intend to entertain any more arguments."

She threw up her hands in defeat. "Okay. I'm not arguing. If you want to come with me, fine." And if she ever learned that he'd done so because he didn't believe her capable of getting her message across coherently, all by herself, she'd let him know what she thought about that. Worse, if he was tagging along because he believed her to be somehow connected with whatever had happened in his room, she'd scratch his eyes out.

"I'll look after Tiny, if you'd like me to," Martin offered.

Mari said in something of a huff, "Don't be silly. Tiny comes to town with me all the time. The Nelsons know him and like him." She cast a so-there glare at Tony, who frowned back.

As Mari stomped off down the hall to the Nelsons' quarters, she grumbled, "I hope we aren't going to be waking them up." She only said it to be perverse; she knew good and well that the Nelsons couldn't have slept through the uproar Tiny'd set up. In fact, she was rather surprised they hadn't come upstairs to find out what all the excitement was about.

Tony made a point of pulling his watch out of his pocket and checking the time. "For God's sake, it's only nine-thirty. Nobody goes to bed at nine-thirty."

"People who have to *work* for a living do," she snapped back. "We aren't all blessed with lives that allow us to sleep until all hours and then fritter our time away."

He didn't speak at once. Mari suspected he was using the time to think up a cutting remark to fling back at her. She was, therefore, surprised when he laughed.

"Very well, Mari, I give up. You win. I'm an idle wastrel who fritters away my time on frivolous enterprises."

Now she felt stupid. "I didn't mean it that way," she grumbled.

"Sure, you did. And I guess you're right. Personally, I really do think the pictures are a waste of time."

"You do? I didn't know that. How come you're working on this one?"

"You already know the answer to that. I'm supervising the spending of my father's money. Also, Martin and I are old friends from college. We just have different notions about the pictures, is all. I'm really happy to be helping him make a success of Peerless."

"Oh." She'd be darned if she'd tell him she thought that was nice of him, even though she did.

"Besides," Tony continued, "maybe he's right and I'm wrong. Maybe the pictures are the conduit to world understanding and peace. I suppose it's possible that, once folks get to know each other, worldwide, harmony will break out. I doubt it, but you never know."

"Hmmm. I suppose so." It seemed more likely to her that the pictures would seduce people away from their rightful jobs and useful work and create a nation—or a world—of idlers, but what did she know?

They continued on their way to the Nelsons, and Tony began whistling. The tune was again "Beautiful Dreamer," and Mari wondered if the song held any particular significance for him. She was on the verge of asking, when she decided not to. For all she knew, the song reminded him of a girl he'd left behind in New York.

It occurred to her that for all she knew Tony Ewing was engaged to be married to some aristocrat back East. The idea settled into her heart and burned there. She was pretty depressed by the time they reached the Nelsons' small suite of rooms at the back of the hotel.

She did her duty, however, and Mr. Nelson agreed to install security locks on all windows and doors, beginning tomorrow. He also offered to rent Martin a room in which to store Peerless's expensive equipment.

Thirteen

Tony was impressed by the way Mari expressed herself to Nelson. She was an articulate little baggage, considering she'd had no exposure to life's finer things.

He wished he could get over this absurd and insistent impulse to lavish gifts upon her. It had been dogging him ever since they'd gone to Los Angeles, when he'd bought her those clothes and compelled her to accept them.

Ever since their sojourn on Olvera Street, he'd been plagued by the mad desire to see her clad in diamonds and emeralds and satins and silks. He wanted to buy her a roadster and watch her tooling down the avenue clad in driving gloves, goggles, and a long, flowing scarf. She'd be elegant. Superb. Tony imagined young girls watching her breathlessly and wishing they could be just like her.

Especially if she had a handsome fellow like him at her side. The image of the two of them, carefree, gay, and laughing, appeared in his mind's eye like one of those modern cigarette advertisements one saw in periodicals that pandered to young people.

Good God, whatever was he thinking? He shook his head to dislodge the errant images and, as they walked away from the Nelsons' door, said, "I'll take you home as soon as I place a long-distance call to my father, Mari."

"You don't have to do that, but thanks."

Dammit, why did she always have to argue with him? "I know I don't have to do it, but I'm going to. It's pitch-dark outside. Besides, it'll take less time in the motorcar."

"It won't, either," she said tartly. "You'll blow a tire because you won't be able to see where you're going. Besides, I'm used to it."

"Damnation, Mari, don't you understand yet that there are bad people hanging around here?" He hadn't meant to yell and lowered his voice. "I'd be worse than a cad to allow you to walk home alone under these circumstances, and you'd be a damned fool to do it."

In an icy voice, Mari said, "Tiny will be with me. Nobody will dare bother me as long as Tiny's there to protect me."

"Protect you? Ha! He'd be more likely to invite a crook into your house for tea and crumpets."

Her laugh sounded both spontaneous and reluctant. "Stop being silly. I'm fine. Especially with Tiny along. He scares strangers, even if he isn't very ferocious, and anybody who'd be likely to want to do me harm would have to be a stranger."

"You don't know that, and neither do I."

"Fiddlesticks. I know everyone in town."

"That doesn't make any difference, and you know it. For all we know, Edison's bribed the whole town to prevent Peerless from making this picture."

From the expression on her face, Tony judged she wasn't buying that one any more than he did. But she only said, "That's silly."

Bother. He hated it when she was right. He wasn't going to give in on this issue, though. "I'm going. If you won't let me drive you, I'll walk with you."

"But then you'll have to walk back to the hotel alone,

and it might be dangerous for you. You don't know the landscape like I do."

"I," Tony said stiffly, "am a man. I'll have a lantern with me, and nobody would dare attack me. I'm strong enough to fight back." Especially with the revolver he carried in his pocket. He didn't mention it, because he sensed Mari wouldn't approve. He was a damned good shot, though, even if he did say so himself.

She huffed. "I can take care of myself, too. I've been doing it for years now."

"I thought your father died only a few months ago."

She hesitated before she said, "Well, yes, but—" She broke off abruptly, and Tony feared he'd prodded an unhealed wound.

"Say, Mari, I'm sorry. I didn't mean to bring up your father. I know you and he were close." No matter how much Tony thought Mr. Pottersby had been a stinky father to her.

Another moment's pause ensued, then she said, "No, it's not that. It's only—" Again, her words broke off, making Tony picture a guy with an ax lopping off the ends of her sentences.

"It's only what?" he asked gently, hoping she'd divulge one or two of her deepest secrets, although he couldn't imagine why she would. Not to him. Hell, for all he knew, she still despised him, both for being rich and for being—well—a little harsh with her at first.

He heard her expel a huge gust of breath. "It's only that my father and I were—well, we were close, but he didn't really help much with anything."

Exactly as Tony'd expected. His antagonism toward Mari's deceased parent grew another yard or so. He tried to keep anger from sounding in his voice when he next spoke, since he knew the quickest way to shut her up was to disparage her, her father, her dog, that damned mine, Mojave Wells, or anything else connected with her life. He cleared his throat and said, "Oh?" There. He was proud of himself for being so absolutely noncommittal. Not even Mari, who was good at it, could take exception to that one teensy word.

"Yes." She shut up.

Damn. Tony had been hoping she'd open up and spill the beans about her idiot father. An idea blossomed in his head, and he decided it was stupid. Then he decided, what the hell, and used it anyway. "I, ah, have never been close with my own father."

"No?"

She sounded interested, so Tony decided to take one more baby step.

"No. He, ah, wasn't home much."

"Too busy earning money, I expect."

He heard the smile in her voice and took heart. Maybe he could do this without getting all maudlin and mushy. He decided he could place his long-distance call tomorrow, and the two of them walked outdoors together. "Yeah. He loves money. More than he loved my brother and mother and me, I sometimes thought."

"Oh, you knew your mother?"

What an odd way to put it. Tony lifted the lantern so he could see her face. She looked nearly avid. "I still do. She lives in New York. You didn't know your mother?"

She shook her head. "She died when I was a baby. I don't even have a memory of her."

Although she spoke lightly, Tony thought he could detect traces of ancient pain. His own heart lurched and ached for her. So, she'd had no mother and an obsessed father. Great life for a darling little girl. He was sure she'd been darling. She still was. "I'm sorry, Mari."

"It's all right." She shrugged.

Tony got the impression of both great strength and

enormous fragility from the gesture. Again, his heart hurt. "Doesn't sound all right to me. No mother and a father who—well, I know he was a good man—" He knew no such thing. Tony thought he was a damned idiot, if not worse. "But evidently he didn't take very good care of you."

He cringed as soon as the words left his mouth, knowing from bitter experience that Mari didn't take kindly to censorious comments about her parent. She surprised him with another huge sigh.

She followed it up with, "No, he didn't. It's not that he didn't love me, but he didn't think about it. I mean, he just figured I was part of his life and would naturally share his ambitions and dreams."

"That mine—that is to say, the Marigold Mine—was what his ambitions centered on, I imagine."

"Yes."

"He named it after you?" That had been a nice gesture, at any rate.

"No. He named me after the mine."

Tony stopped dead in his tracks for no more than three seconds. He didn't want to upset Mari and make her stop spilling her guts. Hmmm. That didn't sound right. He chucked it and went back to the conversation. "He named you Marigold for the mine, did he?" He was pleased that none of his rage could be detected in his voice. "That's, ah, an interesting round-about."

She laughed, and it sounded genuine. "You don't know how much my dad loved that mine. And me, of course."

"Of course." It didn't escape his attention that she'd tacked herself on as an afterthought. His fury against Mari's father had risen to such a proportion that what he said next surprised the socks off him. "I imagine there are lots of ways people show their love. Your dad's might have been a little eccentric, but there you go.

Just because he was, um, kind of an oddball doesn't mean you can't love him, either."

Good God, where had that come from? It sounded like something out of one of those soppy women's magazines his mother liked to read.

Now that he came to think about it, that might say something about his parents' marriage. Shoot, when he'd started this conversation, it had been to get to know Mari better. He hadn't intended to open any of his own cans of worms.

"You're absolutely right." She sounded happy that he'd admitted it. "That's exactly what I think, too. I know a lot of people in Mojave Wells thought my father didn't treat me very well, but—he loved me, and I knew it. We had great times together, even if I did feel rather like I was the parent sometimes. If you know what I mean."

"I know what you mean." He could picture it in his mind very well, in fact. He imagined Mr. Pottersby, an inveterate dreamer, being hauled down to Earth by his little girl. Poor Mari. He wanted to hug her and promise to take care of her for the rest of her life.

That was probably the stupidest thing he'd ever wanted. His train of thought was interrupted precipitately when Tiny gave a sudden, ear-splitting yowl and plunged into the darkness like a locomotive thundering into a tunnel. Tony was so startled, he nearly dropped the lantern.

"Tiny!" Mari yelled, exasperated. "Tiny, you come back here." Lowering her voice, she muttered, "Drat that dog. Must be a jackrabbit."

"You think so?" Tony's heart had started drumming like the timpany in an orchestra. He wasn't accustomed to dogs scaring the bejesus out of him. He hoped, too, that whatever Tony was after really was something as benign as a jackrabbit.

A huge sigh preceded Mari's next comment. "I'm sure it is. They come out at night, and Tiny just adores running them down."

"Yeah? You mean he can catch them?"

"Sometimes. Not always."

Tony saw her glance up at him in the dim lantern light. Her face, shadowed with night and lantern glow, was appealing and mysterious, not at all like the face of the rugged miner's daughter. She was a remarkable woman, he thought in that moment. Beautiful, honorable, tough as rocks, and as hardy a specimen of womanhood as he'd ever encountered. She'd have made an admirable pioneer, his Mari.

His Mari? Good God. This whole thing was in danger of getting out of hand.

He spoke hurriedly in order to dispel the ungentlemanly surge of lust threatening him. "Um, can you do anything with the rabbits after he catches them?"

"Do anything with them?" She sounded puzzled. "Well, I generally bury them, but Tiny just as often digs them up again. It's a losing battle." She chuckled.

"You can't eat them?"

"Jackrabbits? No. They're tough and stringy. The cottontails are pretty good eating. In fact, I eat cottontails and chickens a lot more than beef. I raise the chickens and shoot the rabbits, and they make life cheaper. So to speak."

"I see." Tony never thought twice about ordering thick porterhouse steaks in whatever restaurant he found himself. He could scarcely comprehend having to shoot his dinner. Curious, he asked, "Do you shoot anything else?"

"Oh, sure. Birds, for instance. There are quail around here, and they're pretty tasty, although they have all these little bones that I find tiresome. I'd rather eat a chicken."

"Ah. Yes, quail do have lots of bones, don't they?" Tony knew they did, because, when he wasn't ordering porterhouse, he often chose quail. But he didn't have to shoot it.

"Then, too, you have to be careful not to break a tooth on the buckshot."

Break a tooth on the buckshot? Sweet Lord in heaven. He said, "I see."

"So I generally go for chicken and rabbits."

"Makes sense."

Mari whistled for her dog who, true to form, ignored her summons. Tony heard her sigh. "Will he come back on his own?" he asked after a moment.

"Oh, sure, eventually. Probably with a jackrabbit dangling in his teeth. He brings me gifts, you see."

"I see." Tony chuckled.

"Oh, good, here we are."

"We are?" Where were they? Tony glanced around in the blackness and was disappointed to see a light not far off. "Oh. Is that your cabin?"

"Yup. Home, sweet home, and all that."

"You've made it quite cozy," he murmured.

She laughed outright. "Come on, Tony, you don't really mean that, do you?"

"Well . . ." He thought about it and said, "Yes. I do mean it. I think you're a remarkable young woman, Mari."

"You do?"

Tony knew he shouldn't resent the amazement in her voice, but he did. "Yes, I do."

"Is that a good thing or a bad one?"

"Being remarkable? I'd say it was a good thing. A darned good one, in fact."

"Well. Thank you."

Tony got the impression she didn't believe him but didn't want to say so. Impulse made him say, "I'd better stick around until your dog comes home. Don't want anything to happen to you, all alone out here."

"Don't be silly." There was no exasperation in her tone, which Tony found minimally encouraging.

"No, really. I think I should."

"Well . . ." She hesitated for a few seconds. "Okay. I'll bring out a couple of chairs. It's kind of nice to sit outside and look at the stars once the sun's gone down and the mosquitoes go away."

"You have mosquitoes out here? But it's so dry."

"I know, but I guess they live somewhere, because we sure have them."

"I'll be darned."

She pushed the door to her cabin open, and Tony went inside to retrieve two chairs. He noticed that the one room was neat as a pin. Even though he couldn't even imagine living in such a place, he gave Mari credit for doing the best she could with what she had.

Maybe the money she was going to make with Peerless would go toward making her life easier. As he lugged the chairs outside, he knew he was dreaming. She'd pour all those thousands of dollars down that damned mine of hers, and before long she'd be just as badly off as she was now. The notion riled him.

When he set the chairs down with their backs against the cabin wall, though, and looked up to see Mari serenely gazing into the night sky, his heart plunged crazily. He walked over to stand beside her. "You're right. It's pretty here."

"Beautiful. I think this is when I love the desert most."

"I can understand that." The urge to touch her, to hold even her hand, was so powerful, Tony stuck his hands into his trouser pockets in order to make them obey his command to remain gentlemanly.

"Your eyes get used to the dark after a while, too,"

she said softly. "If you stay outside long enough and are still, eventually you'll begin to see jackrabbits hopping around and sometimes even the wild donkeys will wander by."

"Yeah? The closest I've ever come to nature before this was the menagerie in the Bronx back home."

"The Bronx? My goodness, I've heard of the Bronx. I'd kind of like to travel someday."

Her voice sounded so wistful and her profile looked so soulful that, combined, they succeeded in undoing all of Tony's commands and lured his hands out of his pockets. Carefully, so as not to alarm her, he reached out and took her hand. She whipped her head around, and he read fear and suspicion in her eyes.

"Don't worry," he told her. "My intentions are pure. I just didn't want you to stumble heading to the chairs." If she bought that one, she was a fool. Tony, who already knew she wasn't a fool except when it came to that mine, expected her to slap him.

She didn't. She only sighed, turned, and walked with him back to the cabin. She didn't yank her hand out of his, which, again, he found mildly encouraging. Therefore, he didn't release her hand when they both sat, but kept it in his for several moments. Then he lifted it to his lips and very gently kissed her palm. It wasn't a soft, delicate palm; it was callused from years and years of hard physical work. Tony's heart hitched and pitched, and he stifled the urge to make all sorts of wild declarations and promises to this independent girl.

"Tony . . ." Her breathy voice came to him as if in a fog.

"You're a lovely young woman, Mari," he murmured into her palm. "Beautiful."

"Oh, but—"

To stop her from denying his assertion, which he

knew to be true, he leaned over and kissed her lips. Worked like a charm. She didn't say another word. He did hear a tiny mew of surprise, perhaps even pleasure. As gently as gently could be, he put both of his arms around her and drew her nearer to him. He'd had the foresight to set the chairs close together, so there were no perilous gaps to worry about.

Pressing her hands against his shoulder, she whispered, "Tony, no."

"I won't hurt you, Mari." He meant it. He'd never hurt her.

"But, this is—this isn't right."

"It feels right to me." His sex had stirred and was standing at attention, but Tony felt no urgency to ravish Mari. Perhaps the desert's magic had gotten to him. He thought it was more probable that Mari herself had. As much as he yearned to bury himself in her luscious body, he'd sooner shoot himself than add to her burdens.

She moaned softly, and he got the impression it felt right to her, too.

"I've wanted to do this for a long time," he whispered as he feathered kisses down her chin to her throat.

"You—you have?"

"Yes, I have. Are you surprised?"

"Yes."

"I don't know why you should be. I was afraid I was being too obvious."

She gave a soft, shaky laugh. "I thought you hated me."

"Good God, no." Although he feared he might spook her, he began to caress her with his hands. Carefully, he stroked her back to the waist and a smidgen lower, where her hips flared gently. Lord, he wanted to see her. She had legs that went on forever; he already knew that much, because he'd seen her in britches the first time they'd met. She was lithe and slender, and as womanly as a woman could be.

"I don't hate you, either," she said quietly.

It wasn't exactly a declaration of love, but it was a start. And Tony didn't know if he wanted any declarations of love. He didn't think he was ready for them. He was certainly ready to know Mari, though, both in the intellectual and the carnal sense. Since he knew that he probably couldn't get the latter without some kind of commitment, he wasn't pushy. This was a preliminary investigation, sort of a trial run.

"I'm glad," he murmured against the skin of her throat. She had an elegant neck.

He kissed her lips again, caressing them with his own, gently teasing her mouth open. Taking care not to frighten her, he allowed his tongue to play against her full lower lip. She gasped but didn't draw away from him. His hands finally wandered to right beneath her breasts, and he let them rest there, where he could barely feel the softness of her curves heavy against them. He wanted to cover them and feel her nipples pebble, to taste her, to let his tongue work magic on her.

But that would have to wait. He didn't want to frighten her more than he wanted most things in life. The knowledge came as a surprise to him; almost as much a surprise as his urge to protect her and make her life easier.

She murmured his name so softly he almost didn't hear it, and in a tone that thrilled him. "You're a beautiful woman, Mari," he responded, then deepened the kiss so that his tongue barely penetrated her open mouth. She tasted like heaven.

He wanted her to explore his body with her hands, too, but she was shy. He didn't push her, although the ache in his groin was so strong, he had to restrain himself from grabbing her hand and pressing it to the bulge in his trousers. Lord, he wanted her. He couldn't recall wanting another woman as he wanted Mari, although he'd had women before.

Tony's list of conquests wasn't long. They consisted primarily of society dames who were bored with their husbands. He wasn't proud of himself for playing that game, although he'd done it. The notion of loving a woman and of having her bed another man had stopped him from seeking pleasures of the flesh far more often than he'd succumbed to his carnal urges. Which, he supposed, made him rather like Mari in that regard. He possessed a trace of honor, if no more than that.

He had no earthly idea how long they'd sat on those two hard chairs of hers, kissing and exploring each other in the desert darkness. He'd gotten sidetracked somewhere in a sensual haze and lost track of time, when a sudden noise brought them both to attention.

Tony's arms still held onto Mari, and hers were still wrapped around him, when all at once Tiny bounded into the scene. Tony muttered, "Good God," when the gigantic black shape showed itself against the grayer blackness of the night. "He could pass for the Hound of the Baskervilles without half trying, couldn't he?"

Mari giggled. "Except he's not a hound."

"Whatever he is, if you didn't know it was him, you might be scared."

She sighed, which Tony took for agreement. He didn't want to do it, but he released her, figuring it would be better for both of them to have hands free in order to fend off Tiny's loving advances, should he make any. He wanted to inspect Mari, to see if she was reacting negatively to his caresses. He hoped not. He wanted to love her, not scare her.

Shoot, did he mean that? How very frightening, to be sure.

His thoughts scattered like chaff when Tiny loped

closer to the cabin, his tail aloft and waving proudly, not unlike a celebratory banner. Leaping up to them in a swirl of dust, he dropped a parcel on their feet and let out a huge "Woof!"

"Oh, dear," Mari murmured, pressing her hands to her cheeks. Her nose wrinkled as she stared at her feet.

Tony looked, too. "Good God."

The dog had dropped it right smack on top of their shoes: a big, floppy, very dead jackrabbit. Tony burst out laughing. He couldn't help it. This girl and her dog and her cabin and her mine composed the most outrageous set of theatrical paraphernalia he'd ever seen, and he'd seen Broadway productions aplenty.

"Oh, Tiny, I wish you wouldn't do things like this." But Mari smiled, too.

Hearing his name, Tiny wagged more ferociously still, lowered his big torso until his head was between his front paws, his rump stuck up in the air, and his tail whipped back and forth like a crazed metronome. Then he let out a series of thunderous barks. Tony shook his head. The beast wanted to play. "Does he want us to throw the rabbit for him to fetch?" *Ew.*

"Probably." Mari sighed heavily. "I'll get it out of the way and bury it in the morning."

"If you leave it, won't some animal come by in the night and eat it?"

"I don't know. Probably, but I don't want to attract coyotes, because they're sneaky and might get into the chicken coop."

"Ah, I see." Good grief, it seemed like every three or four minutes, Tony endured another shock over the way Mari lived her life. She shouldn't have to. Things oughtn't to be this hard for her. It wasn't fair. He took her hand and lifted it to his lips. He saw Mari watching him, her dark eyes wide and luminous. Warmth pervaded his body, from his heart to his groin.

"Well," he said. "I suppose I'd better get back to the Mojave Inn." He didn't want to go. He wanted to stay here, in this disreputable cabin, with this astonishing girl and her incredible dog. He knew he couldn't.

"Yes," she said. "I know you need to get back. We all need our rest, I guess."

"Right." She had no idea, he perceived, how very much he wanted her. Why should she? Until he'd kissed her, he'd tried hard to resist. Unfortunately, Mari was irresistible. She was like Circe to his Ulysses.

She turned away and sighed deeply. "Thank you for walking me home. I, ah, suppose something might have happened to me if I'd been alone."

Something *had* happened to her, although she didn't appear inclined to admit it. "Right," said Tony. He forced himself to rise. "I suppose the crew will be at work bright and early tomorrow. I guess tomorrow's your first scene, if the insurance folks don't take too much time."

"Oh, my God, that's right." Her face fell ludicrously.

Tony grinned, not entirely happy to have the former seductive mood dispelled, but understanding it was for the best. Damn it. "Try not to worry too much. You'll be great."

"I doubt it. I'm scared to death."

"We'll all be there to help you. Martin's a great director. And he's also a very understanding and kind man. He's not like me."

She looked up at him quickly and looked away again. "Oh, you're not so bad."

"I'll send a car for you." He hoped he'd be able to come himself.

"There's no need for that," she muttered.

"I don't care if there's a need or not. I'm sending a car. And you can bring that big lug with you." He gestured at Tiny, who had tired of acting cute since no one was paying attention to him, and was snuffling the ground where Tony had shoved the rabbit with his foot.

"Okay," Mari said, sounding resigned.

He had to kiss her again. He knew he shouldn't. Everything in his life and nature rebelled against the attraction he felt for her, but he couldn't stop himself. He lifted her chin with his finger. "You'll be fine," he said softly. "Fine."

Hell's bells, she already was fine. He kissed her once, tenderly, and let his hand fall. "See you tomorrow, Mari."

She nodded. He leaned over to give Tiny a last pat and turned to walk back to the Mojave Inn. He still carried the lantern to light his way, and he turned once before he'd gone very far. He could scarcely discern Mari and her dog standing there, but he distinctly saw her lift her hand in a salute of farewell. He waved back, continued his walk, and didn't turn around again.

The most unsettling combination of emotions roiled in his breast as he trudged back to the hotel. He felt good and bad and heroic and cadlike and brilliant and stupid and happy and sad and exhilarated and depressed.

Could this possibly be love?

It was, Tony decided grimly, something to think about.

Fourteen

Mari faced the morning with heavy eyelids and a headache. After Tony'd left her the night before, she hadn't been able to get to sleep for hours. She'd even gone outside and buried that stupid rabbit carcass sometime past midnight, hoping the exercise would help her sleep.

It didn't, she didn't, and now she felt terrible. Faced, however, with the prospect of ten thousand dollars for a week or two's work, she wasn't going to shirk.

Ten thousand dollars. The notion of sinking all that money into her father's unproductive mine, no matter how many deathbed promises she'd made him, sat like lead on her heart.

"I'm so darned tired, Tiny," she murmured to her wagging dog. "I'm sure I'll feel more cheerful after I rest up."

She wasn't sure though. She feared all of the dogged determination that had kept her going for so long was being seriously eroded now that she'd experienced a little bit of life from a different perspective.

"But that's silly," she announced. Tiny wagged harder. "As soon as all these Peerless people get out of my life, everything will get back to normal."

In a pig's eye. Nothing in Mojave Wells would ever be the same again. Even if Mari herself went back to life as she'd been living it for all of her nineteen years, the memories would persist. And the talk. So little happened in Mojave Wells on a day-to-day basis that a huge upheaval like a moving picture being made in town would keep folks yapping for years. Decades, even.

She handed Tiny a huge bowl filled with meat scraps and vegetables. He ate like there was no tomorrow. He could probably eat up ten grand in no time at all if she weren't accustomed to living frugally.

"Frugally, my foot," she muttered. "Poorly is more like it. Stupidly probably describes it, too."

Good gracious, but she was in an evil mood. Why should that be?

"Stupid question, Mari Pottersby. You know darned well why it is."

That kiss. That wonderful, frightening, spectacular, luscious, deplorable kiss. She lifted a work-roughened hand and pressed it to her lips. "He kissed me, Tony—I mean, Tiny. He actually kissed me."

Although Tiny didn't leave off gobbling his breakfast, he did wag his tail some more. Mari considered it a form of communication and was gratified. At least her dog didn't seem distressed that she'd allowed herself to be kissed by a man so far above her own station in life.

"Lordy, Tiny, I'm beginning to sound like a Gilbert and Sullivan operetta." She and her cousin had seen *HMS Pinafore* in San Bernardino several years before. Mari had adored it. She thought she would really like being able to go to the theater, if she were ever to be, say, rich. Or even comfortably circumstanced. Fat chance of that ever happening.

Then again, ten thousand dollars could make a girl pretty darned comfortable if she didn't have to throw it all down the gullet of a bottomless, money-eating mine shaft.

"Stop it, Mari Pottersby. You have no choice in the matter."

That was a load of junk, and she knew it. The only thing that kept her working in that useless pit was her promise to a man whom she'd loved, but who probably didn't deserve her devotion.

"Nonsense. Love isn't something a person deserves or doesn't deserve. It happens or it doesn't. I loved my dad. He might not have been the world's greatest father, but he was the only one I had, and he was good to me." She had to wipe away a tear, and swore at herself to stop being sentimental and mushy just because she didn't feel well.

Which didn't solve any of her problems. She sighed heavily and wished she had some salicylic powders. She'd heard they were good for a headache. But they cost money, and Mari didn't spend her few pennies on luxury cures for headaches. She didn't have headaches often, anyway. This morning's was an exception, and it was due to not sleeping.

The thrum of a motor penetrated the cabin walls. Mari's heart gave a leap that probably dislodged it from its proper place in her chest cavity, and she raced to the mirror on the wall to see if she looked as bad as she felt. Thank God, she didn't.

Madly patting at her hair, her skirt, her blouse, and everything else she could reach, she tried breathing deeply to still the battering of her heart. "I wonder if it's Tony," she muttered, ostensibly to Tiny, but really because she wanted—needed—to voice her hope, even if she worded it as an idle musing. She longed to see him. She longed to be in his company. To talk to him. To walk with him.

To kiss him.

Oh, dear, this was awful. She ran to the door and reached for the knob, then paused. She wouldn't make a fool of herself over a man. Any man. Especially a man whom she didn't even really trust.

Something in her chest twisted painfully. It wasn't so much that she didn't trust Tony per se, she amended. It was the circumstances she didn't trust. He was as rich as God and lived in New York. She was as poor as dirt and lived in California. Under ordinary circumstances, the twain would never have met at all.

Under the odd and fantastic influence of the motion pictures, the twain had not merely met, but kissed.

"It was only a kiss," she growled to Tiny, as if he'd questioned her on the incident. "I'm sure he kisses girls all the time."

There went the twisting in her chest again, harder this time. So hard, indeed, that Mari pressed a hand to her breast, in an effort to stop the pain.

She didn't kiss men all the time. Far from it. In fact, except for Gordon Shay, who didn't count, she'd never been kissed at all until last night. Anyhow, there was no way on Earth to compare Gordon to Anthony Ewing. They might belong to different species entirely, so different were they from each other.

Gordon and Mari were from the same sphere.

Which meant that Mari and Tony might belong to different species, too.

"By thunder, I'm in a bad mood," Mari muttered. She turned the doorknob and flung the door open, still praying in her heart of hearts that Tony had come to pick her up this morning, even though she tried to deny it.

She watched the dust cloud flung up behind the motorcar, and raised a hand to shade her eyes as she squinted into the bright distance. Her heart was doing an odd-rhythmed jig in her chest, her mouth was dry, her head hurt, and she wished she could get over her fruitless infatuation with Tony. It felt awful. *She* felt awful.

"I thought love was supposed to be a wonderful thing, Tiny," she grumbled into the desert air, the temperature of which had already soared to a hundred, or she missed her guess. "If what I'm feeling is love, it hurts like heck, and I wish it would go away and leave me alone."

But it didn't. And when the motorcar came close enough so Mari could discern the features of its driver, the heart that had been giving her so many problems lately plummeted into the dirt at her feet. "It's not Tony, Tiny."

It was a funny thing, but saying the two names together sounded silly and cheered her up a trifle. So she said them again. "Tony. Tiny. That's funny. Tiny. Tony."

Tiny, wagging cheerfully at her feet, seemed to be enjoying the juxtaposition of the two names as well. He barked a greeting as the driver pulled up in front of the cabin. It was George Peters, the set designer.

That was nice. Mari liked George. Even if he wasn't Tony.

George got out of the motorcar. "Good morning, Miss Pottersby. Tony asked me to pick you up this morning. He and Martin are tied up with the insurance people."

Oh. At least Tony had a plausible excuse for not coming to get her himself. Mari tried to be understanding as she shook George's hand. "Call me Mari, please. I understand all picture people call each other by their first names."

George laughed as he opened the door to the backseat of the big touring car and gestured for Tiny to enter. "I guess they do. I'm just not used to it yet."

"That makes two of us." Tiny didn't get into the car, but stood there glancing from George to Mari and wagging his tail. Mari sighed. "Come on, Tiny, get in the car. Here, I'll show you." She did, and he got in.

George rolled down the glass of the back passenger's window, and patted it for Tiny's benefit. "See? you can stick your big head out there and sniff to your heart's content while we drive to Mojave Wells." He laughed when Tiny took him up on his suggestion. "That's one big dog you have there, Mari. It's funny that you named him Tiny."

George's good humor buoyed Mari's spirits slightly. "Believe it or not, he was the runt of the litter. That's how he got his name."

"Wow. I'd like to see the other pups, if he's the littlest." Gentlemanlike, George opened the front door for Mari.

She thought that was sweet of him. George seemed like a genuinely nice young man. *He* probably wasn't so far above her in life that it would be nonsensical to love him. Unlike Tony Ewing, who was. Unfortunately, while she liked George, he didn't make her heart sing and her blood race and her whole being want to smile.

She had to stop this. "I don't think he's the smallest anymore. He grew like a weed after he came to live with me."

"He must eat a lot." George cranked the motorcar to life, jumped into the front seat next to Mari, and the automobile chugged off toward Mojave Wells.

"He does. He's a real sweetheart, though. He fools people, because he's so big."

"I'll say. Martin told me what happened when he and Harrowgate first came to talk to you." He shook his head and looked wistful. "Wish I could have seen it. Harrowgate's such a pompous old thing. I'd love to see him being given a bath by Tiny."

Mari laughed at the memory. She couldn't help herself, and she blessed George for reminding her.

They chatted amiably as George drove Mari to the Mojave Inn. The first thing she saw as the automobile roared close to the town was the crowd of people gathered around the shed in back of the hotel. They were quite far away yet, and soon buildings would interfere with her vision, so she squinted and tried to pick out Tony's form from among the others.

No use. Before she'd managed to focus on a likely candidate, her view of the scene was obscured behind Mr. Fenster's barn. "How long have the insurance people been there?" she asked. "They must have come mighty early this morning."

"They did." George laughed. "Martin was already up and eating breakfast—he's an early riser—but the rest of us had to be rousted out of bed. Tony wasn't happy about it."

Mari felt herself quiver to attention, like some sort of sharp-eared animal catching the sound of its prey. "Oh? He doesn't like early mornings, eh?"

"I guess not. Don't blame him. I prefer sleeping until around eightish myself. Picture folks usually have to get up earlier than that, so I'm adjusting."

"Eight? That's early? Shoot, for me that's the middle of the day." One more massive difference between poor Mari Pottersby and rich Tony Ewing.

"The middle of the day?" George exclaimed. "For goodness' sake, Mari, that's appalling." He laughed again. "You and my sister-in-law ought to meet each other. She's always telling me I'm a lazy bum because I don't like mornings."

"She is?" Until this moment, Mari had been under the impression that Brenda Fitzpatrick was a nice woman. Now she wasn't so sure.

George set her mind at rest on the matter at once. "She's only teasing. It's just that she had to get up so blasted early for so many years, that it was hard for her to adjust to a life of ease after she married my brother."

"Oh. For heaven's sake." Well, now, wasn't that interesting? Mari had assumed, because of everything she'd read, that famous actors and actresses lived lives of idleness and luxury. Of course, now that she thought about it, it made sense that they had to work, too. Otherwise, they wouldn't be rich and famous, would they? Unlike the Anthony Ewings of the world, they had to labor for their wages. Tony's fortune had descended on him at birth, as if from heaven. Sort of like bird droppings.

That's not fair, Mari, she scolded herself, even as she smiled inside at the image the thought had created.

And anyway, how had she gotten back on that old, bedraggled subject again? She didn't know why her brain insisted on wallowing in the differences between herself and Tony. Recounting them all only made her unhappy. But wallow it did; she felt as if she were the victim of her own rebellious brain, and she didn't enjoy the feeling at all.

George stopped the motorcar in front of the hotel and hopped out to open Mari's door. That was one thing she'd learned since Peerless came to town. She now waited for the gentleman to open her door and didn't jump the gun and open it for herself. It still didn't make any sense that society should consider women incapable of opening doors for themselves, but she was too tired to fight tradition this morning, even if she wanted to. She didn't, either. After all, it had been she who'd asked Tony to teach her how to behave; she'd be foolish to ignore his kindly imparted lessons.

There she went again: thinking about Tony. She wished she could simply press a switch and turn off the Tony-dwelling part of her mind. No such luck.

"Want to go out back and see what's happening?" George asked eagerly.

"Sure. Let me put Tiny's leash on him so he doesn't scare the insurance men away."

George chuckled, and Mari got her dog more or less under control. Tiny was excited and really wanted to be loping up and down the street and greeting all of his old buddies in town, but Mari didn't want any trouble or misunderstandings that might ensue because of the size and disorderliness of her dog. "I'll let you run later, boy," she promised.

Tiny woofed once, wagged his tail, and she guessed he understood. The three of them went toward the shed in the backyard, hastened along by Tiny, who dragged them after he figured out which way they wanted to go.

Once she was close enough to distinguish forms and faces, the first person Mari saw was Tony Ewing. He had his fists on his lean hips and was frowning down at the remains of the two cameras. They had been dragged outside in the sun by pulling the canvas upon which they lay.

Mari's breath hitched. The day was hot already and promised further delights, if one enjoyed broiling in the sun. To accommodate the weather, Tony had shucked off his jacket, unbuttoned several top buttons on his shirt, and rolled up his sleeves. He hadn't bothered to don a celluloid collar at all, and he looked deliciously rugged sans all of his fine trappings. Mari's heart started thudding painfully.

Tiny gave an excited bark, Tony glanced up, and his gaze locked with Mari's for several seconds. Confused by the emotions tumbling inside her, Mari blushed, finally managed to drag her gaze away from his, and lowered her head, pretending to watch where she was stepping.

"Oh, there you are, Mari." Martin left the group of men and hurried over to her. "We're almost through here. Why don't you go inside. We're using Room Three as a change and makeup room. Your costume is in there waiting for you. We should be ready to start filming soon."

"Without cameras?" Her glance kept sliding over to Tony, but she pretended her interest centered solely in the ruined cameras.

"We got two more cameras in this morning, one of which I've already sent out to the mine to do some site testing in the mine shaft. I cabled the studio, and Phin sent them right out. I don't know what this is going to mean, money-wise, but we have to keep going with the filming or we'll get hopelessly behind schedule, and the insurance fellows will just have to catch up with us." He cast a worried peek at the wreckage. "At least, I sure hope they will."

She nodded. "Yes. I do, too. It would be awful if somebody got away with doing this."

"Yeah. That fellow over there"—Martin pointed to a burly man in khaki slacks and shirt—"is investigating from a police angle."

"Oh, it's Mr. Jones." Mari waved at the man, who waved back. "He's been the sheriff here for ages."

Martin nodded. "Why don't you go on in and get ready for your first scene now. The costume and makeup people are waiting for you."

Bother. Mari had wanted to go over, stand beside Tony, gaze at the demolished cameras, and masquerade as an interested bystander. In truth, she just wanted to be near Tony for a few minutes. Even a few seconds. She felt an awful need to have a dose of him, as if that would make her feel better.

Quit being an idiot, Mari Pottersby. You have a headache from not sleeping enough. Which was Tony's fault, too.

Exasperated with herself, Mari said, "Okay." She

was about to turn and do her duty when she remembered Tiny. She didn't know how she'd managed to forget about him in the first place, since he was practically pulling her arm out of its socket, trying to get to where the action, and the people, were. "Um, Martin."

"Yes?" He'd been peering anxiously at the small crowd of people surrounding the entrance to the shed.

Mari hated to ask but knew she had to. "Um, would you mind watching Tiny for me? Or I can take him with me." She hesitated, then plunged ahead. "Except that he really wants to see what's going on. He's a snoopy dog."

Martin eyed Tiny with what looked like a good deal of affection. Mari's heart lightened considerably. "Snoopy, is he? Sure, I'll be glad to renew acquaintances with your cow—I mean, your dog."

Mari giggled. She felt better already. "Thanks, Martin." Casting one last glance at Tony, whose concentration seemed to be wholly on the mess at his feet, she sighed and walked, drooping slightly, to the hotel. Judy Nelson greeted her at the front door with a dust rag in her hands and her hair in a scarf.

"Hi, Judy."

"Hi, Mari. Say, did you see what happened to those cameras out there?" Judy's eyes gleamed with excitement.

Mari understood that. The making of a motion picture in Mojave Wells was probably the most thrilling thing that had ever happened or ever would happen here.

"Yes. I saw them yesterday. What a mess."

"I'll say. They called in Sheriff Jones, too."

This was exhilarating because, as a rule, the sheriff only got to suppress rowdy drunks. He probably couldn't remember the last time a real crime had been perpetrated in Mojave Wells. He must be as excited as the rest of the community now.

"Yeah," she said. "I saw him out there, trying to look official." Both girls giggled.

"That's a stretch. Usually he just looks sleepy."

Out of curiosity, and because she wanted to know if Judy had been given any juicy tidbits of information that Mari had missed from the distance of her cabin, Mari asked, "Has anybody become a suspect yet?"

Judy shook her head. "Not that I know of." Her smile vanished. "You know it's got to be one of them, Mari. Nobody in Mojave Wells would do anything like that."

"You're right. I think so, too." Folks in Mojave Wells had too much respect for personal property rights. Mari couldn't imagine a soul who'd think it a good idea to smash expensive equipment like those cameras. "But who could it be? Aren't all those guys employed by Peerless? They wouldn't want to jeopardize their own production, would they?"

With a shrug, Judy began polishing the furniture in the hotel's lobby. "Search me. All I know is it isn't anybody who lives in Mojave Wells. We simply don't *do* things like that."

Mari nodded and went off to seek out Room 3. She guessed Judy was right, although she wasn't as absolutely positive about the integrity of her fellow citizens as Judy. When folks needed money, they were apt to go a little crazy. Mari knew as much from bitter experience. How else could she account for agreeing to act in this picture, if not for insanity brought about by financial desperation.

"Excuses, excuses," she muttered as she walked down the hallway. "If a person has true moral strength, such things shouldn't matter."

That was downright depressing, when she added it to all the other uncertainties her life contained at the moment. Fortunately, before she could begin to wallow again, she reached Room 3. She considered knocking, decided not to, and opened the door. Everyone in the room turned to look at her, and she paused, embarrassed, before grabbing the bull by the horns and walking in as if she belonged there. Which she did, darn it.

"Hi, there," she said, trying to sound relaxed and friendly. She felt like picking up her skirt and running fast in the opposite direction.

A woman she recognized as the one who'd prepared her face for the camera during her screen test, gestured for her to climb up onto the tall stool beside her. "Hello, Mari," the woman said. "Ready for your first scene?"

No, she was ready for no such thing. "I guess so," she said, and sat on the stool, folding her hands in her lap. "Have at me."

The woman laughed, which made Mari feel not quite so glum. "It'll be all right," the woman assured her. "You'll be great on film."

That was kind of her. "You think so, do you?"

"Sure. I've been at this long enough to spot naturals. You're a natural."

"I hope you're right." The woman's words didn't do much to dispel the aura of gloom under which Mari had been living since opening her eyes that morning. "Say, you know my name, but I don't know yours."

"Helen Bernstein."

"Hi, Helen."

"Hi, Mari."

This was stupid. Because she wanted to calm her anxiety, she decided to get the woman talking about herself. "So, how long have you been working in the pictures, Helen?"

Her ploy worked. As Helen brushed Mari's hair back from her face, slipped a band over her head to hold the hair out of her way, and daubed on the first pancake of dead-white makeup, she talked. "I wanted to be an actress, but there was more work available for makeup artists than actresses, so I decided to do that instead."

Mari asked more questions. Helen answered them, and before Mari was ready to climb down from her stool and seek out her costume, the two women were fast friends. She was pleased. That hadn't been so hard. Even her nerves seemed calmer.

Next, Mari visited Karen Crenshaw, the costume person. She didn't hesitate to ask Karen her name, or to inquire about how she ended up working for the pictures. She was surprised to learn that Karen was employed by Madame Dunbar, the very same dressmaker whom Mari had visited on her trip to Los Angeles.

"Oh, my," she said. "She scared me." Instantly, she regretted admitting how shy she'd been with Madame Dunbar.

But Karen only laughed. "She's okay. She only looks haughty."

That was nice to know. Mari didn't quite believe her. "She sounded pretty haughty when I talked to her, too," she muttered.

With another laugh, Karen said, "Oh, all right, I admit it. She's a hard, difficult woman. But she's a great costumer and a wonderful teacher, and I've learned a lot from her. Also, since I do most of my work on location, I don't mind that she's difficult because I don't have to be around her much."

Made sense to Mari.

She'd been ensconced in Room 3 for three quarters of an hour before the door opened once more. Mari, who had become quite lighthearted and gay as she chatted and joked with the other two young women, immediately became tongue-tied when she recognized Tony Ewing as the person who'd opened the door. She was especially unsettled to note that he was frowning and looked irked—and they hadn't even quarreled yet today.

He rapped out, "Are you ready?"

Mari swallowed and made a quick survey of the room to make sure it was she to whom he had addressed his question. "Um, I think so."

Tony glared at Karen, who'd been fitting Mari's costume with pins here and tucks there. "Is she ready?" he barked at Karen.

Karen gave him a crabby look, which he richly deserved in Mari's opinion. "Sure, I guess so."

He turned back to Mari. "Then come with me," he commanded.

Mari's eyes started to narrow. She didn't like being spoken to in this insulting and peremptory way. Because she also didn't want to start a fight in front of her two new friends, she waited to tackle him until they were outside Room 3 and the door had shut behind her.

She didn't get the chance. Tony turned so precipitately that she bumped into him, and he took her in his arms. The sound that came out of Mari's mouth then couldn't properly be termed a word. It was more like a squeak.

"God, I've been wanting you for hours today already!" he said after he withdrew his lips from hers. "I couldn't wait a second longer."

Absolutely dumbfounded, Mari discovered she also couldn't prepare a coherent sentence. All the words she knew just sort of clumped together at the back of her throat, and she was too befuddled to sort them out.

Once more, it didn't matter, because Tony kissed her again. Her body responded instantly and with enthusiasm. Heat that had nothing to do with the weather prickled her skin, tension puckered her nipples, unfamiliar and insistent sensations danced through her veins like a troupe of ballerinas, pressure built in her private area, and her head buzzed.

Unlike her body, her brain was having a more difficult time reconciling this assault with a lifetime's learned values. This sort of behavior was improper; her brain told her, even as her body rebelled at the prudish commentary. Tony Ewing, a man so rich she couldn't even conceive of his wealth, was taking advantage of her because she was poor, her brain said. If she were as rich as he, he wouldn't dare take these liberties.

"So what?" her heart asked her brain.

"It matters," her brain answered back, "because as soon as he tires of playing with you, he'll go away again. And, unlike you, he will merely resume his old, expensive, devil-may-care way of life. *You* will not be merely emotionally devastated but quite possibly pregnant as well."

Her brain finally succeeded in shocking her body out of its delight in Tony's caresses. She pulled from him so hard, she startled him, and he let her go. "Mari . . ."

"Stop it, Tony!" She patted her hair, which Karen had just succeeded in nudging into the correct state of glamour, tempered with Peerless's notion that a miner's daughter might have to live rough. Mari could have put the notion of any glamour at all out of their heads if they'd bothered to ask her, but they hadn't.

"But— Oh, God, Mari, I've missed you so damned much. I didn't know it was possible to miss somebody this much overnight."

He'd missed her? Had he been pining away all night, as she had, for the sake of her?

No. Such a scenario was downright impossible. Leastways, he'd have to do a lot more convincing before she'd allow him to take liberties with her person again.

Like hell.

Mari groaned when she acknowledged the state of her own mind and heart. She was madly and passionately in love with Tony Ewing. He desired her. No equity of purpose existed in this bleak picture.

Instead of saying anything so certain to cause her acute humiliation as admitting the state of her heart, she said, "For heaven's sake, they just globbed all this makeup on me, and you're rubbing it off. Look at you. Your lips are all white." If her emotions hadn't been rioting, she might even have laughed, because he really did look funny.

He wiped his mouth with the back of his hand and frowned. "I didn't mean to mess up your makeup, but . . ." He looked as if he were struggling to find words.

This was minimally encouraging to Mari, who'd thought she was the only one. Because what she'd just said was true, and because she couldn't think of anything to say, she said nothing, but only continued looking at him.

He took a deep breath. "Listen, Mari, about last night—"

"Are you ready, Mari?" Martin's cheerful voice rang out. He sounded as if he were on the front porch.

It made her jump and Tony swear. But she turned toward the voice and forced herself to call out with aplomb—or as close to it as she could get—"Be right there, Martin."

Anyhow, she wasn't sure she wanted to talk about last night. At least, not with Tony and not now. Maybe, in, say, a century or two, she might be able to relate to her great-great-great-grandchildren that she'd once spent an idyllic evening with the man of her dreams. Not now. Now, if she even tried to talk about it, she knew good and well she'd burst into tears and mortify herself.

"Mari," he said. He sounded fairly desperate, which surprised her. It might even have gratified her, but she was too flustered to tell.

But she couldn't possibly think about his desperation at the moment, not with her own threatening to overwhelm her. "I have to run, Tony."

"But—"

"I'll talk to you later," she said as she started trotting outdoors to her doom. Rather, to her first scene. She heard Tony's soft "Damn" behind her, and an unintentional sob shook her. She ferociously commanded herself to get herself in hand, stopped just before the front door of the inn to gather herself together, yanked the door open, and walked outside, assuming an air of serenity. At any rate, she hoped to heck she looked serene.

Fifteen

The bright sunlight made her blink and squint, and she lifted a hand to shade her eyes so she could find Martin.

She knew she looked pretty good. From a distance. There was no way she'd ever think this dead-white makeup looked anything but ghastly up close. Yet she'd seen herself on screen—well, on a wall—and knew for a fact the makeup carried onto celluloid beautifully. According to Helen and Karen and Martin and a whole bunch of other people who ought to know, white makeup filmed much better than natural skin tones or beige-colored makeup.

So be it. She smiled broadly at Martin when he came up to take her hand and lead her onto what passed as a "set." It was actually a stretch of dry desert on which some storefronts had been erected. Evidently, the real thing didn't look authentic enough for the picture folks, so they'd had George Peters design a mining town out of cardboard and two-by-fours.

As they walked over to the set, Mari had to admit that George's conception of a rugged western mining town was much more picturesque than Mojave Wells. That made her a little sad, although she couldn't have said why. Maybe it had something to do with the fact that this is the way most people in the world were going to view her life forevermore, and it was false.

On the other hand, what did she care? She scolded herself for getting sentimental and prayed for the umpteenth time that the good Lord rid her of her too-ready emotionalism. She had to live a hard life. She needed to be tough minded and hardy, not slushy and weepy.

By the time she and Martin reached the set and Martin showed her the mark on the ground where she was supposed to begin her scene, Mari had herself more or less under control. She was pretty sure she wouldn't collapse or fall into a crying fit or anything. Besides, this first scene was easy. All she had to do was sit on a chair beside a table, both of which were supposed to be inside a miner's cabin, and carry on a silent conversation with Reginald Harrowgate, who was playing her father. She'd met Harrowgate since her first unfortunate introduction to him, and she knew he'd not forgiven her for Tiny's behavior, but she was willing to make the most of it.

Ten thousand dollars, she told herself. *You can do this for ten thousand dollars.* In fact, *ten thousand dollars,* served as her mantra during that first scene.

Harrowgate let her sit in the hot sun for a full five minutes, and Mari had begun to fear she'd slide right out of her chair because of how much she was sweating, before he strode onto the set like a king to his throne. He peered down at her as if she were some disgusting species of fungus. "All ready here, Martin," he said, and he, too, sat.

Mari dared to smile at him and say, "Hello," but he merely scowled and put a finger to his lips.

As if it mattered. The pictures were silent. Nobody'd know if they spoke to each other. With a sigh, Mari let it ride. She didn't care if this silly man liked her or didn't like her. She only hoped she wouldn't make a complete fool of herself.

"All right. And, ready? Action!"

Martin had explained the language of picture making to Mari, so she knew these esoteric commands meant the camera would now start to crank, and she and Harrowgate would assume the roles of father and daughter. Given the strength of the actor's animosity toward her, Mari didn't feel any too confident about her first foray into the realm of fantasy, but she gave it her best shot.

"All right now, Miss Pottersby, as you know, I've just come home from a hard day's work in the mine."

Right. A single glance at the actor's soft, elegant hands put the lie to *that* assertion. Mari reminded herself she was acting, and said, "Right. And I run to the stove to pour you a cup of coffee." She did so, rising from the table, smiling at the man who was supposed to be her father, and going to the potbellied stove sitting in a triangle of wooden walls representing the cabin. This particular cabin had only two sides, so the camera could capture all the action going on indoors.

Speaking of the camera, it sure did make a racket. Even if speech could be recorded, nobody in an audience would be able to make out the words due to the ratcheting noise the camera made. And the sprockets made big chunking sounds when they flew out onto the ground. Mari thought how silly this all was and almost smiled.

She caught herself in time. As her father, Harrowgate was supposed to be recounting the miserable luck the day had brought him. She turned at the stove, as Martin had told her to do, put on a doleful expression, and thought to herself, *I'm sorry, Pa.* She didn't say it aloud, because she'd have felt too darned stupid speaking the words to the actor.

"Wonderful! You're doing a great job, Mari!"

Mari had to remind herself not to smile at Martin's encouraging words. But it was very nice of him to treat her so well.

"All right, Miss Pottersby, bring the coffee to me," Harrowgate prompted. No one would be able to see his lips move, because he'd sunk his head into his hands in a pose eloquent of despair. Mari was impressed.

She'd have been glad to bring him a cup of coffee too, but the pot was filled with water. She brought him a cup of water instead, and decided it was going to be fun to see the end product of all this pretense. Already she expected it would look authentic, even though everything going into its creation was as phony as a three-dollar bill. "Here's the coffee, Pa," she said, and then had to stop herself from grimacing. She hadn't meant to speak aloud.

"Thank you, Gloria." Gloria was the name of Mari's character in the picture. "You're a good daughter."

How sweet. And he sounded so natural, as if he didn't really hate her at all. Mari decided it was a darned good thing she didn't intend to make a career of acting, or she'd be confused all the time instead of just most of it. She found life difficult enough already, living among people who meant what they said.

"So, tell me what happened in the mine today." She almost tacked on another "Pa," but caught herself in time. The very word, *Pa,* reminded her of her own deceased father and made her sad. Her father had been ever so much more jolly than this bag of puff.

"It's bad, Gloria. We're almost played out."

Mari knew the feeling well. "Oh, dear, I'm so sorry."

Harrowgate shot her a scowl from between the fingers of his cupped hands. "You can do better than that. Wring your hands or something."

"Okay." She began to wring her hands and look distressed. "That better?"

"Don't move your lips so much. They'll be able to tell what you're saying."

Mari scarcely restrained herself from rolling her

eyes. He was probably right. He knew a whole lot more about this business than she did.

"Great, you two. Mari, press a hand to your heart. Your emotions have been wrung by the picture of your father in so dire a circumstance."

"Right." She stopped wringing her hands and pressed them both to her heart. What the heck. If one was good, two were undoubtedly better.

Martin confirmed her assumption by shouting, "Wonderful! You're doing great!"

Harrowgate stood up suddenly. Mari was expecting it, because she'd studied the story line carefully, but she still jumped back a pace. She hoped that was all right, because she couldn't help it.

"Great!" hollered Martin through his megaphone. "Wonderful! This is going to be a truly powerful scene!"

Powerful, eh? Well, Mari guessed it might be. She reached out and clutched Harrowgate's arm, as she was supposed to do. He shook her off, as *he* was supposed to do, and headed for the door set into the wall.

"No!" she cried. "Don't go!" Then she thanked her stars for makeup, because she knew she was blushing.

"Fantastic!" shouted Martin. "Perfect! You two are wonderful. Run after him, Mari! Try to stop him!"

She did so. Again Harrowgate shook her off. Then he flung the door open, turned around and, with one hand on the latch and the other splayed over his heart, said, "I'm going, child! I'm not going to let that foul fiend steal my mine from me!"

That foul fiend? Mari had heard of overacting, but she'd never seen it until this instant. Since it seemed appropriate, she decided to do some emoting of her own. She clasped her hands in a gesture of prayer and cried, "No, Pa! Please don't go to that dreadful place!" According to the script, Harrowgate was now going to visit a saloon, where he was going to get drunk and gamble away his mine—and his daughter.

Harrowgate didn't speak again, but wrenched the door shut with a slam that wobbled the scenery. Trying to imagine what a girl in this circumstance might do, Mari clapped her hands over her mouth, opened her eyes wide, and tried very hard to appear both horrified and anguished.

"Perfect! You captured the emotion brilliantly, Mari!"

As well she should, having lived it over and over again in her few short years on Earth. Still, she appreciated Martin's approval.

"Keep it up for another couple of seconds. Walk dejectedly back to the table, Mari, and sink down as if your legs won't hold you any longer. That'll be great!"

She did as Martin directed and, with dragging feet, went back to the table. She looked up once, caught sight of the terrible expression on Tony's face, and had no trouble at all dropping like a rock into the chair.

"Perfect! Splendid!" Martin shouted. "And—*cut!*"

The cameras stopped grinding, the sprockets stopped chunking, and Martin ran over to where Mari sat, blinking against the sun and wondering what was wrong with Tony.

Then she remembered her dog. Because there was no way she'd ask Martin about Tony, she said, "Where's Tony? I mean, Tiny?" Drat. She wished she'd stop doing that.

"You were wonderful, Mari! Great! You—I beg your pardon?"

She stood up and smiled. "Thanks, Martin. I appreciate your words, although I'm not sure I should believe them. I only asked where Tiny was. I don't see him."

Martin laughed heartily. "Oh, Tiny! He's okay. I've got one of the crew holding his leash. And you ought to believe me, because I'm telling the truth. You were wonderful. Wait until you see yourself. You were great! Perfect!"

Wonderful, great, perfect. Mari'd never been any of those things before, at least not that she could remember. Her teachers used to complain all the time about her daydreaming. A couple of them had even whopped her knuckles with their rulers. She'd never thought of herself as anything but a no-account whose head drifted perpetually in the clouds. Except when her body was in the mine.

"Thank you."

"You're more than welcome. I think we got that in one take, too. Now comes the scene where your father comes home after spending all night in the saloon. He's even more miserable than he was when he left, you'll recall, because he's not merely drunk, but he's gambled away everything he values, including you."

Mari shivered involuntarily. It wasn't because of the weather, which was searingly hot, but because of the abysmal portrait Martin had just painted in words. Powerful things, words. She thanked her stars her father hadn't been a drinker. She said, "Okay."

"Super. I'm so glad you agreed to work with us." Martin strode off, tapping his bullhorn against his leg and looking happy as a clam.

Mari thought he had a very pleasant nature, and one that was easy to be around. She wished some of the other people connected with this picture were more like him. She shot a glance at Tony, but he still looked like he wanted to kill something. Mari had a hunch it was her whom he wished to slay, but she had no idea why. She'd not done anything wrong that she could remember.

With a sigh, she settled in the chair ready to assume

the pose of the anxiously waiting daughter whenever Martin gave her the signal.

Tony scowled at the cabin set and beat himself up inwardly. For the love of God why had he lost control of himself this morning? If he did that again, Mari was sure to get scared and back away from him. Unless she ran off screaming, which was another possibility.

He glowered at the broiling-hot set and called himself every vile name he could come up with. What had he been thinking of when he'd grabbed her like that?

He hadn't been thinking at all. He'd been so damned glad to see her, all thought had fled, and he'd reached for what he craved. That what he craved was Mari and that he had no right to embrace her hadn't entered into the equation.

She was damned good as the leading lady in this picture. Tony didn't know how he felt about that. He feared she might be too successful for him. Hell, if she got to be famous and sought after as an actress, what would she need him for?

Not, of course, that she needed him now. At least she didn't think she did. But that was only because she hadn't stopped to consider how much better her life could be if she'd allow him into it.

Blast, there he went again, thinking about permanence. Permanence meant marriage for a woman like Mari. He sincerely doubted that he'd ever be able to persuade her into a more casual alliance, because such affairs weren't considered proper in her realm of society. They weren't considered proper in his, either, but that didn't seem to stop a whole lot of people from establishing illicit alliances. Mari was too obstinate to go for anything like that.

It occurred to him that a Mari without her strict values wouldn't be the Mari he wanted, which was a moderately discouraging thought. He wasn't sure where that left him, but he feared it might be without Mari.

Something on the set caught his eye, and his gaze zeroed in on the left cabin wall. Was it swaying slightly? Maybe it was rocking in the wind.

"Balderdash," he growled. There wasn't a hint of a breeze today, much less a wind. He started walking closer to the set.

Martin had given the command, Ben had begun cranking the camera, and the god-awful noise of filming filled the air. Harrowgate staggered through the door, slamming it behind him, and Mari ran to meet him, then backed away, as if his condition horrified her. As well it might, Tony thought cynically. Harrowgate was a pompous old bore and nearly always made Tony feel horrible.

He did a pretty good job as Mari's sodden father, though. When he faked a slap that was supposed to send her to the ground, it looked so real, Tony almost objected. He didn't, thank God. Then Harrowgate staggered back out the door and slammed it behind him again.

"Good God!"

He wasn't imagining things. That damned wall was going to collapse—and it was aimed straight at Mari.

As he started running toward the set, Tony called out, "Mari! Get out of there! The set's falling!"

Tony was vaguely aware of other people, at first startled, then appalled, and then in motion. Mari herself looked up, surprised, blinked, and glanced around, obviously wondering what this interruption had to do with the scene being filmed.

"Move! Get the hell out of there!" Tony bellowed.

Damn, he wasn't going to get to her in time. He skidded to a stop that churned up a mountain of dust when the wall toppled, his heart in his throat. *"No!"* he thundered.

That did no good at all, naturally. He heard Mari scream when she finally understood what was happening. He thought, but he wasn't sure, that he saw her lift her arms to cover her head. The wall went down with a crash like two locomotives running into each other at full speed. The cloud of dust was so huge it blocked out the sunshine.

George Peters, the set designer and builder, raced past him, and Tony shuddered once, then sprinted to catch up with him. If George had built a faulty set, Tony would kill him with his bare hands. Since meeting George, he'd been under the impression that the young man was both a brilliant set designer and a careful carpenter. But this . . . God, if Mari was hurt, Tony didn't know what he'd do.

"Mari!"

Nothing answered his shout.

Tiny bounded onto the scene from somewhere and ran directly over to the crash site. He began snuffling around the fallen wall as if he, too, were trying to reach Mari.

"Help me lift this thing," George said. His voice was so full of consternation that Tony decided to wait awhile before killing him.

Martin joined them and reached out to grab hold of the massive structure. "Good God, what happened?"

George's voice trembled when he answered. "I don't know. If it's something I did, I'll—I'll . . ." He didn't say what he'd do, undoubtedly because he didn't know. It didn't matter; Tony'd do it for him.

"Everybody grab," Tony commanded. "I'll give the signal. When I say 'three,' lift the damned wall."

A variety of grunts and noises signified agreement

to this proposal. Several other crew members had joined Tony, Martin, and George.

With his heart pounding out a death march, Tony said, "One. Two. *Three!*"

Putting all their strength into it, the men raised the fallen wall. Whining piteously, Tiny dashed underneath, presumably to get to his mistress.

Straining because the wall was heavy, Tony managed to call out, "Mari? Mari, are you there?"

Again, no answer came forth. His whole being cried out in agony. "Mari! Dammit, answer me!"

Tiny emerged first, dusty but unbowed, grinning and wagging his tail. Tony blinked, sure he was imagining that grin.

His heart leaped almost out of his chest when a bedraggled Mari crawled out from under the wall. "There's no need to swear at me, Tony," she said tartly. "I've just been through an ordeal. I don't need people swearing at me, too."

As soon as she was free from the wall, Tony let go, wheeled around, and grabbed her to his chest. "Mari! Thank God! I thought you'd been crushed."

Tiny jumped on them both in an ecstasy of doggy delight. Tony scarcely noticed. He figured Mari's dog had as much right to be happy as he did.

She wriggled in his grasp, and he realized they were in a very public place. From all over town people were rushing toward the scene of the big crash. The huge noise made by the wall when it fell had been heard throughout Mojave Wells.

"I'm okay, Tony," she said. "Please don't make a big scene. It's embarrassing."

"A big scene? Good God, Mari, that wall fell on you. I was afraid you'd be crushed." It went against the grain, but he let her go.

Dust covered her from head to foot. It clung to her

white makeup like frosting on a cake. She tried to brush it away from her eyes. "I must look awful."

"What you look like doesn't matter. How in the name of glory did you manage to come away from that wreck unscathed?"

Martin, George, Ben, and at least three dozen other people had run up to the two of them and were now hovering around. They didn't completely invade their space, but left a smallish circle of empty ground around them. Tony wondered if his inner ferocity was helping to hold them at bay, but he didn't dwell on it.

Peering down at herself and beginning to test her limbs, Mari said, "I'm not sure I'm unscathed, but at least I'm alive."

George broke out of the circle, almost jumping at Mari, and grabbed her hands. "God, Mari, I don't know what happened. I'm so sorry. If it's anything that I designed wrong, I—I—" Again, he ran out of words.

Following George's precedent, Martin also came up to the couple. Glumly, Tony decided his aura must not be all that powerful. If he had his way, the crowd would disperse, leaving the two of them all alone in Mojave Wells. Then he and Mari would discuss the matter, dress her wounds, if any, rest up, and come to some kind of conclusion about the cause of the accident. No such luck.

"I can't believe the wall didn't crush you, Mari," Martin told her. Tony could tell how shaken he was because he'd gone white as a sheet and his hands were trembling when he wiped his brow with his handkerchief. As soon as he'd stuffed it back into his pocket, he started pulling on a tuft of hair.

Taking a clean handkerchief from Tony, who'd finally thought to hand her one, Mari pondered the near-catastrophic accident. "I didn't know what was going on at first. I heard someone holler at me—"

"That was me," Tony said gruffly, unaccountably miffed that she didn't already know.

She shot him a small smile. "Oh, yes, I remember now. I remember it was your voice, and I wondered what I'd done wrong this time."

How embarrassing. Did she really think of him as some kind of mean-tempered disciplinarian? Tony guessed he'd better work on that aspect of their relationship.

What relationship? Good God, he was so confused at the moment, he didn't know whether he was coming or going.

"When you yelled again—I don't remember what you said—I realized the set was collapsing and dived under the table."

"The table," Tony whispered. "Of course."

"The table," said Martin, sounding relieved.

"The table," George muttered. "Thank God we used that old metal thing. If we'd used a wooden one, chances are it would have been crushed under the weight of the wall, and you with it."

Mari shuddered, and Tony decided he didn't give a rap if people started talking. He put an arm around her. In order to give the impression of a brother rather than a lover, he said, "Here, Mari, let me help you back to the inn. You ought to wash up and see if you need medical care."

"Right." Martin snapped to attention. "I'll call that doctor who came when Gilman was taken sick."

Gilman? Oh, yeah, the first director. Tony frowned. Something was definitely wrong with this production. "Thanks, Martin. I'll get her inside."

"If it's all right with you," George said, speaking to Martin and Tony, "I'll take a look and try to see what happened to that set. It shouldn't have collapsed like that."

"Good idea," Martin said.

A suspicion touched Tony, and he asked Martin, "Say, are those insurance fellows still here?"

Martin and Tony shared a glance, and Tony saw that Martin understood his unasked question. To George, he added, "You might want to get the sheriff to look at it with you."

George, too, caught on. "My God, you don't think it was sabotage, do you?"

Mari gasped. As well she might, thought Tony grimly. She might have been killed. "I don't know," Tony said. "But I really want to. If the insurance guys have gone, at least make sure the sheriff inspects it thoroughly. If it is sabotage, whoever did it almost committed murder today."

This time the entire crowd, which included everyone who lived in Mojave Wells unless Tony was completely deluded, gasped. George looked stricken.

"Right," he said. "Sure. I'll get the sheriff first. He might want to post men at the scene of the accident so nothing is disturbed."

"Good." Although Tony wasn't ready to give George a pardon yet, he did give him a smile. "That's a good thought, George." In his heart of hearts, Tony didn't think George was at fault here. But the lad was young, and he might have been careless. Tony wasn't sure if he'd rather they find the accident had been caused by George's mistake or by a saboteur. If it was George, they could probably consider the episode ended, and it was a certainty that George would never make the same mistake again.

If it turned out to be vandals or saboteurs, the good Lord alone knew when or where they'd strike next.

Sixteen

Too shaken by her recent brush with injury or death to protest, Mari allowed herself to be led upstairs by Tony to his room. There were too many people around for such a maneuver to be improper anyway. Darn it.

Mari shook herself, knowing that if she allowed her present state of agitation to dictate her actions, she'd be in Tony's bed in no time at all. That would be a worse calamity than having a wall fall on her, albeit not as unpleasant.

"Really," she said, "I'm all right. I don't need to lie down."

Tony, with help from Judy Nelson, had led her into the hotel, where she'd had brandy forced upon her and been made to sit still while Judy and Mrs. Nelson palpated every exposed surface on her body as Tony watched, eagle-eyed. It had been very embarrassing.

"Don't be silly," Mrs. Nelson had snapped when she'd said as much. "You might have been killed out there, Mari Pottersby, and I don't take it kindly when people are injured on my property."

"I'm not injured," Mari had muttered to no avail.

It didn't seem fair to her that she, the one upon whom the wall had almost fallen, should be ignored while everyone else ordered her about. If her wits hadn't been so rattled, she'd not have permitted it. Her wits *were* rattled, though, and she couldn't drum up a coherent protest to save her life.

At least Tiny wasn't bullying her. He'd trotted along with her wherever people led her, sat next to her wherever she sat, and laid his huge head on her lap whenever possible. She'd petted him at every opportunity and would have told him how much she appreciated his unequivocal, and undemanding, love except that she didn't want to hurt anybody else's feelings.

"I wish this place had an elevator," Tony grumbled as they walked, with excruciating deliberation, up the staircase.

"Your room's only on the second floor, for Pete's sake." Mari hadn't meant to sound peeved, but she was getting sick of people treating her like an invalid. The blasted wall had fallen at least an hour ago, and thanks to George's metal table, she was totally unscathed. Almost totally. She admitted to a few bumps, bruises, and scrapes, but they were nothing. She was fine now. "If you'd only let go of me, I could get there in a couple of seconds."

Not that she wanted him to let go, but the circumstances aggravated her. She'd be happy to have him hold her if he were, say, wildly in love with her or something, not because she'd had an accident.

As if. Mari told herself to stop dreaming immediately, because, she reminded herself as she'd been doing forever, daydreams only led to disappointment, as she already knew too well.

"Quit complaining," Tony grumped. "You've endured a bad accident, and it's time you left off moaning and groaning just because we want to make sure you're not seriously injured."

"If I were seriously injured," Mari ground out between her teeth, "I'd hurt somewhere."

"Not necessarily." Tony sounded as if he were trying

to convince himself. "You might have . . . internal injuries. Or something."

"Right." The truth of the matter was that Mari was exhausted. There was something about stark terror, even if it only lasted five minutes or so, that wore a body out. What she really wanted was to take a bath and get all the makeup and dust off her, wrap herself in something clean, loose, and comfortable, and sit on Tony's lap while he petted her. After a few hours—or years—of that, she might feel good enough to finish the picture. Maybe not.

She didn't tell Tony any of that.

"Here we are," Tony said, fumbling for his key. "As soon as the doctor arrives, we'll know better what's going on."

"Fiddle." This was insane.

Insane or not, Mari couldn't help but have an unsettled feeling about the wall incident, and it wasn't only because it had nearly flattened her. All these episodes weren't natural. Oh, sure, accidents happened. But not so many, so often, and having to do with one subject. It seemed to her that a malign force was at work here. Somebody had it in for the Peerless Studio, or at least for this production of *Lucky Strike*.

But she was too tired and wobbly to think about evil beings at the moment. Meekly, she allowed Tony to help her into his room, and she didn't even balk when he told her to sit on the bed.

"I'll take off your shoes and stockings," he told her, clearly making his voice tough to forestall any argument from her.

She was too bushed to argue. When he knelt in front of her and reached for her foot, she lifted it obligingly. He set it on his bent knee and unlaced her shoe, and Mari's eyes filled with tears. She brushed them away, angry with herself for succumbing yet again to a fit of emotion.

What in the world was wrong with her? She'd lived a tough life; she ought to be tough, too. But she wasn't, and when she saw Tony there in front of her, in a pose now considered a classical one for proposals of a romantic nature, she gave up pretending.

It was all too much for her. The tears continued to fall, and she kept wiping them away, all the time hoping Tony wouldn't look up and notice. Blast it, this wasn't fair.

"Other foot." He didn't glance at her face, thank heaven, and Mari lifted her other foot.

He unlaced the shoe on that one, too. Mari saw him lick his lips.

"All right. Now for the stockings."

It was too much. Tears be damned. Mari snapped, "I'll do them." She wasn't going to allow any man, and particularly not this one, to whom she felt an almost violent physical attraction, to roll her stockings down. She might be poor, and she might have no knowledge of how society snobs acted, but she knew proper behavior from improper. "Turn around."

"For God's sake." He was peeved now.

Too bad. "Darn it, Tony, turn around."

He did. Mari lifted her skirt, untied her garter, and rolled down first one stocking and then the other. Her legs, she noticed, sported a variety of colorful bruises. Swell. Just what she needed. It wasn't bad enough that she had to slave away in a worthless mine eleven months out of the year. Now, during the one month when she might expect at least some respite from her toils, she got battered by the scenery.

"All right," she growled when she was through. "Now what?" She plumped herself back on the bed and scowled. She expected she now bore muddy tracks down her face from tears slogging through dust and makeup, and she didn't even care. Much.

Tony turned around—at least when he'd complied with her command, he'd not cheated and peeked—and scowled down at her. She saw his frown vanish and an expression of concern replace it. "Why are you crying? Where do you hurt?"

She lifted her chin and glowered up at him. "I don't hurt anywhere." Except her feelings. They hurt like fire. "I'm just tired of everything."

Comprehensive. But comparatively true. At the moment, Mari longed for peace. Tranquility. Respite. All of those delicious things she, being who she was, couldn't expect from life. Ever.

Tony surprised her by sitting next to her on the bed and encircling her shoulders with a strong arm. "Here, Mari, I know you've been through it today. If you need to cry, go ahead. It's all right. Hell, women cry all the time."

Oh, they did, did they? Mari Pottersby didn't. Mari was tough. She was rugged. She was strong and independent and steadfast. She was . . .

Who was she trying to kid? She was a puddle of slush inside. Balling her hands into fists, she concentrated on not crying. She wouldn't cry. She wouldn't. Never again.

"Oh!" she blurted out, suddenly forgetting all about tears. "Where's Tiny?"

"Tiny?"

"Tiny. He was with us downstairs. Did he stay there? Why didn't he come up with us?" He'd been dogging, so to speak, her footsteps ever since she'd crawled out from underneath that blasted wall.

A scratch came at the door, accompanied by a rumbling whine. Mari, her relief so sudden and intense she became lightheaded, whispered, "Thank God."

Tony didn't. Rather, he rose from the bed in what looked like a huff and stomped to the door. When he opened it, Tiny bounded in and made a flying leap at Mari and the bed, sending her over backward.

"Damn it! Why don't you train that beast?"

Although she couldn't see him, since she was being joyously greeted by her monumental dog, Mari knew Tony was furious.

"Don't blame him," she said. "He's only glad to be with us again. I think you probably shut the door on him."

"I'm not blaming him. I'm blaming you. Anybody with a dog that big owes it to the rest of humanity to train it."

It was a struggle, but Mari managed to get herself upright again. Tiny lay on Tony's bed, grinning up at Tony, and whipping his tail back and forth so hard he dislodged the pillows.

Feeling much better now that her dog had returned to her side, or her back, Mari said, "Nuts. You're just jealous because you don't have a nice dog like Tiny." She didn't resent it when Tony grimaced with disgust, because she'd expected him to do something of the sort.

Before hostilities could build into something explosive, Martin arrived with the doctor, a kindly old soul named Crabtree who'd been treating the ills of Mojave Wells's citizens for as long as most of them could remember.

Mari lifted a scraped hand in salute. "H'lo, Doc."

Dr. Crabtree shook his head. "You look like hell, Mari Pottersby. You already knew that, I suppose."

She grinned, feeling better already. "Yup. I had a peek in the mirror."

"To conduct a proper examination, I think it would behoove us if you'd get that makeup off your face and wash up a bit." As he set his black bag down on the night table, he eyed her closely. "Unless you think you have injuries that ought to be attended to immediately."

Mari shook her head and rose from the bed. "No. I think I'm fine, actually. But I know the studio wants to make sure their goods haven't been damaged, so I'll retire to the bathroom for a few minutes." She thought of something. "Um, what shall I wear, Doc? This dress?" She glanced down at the frock she wore. Because of the poverty of the character she played in the picture, the dress had been shabby to begin with, but it hadn't started out this dirty.

"No. You ought to have a robe of some kind."

"You can use one of mine, Mari."

Mari was glad she hadn't washed up yet, because when Tony spoke, she blushed, but she figured the makeup and dirt would disguise it. In an attempt to pretend she wasn't embarrassed, she merely smiled and said, "Thank you," when he handed her a silk dressing gown that probably cost more than Mari had spent on provender during her entire nineteen years.

The bathroom was something. Mari had never bathed in anything but a wooden tub. This porcelain thing was a work of art. She filled it, wishing all the while she didn't have to hurry. The water, warm from the tap, felt like heaven when she dipped her toe in it. When she submerged her body, she wished she could stay there forever.

Such could not be, however. Grabbing the sweet-smelling soap lying in the dish and lathering her arms, Mari thought it was a good thing she'd committed to doing this one picture only, or she might become addicted to luxuries. And that, given her role in life, would never do.

Her role in life. She scowled as she scrubbed makeup and dirt from her face.

What was her role in life, anyhow? Was she doomed

to struggle fruitlessly in that stupid mine for the rest of it? It sounded a dismal future to her. Yet she'd promised her father as he lay dying that she'd keep his dream alive.

"Pa's dead," she reminded herself as she splashed clean water on her face to remove the suds. "And he'll never know."

But she'd know. If she turned her back on the Marigold Mine, Mari feared the guilt would haunt her forever, and she'd end up hating herself. She had enough to contend with, what with poverty, lack of family support, and unrequited love—damn Tony Ewing, anyhow—without adding self-loathing to the mix.

It was all too much for her. She told herself to stop thinking and wash and almost succeeded in obeying herself. Probably her state of exhaustion helped. As she lathered her hair, which was dulled with dust, she allowed herself to suspend worry and merely feel for a few minutes.

Tub baths were really quite delightful. She could hardly imagine the fabulous wealth that allowed people like, say, Tony Ewing, to take tub baths whenever they felt so inclined. Mari thought if she were ever to have access to a bathtub and hot and cold running water, she'd spend the rest of her life soaking in it.

This wasn't the day for that, however. As quickly as possible, she finished washing the makeup and filth away, then rose, dripping, from the water and looked around for a towel. Ah, there was one. She reached for it, noticed the initials *A.W.* embroidered in fancy script on it. "Anthony Ewing," she whispered, and buried her face in the pillowy softness of Tony's towel.

She was drying her body with Tony Ewing's own personal towel. She felt both decadent and fortunate in so doing, and she allowed a couple of fantasies to keep her company as she toweled herself dry. Then she brushed her hair with Tony Ewing's very own hairbrush, and her fantasies multiplied.

What, she wondered, would it be like to have enough money? To carry the question further, what would it be like to have lots of money?

Mari's imagination, always pretty good, stumbled as she tried to conceive of such a scenario. Her life had been so restricted that, for her, luxury would be indoor plumbing. Running water of any kind would be nice. Hot water was so outrageously off the scale of what the Mari Pottersbys of the world could expect that she couldn't manage to expand her fantasy that far.

Enough money to go to the doctor when she was sick would be nice. Doc Crabtree didn't mind being paid with chickens, but Mari really needed the chickens for herself, to eat and to sell to the Mojave Inn. She knew, because she read extensively, that most middle-class families in America had at least one person to help with the housework. She wouldn't need that, since she lived in a one-room cabin, but she sure wouldn't mind being able to buy a meal at the Mojave Inn every once in a while.

She chided herself for being stingy with her fantasies. Heck, if she was going to imagine, she might as well do it big. So she imagined a real house with more than one room. It would be nice to have a separate kitchen. And a bathroom. And electricity! The weather in this desert might almost be tolerable if one could stir the air a bit with an electrical fan.

By the time she knotted her still-damp hair into a bun and pinned it in place, Mari had succeeded in expanding her daydream to include a house with a green lawn and a motorcar, so she could take trips to pretty places like, say, Pasadena. It was lovely there, near the mountains. And so green. Mari wondered if everyone who lived in deserts craved green as she did.

She felt almost decadent as she slipped into Tony's robe. She'd never worn silk before. It felt like heaven against her skin. With a sigh, she opened the door and stood there, slightly taken aback when a room full of men turned to stare at her. She frowned and turned to Dr. Crabtree. "Where do you want to do this examination, Doc?"

Her prosaic question seemed to jolt the men out of their trance. Dr. Crabtree cleared his throat and said, "I suppose we can carry it out here, if these gentlemen will kindly leave us be. I don't think you want an audience." He smiled at her in his kindly way.

"Good Lord, no." Mari shuddered. This was going to be bad enough without Martin and Tony and Ben and everybody else in the world watching.

A knock came at the door before the men could get themselves organized and depart. Martin was closest, and he opened the door. Frowning and clearly upset, George entered the room with a graceless lurch. He held his hat in his hand, and his face was so pale, Mari wondered if he, and not she, might benefit from a medical examination.

Martin took George by the shoulder, his face expressing concern over his colleague's state of mind. "What is it, George?"

George, whose brown eyes held an intense expression at the most relaxed of times, now appeared almost maniacally fervent. "Sabotage," he declared, his voice rasping and sharp-edged. "Deliberate, cold-blooded sabotage."

All talking ceased. The only discernible noise in the room was Tiny's tail as it swished back and forth across the floor. Nothing, not even deliberate sabotage, could get Tiny down.

Finally, Tony broke the silence with a short, brutal curse. The men swarmed around George. Dr. Crabtree

shooed them out of the room to discuss the matter else-
where, and directed Mari to sit on the bed so he could
test her reflexes and eyesight, and judge for sure if
she'd been concussed by the falling wall.

Mari wanted to rush off with the men and hear what
George had found out. Darn it, she hated being left
out.

It was a glum group that gathered in a corner of the
Mojave Inn's dining room. Understanding the needs of
men, Mr. Nelson dismissed his wife's objections and
carried over a tray of mugs, frothy with beer foam.
Tony tipped him handsomely, grateful for the proprie-
tor's consideration.

"My old man's going to have to know what's going
on here," he said to Martin unhappily. "I haven't called
him yet and was hoping I wouldn't have to; but if somebody's seriously trying to undermine the picture, he'll
have to be told. I'll try to get a long-distance trunk call
put through before the end of the day."

"I suppose you'd better." Martin took a swig of his
beer, looking more grim than Tony could remember
seeing him. "It's his money, after all."

Feeling apologetic about it, Tony agreed. "Right. I'm
sorry, Martin."

Martin waved away the apology. "It's okay, Tony.
This is serious, and our backers need to know about it.
I've already placed a call to Phin. I'm hoping the long-
distance operator will ring back soon with the connection."

"Yeah, he ought to know what's going on, too."

Martin uttered something between a growl and a
snort. "I'm going to ask him to send out two or three
private detectives. And maybe a couple of other men
to work as guards at night."

Tony lifted his eyebrow. "Good idea. Why didn't I think of that?"

Martin grinned at him. "It's not your baby. You're only minding your daddy's money. My career and the future of Peerless might rest on this venture."

George, who had remained silent and seemed shrouded in gloom, shuddered. "Career?" he muttered. "I don't even have a career yet, and it's being ruined as we speak."

That put everything in a disagreeable light. Tony frowned into his beer mug. "You're right. Blast it, I sure hope your detectives can find out who's behind all of this vandalism, Martin. This whole series of malicious acts is an outrage."

With a sigh, Martin said, "It's gone beyond vandalism, I think. It looks to me as though whoever's doing this is seeking outright ruin for Peerless."

"Hmmm." Tony eyed Martin. "You don't think Edison has anything to do with this series of . . . mishaps, do you?" They weren't mishaps, but Tony couldn't think of another word to describe them.

For a moment, Martin gazed off into the gloom of the dining room; luncheon was still a couple of hours away, and the lights hadn't been turned on. Then he shrugged. "I don't know. Edison's more likely to use the courts and claims of patent infringement to undercut his competitors. I've never heard of him doing overt malicious mischief to a rival's production."

Tony downed the rest of his beer. "Yeah. I never have, either."

"And if whoever was behind today's villainy had succeeded in killing Mari, you can be sure that would be the end of Peerless."

Tony's heart contracted so suddenly and painfully that he couldn't have responded even if he could have thought of words to say, which he couldn't.

George didn't speak either. He only moaned softly.

When Tony looked up at last, he beheld Mari standing and blinking at the door to the dining room. She'd come from the light-infused lobby area, and probably couldn't see the men in their corner. She'd dressed in the clothes she'd worn to town that morning. He rose abruptly, and his chair scraped the floor with a noise that made Martin and George jump and Mari turn toward the sound.

He hurried over and took both of her hands in his. She appeared a little shocked by this intimacy, but Tony didn't care. She might have had the life crushed out of her this morning, and it had scared the bejesus out of him. Although he still wasn't able to put words to his innermost feelings, he did know good and well he wasn't going to let her get away from him without putting up a damned good fight first.

"What did the doctor say?" he asked before she'd had a chance to find her wits. "Are you all right? Is anything broken? Was there a chance of concussion? What about bruises? Are you sore? Do you need medication? Carbolic? Headache powders? Bandages? Anything?"

She stared at him as if he'd lost his mind. Which he might well have done. He'd never experienced this desperate need to protect another human being before he met Mari. Not only that, but the need extended only to Mari, although it encompassed her and everything she was, did, owned, and thought. Even her stupid dog.

"Um, I'm fine, thanks." Glancing at the table, she squinted for a moment, then said, "Oh, is that Martin? And George? Is he there? What happened?"

"What happened? The damned wall fell on top of you!" Modesty was all right in Tony's book, but this was pushing things. She knew damned well what had happened to her, and this pose of coy timidity didn't wash with him.

She gave him an "oh-for-goodness'-sake" look. "I know the wall fell, Tony. What I was asking was, did George discover *why* it fell."

"Oh." That made sense. He guessed he was being slightly aggressive about his protector's mode. He took her by the elbow and guided her to the table he'd lately left. "Yes, he did find out. I'll let George tell you about it."

He pulled out a chair for Mari to sit upon and asked her, "Would you like something to drink? We're having beer, but—"

"Beer?" Mari's eyes opened up as wide as platters, and she grinned. "Good heavens, however did you persuade Mrs. Nelson to serve you beer before four o'clock?"

Martin chuckled. Tony, who was too worried about Mari's health to find much of anything amusing, answered her question seriously. "Mr. Nelson thought we could use it to calm our nerves."

"That was nice of him." Mari thought for a second. "I could use some lemonade, if there's any made. I'm awfully thirsty. If there's none made, I'll just take water."

If there's any made? Tony would see to it that Mari got lemonade, if Mrs. Nelson and her whole tribe had to grow the lemon trees, harvest the lemons, grind the sugar beets to powder, and dig a well to get water for it. "Be right back," he said. Before he'd taken more than a couple of steps, he turned and asked, his brow furrowed, "Do you need anything else? A bite to eat? Crackers? A sandwich? Something to settle your stomach? Anything?"

Again, her expression told him she doubted his sanity. "Um, no, thanks. I'm fine. Lemonade would be nice."

Tony wheeled around and beat a retreat to the

kitchen, where he barged in, thus surprising Mrs. Nelson and Judy, who were making preparations for lunch. He demanded and received a whole pitcher of lemonade and then went to the icehouse behind the hotel and chipped out a bucket of ice in case Mari wanted it.

When he returned to the table, he stopped in his tracks when he observed Martin patting Mari's hand. He was about to roar over to the table and demand satisfaction from Martin—what kind of satisfaction, he didn't know, since men no longer fought duels over women—when he caught Martin's words.

Laughing softly, Martin said, "No, he's not crazy, Mari. I think he might be developing some tender feelings for you, though."

Now Mari looked at *Martin* as if he'd gone mad. Dammit. Tony tromped up to the table, annoyed that Martin should be talking about him behind his back. Although, he had to admit, he was glad Martin seemed to have no designs on Mari. He'd hate it if he lost Martin's friendship or had to shoot him or anything.

"Here's your lemonade," he growled, and plunked the pitcher on the table.

Mari jumped back a bit, startled. "Oh! Thank you, Tony. I'm not sure I can drink all of that."

"It doesn't matter," he grumped. "Here's some ice." He put the bowl of ice down with a loud clunk.

"My goodness, thank you. This is a real treat, getting to drink ice-cold lemonade. Maybe I should have a wall fall on me every day if I get rewarded with such luxuries."

All three men stared at her, and Mari blushed. "I didn't mean that." She fixed herself a glass of lemonade, liberally cooled with chipped ice, and smiled at Tony, who'd resumed his chair. "Thank you very much. I really appreciate this."

Tony nodded and tried not to look like a lovesick

schoolboy. Martin's words had horrified him. Was his attraction to Mari so obvious? He turned abruptly to George. "Did you tell her about the wall?"

George nodded gloomily. "Yes. I told her about the crosspieces that had been sawed nearly through."

Martin took up the theme. "It's as though whoever did it didn't want anyone to see what he'd done. It was very subtle. The wall might hold up during several rehearsals or even several scenes, but sooner or later, when Harrowgate slammed the door, the crosspieces would break, and the set would collapse."

Mari set her lemonade glass on the table and rubbed her hands up and down her arms, which had apparently sprouted gooseflesh. Tony clenched his jaws. He wanted to do that. The rubbing of her arms part.

"That's—that's really awful," she said in a small voice. "I guess whoever's doing these things doesn't care if people get hurt."

"Obviously," snarled Tony, feeling excessively crabby. Dammit, he wanted to be alone with Mari. He needed to ask her every detail of her doctor's examination, to learn exactly what Crabtree had told her, to find out if she was supposed to be resting, or sleeping, or what. Dammit, she ought to have a specialist look at her. He wondered if he could get someone from New York.

When Mari and Martin glanced at him briefly, Tony realized where his thoughts had flown and concentrated on the conversation. A flicker of a smile crossed Martin's face before he said to Mari, "We're not going to resume work on the picture until detectives arrive from Los Angeles. That will probably be tomorrow, depending on how quickly Phin can get them here."

"Detectives?" Her eyes opened wide, and for a split second, Tony wished he were a detective and could have such an effect on her. Then he mentally slapped himself and told himself to get a grip.

"I'm going to post guards, too," Martin told her. "I'm sick of this. It's getting dangerous. We've got to protect our investment, but even more important, we have to protect our people. We all nearly had heart attacks this morning when we saw that wall fall."

Mari shivered. "You're not alone. I couldn't believe what was happening."

Suddenly, Tony stood. "I'm taking you home in the motorcar, Mari. Do you have to get anything together first?"

The three people still seated at the table gaped up at him. Blast. He frowned at them. "We're not doing any more filming today, and Mari needs to rest."

Hesitantly, Martin nodded his agreement. "Right. Sure." He turned to Mari. "Do you need anything, Mari? Food? Medicine?"

Dammit, Tony was supposed to ask her those things, not Martin. He snarled, "I'll take care of Mari."

Again, a fleeting grin touched Martin's lips. "Okay, Tony." He kept his tone of voice mild, as he might do if he were dealing with a lunatic.

Tony resented it. He glowered at Mari. "Come on, Mari."

"I haven't finished my lemonade," she pointed out without rancor. "Can you wait just a minute?"

"I guess so." He thought of something that would prove to be an impediment if not taken care of immediately. "I'll ask Mrs. Nelson to pack something for your dinner, and find Tiny."

She smiled up at him, which almost made life worth living. "Thank you. That would be swell."

Seventeen

Tiny, in the backseat of Tony's elegant black motorcar, stuck his head out one open window while his tail churned a whirlwind out the open window on the other side of the car. Mari, who'd been through a great deal, now felt peaceful and pleasantly sleepy. She wished she could stay in Tony's machine and have him drive her and her dog around for hours. Being a passenger in a moving vehicle could be a very relaxing experience.

"Your dog likes the fast life," Tony commented with a grin.

Mari glanced first at Tiny, then at Tony. Tony was absolutely perfect for this setting. At ease, both with himself and the world, confident, young, and handsome, he belonged to a future filled with motorcars, moving pictures, investments, and modern inventions.

She sometimes believed herself to be mired in the past. And it wasn't even her past. It belonged to her father's generation. What's more, it hadn't paid off then, and it didn't show any signs of paying off now or ever. She sighed.

"Yes, he likes riding in your motorcar."

He slanted her a peek and a grin. "And you, Mari? Do you like riding in my motorcar?"

Oh, boy, she *loved* riding in his car. She said, "Sure. It's fun."

He nodded, but she noticed his grin fled. Should she have been more enthusiastic? But she didn't want him to know how much of a crush she was developing on him, if *crush* it was. *Crush* was a safe word for a condition in which Mari felt not at all safe. Besides, crushes didn't last. She feared what she felt for Tony was going to last far too long.

Frightened by the noise of the motor, a jackrabbit sailed across the road in front of the car and sped off, sending Tiny into a gleeful frenzy. Her dog's antics took Mari's mind away from fruitless contemplation, and she laughed. So did Tony. She sighed again.

If only, she thought, this day could last. Just like this. Never coming to a conclusion, and not having to start over again with all of its attendant frights and flurries. This was so—nice, she guessed was the right word, although it didn't exactly capture her mood. Blissful? Sweet? Heavenly? Yeah. Those, too.

It occurred to her that while she'd been spinning fantasies, she might have included Tony and his motorcar in at least one of them. But like a grand house in Pasadena and lots of money, Tony was so far beyond her reach that it seemed idiotic even to daydream about him.

"There's the old homestead."

Tony's voice penetrated the fuzz of Mari's thoughts, and she sat up straight and looked. "Oh, yes." There it was, all right. "The old homestead."

How poetic a phrase for that pile of junk. And how pathetic that her whole life contained so little more than that. She took herself to task for sinking into the dismals. She even tried to convince herself that more people lived in something like her circumstances than in Tony's.

That was all well and good. But Mari suspected in her heart of hearts that not too darned many people were as poor as she, or as alone in the world. What a fruitless line of thought, but that didn't make it inaccurate.

She shook herself and reached around to pet Tiny. "We're almost home, boy, and you can go find yourself another jackrabbit to chase." And kill. She didn't add that part, sensing that a reference to Tiny's predatory habits might spoil the mood, whatever it was.

Tony braked the motorcar in front of Mari's door. Since Mari had lived in the cabin forever, and since she was used to it, she seldom noticed its almost perfect shabbiness. She noticed today. Turning to Tony, she said with a wry grin, "Not exactly what you're used to, is it?"

He caught and held her gaze for a minute before answering. "No." As if shaking off a mood, he hooked the basket packed with provender that Mrs. Nelson had provided and that had been sitting on the front seat between them. "Here. Let's have a picnic."

"A picnic sounds nice, but it's going to be dark pretty soon." She tried to sound enthusiastic but feared she didn't quite make it.

Mari's idea of a picnic, fostered by copious novel reading, should be held on a quilt spread out at the seashore. Or on some vast green lawn somewhere overlooking a lake. Something like that. Squinting at her cabin, the two half whiskey barrels in which she'd planted geraniums in an effort to perk the place up, and the bare earth spreading out on every side thereafter, she decided this scenario didn't fit her mental pictures of proper picnic places.

But that was nothing to the purpose. She smiled up at Tony when she exited the car, having waited without murmur as he walked around to open her door. "A picnic sounds very nice. We can set out the food on my table and pretend we're in the mountains." What the heck, she was good at pretending, wasn't she?

As soon as Tony opened the back door, Tiny bolted out of the automobile and frolicked around his two human friends for several seconds. Then he bounded away, celebrated his return home by lifting his leg against a cabin wall, and proceeded to gambol off into the desert.

"He looks like he's dancing," Tony commented with a smile.

"He likes to be home." Even this home. Mari pushed her door open and stepped inside. She frowned. "Something's not right in here."

Instantly Tony shot past her into the cabin, looking around as if he were searching for bandits. "What? Where? What's wrong?"

"Oh, dear, will you look at that?" Mari walked over to the fireplace, where faded photographs of her parents were displayed in yellowing paper frames. Both photographs now lay facedown on the mantel. She picked them up and set them in their proper places. "That chair wasn't on its back when I left, either."

Tony's nose wrinkled as he scanned the tiny cabin. As he picked the chair up and set it right, he asked, "What could have done this?"

"I have no idea. I know we didn't have an earthquake since this morning."

"Do you think somebody's been in here?"

Slowly, Mari circumnavigated her home. It didn't take long. The box where she kept her clothes neatly folded had been moved, and her clothes looked as though they'd been gone through. "Yes," she said at last. "But I don't know why."

Tony rubbed his chin and frowned. "I don't like this. It might be part and parcel of the other things that have been going on."

Shaking her head in bewilderment, Mari asked, "But why go through *my* house? I don't have anything worth taking." Pathetic, but true.

"I don't know. Can you lock the door?"

"I can bolt myself in at night, but there's never been any need to have a lock on the door. Heck, sometimes prospectors pass by, and it's customary to leave the latch ring outside the door so they can come in and grab some water and bread and butter if they're hungry and no one's home."

Lifting his eyebrow in a faintly ironic gesture, Tony murmured, "Magnanimous."

Miffed, Mari snapped, "We share what we have. It may not be much by your standards, but it's what we can do."

He held up his hands, as if surrendering to superior forces. "I didn't mean anything by my comment, Mari, honest."

She didn't believe him, but she let it pass. "But this doesn't look like a miner's doing. This looks—strange."

"Is anything missing?"

She shook her head, since her one walk around the cabin had been sufficient for her to know the answer to that one "Nope. Like I said, I don't have anything to steal."

"Maybe they were looking for money."

"Don't have any of that, either," she said sourly.

"What about your Peerless pay?"

She gaped at him. "I don't keep money lying around my house, for heaven's sake. That first check I got from Martin, I put in the bank as soon as I could."

He eyed her curiously. "You didn't spend any of it? None?"

She shrugged. "On what?"

"I don't know. Food? Clothing?" He glanced around her pathetic home. "Curtains? Rugs?"

Her heart gave a painful spasm. "For this place? Be serious, Tony. Why would I waste money on luxuries for this dump?" She hadn't meant to sound so bitter. Bitterness was an unbecoming and unpleasant characteristic, and Mari tried never to give in to it.

He stared at her for several seconds, fully long enough for her to get itchy. At last he said, "Mari . . ." But his voice petered out, and he didn't continue.

Irked with herself and annoyed with him for making her nervous, she said curtly, "Yes?"

"Mari, there's something I want to ask you."

"Oh?" Figuring there was nothing to do about a long-departed intruder but pick up after him, Mari refolded her clothes as Tony thought and shoved the box back into the corner where it belonged. Then she got the checked tablecloth she used for company from the shelf where she stored it, flapped it open, and laid it on her rickety table. She might not be able to create elegance, but she could at least use a tablecloth for company.

Tony didn't speak again for several moments, and she glanced up at him, curious. He looked remarkably ill at ease for such a man of the world. She raised her eyebrows in a question. He licked his lips.

Strange. Mari'd never seen him disconcerted before. Well, except when he'd been mad at her. But that was only natural. She'd probably be pretty peeved if somebody hit her with a rock, too. She grinned as she went to the kitchen area of her cabin and found two forks, two knives, and two spoons. None of them matched, but a body didn't need matched flatware to eat a basket lunch. No matter what the Tony Ewings of this precious world might think.

He started speaking again when her back was turned. "You see, Mari, it's like this. I—well, I've been doing a lot of thinking lately and—"

Tony didn't finish that sentence either, but only because both he and Mari had their ears assaulted by the report of a gun, followed instantly by a hideous howl from Tiny. Mari, whose heart stopped at the sound of her dog in distress, dropped her silverware and bolted toward the door. Tony caught her before she could race outside and rescue Tiny.

"Wait!" he shouted.

"Tiny's hurt!" She started crying, in spite of telling herself she wouldn't. "I have to get to him!"

"Dammit, wait a minute. Somebody's out there with a gun, for God's sake, and he might be just as happy to shoot you as your dog."

"I don't care! I don't care! Tiny's all I have!" If she'd been in possession of her senses, she'd have been embarrassed by her pitiful wail, but she wasn't. All she could think about was the possibility of losing Tiny, and she couldn't bear it.

"Stop it, Mari. Here, I'll help you look for him. But don't run out until I find out if it's safe."

"No!" It was no use. She knew he was right. With her heart breaking and her life crumbling around her, Mari crumpled up onto a chair and buried her face in her hands. "Go ahead," she sobbed. "Go ahead and see if it's safe. If Tiny's been hurt, I—I'll—"

But she had no idea what she'd do. Kill herself? Already she wanted to. Life was hard enough. If she had to face it without Tiny, she was pretty sure she wouldn't survive.

Tony watched Mari for a minute to be sure she wasn't going to dash out the door when he opened it. Damn, she looked awful. He wished he could hold her and pet her and tell her he'd take care of everything. But he had no right to do that. Anyhow, that might be a lie, and he discovered within himself a distinct reluctance to lie to her. The poor kid had it hard enough already. She didn't need to contend with lies, too.

If he ever caught the person who was doing these things, he'd kill him with his bare hands. Thinking quickly, he got Mari's battered old hat from its peg by the door, grabbed the broom from a corner, and stuck the hat on the broomstick. Carefully, he opened the door and showed the hat-on-a-stick in a way that he hoped resembled a person cautiously peering outside.

Nothing happened. A faint, faraway whine came through the open door, and Tony turned his head to see if Mari'd heard it. She had. She lifted a tear-stained face, eloquent with longing, and stared at the open doorway.

"Tiny?" she asked in a small voice.

"I'll get him," Tony promised. "As soon as I know it's safe."

She nodded. He hadn't known she could be so reasonable. He had a strong hunch this was an aberration brought about by too much excitement, too many bad things happening, and sheer terror over the fate of her dog. He understood, even though he'd never been in a similar position himself. It was astonishing how having sufficient money could shield one from the rough side of life.

Taking a chance and hoping he'd survive it, Tony sucked in a deep breath and stepped into the doorway. Nobody shot him, so he ventured a step away from the cabin. Tony's whine became louder, as if he were begging for help.

The chair scraped behind him, and Tony turned in time to catch Mari before she could rush past him and out to her dog. "We'll go together," he said calmly. He didn't feel calm. He felt like hell. As a precaution, he took his revolver out of his jacket pocket.

Mari eyed the gun with astonishment. "I didn't know you carried a gun."

"It's a concession to the Wild West," he said ironically. The truth was, he hadn't known what to expect when he'd agreed to come to California. For all he'd known, there were desperadoes on every corner, and life was as cheap as depicted in those torrid yellowback novels. He hadn't expected to discover California to be almost as civilized as the eastern seaboard.

Mari didn't question his assumptions about her home state. He had to hold her back from running out onto the desert. "Stick by my side, Mari," he said in a hard voice. "If we separate—well, I don't know."

For all he knew, someone wanted to kidnap Mari and hold her for ransom. What with all the other kinds of vandalism going on, that didn't sound as fantastic to him as it might have a couple of weeks ago.

"Oh, please, Tony!" she begged. "I've got to get to Tiny."

"I know, sweetheart, I know." Tears still rolled down her face, and his heart swelled with compassion.

Daylight was fading fast out there in the desert, where light didn't linger long after the sun went down. Tony snagged the lantern Mari kept on a hook beside the door and handed it to Mari. As they warily walked farther away from the cabin, he patted his pockets until he found a box of matches. Then, not daring to stop to be efficient, for fear Mari would get away from him, he fumbled around until he'd gotten the wick lighted. The lantern didn't help much now, but if they had to search very long for Tiny, it would come in handy. "You'd better call him, Mari."

She obliged in a voice trembling with emotion. "Tiny? Tiny! Where are you, boy?"

If her dog had been killed, Tony wasn't sure what he'd do, but he'd never stop looking for the perpetrator. Mari loved that nonsensical horse of a dog and, therefore, so did Tony. The realization came upon him suddenly and didn't surprise him. He'd almost given up pretending he didn't care about Mari. Hell, he'd been on the verge of proposing marriage when Tiny'd been shot.

He shivered in the cooling evening air, wondering if that had been a propitious escape or the other kind. As he'd never even considered marriage before he'd bumped into Mari, he wasn't sure. However, although he deplored the reason for it, he couldn't help feeling somewhat relieved that his proposal had been thwarted. He really ought to think good and hard about what marriage entailed before popping the question.

After all, he and Mari were about as far apart socially as a bird was from a mole. Which wasn't an altogether inapt comparison if he did say so himself.

Deciding to help out on the calling front, Tony called softly, "Tiny, where are you, boy?"

"Do you think we need to be so quiet, Tony? Do you think whoever shot him is still lurking?"

Lurking. Good word. Made Tony's skin crawl. Before he could answer her, they both heard the distant rumble of a motorcar starting up. Mari gripped his arm convulsively. Tony's lips tightened.

"I guess that answers your question," he muttered. "Whoever did the deed is evidently escaping."

A strangled sob greeted this piece of conjecture. Tony put his arm around her waist. "Buck up, Mari. I'm sure we can save him."

"Oh, Lord!" For only seconds, Mari seemed in danger of total collapse. Then, as Tony might have expected, she pulled herself up straight, wiped the back of her hand across her eyes, and shouted, "Tiny! Tiny, where are you!"

A pathetic whimper, totally unlike anything else Tony'd heard issue from the Great Dane's throat, responded to her call. Mari cried out and broke away from Tony.

"Damnation." He pelted after her, disconcerted because she was only a couple of yards away and already fading into the twilight gloom. Having longer legs than she, he caught up at once.

They both stopped dead at the sight of Tiny huddled on the ground, a large black heap, looking as though he'd been cut down in full stride. Mari clapped her hands over her mouth, and Tony heard another sob break from her lips. He felt like crying, too.

He'd never have imagined Tiny in such a pitiful condition. The dog lay on his side, evidently unable to lift his head but staring at them as if they were his salvation. As incongruous as it seemed, his tail began to wag. Tony thought what a great pair this girl and her dog were. They both had more spirit than brains, and he couldn't think of any two beings on this Earth that he honored more.

Snapping out of his stupor almost immediately, he barked at Mari, "Stay with him and give him what comfort you can. I don't want to try to lift him and carry him back to the cabin. He might not make it—"

Another strangled sob from Mari.

"So I'll get the motorcar."

"But the tires . . ."

"To hell with the tires. Tiny's more important than a dozen Pierce Arrows."

As he loped back to the cabin, Tony couldn't believe he'd actually said that. Even more, he couldn't believe he'd meant it. But he had. Still did, for that matter.

Cursing the minutes as they passed, he cranked the car's motor to life, leaped behind the wheel, and as carefully as could be, drove to Tiny. Mari'd been right to worry about the tires, he thought grimly as something spiky pierced one of them and he heard air whooshing out of it.

But to hell with the tires. To hell with the whole car if it came to that. Mari's dog was in peril, and Tony was going to rescue it or die trying.

Perhaps not anything that dramatic. But he was going to do his very best to see that Tiny survived this ordeal.

For one thing, he felt responsible, even though he knew intellectually that he wasn't. It wasn't his fault someone was trying to disrupt production of *Lucky Strike*. Still, his father's money was backing the picture, and Tony was presently in charge of his father's movie money. Ergo, he did feel responsible, logical or not.

He was grateful he'd thought about a lantern when he came upon the tableau created by Mari and her pooch. The lantern light directed Tony to a perfect spot. Mari, huddled beside her huge dog and smiling pathetically, waved at him. As if he could ever misplace her. Still, the lantern helped.

Driving as close as he could get to the pair, he let the engine idle while he scrambled out of his jacket, rolled his shirtsleeves up, and snatched a blanket out of the car's rumble seat. "Let me look at him before we do anything."

"He—he's got a hole in his side, and it's bleeding. I think the bullet's still in him."

The brokenhearted comment almost broke Tony's heart, but he swore at himself to be strong. "I'm sorry, sweetheart. But lots of folks survive bullet wounds. And so do lots of animals." As if he knew anything about bullet wounds. Still, it was probably true.

"Oh, I hope so."

Her tone of voice was so fervent that Tony very nearly dropped the blanket and kissed her. She wouldn't have thanked him for that, however, so he didn't.

Kneeling beside Tiny, he spoke softly to the beast. "It's okay, boy. We'll just see what's going on here, and then we'll get you back home to rest and recuperate."

Although Tiny whined and whimpered with pain when Tony felt around the bloody hole, he didn't try to bite, which Tony thought was quite magnanimous of him, considering he was a dumb animal, in pain, and didn't know what was going on. "I think he's only shot in the one spot."

"That's all I could find, too," confirmed Mari, again wiping her eyes.

"Okay. Let's see if we can get him onto the blanket. Then we can lift the blanket and carry him to the motor."

"All right."

Tony heard her take a big breath, as if she were bracing herself for the coming ordeal. He did the same thing. "All right, Tiny," he whispered, trying to make his voice as soothing as possible. "This might hurt, boy, but we're trying to help you."

"It's all right, Tiny," Mari added. "That's a good boy. Come on now."

Inch by painful inch, they maneuvered the gigantic dog onto the blanket. Tony had to pass a sleeve over his dripping forehead to wipe away perspiration when they finally succeeded. It wasn't all that hot, but his heart was hammering like a bass drum, his nerves were jumping like frogs in a pond, and he was sweating like a pig. He breathed a silent prayer of thanks, and asked God for a little more good luck. "All right." He glanced at Mari over the inert body of her dog. "Do you know how much Tiny weighs?"

It touched Tony when Tiny, hearing his name, tried

to wag his tail. Damn, this was a fine dog. Spirited. Gallant. Exactly like his owner.

She thought for a second and shook her head. "No. I think he weighs more than I do, though." She managed a damp chuckle.

"That doesn't surprise me." He pondered the problem of getting Tiny into the backseat of his automobile. He'd left the door open, so all they had to do, really, was slide him in. Unfortunately, Tiny wasn't like Tony's mother's pampered Pomeranian that weighed a couple of pounds. He was more likely to weigh in the neighborhood of a hundred and twenty or more.

Still and all, he could have lifted him on his own if he hadn't been worried about his wound. And Mari was strong. Wasn't she? "Do you think you can lift one side of the blanket with him in the middle if I lift the other side? If we drop him, it won't be good for him."

Although the lantern didn't provide much light, it gave out enough for Tony to see Mari's eyes widen with horror. *"Drop* him? I'd never drop him!"

"I know you wouldn't want to," he said, nettled. "But are you strong enough to lift him up. He's no lightweight, Mari."

"Oh, for the love of— Tony, I wield a pick and shovel six days a week, and I'm strong as an ox."

She didn't look like one. Nevertheless, he grinned at her, admiring her spunk. "All right, then. I'll take his front half, and you take his back half, and we'll carry him to the machine. Let's try not to jostle him."

"Of course." Her voice was tight, and he sensed that she was steeling herself for another ordeal.

So be it. He positioned himself at Tiny's head. Looking down, he saw Tiny's huge head bent upward, and he knew the dog's eyes, trusting and in pain, were upon him. For the umpteenth time that day, his heart was wrenched. He whispered to the dog, "It's all right, boy. We'll fix you up."

"Oh, I hope so." The words sounded as if they'd been choked out of Mari's throat without her consent.

"We'll do our very best," he promised them both. "All right now. Gently. Heave him up."

The maneuver went surprisingly smoothly. Mari proved herself to be as strong as an ox, in truth. She was a marvel. Tiny whimpered a little as they transported him the few feet to the motorcar's back door. Tony cursed himself for not thinking to open both back doors. But he managed it well enough, crawling into the automobile butt first and twisting to get the opposite door open so that he could crawl out on that side.

When they were through, he hurried to Mari's side of the car. She stood there, looking at her dog, patently in distress, and crying. Until tonight, Tony hadn't known there were so many tears in her. She was so damned strong for the most part, he hadn't anticipated this emotionalism from her. He actually liked it. Made her more human or something.

He put an arm around her shoulder and guided her to the passenger's side of the automobile. "Here, Mari," he said tenderly. "Climb in next to me, and we'll get this big lug back to your house." He thought of something. "Unless you think we ought to take him to town."

She shot him a surprised glance. "To town? Why to town?"

He shrugged. "I don't know. To see the doctor?"

She shook her head. "We don't have an animal doctor in Mojave Wells, and I don't think Doc Crabtree would appreciate having Tiny in his surgery. Although I could pay him," she added, as if suddenly struck by a happy thought.

"Forget it," Tony said, irked. He didn't want Mari to

pay for the doctoring of Tiny out of her own pocket. Hell, it wasn't her fault a moving-picture company had invaded her life. "Let's take him home."

She consented with a nod, and after retrieving the lantern, Tony drove them to the cabin. Since he knew now how to work this transportation business, he made sure the front door of the cabin was open, and a pad set out for Tiny before they carried him into the house. Then they had to get down to brass tacks.

"I don't know anything about doctoring pets, Mari," he confessed, wishing he could play hero in this situation but fearing if he tried, he might damage Tiny.

"I can do whatever can be done," she said.

Tony didn't doubt her. He'd learned long ago that Mari had served as her own doctor, nurse, and parent for most of her life. Because he wanted to be useful, he said, "I'll boil some water and get a couple more lanterns lit. You'll need lots of light."

"Right. There's some laudanum and carbolic acid in the cupboard. Will you please bring them, too? And the witch hazel and rubbing alcohol and the tweezers in the box beside the sink."

"Right."

It didn't take long before Mari was ready to begin. "You might have to hold his head, Tony. Be gentle, but he's very strong, so you might have to use force."

"I can handle it," Tony declared quietly, praying he wasn't lying. She deserved all the help he could give her. And then some. Not only that, but it would be humiliating to allow Tiny to bite him.

With assurance and agility, Mari doctored her dog, first cleaning the wound, then finding where the bullet had lodged and pulling it out with sterilized tweezers. Tony didn't know how she could be so efficient under the circumstances. His own stomach heaved, he felt like cringing, and it was all he could do to keep from crying out several times when Tiny protested the pain of the operation.

It was soon over, and at last Tony could help when Mari bandaged her dog. Fortunately, by that time, the dose of laudanum they'd dribbled down Tiny's throat had taken effect, and the poor dog was too sleepy to protest. When Mari'd tied the last bandage and washed her hands, she sat back, staring at her pet.

"There," she said. "I guess what we have to do now is wait and see what happens."

Tony nodded. "You did a great job, Mari." He was terribly impressed, actually.

"He lost a lot of blood," she murmured.

"He'll be okay," Tony told her with more assurance than he felt.

She looked up from her dog to his face, and he saw how drawn and weary she was. "I hope so. I don't know what I'll do if Tiny doesn't make it."

Then she sat back on her heels, bent her head, lifted her hands to her face, and started to sob as if her heart were breaking.

Tony couldn't stand it. On his knees, he went to her, took her in his arms, and cradled her, rocking her and crooning to her as if she were something precious. Which she was.

Eighteen

Mari knew Tony was holding her, and she appreciated it, but she couldn't seem to stop crying. She was so tired and so worried about Tiny. The day had been horrible. She'd almost been killed, and now her dog was in peril.

Burying her head against Tony's hard shoulder, she sobbed until exhaustion even robbed her of tears. His hand, stroking her hair as if she were his pet, comforted her strangely. She couldn't recollect anyone ever trying to soothe her this way. Is this what mothers were for? she wondered. Or fathers?

Or lovers?

In the faint hope that the last might succeed in this instance, she lifted her head and gazed at Tony's face. It looked pale and drawn in the lantern light, as if he were bushed, too, and was only holding on to his strength because she needed him. She loved him very much and wondered if he'd like to know it, or if he'd be appalled. She didn't want to risk whatever tenuous hold they had on a relationship by admitting the state of her heart. She did, however, feel compelled to thank him for helping her with Tiny. And for offering her a shoulder to cry on. Literally.

"Thanks for all your help, Tony."

Slowly he opened his eyes and gazed down at her. "You don't need to thank me, Mari."

"That's very nice of you, but I'm grateful anyway."

"I'm always available for you, sweetheart. You ought to know that by now."

She blinked up at him, unsure what those very kind words meant exactly. They sounded rather like a lover's, but Mari'd lived a hard life and wasn't accustomed to good things happening to her. Also, she'd hate like the devil to make a fool of herself.

He had, however, called her *sweetheart* several times this evening. This was the first time Mari's brain had been unoccupied enough to register the fact. *Sweetheart* was an endearment not often used on casual acquaintances. At least, it wasn't in Mari's circles. She wasn't sure about the customs prevailing in Tony's more lofty society.

His grin came out of nowhere. "You're staring at me. Do I have dirt on my nose or something?"

Startled because she'd gotten lost in a fog, she grinned back. "No. I'm just . . . looking."

"Like what you see?"

His soft voice caressed her senses as his hand had been caressing her hair. It was only then Mari realized he'd taken out the pins and begun running his fingers through her hair, as if he were combing it out.

Afraid to speak for fear of sounding or looking like a lovesick idiot, Mari nodded. She sure did like what she saw. What's more, she no longer thought of him as only a rich, handsome man. She'd come to know that, while he might be unfamiliar with the hard side of life, he wasn't a snob. He was very nice, in fact. Kind. Magnanimous, even. And he wasn't afraid of working hard. Or of blood. She shivered, and he hugged her more tightly.

"Are you cold?" he asked solicitously.

"No. I'm warm."

"Me, too."

She felt him kiss her hair where his hand had just stroked, and she sighed deeply, wishing they could stay wrapped up in each other forever. Because she wanted to, she tilted her head up and sought his lips.

He took in a sharp breath when he realized what she wanted, but he obliged her, kissing her slowly, caressingly, lovingly. At least—Mari tried to be realistic about things—the kiss felt loving. Her half of it was; she wasn't sure about his. She kissed him with all the love in her body, soul, and heart, bestowing it upon him freely.

"Mari . . ." His voice was thick.

"Yes?"

"I . . . I . . ."

"Yes?"

"Oh, God."

Evidently unable to think of anything to say that meant anything under these circumstances, Tony gave up and showed her what he meant. That's the way Mari interpreted his actions. He kissed her passionately, using his lips and tongue in ways Mari hadn't known were possible. She was an eager student and caught on immediately, kissing him back in kind.

"Here," he said after several delicious minutes. "We can't stay here on the floor."

"No," she agreed. "Let's use the bed."

By the light of the lanterns, Mari saw that he was shocked at her suggestion. Naturally, she became defensive. "That's what you want, isn't it?" She hadn't meant to sound quite as challenging as all that.

He gazed at her soberly. "Yes, it's what I want, Mari, but I won't do anything to hurt you."

She shook her head. "You won't hurt me." She wasn't really all that sure of herself, but she did know she didn't want Tony to quit now. Mari knew what went on between men and women. She'd honestly not thought about herself ever being with a man, but she knew that if ever she were to experience the physical side of love, she wanted it to be with Tony. If she lived and died alone after this, so be it. At least she'd have known the man she loved, in the most intimate way possible.

Still, he hesitated. Puzzled and a little hurt, Mari said, "What's the matter, Tony? Don't you want me?" That would be about the most humiliating circumstance she could conceive of, but she felt compelled to ask.

"How can you ask me that?" He sounded cranky. "It must be obvious even to you that I want you. But— but, we're not married."

Self-evident, Mari thought sourly. "Listen, Tony, if you're going to talk this to death, then forget it." If he went on in this vein, the moment would be spoiled and the opportunity lost. Once thought entered into a spontaneous activity, the activity lost all its fun.

He gazed at her for approximately ten more seconds, then gave up. Mari could detect the exact moment when his caution was subsumed by his desire, and she thanked her stars for small favors. She rose and took his hand and led him to her small bed, shoved against a wall.

The rag rug beside the bed was one Mari had made herself, during the cold winter of two years prior, when it had been too cold to work the mine and she'd had nothing else to do. She'd always been glad she'd done it, since the bare wooden floor could be perniciously cold of a winter's morning. Now she was glad she'd done it because it made the room look less pitiful.

During the day she covered her bed with a shabby, but colorful spread and propped cushions on it so it could serve as a sofa when folks came to call. She shoved the cushions aside and sat, guiding Tony to do likewise. He did and took her in his arms.

He didn't kiss her again at once, but whispered tenderly, "Will this be your first time, Mari?"

Shocked that he'd even ask her that, she jerked back and stared at him. "I beg your pardon? What kind of girl do you think I am, anyhow?"

She was surprised when he threw his head back and started laughing. She didn't know whether she should be offended or not, and was still contemplating whether to laugh with him or slap his mouth shut when he solved her problem by saying, "I think you're the most wonderful kind of girl, Mari Pottersby. You're a true original, a paragon of hardy womanhood, a glorious natural creature. You're not only lovely to look at, but marvelous to know."

Oh. That kind of took the wind out of her sails, but she enjoyed hearing it. In fact, she felt herself flush, and tucked her chin in, embarrassed. Tony tilted it up again. "I like it when you lift your chin, Mari. I can always tell when you're going to light into me by that chin of yours."

"Really?" She'd had no idea.

"Your chin is like Tiny's tail. It's a clue to your mood."

Because she didn't want to make too much out of his words, in case they were only flattery, she said jokingly, "Are you comparing me to a dog?"

"I sure am. You're as unusual and perfect as your unusual and perfect dog. I can't think of another creature I'd rather be like than Tiny."

"I'm still not sure I find the comparison complimentary, Tony Ewing. Tiny's big as a house, and I'm not."

"No." His voice went low and caressing again. "You're definitely not. You're slender and lithe and marvelous. I've been wanting to make love with you for the longest time, Mari."

"You have?" Good heavens.

"I have." He held her by her shoulders and gazed into her eyes. "But I won't do it unless you want me to."

She swallowed. Blast. She was always having to make decisions. Didn't anything in life ever just happen naturally? As ever, Mari took the bull by the horns and dealt with it. "I want you to."

Tony's fervent "Thank God" sounded genuine to Mari. She guessed he really did want her.

Then he kissed her, and her question about things happening naturally was in a way being answered. His passion was so hot, it seemed to melt her very bones; and she sank against him, willing him to do whatever he wanted with her.

He made her body sing. She hadn't realized how delightful a man's hands could feel against her skin. Which made sense. How should she?

"You're beautiful," he whispered at one point as he was unbuttoning her shirtwaist.

Mari almost believed him because he sounded so sincere. She wondered if he found her tanned skin off-putting, since refined ladies were always depicted with skin as white as snow. But she decided to give herself a break. If the man said she was beautiful, she'd believe him. At least for tonight. She'd deal with tomorrow when it came.

When he'd undone the last button, he slid his hands inside her shirtwaist and slipped it aside, gazing at her modestly covered torso, his eyes hot with desire. Mari figured she ought to be shy, but she wasn't. She loved the way he looked at her; she'd never even imagined she could stir Tony Ewing to lust. It seemed so incongruous.

"You're a beautiful woman, Mari."

There he went again, calling her beautiful. She liked

it. A lot. She didn't respond in words because she didn't know which ones to use. Instead, she closed her eyes and let her body take over and do what it wanted to do. She was tired of thinking all the time.

He leaned toward her and pressed his lips to her naked flesh, on that little dip between her neck and her shoulder, and she darned near fainted. When he feathered warm kisses across her shoulder and down to her chest, she uttered a low moan that meant nothing but pleasure.

"Don't be afraid, Mari," Tony whispered raggedly. And he slipped her shirtwaist from her shoulders until it puddled around her hips.

"I'm not afraid." And she wasn't. How strange.

"I'm going to take your shoes off."

"All right."

In a trice, he was on his knees in front of her, and Mari's heart lurched. This pose was the same one he'd adopted earlier in the day, and it still reminded her of illustrations she'd seen of gentlemen proposing to ladies. Only Tony's proposal wasn't the same as the ones proffered by those fictional gentlemen. Her insides somersaulted once in a sickening fashion before she squelched these most recent thoughts as unproductive. She reminded herself that this might well be the only chance in however long her life lasted to experience the act of love with Tony Ewing. She wasn't about to allow scruples to spoil the experience.

Her footwear might have embarrassed her, had she still been worried about the discrepancies in their relative social situations. This evening, what society thought didn't matter. Mari decreed it so. Nothing would ruin her first—perhaps her only—adventure with love.

"We have to get you some new shoes, Mari," Tony murmured as he pulled her right shoe off.

We do, do we? Mari watched Tony without speaking, even though she knew good and well her footwear was her concern, not his. She was fully willing to make love to Tony Ewing tonight, but she wouldn't be a kept woman. Ever. She had a mine to run.

Oh, Lord, there was the blasted mine again, intruding, as it always did, into every aspect of her life. Resolutely, she thrust the Marigold Mine into the corner of her mind where her scruples lay huddled.

Tony was shaking his head now. "How long have you had these stockings, Mari?"

She blinked down at his head. His hair looked dark in the lantern light, although Mari knew it to be ash blonde almost golden. He carefully rolled one of her stockings down her right leg, then dangled it in front of her face, his mouth curled in an impish grin. His eyes looked green now.

"I beg your pardon?" She'd forgotten his question.

"How long have you had these? It looks as if they'd been mended a million times."

She grinned back at him, finding humor in the situation instead of a reason to feel humiliated, which seemed a step in the right direction. "They probably have. Stockings aren't the first thing I buy when I get money."

"I should say not. We'll have to remedy *that* situation, too."

"Tony . . ."

"Yes?" He glanced up from rolling down her left stocking.

It had been on the tip of her tongue to tell him she'd be no man's mistress and that she'd buy her own shoes and stockings in the future, thank you very much, but the words wouldn't come. A declaration of such a nature would put a damper on the evening, and she wouldn't make it. "Nothing." He still gazed up at her with that heart-stopping grin on his beautiful mouth, so she said softly, "I like what you're doing."

His grin broadened into a smile. "Good. I do, too."

He tossed the second stocking aside and surprised Mari by lifting her feet, one at a time, and kissing them. She hadn't known people did such extraordinary things. How—how—how stunningly sweet.

"I don't want you to live in want anymore, Mari," he whispered as he gently lowered her feet to the rag carpet once more.

That one was easy. "I don't want me to, either." As if there was anything she could do about it. Still, she gave him an answering smile.

"Good."

Good? Whatever did that mean? Mari didn't ask for fear she wouldn't like his answer.

He stood abruptly, and Mari found herself at eye level with the front of his trousers, the fabric of which bulged alarmingly. She swallowed, knowing what that extremely large bulge meant.

"Be with you in a second," Tony muttered as he fumbled with his shirt buttons. He wore no collar or jacket in deference to the heat of the day, and he made quick work of his shirt, shucking it off in seconds.

Too disconcerted by that bulge to stare at his trousers, Mari lifted her head and looked at his chest instead. At the moment, it was covered with a cotton undershirt—oh. No, it wasn't. Not any longer. Tony had ripped the shirt over his head in one graceful, shrugging gesture, and Mari got to see a man's naked chest for the very first time.

And what a chest it was. Covered with light brown, curly hair, Tony's chest was a work of art. When her gaze slid sideways, and she inspected his arms, she swallowed again. She stared, rapt. "Merciful heavens, Tony, where did you get those muscles?"

"I was on the rowing team in college. It's hard work, although it's a pretty useless occupation, compared to most. I mean, we used our muscles to propel a sporting craft, not do anything worthwhile with them."

The results of plying those oars looked worthwhile to Mari. "Um, I think sports are good for boys." And if all sports resulted in muscles like those, they were good for girls, too, albeit in a different way.

But Tony shook his head. "Knowing you has made me reevaluate everything I've ever believed about life."

His words so shocked her that she left off devouring his musculature with her greedy gaze, and her glance flew to his face. He looked down at her with such warmth and tenderness, Mari at once became skittish and let her gaze slip to the rag rug.

"It's true, Mari." He unbuckled his belt, then unbuttoned his trousers, and slid them down his legs. As Mari gaped at his muscular thighs, he sat beside her and took her hands in his. "I didn't understand how frivolous my life was until I met you."

"Um, really?"

"Really. You made me ashamed of the way I lived."

That was so sweet. And so utterly ridiculous. "Let's not get carried away here, Tony. If I had a choice, I'd live the way you do, believe me. Anyone would."

He laughed and lifted her hands to his lips. As soon as her flesh touched his, gooseflesh sprung up on her arms, traveled across her torso, dimpled her nipples, and continued down the rest of her body, until she felt as though she were one massive, throbbing tingle.

"Of course, everyone wants money. Money's important. What I meant was that, until I met you, I didn't know what selflessness was. I'd never seen it in action before."

"Oh." Selflessness? Her? The word didn't mean a

thing to Mari. She'd always only thought she was trying
to survive.

"Yes," he said. "Oh, forget all that, and come to me.
Come here."

Thank God he pulled her into his arms, because
Mari's brain had started working again, and she knew
better than to trust it not to spoil everything. His kiss
was more fervent this time; harder, more insistent. Mari
responded with gusto.

Little by little, he lowered her to the bed, so that she
lay on her back. She didn't realize he'd been skillfully
undoing the ties to her camisole until the garment fell
away, leaving her bare bosom exposed to his avid gaze.
She wasn't shocked. She knew she had nice, firm
breasts. They weren't massive, thank God, but she believed they'd make a nice handful for Tony Ewing.

He proved her correct in mere seconds. As his hands
cupped her breasts, Mari's eyes slid shut. She reveled
in the sensation of his fingers caressing her sensitive
nipples. When his tongue flicked one nipple, she didn't
think she'd ever felt a more exquisite marvel. Every
cell in her body sang with pleasure.

Then he took her breast into his mouth and Mari
wasn't sure she'd survive so much glory. The only way
to bear it was to use her own hands, so she did, exploring Tony's hard body with as much interest as he was
investing in hers.

She'd not understood before how intensely stimulating a man's body could be. She'd never felt any inclination to explore, say, Gordon Shay's lumpy muscles
and hairy arms. She wanted to feel every inch of Tony's
smoother, more refined musculature. And more besides. She wanted to taste him, to nip parts of him, to
discover every nuance of his flesh.

Because her resolve not to allow her thoughts to interfere with her pleasure was still locked in a corner

of her mind, she acted on her desire. Tony groaned with pleasure when she found his nipples and tasted them as her hands explored his marvelous chest.

Although Mari knew her body was slim, almost sinewy, by modern standards, molded into strength by hard work rather than into softness by feminine pursuits, Tony didn't seem to mind. His hands explored every nook and cranny of her naked flesh with evident rapture. Which was all right by Mari. She was every bit as enraptured by his body.

"You're so soft, Mari. But you're so damned strong."

Although she wasn't sure she should ask, she did it anyway. "Is that a good thing?"

He chuckled. "It's a very good thing."

"Oh. Good." What a relief. When he'd spoken of her strength, she'd feared he'd been put off by her lack of womanly fleshiness.

"You've got a strong body and a strong mind. You're the perfect woman."

Good God. Mari couldn't believe he'd actually said that, although she decided not to ask in case she was right. It was much nicer to think he truly found her body attractive. And stimulating.

His hands had been exploring, inch by inch, until they'd reached a crucial part of her anatomy. Although a little disconcerted, Mari was yet more interested than shy. She wondered what he'd do when he got to that thatch of curls between her legs. Those curls were even darker than her hair, and the portion of her body they hid was at present creating all sorts of havoc in the rest of her body.

She didn't have long to wonder. As his hand cupped her femininity, Mari bucked involuntarily. That's where all the pressure was building. That was the spot, all right. She whispered, "Oh, Tony!"

"Don't be afraid, Mari."

He sounded fairly desperate, and Mari longed to put his fears to rest, but she didn't know how to without sounding like a wanton hussy. Instead, she did what her body wanted her to do, and lifted her hips so that the nub of her pleasure pressed against his palm. He responded instantly by probing her passage with a finger.

She swallowed and let go of an involuntary "Oh!"

"You're beautiful, Mari," he murmured, again sounding moderately desperate. "So beautiful."

How nice. She wanted to shriek at him to keep doing what he'd been doing with his fingers, but again modesty held her back. That was a laugh. There was absolutely nothing modest about this situation any longer.

Since that was the case, Mari decided she couldn't lose any respect in his eyes, provided he still had any for her, so she whispered, "Oh, please, Tony, keep doing that."

Rather than horrifying or repelling him, her words seemed to give Tony's hands a new life. He murmured something she didn't catch and renewed his ministrations to her most secret place, leaning over to kiss her at the same time. She threw her arms around his neck and kissed him back. The kiss progressed as her passion mounted, until their tongues were thrusting as furiously as Tony's fingers.

Then the climax came, and Mari's few remaining inhibitions flew out of her body. Waves of pleasure claimed her, and she cried out with amazement, not having anticipated the intensity of the joy a man and a woman could share.

She realized Tony had been watching her only when her spasms of pleasure subsided and she opened her eyes. He smiled down at her.

With a hand that felt as heavy as lead, Mari stroked

his lovely hair back from his head. She didn't know what to say. Or do.

Fortunately for them both, Tony knew exactly what to say and do. "That was the most beautiful thing I've ever seen, Mari."

She blinked up at him, thinking how nice he was, really. Even if he was as rich as Midas. Although she was vaguely aware that he hadn't enjoyed himself quite as much as she had, she was rather surprised when he suddenly stood up.

When he stripped his underwear down his legs, and his enormous sex popped into clear view, she gasped. Good heavens. A tiny doubt wriggled its way into her chest for only a moment, before Tony spoke once more, again reassuring her.

"Don't be afraid."

Mari couldn't recall the number of times he'd told her not to be afraid this evening, but so far he'd been absolutely right. This was nothing to be afraid of. In fact, it was spectacularly exciting. Glorious, even.

He got back onto the bed, straddling her body with his powerful legs. "I hope this won't hurt you, Mari," he whispered.

She only shook her head, hoping he'd understand that she meant the shake to mean it didn't matter. Tony Ewing had just given her the greatest physical pleasure of her life. She wasn't going to begrudge him a twinge or two when she lost her virginity.

As it turned out, it didn't hurt at all. Perhaps because she'd had to work so hard in her life, her maiden's barrier gave up its hold at once and without a trace of pain. The sensation of fullness she experienced was a novel one, but she accustomed herself to it quickly. Tony was panting as if he were running a race. It took Mari a moment to realize his condition was brought

about by the great restraint he was showing in deference to her recent virginity, and her heart was touched.

"I'm fine, Tony," she whispered, stroking his hair
and arms and back and everything else she could reach.
She loved him so much. If she hadn't been concerned
with his feelings on the matter, she might have wept
with the overwhelming love filling her heart and soul.
But she didn't want to scare him.

Which was really rather amusing, since he'd been
concerned about her own fears and physical well-being.
He was so sweet.

"Are you sure?"

She heard the strain in his voice and hastened to
assure him. "I'm very sure. You feel good inside me,
Tony. Wonderful."

Apparently that was the right thing to say, because
the bonds of his constraint snapped at once, and he
began to plunge almost wildly inside her. Merciful
heavens, what an interesting phenomenon.

She'd just begun to understand where this could lead
when Tony, unable to hold himself back any longer,
cried out and with one last thrust, spilled his seed inside
her. He strained for another couple of seconds, as if
squeezing the last ounce of himself into her, and then
he collapsed at her side.

Unable to help it, Mari allowed a very few tears to
escape. They trickled down her cheeks, and she was
able to wipe them away before Tony opened his eyes.
He still panted, as if he'd run a marathon.

Nineteen

Sweet Lord, he cherished this woman. Exhausted and with his soul afire with love, Tony lay beside Mari, marveling at how much a man's life could change in so short a time.

Only a few weeks ago, he'd come out to California hoping to find something; he didn't know what. And, by God, he'd found her. He'd been seeking Mari and didn't even know it.

He knew it now. The only thing he wasn't sure of at this point was how to get her to marry him. She was so damned independent and stubborn. Maybe if he allowed her to keep her crazy father's mine, she'd agree to a permanent alliance with him. What the hell, he had enough money to keep the mine operating, forever, without any hint of profit, if he wanted to. Tony didn't like wasting money, but Mari would be worth it.

After he'd regained his breath, he whispered, "Mari?"

She stirred next to him, and he opened his eyes to watch her. She turned her head, and he smiled at her expression. Damned if she didn't look shy. After what they'd just shared together! She was so perfectly delightful, Tony wasn't sure he could stand it. His heart was so full, it felt near to overflowing.

"Yes, Tony?" Her voice, whisper soft and caressing,

made him go all mushy inside. It made another part of him begin to stir to life. How interesting.

He cupped her cheek with his hand, then smoothed the hair back from her face before drawing her into a closer cuddle. "Are you all right, sweetheart? Did I hurt you?"

Her eyes gazed at him with such tenderness, his insides squeezed and his heart soared. "You didn't hurt me. I'm fine. Grand, even."

"Grand?" His masculine pride took a bow. He was pretty sure his grin showed how cocky he felt about his performance. "So am I. Very grand."

"I'm glad." She dropped her gaze. "Um, I'd never done—that—before, and I'm not sure if I did it right."

She hadn't been able to tell? Good God. On the other hand, Tony guessed that, as a recently deflowered virgin, she had nothing with which to compare their recent activities. Gratitude flooded him and again his heart pitched when he considered he'd been the first. He'd be the only, if he had anything to say about it. "You did it perfectly. Better than perfectly. You're—you're perfect." Shoot, he wished he could think of a word meaning better than perfect.

"I'm glad." She kept her eyes lowered. "I thought you were wonderful, too."

His masculine pride quit taking smug bows and started dancing a triumphant jig. "Thank you. That makes me happy. *You* make me happy."

Her gaze darted to his face. She appeared uncertain. "Do I? Honestly?"

"Honestly." Absolutely. Phenomenally.

"Good."

They stayed wrapped up in each other without speaking for several minutes. Tony savored each one of them as if they were pure gold. He was bracing himself to pop the question. He wasn't nervous. Not exactly. Not precisely. It was only that he'd never asked a woman to marry him before, and he wasn't quite sure how to go about it.

He also feared she might refuse his proposal. Any other female in the universe would jump at the chance to marry him—or, rather, to marry his money. Which pretty much summed up why Tony had never proposed to anybody before.

But Mari . . . Well, Mari was different from the rest of the women in the world. She was special. Unique. Magnificent.

He cleared his throat. "Mari . . ."

"Yes?" She smothered a yawn in the pillow.

Tony thought she was adorable. "I need to ask you something."

"Yes?"

This was it. He was going to do it. Right now. He was going to open his mouth and just blurt it out before he could get scared. He was going to say it. Right now. Outright. He was going to get it over with right this very minute. He was—

On the floor a few feet away from them, Tiny whimpered.

Mari sat bolt upright as if she'd been shot from a gun. "Tiny!"

Blast. Tony had forgotten all about the dog. He considered the relief flooding through him in the light of cowardice, but he couldn't stop it. He sat up, too. "We'd better check on him."

Mari had already slid out of the narrow bed. Tony had a splendid view of her naked backside as she reached up to grab an old flannel bathrobe from a hook beside the bed. She had a body a man might die for. She rushed to the side of her dog and knelt beside him.

Tony climbed out of the bed more slowly, savoring

the delicious postcoital lassitude infusing him. With a sigh, he stood and glanced around, trying to find his trousers. Ah, yes, there they were. He went to them, picked them up off the floor, shook them out, and pulled them on. He'd as soon live naked for the rest of his life, as long as Mari did likewise. Unfortunately, the world was going to sneak in and interrupt this idyll all too soon.

He padded softly over to the girl and her dog and he, too, knelt. "How's he doing?" The slow smack of Tiny's tail against the floor as he wagged it seemed encouraging to Tony.

"I'm not sure." Mari sounded concerned, but not overly worried, which also seemed like a good sign. "At least he's happy to see us."

"He's a good dog." Tony scratched Tiny behind his massive ears, and the tail sped up a trace. With a grin, he said, "I think he might make it, Mari."

"I sure hope he does." She leaned over and gave the giant pooch a careful hug. "I love him so much. I'd be lost without him."

"You wouldn't be lost, Mari," Tony said tenderly. "You'd be sad, but I don't believe you'll ever be lost. You're too strong for that." Besides, he'd buy her a dozen Great Danes if she wanted them. A hundred. A thousand. He could almost see them in his mind's eye, spreading across the landscape like a herd of cows.

He was a little disconcerted when she glanced at him over the dog's huge black head. He detected a hint of bleakness in her eyes, and he didn't understand it. She should be gloating. After all, no other woman in the world had ever succeeded in roping Tony Ewing.

"Yes," she said slowly. "I guess I'm strong, all right."

She didn't sound awfully thrilled about it. Tony decided she was merely undergoing a few moments of maidenly—formerly maidenly—qualms. He smiled at her to make up for them. After a moment, she smiled back.

Gazing at the dog, he asked, "Do you think we ought to dose him with another couple of drops of laudanum?" He thought it might be nice to get a few hours of sleep, since the film crew was supposed to arrive bright and early in the morning. Martin wanted to get the shots of Mari in her mine done in one day, because of the intense heat. He didn't want anyone dying of sunstroke, a policy with which Tony agreed wholeheartedly.

She stroked the gigantic black beast thoughtfully for a second or two. "I think so. I don't think it would hurt him, and it might help him rest better. If he gets too frisky, he might open that wound, so it would probably be better to keep him sort of sleepy for a while."

"Probably wouldn't hurt us, either," Tony mentioned. "We ought to get some sleep, I suppose." He wouldn't mind losing a night's sleep in pursuit of a good cause, and he couldn't think of a better one than making love to Mari all night. However, she probably shouldn't do any more exercise of that nature for a day or so. No matter how much she professed to having not been hurt, Tony didn't want to take any chances.

When he brought his gaze away from Tiny and directed it at Mari, he was surprised by the expression on her face. She appeared troubled. Unable to help himself, he reached across the dog and touched her cheek. "What is it, Mari? What's the matter?"

She licked her lips. "Um, does that mean you want to stay here? All night?"

He stared at her, thunderstruck for a moment. It hadn't occurred to him that she might want him to leave her after that spectacular bout of lovemaking. He wasn't sure, but he thought his feelings were hurt. "I figured I would. Why? Don't you want me to?"

She swallowed. "Um, it's not exactly that I don't want you to. It's—" She stopped speaking and licked her lips again.

"It's what?" His euphoric mood suffered a puncture. Dammit, she was supposed to be as in love with him as he was with her. Although Tony was willing to entertain some pretty novel eventualities with regard to Mari, given her background and all, the notion that she might not love him hadn't occurred to him until this minute.

She stopped petting Tiny and made a small gesture with her hand. "Well, I mean—" Again, her words faded out.

"You mean what?" He felt his temper begin to rise and tamped it down with difficulty.

Her temper was evidently having the same trouble as his, because she snapped, "Well, for goodness' sake, Tony Ewing! What will everyone think if they know you spent the night here? I'd be run out of town!"

Tony could hardly credit the sensation of relief that washed over him. So *that* was her problem! It was foolish of him not to have thought of it first. After all, he had grown up abiding by a stuffy society's many rules and regulations. He was so comforted to know she hadn't merely used him for her own ends that he laughed. Tiny's tail started thumping again.

She scowled. "I don't think it's funny. You might not be ruined by something like this, but *I'm* not rich and famous like some people."

Shaking his head, he again reached across Tiny to

touch her. She jerked away from him, incensed. "Mari, it's not that. I'm not laughing at you. And I don't think your worries are unfounded or nonsensical. I'm only relieved that you don't want to kick me out because you hate me."

She opened her mouth, shut it, then opened it again, as if at a complete loss for words.

Tony said humbly, "May I please stay here with you tonight? When the crew shows up tomorrow, we can tell them about Tiny being shot. I can say I stayed here to help you with Tiny and because I didn't want you to be alone out here in the middle of nowhere without anyone to guard you, knowing there's a gun-happy lunatic somewhere in the area."

She looked skeptical. "Do you think they'll buy that one?"

"Why not? It's the truth. Martin knows me well enough to understand that I'd never desert a lady in distress."

"I wasn't in distress," she said stiffly. "Tiny was."

Tony only nodded. "Of course. That's what I meant to say."

She thought about it for another several tense seconds. Tony realized he meant the part about not leaving her alone. If she kicked him out of her cabin, he'd sleep in the Pierce Arrow. He'd be damned if he'd leave her at the mercy of whoever was trying to ruin the making of the picture.

At last, she said, "Okay." She stared at him with those gorgeous, solemn brown eyes and added with a hint of reserve in her manner, "I'd like you to stay."

Thank God. He smiled back. "Good. Then it's settled. We can be up and about before the crew arrives, and nobody will ever know a thing."

"Okay. Let me get some more laudanum down poor old Tiny."

Together they doctored the dog, who was an admirable patient. Then they retired to Mari's extremely small bed. Because he didn't want any more temptations to attack him than were absolutely necessary, Tony kept his trousers on. Mari donned a big flannel nightgown—a hand-me-down from her deceased mother unless Tony was much mistaken—thereby putting another barrier between the two new lovers.

That was all right. Tony fell asleep almost instantly once they'd wrapped themselves comfortably in each other's arms. He had the rest of his life to make love to Mari. The rest of his life. He was so happy, he was surprised his body even touched the bed because he was floating on air.

Right before his brain shut off and sleep claimed him, he realized he hadn't gotten his proposal of marriage made.

Tomorrow morning, he assured himself. There'd be plenty of time to propose tomorrow morning before filming started.

It was the rattle of wagons and the purr of motorcar engines that awoke Mari in the morning. Blinking into the sunshine streaming through her window, it took her only a heartbeat to realize they'd overslept. She rolled out of bed with a gasp, flew to the window, and peeked outside, holding the curtain so that no one could see inside the cabin.

Yup. There they were. A caravan of motion-picture people. Darn it all. She raced back to the bed and shook Tony as hard as she could. "Tony! Wake up this instant! They're here!"

"Grmph. Wh—huh?"

Lord, the man was gorgeous. But, at present, he was

such a blasted lump. She shook him again and hissed, "Get up! Martin's here!"

"Mm—Martin?" His eyes flew open. "Good God, what time is it?"

"I don't know." She saw Tony's pocket watch on the table next to her bed and snatched it up. "It's seven-thirty."

"Seven-thirty?" He flung his long legs over the side of the bed and yawned hugely. "Good God, picture people get up early. It's a damned uncivilized profession, if you ask me."

"Yes," she said through clenched teeth. "Don't they, though. Will you get moving? I have to see to Tiny and get dressed."

"Right." Tony stood up and stretched.

Dear Lord in heaven. Mari wished he hadn't done that. He was as much like a Greek god as made no matter, and she really just wanted to stay here and look at him all day. She'd give anything not to have to work.

As if she had anything to give. Which was the whole point, she reminded herself sternly. She was working on this picture in order to earn money, and she'd better get ready to do it. This was supposed to be a big day for her character, and there'd be a lot of climbing in and out of the mine to do.

In other words, it would be almost like a normal day for her. But she wasn't normal. She was a whole new Mari, after last night. She wanted to sing and dance and whistle and tell the world how happy she was.

She did none of those things; she retied her bathrobe and went to her dog. She had to wash up, but Tiny came first. Praying like mad that no one from the picture crew would knock at her door, she inspected Tiny's wound, gave him some water, and hand-fed him a few bites of food.

"Don't give him too much," warned Tony from the far corner of the room.

When Mari turned to see what he was doing, she was gratified to note that he'd already dressed and was brushing his hair with her hairbrush. Her heart gave a brief leap, and it crossed her mind never to wash that brush again. Which was patently stupid.

"I won't," she said. "But I'm sure he needs to eat a little something."

Tony walked over and grinned down at the girl and her dog. "I suppose so. He probably eats more than you do."

"He does," she said dryly.

Tiny wagged his tail and whined. Mari was pleased when Tony correctly interpreted this message as an invitation to say good morning in Dog and leaned over to pet him.

"You're going to be all right," Tony assured Tiny. "Just rest up today and don't do any rabbit chasing or anything."

"I'm going to leave him inside the cabin," Mari said. "Although I suppose I ought to take him outside to do his duty first."

"Why don't you let me do that," Tony suggested. "I'll walk him outside, explain everything to Martin, and you can be getting ready in here. Then he can stay outside with me if he wants to. Tiny," he clarified, "not Martin."

If he wasn't the kindest, most thoughtful man in the universe, Mari didn't know who was. "Thanks, Tony. I—" Good God, she almost said *I love you*. Fortunately, her brain was quicker than her tongue, and she said, "I appreciate it."

He tipped her a wink and went to where Tiny's leash hung on a hook beside the door. Seeing this, Tiny struggled to his feet, whimpering only once. Mari helped him to stand, wincing for his pain. "That's a good boy," she whispered in his big pointy ear, exaggerating somewhat for the sake of Tiny's self-esteem. "You're such a very good boy."

"Come on, you big lug," said Tony, who evidently wasn't worried about the dog's ego. "Let's go outside and show off your battle scars."

Mari's heart seemed to swell in her chest. She'd believed she had only one male to love in the world: Tiny. As she watched Tony carefully guide Tiny out the door, she realized her capacity for love had grown by one. She sighed and wondered dreamily where it would end. No matter how many fantasies she spun in her head, she had no doubt whatever that it *would* end, and that the end would hurt her deeply.

In spite of her doubts and fears, Mari washed and dressed in record time, rushing outdoors to see Martin and the rest of the Peerless crew huddled around Tiny, who was obviously enjoying the attention. Although his tail sagged slightly—when he felt really well, he held it in the air like a flagstaff—it was wagging, and his huge doggy grin was visible from where she stood.

Martin waved to her. "Mari! Tony's just been telling us what happened. Good Lord, I can't believe it!"

She walked over to the clump of people. "I couldn't believe it, either, but I saved the bullet I tweezed out of him. It's in a jar in the cabin." She hooked a thumb over her shoulder.

A troubled frown marred Martin's handsome face, and creases appeared in his brow. He'd already begun tugging on his worry lock. "This has got to stop. We can't have someone shooting dogs."

"I'm sure Mari won't agree with me," said Tony, "but I suppose it's better than shooting people."

Mari shot him a scowl. "Whoever it was might have thought he *was* shooting people," she pointed out. "It was getting dark." She was almost sorry for losing her temper when Tony paled in front of her eyes.

"Good God."

Martin clapped him on the back. "Buck up, Tony. The detectives are here, and I'll post them at Mari's cabin tonight." A thought struck him, and he turned to Mari. "Unless you'd rather take a room at the Mojave Inn until this thing is in the can. Peerless will be happy to pick up the tab." He saw Mari glance quickly down at her dog and hurried to add, "I'm sure they'll let Tiny stay there, too."

"That might be a good idea, Mari," Tony said.

She eyed him narrowly, wondering if he had her interests at heart, or merely thought it would be easier to get into her drawers if she stayed at the hotel. Then she told herself not to be silly; he'd have had no trouble in that regard, no matter where he attempted a seduction. If seduction it had been. Mari didn't even know at this point. All she knew for sure was that she'd been willing. More than willing. Eager.

"Let me think about it, please," she said after lecturing herself severely about the futility of afterthoughts.

Martin readily agreed with this plan.

Tony sat on a chair in the shade of an umbrella with Tiny lying on a blanket at his side. They both watched as the Peerless crew filmed scene after scene featuring Mari and her mine. Reginald Harrowgate staggered into the picture here and there, playing his part of Mari's drunken father to the hilt.

Another actor, a handsome devil named—or renamed, if Tony knew anything about actors—Xavier Joaquin, acted the part of the gent who'd won Mari in a poker game. He swaggered and strutted, and it was all Tony could do to contain himself when Joaquin pretended to manhandle her in one scene.

"It's only a picture," he grumbled to Tiny in an effort to subdue his raging temper. "It's only a picture."

Tiny lifted his head and gazed at him mutely, but Tony felt sure he understood.

Around one o'clock, a wagon arrived with sandwiches and lemonade, and everyone was happy to rest for a half hour or so. They all tried to stay out of the scorching sun, using the umbrellas Peerless had provided, but the heat was still enervating. Tony made sure Mari ate her lunch with him. Although he wasn't overjoyed when Martin joined them, he didn't protest, understanding Mari's reluctance to advertise the change in her and Tony's relationship.

He was going to propose to her as soon as they were alone together. He could kick himself for not doing it last night.

Filming continued after lunch. Mari looked exhausted as she rested on the sidelines, and Tony was proud of how well she hid her tiredness as soon as the cameras commenced their ungodly racket.

At one point, she had to enter the mine, climb down the rope ladder suspended from the mine scaffolding— scaffolding that had been reinforced by Peerless carpenters before filming had ever begun—and pretend to hide from Joaquin. Scenes depicting her escape from Joaquin would be filmed later on a set George Peters had designed specifically to resemble the intricate tunnels inside the mine.

Tony watched, frowning, as, with every evidence of terror, Mari disappeared into the mine shaft. He didn't like thinking of her in that damned hole in the ground. No matter how much effort Peerless had put into making it safe, Tony didn't trust it.

He knew he was being foolish. Mari had worked that

blasted mine all her life. She knew it like the back of her hand. If anyone was safe in that damned pit, it was she.

When a frightened cry rose from the hole in the ground, he was on his feet in an instant and racing toward the mine entrance.

Martin called out, "Hey, Tony! What are you—"

His question was drowned out by a series of loud crackling noises that sounded like fire from a Gatling gun, followed at once by a huge *boom,* and another louder, and more frightened scream from Mari.

Tony's heart lurched sickeningly when a noise like an avalanche issued from underground and a gigantic cloud of dust rose from the mouth of the mine. *"Mari!"* he shouted. "Mari! Mari!"

He heard someone running up behind him, and then Martin's voice joined his. *"Mari!* For God's sake, what's happening in there?"

Tony feared he knew exactly what was happening. Or, rather, what had happened. The saboteur had been at the mine; that's why he'd been here last evening, and why Tiny had scared him so much that the vandalizing bastard had shot him.

Both men halted at the mine opening. All Tony saw from where he stood was rubble. The entrance to the mine was completely blocked by shattered scaffolding and rocks. Everything inside of him throbbed with fear and pain. "Mari," he breathed.

Martin grabbed his arm. "Good God, Tony. This is terrible."

It was worse than terrible. If anything had happened to Mari, it would be the worst tragedy of Tony's entire life. After pausing for no more than ten seconds, trying to assimilate the magnitude of his possible loss, he fell to his knees and started heaving rubble away from the mine entrance. "For God's sake, help me!" he cried, his throat so tight the words barely squeezed out.

"Wait, Tony," Martin said in a calm voice. "Wait a minute. Let George take a look. He'll know better than we what should be done, since he's the construction expert."

"Expert? I swear to God, Martin, if he's responsible for this, I'll kill him."

"He's not," Martin said crisply. "And if you weren't so scared, you'd know it."

Sitting back on his heels and taking a deep breath, Tony breathed in and out twice before he whispered, "Right." He buried his face in his cupped hands, feeling as though his heart were being hacked in two with a dull ax. "You're right. Of course, you're right."

He heard something from inside the mine shaft. At once, he resumed scrabbling to get rocks out of the way. "Did you hear that? Did you hear it? Was it Mari?"

"I don't know."

Tony heard Martin turn, but didn't look up to see what he was doing. Then he heard Martin's voice, sounding slightly relieved, which didn't make sense to Tony, who was in a full-fledged panic now.

"Thank God, you're here, George. What should we do?"

"I'll get the men fitted out with the proper equipment, and I hope we can clear this out in no time."

Tony felt a hand on his shoulder and he jerked it off. "Leave me alone. I'm going to get Mari out of there."

"Tony," Martin said gently, "George has the proper equipment for moving these rocks. You can't do much with your bare hands."

"Maybe, but at least I'm doing something," he growled.

Evidently, Martin realized how futile it would have

been to argue further. Tony heard him walk away, and he continued chucking rocks aside.

He'd been working for what seemed like hours but was probably only ten minutes or so, when two things happened. The first was that George's crew showed up carrying heavy equipment and started removing rocks. The second was that he heard Mari's voice, slightly muffled but still clear as day, from inside the mine. His heart gave such an enormous heave, he wouldn't have been surprised if it had jumped right out of his chest and plunked onto the ground in front of him.

"Mari! Oh, God, Mari, are you there?" Stupid question, he knew, but he couldn't make himself ask if she was alive. Anyhow, clearly she was alive. Good God, his brain had ceased functioning. "Are you hurt?"

"Um," came her voice, sounding sort of weak. Of course, that might have been because he was hearing it through who knew how many tons of granite. "I'm not sure. I don't think so. It's very close in here, though."

Good God. Tony had forgotten about air. He almost cried out to her not to breathe, but caught himself before he'd blurted out anything so utterly stupid. "Take it easy," he said instead. "Don't move around too much. George and his crew are working on getting you out of there."

"Good. I'm glad. Okay."

She sounded weak. Lord, Lord, if she was hurt, Tony didn't know what he'd do. Kill whoever did this, for a certainty, but there must be something more he could do. Besides pay for her funeral.

No. He wouldn't—couldn't—start thinking things like that.

Tiny, whom he'd forgotten altogether, nudged his back with a huge wet nose, and Tony turned to see that the dog had dragged himself to the mouth of the mine.

Knowing he could do nothing more there, Tony first hugged the dog, then led him back to the shade. "She'll be all right, boy," he assured Tiny. "She'll be fine. They'll get her out of there in a jiffy."

Then, for the first time since he could remember, Tony shut his eyes and prayed. Hard.

Twenty

Mari had never been so frightened. When the collapse came, she'd thought for sure she was a dead woman. But the scaffolding fell around her in a way that kept most of the rocks away from her. Some of the smaller ones had battered against her, but she was relatively unscathed except for some scrapes and scratches. One of her ankles hurt like the devil, but other than that, she didn't think she was injured.

On the other hand, the dust had all but smothered her before it had settled. Only then did she pause to think about air. There wasn't any coming in from outdoors any longer. Unless the men working to free her did their job in a hurry, she wasn't sure how long she'd last.

When she'd heard Tony's voice calling to her, she'd experienced a moment of elation. She couldn't be buried that deeply if she could still communicate with the outside world. She'd called back to him and was moderately reassured for a few minutes. Then the reality of her situation began to creep over her, and her spirits started to flag.

She couldn't recall ever being so uncomfortable. The heat was insufferable, the air smelled close and stuffy, her ankle throbbed, her scratches hurt—those that didn't itch—and she couldn't see anything for the stifling blackness. She wondered if hell was like this. It was something to ponder. If this was a foretaste of hell, Mari'd be more diligent about attending church. Provided she got out of this latest predicament alive.

Who in the name of all that was holy could be doing these terrible things? It was bad enough when whoever it was had crushed the cameras, but now the person was getting perilously close to murder. Mari couldn't imagine why anyone would wish to interfere with a motion picture in such a catastrophic way.

Of course, there were those religious zealots who considered all forms of entertainment sinful. Mari had read letters to the editor of the San Bernardino newspaper from some of them. But moving pictures were so popular nowadays, Mari didn't believe the fanatics were awfully numerous.

Then again, sometimes when people felt their positions to be especially weak, they resorted to desperate measures. As she squinted into the blackness of what might yet become her tomb, she decided this act had been pretty darned desperate. So had shooting Tiny. In fact, those two acts were criminal; and if they ever found out who was behind them, Mari hoped the perpetrators would rot in prison.

She sat back against the smoothest boulder she could find and tried to get comfortable. When this proved impossible, she began singing to herself. Realizing singing would only use up what air she had left even more quickly than mere breathing, she ceased singing aloud and commenced humming in her head.

After a minute or two of that, Mari realized the humming wasn't being created by her brain, but by some physical phenomenon, probably lack of oxygen. A surge of panic swept through her, but she held her breathing steady by an effort of willpower. A moment or two later she understood the humming that had so alarmed her was coming from outside. She would have

collapsed from relief if she hadn't already been as collapsed as she could get.

A drill. They were using a drill. Of course. She ought
to have anticipated it.

Although she'd never have believed it possible, she
drifted off to sleep a few minutes later, her senses
dulled by the darkness and her muscles numb from
inaction.

Mari was rudely awakened to reality when a rock
fell on her. She sat bolt upright, banging her head
against a piece of broken scaffolding and dislodging a
miniature avalanche of pebbles and dust. For a second,
she feared she'd damaged the fragile structure keeping
the tons of rock over her head from crushing her, but
she hadn't. Not even her head was hard enough to move
a ton of rock, she decided dryly.

Another rock fell on her. Good heavens, what was
happening? Was the structural damage such that the
fragile wooden scaffolding protecting her was going to
give way after so many minutes or hours of stress?
Mari strove to stave off a mounting sense of horror.

The sound of scraping stone almost caused her heart
to give out. Oh, Lord above, this was it. She was a
goner. In a second, the entire structure would cave in,
and there would be nothing left of her but a squished
heap of human refuse.

Tears stung her eyes. For several moments, she tried
to hold them back. Then she decided she might as well
spend her last few seconds on Earth not holding anything back, so she let them flow, wringing her hands
and sobbing like the heroine in a melodrama. Martin
would have been proud of her.

A tremendous crash made her scream. Rocks and
rubble seemed to rush in upon her. A ray of sunlight
nearly blinded her, and she covered her eyes with her
hands.

Great God in heaven, was life extinguished whilst accompanied by a flash of light? Is this how it all ended?

Two hard hands seized her by the wrists, and she screamed again. She'd never read *anywhere* that one was transported out of this world and into the other one by being hauled there manually.

"Try, Mari, *try!*" a well-known and well-beloved voice urged her. Tony must have died, too. How strange.

It took another couple of seconds for her to realize she was being rescued. A wave of joy was quickly subsumed by one of foolishness for how far her fancy had carried her. She scrambled to help in her own salvation. "I'm trying," she said testily. "I think my ankle is sprained."

"Sprained? Good God, I hope it's nothing worse than that."

"Easy for you to say. It hurts like the dickens."

"I know. I'm sorry, sweetheart. Here, then, be careful."

She couldn't tell for sure, because she was too rattled, but she thought he sounded as if he might be worried about her poor sore ankle. Which made sense, she guessed, since he undoubtedly didn't want a piece of property in which his father had invested to be damaged. That might cost money.

When had she become so unpleasantly cynical? she wondered. Although, she had to admit, being buried underground and in imminent peril of being squashed like a bug did tend to make one reassess one's prior notions about things.

Tony was dragging her by her wrists now. Mari wondered if he was deliberately hauling her over every jagged rock he could find, or if it was only happenstance. She tried to scramble after him, but her ankle wouldn't cooperate. Every time she even tried to put weight on it, it gave out and a wash of violent pain went through her. Blast it, this wasn't fair.

"We're almost there, Mari," Tony panted.

She could hear the strain in his voice and instantly forgave him for dragging her over a couple of sharp rocks. "It was good of you to come after me, Tony. I'm sure Martin would have been glad to send someone else."

"He tried to," Tony said grimly. "I wouldn't let him."

"Oh." Good grief, he really was worried about his father's money, wasn't he? "That was nice of you."

"Nice?" He paused for only a second and looked back at her. Mari couldn't decipher the expression on his face, except to note that it was very intense. "Nice?" he repeated. "Good God."

She didn't have time to ask him anything else because he started tugging at her wrists again. She wanted to know how the accident had happened, and if they thought it had been natural—unlikely, since Martin and his crew had spent days shoring up the infrastructure of the mine—or if it had been another act of vandalism. Mari's money was on vandalism. Or it would be, if she had any.

"Only a few more feet to go," Tony told her after several minutes. "It won't be long now, Mari, and you'll be free again."

Free again. That sounded so pleasant. She hoped her blasted ankle wouldn't interfere with her job in the picture, because she really, really needed that money.

"The doctor's waiting to check you over."

"That's nice."

"I had him look at Tiny while George and his men were digging you out."

"That's *very* nice." For the first time since her father's life's work had fallen down around her, Mari smiled. "Thank you very much."

"You're welcome."

He sounded grumpy again. Mari didn't know why.

All at once, Tony, who had been faintly outlined by the one ray of sunlight streaming into the mine's shaft, vanished from her sight. She cried out, "Tony!" and feared the last few minutes had been the product of her fevered imagination.

Then light poured down upon her, and she realized Tony had merely climbed out of the pit. He still held on to her hands, and he was tugging her out, too. She had a feeling she wouldn't have an inch of skin left after she got through this ordeal, but at least she was still alive.

That being the case, she ought to be much happier than this, oughtn't she? Of course, she should.

Worry. That's what it was. She was too worried about the consequences that might befall her after this latest catastrophe. Surely Martin wouldn't want to use her mine any longer. Would he still pay her?

A deafening noise greeted her when Tony finally hauled her out into the light of day. The noise puzzled Mari until she realized the cast and crew of Peerless, plus most of her friends and neighbors from Mojave Wells, were standing around the collapsed entrance to the mine and cheering her rescue. She glanced up, smiling, and was taken completely by surprise when Tony wrapped his big, strong arms around her and lifted her right up off the ground.

Then he kissed her. Her feet dangled in air, and the crowd's cheers became even more raucous. Mari experienced one fleeting moment of abject embarrassment, before she chucked her cares to the wind, threw her arms about his neck, and kissed him back.

Tony was panting and she was brick red when he finally lowered her slowly to the ground. "Thank God, you're all right," he whispered fervently.

"Thank you." She brushed dirt from her face, forgetting about her ankle until her left foot hit the ground. With a sharp cry of anguish, she crumpled and started to fall. Tony caught her. She thanked him again.

He didn't seem to hear her. Sweeping her up into his arms, he called out, "Where's the doctor? I think she's broken her ankle. It needs to be looked at right away."

"I'm right here, son."

Mari glanced toward Dr. Crabtree's voice, and saw the kindly old man grinning at the two of them. Knowing he was doing so because she and Tony had kissed, she lifted her chin and smiled, trying for a dignified expression. "Thank you, Doc."

She heard Martin's voice say, "Lord, Mari, I was afraid you were done for. I'm so glad you're out of that pit."

Martin, Mari realized, was there at Tony's side. She wondered if he'd been there all the time. Might have been. She'd had eyes for no one but Tony. "Thanks, Martin. I'm kind of glad about it, too."

She'd expected a little bit of laughter to honor her attempt at humor, but none greeted her. She guessed they were all too rattled about the accident. Giving up on humor, she asked, "Does anyone know how it happened?"

"Yes." This, from Tony, who sounded even more grim than he usually did when he was annoyed about something having to do with Mari.

He carried her into the cabin and set her on her bed. Gazing up at him, she said, "What was it? Was it . . ." For some reason, her mouth refused to form the word *sabotage*. Perhaps because she'd almost been killed, she didn't want to think about someone deliberately doing these things.

"Yes. Someone cut the cables holding the scaffolding together and hacked through several of the supports."

"Merciful heaven."

"In a manner of speaking," Tony agreed wryly.

Dr. Crabtree plunked his black bag on a chair. "You might well say so. It was some kind of merciful heaven that saved your life, Miss Mari. I've never seen anything like it."

"No," said Tony. "Me, neither."

He sat on another chair with a plunk, and Mari was astonished to see how terribly pale and shaken he looked. He buried his face in his hands. "My God, I thought I'd lost you."

She gaped at him. He sounded as if losing her would be a bad thing. Before she could ask, the doctor started working on her left foot, untying her shoe and cutting away at her stocking. It was all she could do to keep from screaming in agony. She succeeded, but it took all of her concentration.

A whole bunch of people crowded into the cabin. Tony made them stand back in order to give Doc Crabtree plenty of room to maneuver. Martin smiled encouragingly at her, as did George and Ben and Gordon Shay. Mari was surprised to see Judy Nelson, a corner of her apron stuffed into her mouth and her eyes as wide as pie plates, staring at her. She waved her fingers. "Hi, Judy."

Judy said, "Hi, Mari," and burst into tears. How strange.

"We're going to have to get you a bath, young lady, before we doctor the rest of your wounds. As soon as I check out this ankle of yours, Mr. Ewing is driving you to the Mojave Inn. You'll be staying there for a few days until this matter is sorted out."

"I will?" She stared at Doc Crabtree's old gray head as it bent over her foot.

The doctor nodded. Sensing she'd get no more information from that source, Mari glanced up and caught Tony glowering at her. She blinked, not having anticipated anger from him and feeling rather put out about it.

"No arguments," Tony announced in a stony voice. "You're going to the Mojave Inn, and that's it. Peerless can't afford to post guards for you and your dog now that we know there's an evil intention behind all of these goings-on."

"An evil intention?" That sounded almost romantic. Mari didn't find any of these blasted accidents romantic. Especially not this one, because it had cost her the use of her left foot, and she resented it.

The doctor moved her foot, and she forgot everything but pain. "Ack! Oh, my, that hurts, Doc." She tried to smile, but a smile wouldn't come. Tears did, though, and they embarrassed her.

Tony bolted up from his chair and went to the bed. "What are you doing to her?" he asked angrily.

Dr. Crabtree glanced up, grinned, and shook his grizzled head. "No need to beat me up, son. I'm trying to figure out if it's broken or sprained. She'd be better off if it's broken, because it'll heal faster."

Mari passed a shaky hand across her cheek to wipe away tears. "Really? I didn't know that."

The doctor nodded. "Sure. When you get a sprain, the ligament gets torn, there's lots of internal bleeding, and it can take months for everything to go right again, if it ever does. If you break it, it's a bone, and bones knit faster than torn ligaments."

"Oh." She thought for a minute. "Never thought I'd ever say anything like this, Doc, but I hope it's broken."

He chuckled. Tony let out a hiss through his teeth. When Mari glanced up at him, she got the impression he wanted to lift the doctor up from the ground and throw him out a window. On impulse, she held out her hand to him. "Maybe if you sat beside me, you could help me be strong."

Oh, ick. Had she really said that? She feared she had. What's worse, she feared she meant it.

However, her ploy gave Tony something to do besides stand there and seethe. He sat down next to her on the bed, took her hands in one of his, put his other arm around her shoulder, and held her tight. She tried to hide her sigh of pleasure with a cough.

After another couple of minutes of poking, prodding, and feeling, all of which hurt like the very devil, Dr. Crabtree looked up at Mari. "It's a sprain, young lady, and a bad one. I'll get it wrapped up now. After you get your bath at the hotel, I'll rebandage it and put carbolic and bandages on the worst of your scrapes. You'll have to elevate the foot and won't be able to walk on it for a week or so, and then you'll have to be careful with it. It's going to hurt for months, so prepare yourself."

"But—" Mari was appalled. "But what about the picture? I've still got scenes to do."

The doctor rose from squatting on the floor, using the bed to help himself stand, and huffed. As he threw his stethoscope into his black bag, grabbed a role of bandages, and snapped the bag shut, he grumbled, "You're more important than that silly picture, Mari Pottersby. You've got to take care of that ankle if you ever want it to get better."

"Don't worry about the picture, Mari," Martin said, capturing her attention because she'd forgotten he was the mastermind behind this endeavor. "We can work around you. Change scenes so you can do them sitting down and hide bandages with furniture, and stuff like that." He made a careless gesture with his hand. "We do that sort of thing all the time."

"You do?" She began to feel better.

"Well," Martin amended, smiling, "perhaps not *all* the time, but you're not the first actor who's been hurt on the job, and you probably won't be the last, more's the pity."

Tony had carried Mari out to his car and had driven carefully back to town. They'd put Tiny in the backseat, after giving him a sleep-inducing dose of laudanum. Tony had made Mari sit next to him in the front seat and prop her swollen foot on his coat, which he'd removed and rolled up to make a pillow and placed next to the passenger's door. This, of course, meant that Mari had to lean against him in order to take advantage of the prop. She hadn't objected, which was a damned good thing, because he was spoiling for a fight.

He'd been appalled when the doctor had removed her footwear and revealed the ankle. It was as big as a tree trunk and purple to the knee. Her whole foot was bruised and swollen, even the bottom of it.

Dr. Crabtree had explained that the bruising had been caused by blood leaking under the skin and would probably hurt more than the torn ligament when she started walking again.

When they got to the hotel, he carried Mari inside first and would have fussed over her indefinitely if she hadn't all but shouted at him to take care of her dog. He did so rather huffily, but pleased that at least she hadn't called him Tiny.

She wouldn't let him enter the bathroom and help her undress to take a bath, either. "For heaven's sake, Tony! I want some privacy. Do you mind?"

"Yes," he growled, but he let her have her way, staying in the parlor with Tiny. Tiny appreciated him, if nobody else did. He did make himself useful by fetching Mari a robe to put on after her bath.

Because he thought he should, he had Mrs. Nelson place a long-distance telephone call to his father in New York. The old man ought to know what was happening, even if Tony didn't particularly want to be the bearer of the evil tidings. Although he knew none of these disastrous happenings were his fault, and even though he hadn't wanted the old bastard to invest in a motion picture in the first place, he felt responsible for his father's investment.

Mari was finished with her bath and had just settled herself into a big, overstuffed armchair in the parlor with her foot propped on a pillow Tony'd set on an ottoman, when a commotion from outdoors captured their attention. With a frown, Mari murmured, "What's that? I wonder."

"I hope to hell it's the doctor come to put another bandage on that ankle and check your scratches." Every time he looked at her, his heart cramped. She was so bruised and battered. If he hadn't feared he'd hurt her, he'd have gathered her in his arms and held her close.

"Doc Crabtree will be here as soon as he can be," she told him. "He's a busy man."

"Right." Irate about the conditions prevailing in this backwater, and wishing he could send for a doctor from New York City—which would be ridiculous, since Mari would doubtlessly have healed by the time a New York doctor could make his way out west—Tony stamped to the door and yanked it open. "Oh," he said. "Hi, Martin."

Martin entered the parlor, followed by a phalanx of Peerless men. He smiled at Mari. "You look a little more the thing now, Mari. I'm awfully sorry about your ankle."

She waved her hand in the air. "It'll be okay. It's only a sprain."

"Only a sprain?" Tony bellowed. "The doctor said a sprain was worse than a break!" He resented it when Mari rolled her eyes.

Martin didn't seem to notice the interplay between the two. He was distracted, although Tony didn't realize it until Mari asked, "What's the matter, Martin? What's going on? Good heavens, there hasn't been another accident, has there?"

"No, thank God."

Tony stopped being angry and worried about Mari, and focused his attention on Martin. The poor guy did appear rather rattled. "What happened, Martin?"

Martin flopped onto a sofa near Mari's chair. Removing his sporty tweed cap and holding it on his knee, he looked up at Tony, a troubled frown on his face. "The sheriff caught two men trying to leave town. In their possession was a twenty-two caliber rifle with a spent cartridge, and several tools that could easily have been used to cause the problems with the mine and with the set."

Tony, who had been pacing nervously, his mind cursing the doctor who seemed determined not to come to Mari's aid, stopped pacing and stared. "You mean, Jones caught the perpetrators?"

"Oh, my!" exclaimed Mari. "This is wonderful!"

Martin grimaced. "It might not be quite as wonderful as all that."

Tony and Mari exchanged a glance. Tony asked, "What do you mean?"

After heaving a dispirited sigh, Martin said, "It's kind of complicated."

This time it was Tony who rolled his eyes. "Out with it, Martin. Who was it?" He hoped to hell it wasn't

George or Ben or another of the Peerless men Martin had trusted for years.

Martin stood again and started twirling his hat nervously. "Maybe you'd better come out to the main lobby with me, Tony. I don't want to upset Mari."

Mari sat up and fairly shrieked at the two men, "Don't you *dare* leave me to wonder what's going on! If you don't do whatever you need to do in here, I'll hobble out there if it kills me!"

The two men gazed at her, Martin with concern, Tony with fury. "Damn it, Mari, you're not supposed to move." He hurried to the door and looked out, scanning the hallway in both directions. "Where the hell's the doctor?"

"He's coming," Martin said. "He had to, ah, take care of an emergency first."

"What's more of an emergency than Mari?" Tony demanded.

"Oh, for heaven's sake." Mari pushed herself away from the chair back, preparatory to standing.

Seeing this maneuver on her part, Tony bellowed, "No! You stay right where you are, damn it!"

Through a barely opened mouth and seriously clenched teeth, Mari snapped, "I intend to know who did this to me, Tony—and you can't stop me."

"Hold on, you two." Martin held up his hands in a placating gesture. "I'll bring everyone in here, so you can hear the news firsthand, Mari. Will that be all right with both of you?"

Tony still looked like a bull about to charge, but he said, "Yes. That will be fine."

Mari gave Martin one of her more glorious smiles. Tony begrudged him that smile. He wanted all of Mari's smiles for himself. "Thanks, Martin," she said. "You're a real pal."

As Martin left the room, Tony grumbled, " 'You're a real pal.' I can't stand it."

"Quit whining," Mari snapped. "And where's my dog?"

"Last I looked, he was sleeping it off in the hotel lobby."

"Oh." She settled back against the chair cushions. "Is he all right?"

She looked so unhappy, Tony's heart flipped. Relenting slightly, he said, "I'll see if he's fit to come in here. I'm sure he'd like to be with you as much as you'd like him to be." There. If she wouldn't marry him after that magnanimous speech, Tony didn't know her.

That reminded him, he still hadn't proposed. What the hell! A man could only do so many things at once. He hurried out to the front lobby, not wanting to miss Martin and the perpetrators.

Twenty-one

The doctor arrived before Martin and the sheriff did, a circumstance for which Mari was grateful. She was in a lot of pain.

But Doc Crabtree soon had dabbed carbolic on the worst of her scrapes and scratches and applied gauze bandages, rebandaged her foot and ankle, given her a bottle containing a laudanum solution that she was to take if she needed it, and told her she'd be okay.

"Eventually," he added, replacing the roll of bandages, considerably diminished now, in his black bag. "You had a narrow escape, young lady."

"Don't I know it." Mari stared gloomily at her bandaged ankle. The bandage ran halfway up her calf, but the purple bruising went all the way to her knee. The doctor told her she couldn't have done a better job of spraining it if she'd tried. She didn't think it was funny.

"But I suppose everything will be all right now. I understand they caught the fellows behind all the so-called accidents."

"Yes, Martin told us. They're going to come here and explain everything." She scowled at the door, through which not a soul had passed since Doc Crabtree's arrival. If they'd lied to her, she'd be extremely angry.

But before the doctor had left the room, a procession of people entered. Tony wasn't with them, but Martin,

George, Ben, and several other Peerless people accompanied the sheriff. Sheriff Jones was leading a handcuffed man sporting a bandaged head whom Mari vaguely recognized as being one of the stage crew. She gazed at the men curiously.

They were all milling around in front of the door, as if they were trying to decide where to sit, when Tony's voice sounded behind them in a peremptory command. "Out of the way, everybody. Dog coming through!"

The men parted like the Red Sea for Moses, and Mari's heart was touched when she saw Tony, struggling under the weight of her oversized dog. "Oh, Tony!" she cried. "You carried him to me!"

Scowling hideously, Tony said, "Yeah, I carried him, the big lug."

Despite his irritated words, Tony was as gentle as gentle could be when he laid the monster dog on the rug beside Mari's chair. She hadn't thought she could love him—Tony, that is to say—any more than she already did, but his care with Tiny revealed her mistake. She didn't think she'd ever get over her love for Tony Ewing. Pathetic, but true. She sighed deeply. "Thank you, Tony."

"You're welcome." He stood, glowered down at the dog for a moment, then turned.

Mari was startled when Tony caught sight of the villain. His eyebrows soared, his eyes all but started from their sockets, and he blurted out, "Sidney! What the devil are you in handcuffs for? What happened to your head?"

The sheriff asked, "You know this man, Mr. Ewing?"

"*Know* him? Sure, I know him. He's one of my father's men. One of the guys who came out here with me to work on the picture."

Mari gasped. "Good heavens."

Sidney, head bowed and looking as if he wished he could fade into the woodwork, said not a word.

Tony exploded when the light dawned. "Do you mean to tell me *you're* behind these accidents, Sidney?"

Sidney remained mute.

Tony took a step toward Sidney, who backed up an equal distance. He'd probably have backed up even farther, but Sheriff Jones didn't budge, and the chain on his handcuffs wouldn't let him. *"Why,* for the love of God? Are you insane?"

Still Sidney didn't speak. After frowning at him for a minute, the sheriff looked up at Tony. "I'm afraid it's worse than that, Mr. Ewing." He gave Sidney an ungentle nudge. "Speak up, Sidney. It's got to come out someday. You've already told me about it. You'd best make your confession to Mr. Ewing here. It's his lookout, after all."

Looking as if he'd rather be dead than explaining the matter to Tony and Martin, Sidney at last lifted his head. "I'm sorry, Mr. Ewing. We didn't mean to hurt nobody."

"Who's we?" Tony demanded.

"Me and Clifford. But we really didn't mean to hurt nobody."

Tony snorted. Because he was close enough, Mari whacked his arm to get him to be quiet. He glared at her but didn't make any more noises.

Sheriff Jones put in, "When the citizens of Mojave Wells realized I'd arrested these two, they got a bit out of hand. Clifford's still out from being hit by Clyde." Clyde was the local blacksmith.

Mari murmured, "Oh, my." Her friends in Mojave Wells had attacked her injurers. Mari's heart swelled

with pride for her fellow citizens. It was nice to belong
to a community that took care of its own.

"It's your father, you see," Sidney went on in a
quavery voice. "The insurance on the picture would
have paid more than if the picture went into distribu-
tion. Mr. Ewing—the senior Mr. Ewing, I mean—paid
me a big bonus to sabotage the production."

"My *father* is behind this?" Tony's eyes were fairly
starting from his head. "My *father?*"

Sidney nodded miserably. "Yes, sir. I'm sorry, sir."

"My *father?*" Tony's voice rose. "My goddamned
old man nearly killed the woman I love for *money?*"
He'd begun shouting. "I'll *kill* the bastard! *I'll* give him
money! I'll give him a bullet in the brain pan! I'll *ruin*
him, damn his eyes!"

Because she was still close enough to grab a hunk
of his shirtsleeve, and she wanted clarification on a
particular matter, Mari yanked hard. Tony turned
abruptly. *"What?"*

"Tony, calm down," Mari begged.

"Calm *down?"* he roared. *"Calm down?* I'm going
to rip that son of a bitch apart with my bare hands! He
almost murdered my *wife!"*

"Wait a minute, Tony," Mari said.

"No! Damn it, Mari, you might have been *killed!"*

"I know it, Tony, but I need to ask you something."

"Damn it, I'm in no mood to be answering questions!" He turned to Sidney, shook off Mari's restrain-
ing hand, and barreled up to the man. The sheriff held
him back from doing mayhem to Sidney by barring
Tony's advance with his billy club.

"Calm down, son. Nobody got killed. I'm sure it's
a bad shock to you—"

"A *shock?"* As if he were incapable of continuing,
Tony stood still and shook his head hard.

Mari watched intently. Dagnabbit, had he said some-

thing about Sidney hurting the woman he loved? His
wife? If he had, was that woman herself? Mari Pottersby? Because she didn't trust luck or hunches or
wildly delicious daydreams, Mari felt a compelling
need to clarify the comment before falling either into
raptures or despair.

But it had to be her, didn't it? There weren't any
other women around here, were there? Well, there was
Judy Nelson, but if Tony was in love with her, Mari'd
shoot herself. No, no, no. She meant, she'd be surprised,
is what she meant.

Mrs. Nelson appeared at the door, and everyone
turned to stare at her. Clearly ill at ease under the scrutiny of so many people, two of whom were bandaged
up and one of whom wore handcuffs, she twisted her
hands in her apron and said with a squeak in her voice,
"Your long-distance call's come through, Mr. Ewing."
She didn't wait for anyone to respond or for Tony to
quit gaping, but fled as soon as she'd delivered her
message.

Silence prevailed in the room. Mari's attention was
focused exclusively on Tony, who was blinking at
where Mrs. Nelson had stood as if he'd just seen an
apparition. Suddenly he lunged forward, and the group
of men jumped backward.

"My father," Mari heard him say as he headed out
the door. "My damned father. I'll talk to him, all right.
I'll talk to him."

His voice reeked with menace, and Mari wished she
could hurry out with him and try to calm him down
some. Unfortunately, she couldn't move. Not only that,
but if Tony's father truly was behind these awful
things—and Mari could conceive of no reason to doubt
Sidney's veracity, especially since he'd confessed under
extremely perilous conditions—Mari thought the horrid old beast could use a good talking-to.

Maurice Ewing received more than a mere talking-to from his son. Even in the parlor, Mari and the rest of the folks gathered there could hear snippets of his roaring condemnation. The words *bastard, kill, dog, love,* and *lawsuit* seemed to prevail, although many others filtered through the Mojave Inn's thick plaster walls. Mari wasn't sorry the evil Mr. Ewing was getting a good dressing-down from Tony, but she still needed to clarify matters with Tony herself.

She didn't get the chance until later that afternoon. The doctor had provided her with a pair of crutches and showed her how to use them, but he had advised her to sit still with her foot elevated for three or four days before she tried getting around much. Exhausted and sore, Mari complied with something akin to relief. There was something about being laid up, she realized, and knowing she couldn't work even if she wanted to, that allowed her to relax.

After the men had cleared out of her room, she fell asleep in her chair, Tiny snoring peacefully at her side. When she awoke, it was to the aroma of fried chicken, which Mrs. Nelson brought her for lunch. Mari was grateful, although the chicken did bring to mind her own chickens, and she asked Mrs. Nelson about them.

"Don't worry about your garden or your chickens, Mari," Mrs. Nelson advised her. "Your Mr. Ewing hired Judy to go out to the cabin and take care of it while you're laid up."

Her Mr. Ewing? Mari didn't feel up to asking. Instead, she said, "How kind of them both. But it's too far for Judy to walk, Mrs. Nelson. I don't want her to have to—"

Mrs. Nelson cut her off with a laugh in midprotest. "Don't be silly, Mari. There's nothing the least bit shabby about your Mr. Ewing. He's hired a man to drive her there in the morning and in the evening, so it won't take hardly any time at all, and you can be sure your place is secure and your chickens are fed."

"How—how nice of them both," Mari murmured, too dazed to think of anything more cogent to say.

Mrs. Nelson patted her hand. "Don't be silly, girl. You know we'd have taken care of you even without Mr. Ewing's money, but it's nice to know he cares so much." And with a wink, Mrs. Nelson left Mari to her fried chicken, which was delicious.

Mari hadn't realized how hungry she was until she recalled she hadn't eaten a bite since breakfast, and it was now getting on toward four in the afternoon. Blast it, where was Tony?

Tiny, smelling chicken, awoke from his drug-induced slumber and slowly staggered to his feet. Eyeing him critically, Mari decided it was a good thing he had four of them, or he'd never be able to stand. She pulled the meat from a leg bone. "Here, boy, this isn't enough, but maybe it'll keep your tummy from growling until we can get some more food for you."

"What's going on in here?" an imperious voice demanded from the doorway.

Looking up from her plate, Mari beheld Tony. Instantly her appetite fled, her heart raced, and the blood began pounding in her veins. "Tony."

He stomped toward her. "Why are you giving Tiny your dinner? Are you sick? Aren't you hungry? Do you want something else? Do you feel queasy?"

"Hold on there, Tony," she pleaded. "I only gave Tiny a little chicken meat because he said he was hungry." Interpreting the look on Tony's face and shooting a glance at her dog, she amended, "That is, he looked hungry." She didn't expect anyone else to understand the communication extant between herself and Tiny, although it existed.

"Well, stop it," Tony commanded her. "I'll get something for Tiny to eat."

Before Mari could voice approval or her thanks, he was gone. She sighed. "Gee whiz, Tiny, I really need to talk to him." She heard the thump of Tiny's tail on the floor. "Oh, all right, I'm glad he went to get you some food first." She gave her dog a mock frown. "I don't want you eating all of *my* dinner."

Tony came back pretty soon with a big bowl overflowing with scraps for Tiny. "Here. This ought to do the beast."

Although she didn't approve of people calling her dog a beast, Mari thanked him.

So did Tiny, although he didn't do so in words.

As soon as Tony had straightened from putting the bowl on the floor, Mari said, "Tony, we have to talk. I need to ask you something."

"Not until after you've finished with your meal. You have to keep your strength up, Mari. You've been through an ordeal."

"Yes, yes, I know, but I still need to talk to you."

"You're not going to do it now. I'm going to talk to you while you eat."

She sighed but knew it would be useless to argue. It's probably because he's so darned rich, she thought sourly. He's not used to anybody doing anything unless he okays it first.

Still, she was very hungry, so she capitulated without argument. As she ate fried chicken, mashed potatoes, green beans, and sliced tomatoes, Tony talked.

"It was my father," he started out in his blunt way. "He said he has no faith in the pictures, but he figured he might as well make some money from them. His idea, however, was to earn it on the shady side, the bastard."

Tony's entire monologue was peppered with criti-

cisms of his father. Mari didn't mind, since she agreed
with him.

He went on to explain the deal Maurice had struck
with some business partners on the West Coast, and
how he'd paid Sidney and Clifford an enormous sum
of money to sabotage the production. It was all sort of
interesting, although Mari still itched to ask him what
he'd meant by his comments earlier in the day.

When, however, he went on to say, "I took some of
the rocks that were dislodged to an assayer in town
today, Mari," she looked up from her chicken bones
and gazed at him curiously.

"Why? Don't tell me you think there's really ore
down there?"

His brow remained furrowed, as if he were still la-
boring under strong emotions. "I don't know. I've studied a lot about mining, you know."

"I remember you said you studied mining engineering."

"Right. Well . . . Let's just say I have a suspicion."

"A suspicion? About what?"

"I'll tell you later."

Mari wasn't up to entertaining mysteries today. She
snapped, "Just remember that my contract states any
ore discovered in the making of this picture is mine."
She thought of something. "And don't think that you
can get out of it by saying it wasn't discovered in the
making of the picture, but rather in the sabotaging of
it, either, because it won't wash."

For the first time in what seemed like forever, Tony
grinned. "Don't worry, sweetheart, I won't try to cheat
you."

"Humph. It's a good thing." She was finished with
her chicken and potatoes and was ready to start in on
the apple pie when Tony's next words made her freeze
with her fork halfway to her lips.

"Anyhow, I think California has community property laws, so what's yours will be mine and what's mine will be yours, and it won't matter who started out owning the Marigold Mine."

She blinked and slowly replaced her fork on her dessert plate. After clearing her throat, she said, "Um, I beg your pardon?"

His eyebrows lifted. "What? I only mentioned California's community property laws."

"What does that have to do with anything?"

"Why, it means that married couples have an equal right to property owned during marriage."

Mari glanced around the room. "Um, I don't see any married folks in here, Tony."

His smiled made her heart hitch. "Maybe not now, but there soon will be."

"Wh-what do you mean?"

She jumped and almost spilled her dinnerware when he bounded out of his chair and fell to one knee in front of her. Even Tiny was rattled. He uttered a short whimper and slid sideways on the rug.

Tony took up the hand that had lately held her fork and lifted it to his lips. "Mari, I've been meaning to ask you this for what seems like a lifetime now, but something always interrupted." He paused and sniffed. "Yum, smells like chicken."

She didn't know whether to laugh or cry.

"I want you to marry me, Mari. I want you to be my wife. I want you and Tiny to live with me here in Southern California." He grimaced. "In Mojave Wells, if you must, although I'm going to insist on building a house. I'll be damned if I'll live in a one-room cabin."

"You—you want to marry me? *Me?*" She pointed to her chest with a shaky finger.

"You bet. You're the only woman I've ever met I can even conceive of marrying."

"My God."

"Is that a yes?"

She nodded. "Yes. It's a yes."

In one fluid movement, Tony removed the tray from Mari's lap and set it on the floor. Then he joined her on the overstuffed chair, pulled her into his arms, and kissed her as if there were no tomorrow. Mari didn't care if there wasn't one. This moment would last her forever.

Tiny ate her pie.

Epilogue

Filming on *Lucky Strike* was delayed for a week while sets were redecorated so Mari could sit as she played her remaining scenes, and her condition could be hidden from the camera's inhuman eye.

Because she refused to stay in Tony Ewing's hotel room with him as a single lady, the minister of Mari's church, Mr. Grubfield, performed a marriage ceremony in the large parlor of the Mojave Inn. Considering the shortness of the time folks had between the announcement and the ceremony—a day—Mrs. Nelson, Judy, and the rest of Mari's friends in Mojave Wells did a splendid job of decorating. Mrs. Nelson even made a three-tiered wedding cake. It tilted slightly to one side, and the decorations were lovely.

That night, in spite of Mari's damaged foot, Tony gave her another lesson in the art of lovemaking. An apt and ingenious student, Mari then taught Tony some very creative ways to achieve glorious satisfaction in unusual positions (said positions made necessary by the state of her health).

Tiny improved daily, much to Mari's delight. The Nelsons and Tony tolerated the monster dog's presence in their lives with more grumpiness than they felt. Tiny was too lovable to make enemies.

Now that the problem of who was behind the acts of vandalism was solved, Martin fretted for approximately one and a half days. He was worried about money to finish the project now that Maurice Ewing had been revealed as a wolf in sheep's clothing. Although he still didn't share Martin's love of the moving pictures, Tony offered his own funds. With a grim smile, he told Martin not to worry. Tony aimed to make absolutely sure his father paid eventually for all the harm he'd done, both to Peerless and to Mari.

The assayer's report on the Marigold Mine revealed a rich vein of borax. Tony invested more of his money in repairing and reviving the mine. Because he could afford to hire sufficient men and machinery, the Marigold Mine was soon one of the most profitable borax mines in the San Bernardino area.

Although Tony had meant it when he'd assured Mari he'd live in Mojave Wells if she wanted to, Mari decided she and Tiny would enjoy life more if they had more green around them. Therefore, the Ewings built a magnificent estate on Orange Grove Boulevard in Pasadena, where the Ewing clan flourished.

It became more and more difficult to avoid movie people as more of them flooded from the East Coast to the West. Bowing to the inevitable, Tony invested heavily in the Peerless Studio, which also flourished. Martin Tafft was a frequent visitor to the Ewing estate, and stood godfather to the first Ewing offspring, a little boy whom they named Theodore, after Mr. Roosevelt.

The only contact Tony ever had with his father again was via the courts. Maurice Ewing paid heavily for his underhanded dealings with Peerless although, naturally, he was too rich ever to go to prison.

Ten years after they'd met, Tony and Mari stood on the massive front porch of their estate and gazed out upon acres of rolling green, dotted here and there with frolicking children and Great Danes.

"Are you sure you wouldn't prefer horses, Mari?"

It was an old argument, and not a heated one. In truth, it had become a family joke.

"Not on your life," Mari told him, as she always did. "Horses are too darned big."

"Right."

It didn't matter anyway, since Tiny and his kin were happy to allow the little Ewing children to ride on their backs.

Tony had never been happier.

Mari, whose life had been rough from the beginning, still had trouble believing in her luck. When she glanced from her husband's beloved profile to her children shrieking with delight on the green, green grass of her home, she decided it wasn't luck.

Her father's dream had finally paid off.

If you liked THE MINER'S DAUGHTER, be sure to look for HER LEADING MAN, the next in Alice Duncan's The Dream Maker series, available wherever books are sold in November 2001.

For beautiful Christina Mayhew, film acting is simply a surefire way to earn money, which she'll need to get into medical school. At least she has intellectual, gentlemanly producer Martin Tafft to talk to. But while Martin is more than happy to discuss matters of the mind with Christina, his reaction to her secret goal is a crushing disappointment—especially since she has come to see Martin as more than just the boss. Then an accident on the set forces Martin to take the male lead, and Christina gets a taste of his kisses—on screen, at least. Now all she has to do is convince him that he would be perfect for another role . . . namely her lifetime leading man?

COMING IN OCTOBER 2001 FROM
ZEBRA BALLAD ROMANCES

__SULLIVAN: The Rock Creek Six
by Linda Devlin 0-8217-6745-3 $5.99US/$7.99CAN

A half-breed, Sinclair Sullivan knows he has no place in the world. Not with white men, not with the Comanche—and certainly not with beautiful Eden Rourke, the sister of one of his few friends. She's certain that their love is written in the stars . . . and yet, Sullivan must first convince himself that he's the man his lovely Eden deserves.

__AT MIDNIGHT: Hope Chest
by Maura McKenzie 0-8217-6907-3 $5.99US/$7.99CAN

Newspaper reporter Trish "Mac" McAllister is hot on the trail of a notorious murderer. She picks up an old pair of handcuffs with the initials EJY and instantly plummets back to 1892—where she comes face to face with sinfully sexy Everett "Jared" Yates. Mac is sure that together, they can capture this elusive time traveler.

__WINTER FIRE: The Clan Maclean
by Lynn Hayworth 0-8217-6884-0 $5.99US/$7.99CAN

Lachlan Maclean is an outcast in his own land—and from his own family. Then, from America, comes Fiona Fraser, a bewitching widow with a healer's touch. The future of the clan Maclean rests in their hands, if only they can see beyond the treachery that threatens their unexpected love.

__THE INFAMOUS BRIDE: Once Upon a Wedding
by Kelly McClymer 0-8217-7185-X $5.99US/$7.99CAN

When Juliet rashly declares to her family that she will have Romeo at her feet within the month, she imagines only the sweet satisfaction of success—not a scandalous kiss that leads to a hasty wedding! Can she convince him that the frivolous girl he wed deserves what she suddenly desires . . . his wholehearted love?

Call toll free **1-888-345-BOOK** to order by phone or use this coupon to order by mail. *ALL BOOKS AVAILABLE OCTOBER 01, 2001*

Name_____

Address_____

City_____State_____Zip_____

Please send me the books that I have checked above.

I am enclosing $_____

Plus postage and handling* $_____

Sales tax (in NY and TN) $_____

Total amount enclosed $_____

*Add $2.50 for the first book and $.50 for each additional book. Send check or money order (no cash or CODS) to: **Kensington Publishing Corp., Dept. C.O., 850 Third Avenue, New York, NY 10022**

Prices and numbers subject to change without notice. Valid only in the U.S. All orders subject to availability. **NO ADVANCE ORDERS.**

Visit our website at **www.kensingtonbooks.com.**

Complete Your Collection of
Fern Michaels

___**Dear Emily**   0-8217-5676-1   **$6.99**US/**$8.50**CAN

___**Vegas Heat**   0-8217-5758-X   **$6.99**US/**$8.50**CAN

___**Vegas Rich**   0-8217-5594-3   **$6.99**US/**$8.50**CAN

___**Vegas Sunrise**   0-8217-5893-3   **$6.99**US/**$8.50**CAN

___**Wish List**   0-8217-5228-6   **$6.99**US/**$8.50**CAN

Call toll free **1-888-345-BOOK** to order by phone or use this coupon to order by mail.

Name _____

Address _____

City _____ State _____ Zip _____

Please send me the books I have checked above.

I am enclosing $_____

Plus postage and handling* $_____

Sales tax (in New York and Tennessee) $_____

Total amount enclosed $_____

*Add $2.50 for the first book and $.50 for each additional book.

Send check or money order (no cash or CODs) to:

Kensington Publishing Corp., 850 Third Avenue, New York, NY 10022

Prices and numbers subject to change without notice. All orders subject to availability.

Visit our web site at **www.kensingtonbooks.com**

Contemporary Romance by
Kasey Michaels

__Can't Take My Eyes Off of You
0-8217-6522-1   **$6.50US/$8.50CAN**
East Wapaneken? Shelby Taite has never heard of it. Neither has
the rest of Philadelphia's Main Line society. Which is precisely
why the town is so appealing. No one would ever think to look
for Shelby here. Nobody but Quinn Delaney . . .

__Too Good To Be True
0-8217-6774-7   **$6.50US/$8.50CAN**
To know Grady Sullivan is to love him . . . unless you're Annie
Kendall. After all, Annie is here at Peevers Manor trying to prove
she's the long-lost illegitimate great-granddaughter of a toilet paper
tycoon. How's a girl supposed to focus on charming her way into
an old man's will with Grady breathing down her neck . . .

Call toll free **1-888-345-BOOK** to order by phone or use this
coupon to order by mail.
Name_____
Address _____
City_____ State _____ Zip _____
Please send me the books I have checked above.
I am enclosing $_____
Plus postage and handling* $_____
Sales tax (in New York and Tennessee only) $_____
Total amount enclosed $_____
*Add $2.50 for the first book and $.50 for each additional book.
Send check or money order (no cash or CODs) to: **Kensington Publishing,
Dept. C.O., 850 Third Avenue, New York, NY 10022**
Prices and numbers subject to change without notice.
All orders subject to availability.
Visit our website at **www.kensingtonbooks.com**

Discover the Magic of
Romance With

Kat Martin

__The Secret
0-8217-6798-4 $6.99US/$8.99CAN

Kat Rollins moved to Montana looking to change her life, not find another man like Chance McLain, with a sexy smile and empty heart. Chance can't ignore the desire he feels for her—or the suspicion that somebody wants her to leave Lost Peak . . .

__Dream
0-8217-6568-X $6.99US/$8.50CAN

Genny Austin is convinced that her nightmares are visions of another life she lived long ago. Jack Brennan is having nightmares, too, but his are real. In the shadows of dreams lurks a terrible truth, and only by unlocking the past will Genny be free to love at last . . .

__Silent Rose
0-8217-6281-8 $6.99US/$8.50CAN

When best-selling author Devon James checks into a bed-and-breakfast in Connecticut, she only hopes to put the spark back into her relationship with her fiancé. But what she experiences at the Stafford Inn changes her life forever . . .

Call toll free **1-888-345-BOOK** to order by phone or use this coupon to order by mail.

Name_____

Address_____

City _____ State_____Zip_____

Please send me the books I have checked above.

I am enclosing $_____

Plus postage and handling* $_____

Sales tax (in New York and Tennessee only) $_____

Total amount enclosed $_____

*Add $2.50 for the first book and $.50 for each additional book.

Send check or money order (no cash or CODs) to: **Kensington Publishing Corp., Dept. C.O., 850 Third Avenue, New York, NY 10022**

Prices and numbers subject to change without notice. All orders subject to availability. Visit our website at **www.kensingtonbooks.com**.